The Oath

STEPHEN ROBERT
STEIN

The Oath

STEPHEN ROBERT
STEIN

A Genuine Vireo Book | *Rare Bird Books*
Los Angeles Calif.

THIS IS A GENUINE VIREO BOOK

A Vireo Book | Rare Bird Books
453 South Spring Street, Suite 302
Los Angeles, CA 90013
rarebirdbooks.com

FIRST TRADE PAPERBACK EDITION

Set in Dante
Printed in the United States

This book is a work of fiction. Names, characters, businesses, organizations, places,
events, and incidents are either a product of the author's imagination or are used
fictitiously. Any resemblance to actual persons, living or dead, events, or locales is
entirely coincidental.

10 9 8 7 6 5 4 3 2 1

Publisher's Cataloging-in-Publication data

Names: Stein, Stephen Robert, author.
Title: The Oath / Stephen Robert Stein.
Description: Includes bibliographical references | A Vireo Book
New York, NY; Los Angeles, CA: Rare Bird Books, 2016.
Identifiers: ISBN 9781945572920
Subjects: LCSH Holocaust, Jewish (1939-1945)—Fiction. | Auschwitz (Concentration
camp)—Fiction. | Concentration camps—Germany—Fiction. | Jews—Crimes
against—Germany—History—20th century—Fiction. | Concentration camp inmates—
Crimes against—Germany—History—Fiction. | Torture—Germany—History—20th
century—Fiction. | Human experimentation in medicine—Germany—History—20th
century—Fiction. | Jews—United States—Fiction. | BISAC FICTION / Historical |
FICTION / Jewish
Classification: LCC PS3619.T4761 O28 2016 | DDC 813.6—dc23

PROLOGUE

Dead, yes, they said I was dead. Dead along with five hundred poor souls, coiled up grotesquely intertwined with each other, the gas suffocating every last ounce of life left in them. I imagined their pain and felt it as if it were my own, but I recalled nothing beyond walking into that shower room. For years, I did not remember the screams; they stayed silent within me. I lived while others had died, and I carried that burden alone, unable to release the weight of it besieging my soul. I lived because of a doctor who had saved me twice—once from the edge of death and later from the guilt of survival. For this, I was determined to help salvage him, so entombed in the guilt and shame of his own actions with the SS. And yet I didn't know if I could save him from becoming like them...

Tamara Lissner, age fourteen
Auschwitz, Poland
January 1945

"I swear by Apollo, the physician..."

1

May 18, 1974
San Francisco, California, USA

The screen in the large convention hall lit up with the image of a German Messerschmitt Bf-109 fighter crashing in the foreground as a pilot drifted in his parachute, down towards a blue-black sea. The roaring sound of the diving fighter-bomber awoke those doctors dozing in their seats after their midday meal. *Quite an unusual way to start a medical paper,* mused Doctor Michel Katz as the audience hushed.

The presenter was standing at the podium. Doctor Robert Small, the moderator, had introduced the speaker, Doctor Jürgen Hauptman. The topic: "Hypothermia in Trauma."

The name Hauptman—was that the name Martin had mentioned? I can't remember...I was so disturbed at the time.

Doctor Katz felt queasy. And something else was bothering him...the strong German name, Hauptman...a "hypothermic study." *Martin said I would see Hans Bloch at this presentation, but it's been thirty years. Will I recognize him?*

"Doctor Hauptman is a practicing general surgeon who has studied hypothermia in surgery over the past thirty years," said Doctor Small. "He is one of the few investigators who has gathered his data outside of a university system.""Thank you for that grand introduction," said Doctor Hauptman with a curt nod.

Oh my God, Hauptman is...Bloch?

Michel's world started to spin. It took everything he had to stay in the present moment.

"I am pleased to be here among this world-renowned faculty," Doctor Hauptman was saying.

He had the air of a distinguished German professor, his English perfect with just a slight German accent. His hair was white and perfectly combed, and he sported the traditional navy blue suit worn by most of the speakers.

"During World War II, many airmen lost their lives after successfully parachuting out of their planes into the cold Atlantic waters. The winter temperatures of the Baltic and North Seas hovered around five to ten degrees Centigrade. Even if the pilots were able to get into a rubber raft, the cold air and wet clothing caused them severe hypothermia within two hours of entering the ocean."

Doctor Hauptman spoke with a confidence that bordered on arrogance. "These tragedies led to studies which demonstrated the various stages of hypothermia leading to death. Initially, with the body's core temperature cooling down to thrity-six degrees Centigrade, there are findings of tachycardia, increased blood pressure and peripheral vascular resistance, as well as an increase in cardiac output. Taking the body temperature below thirty-five degrees Centigrade is associated with bradycardia, decreased blood pressure, and markedly reduced cardiac output."

Becoming animated, Doctor Hauptman described the sequence leading to death. "As the core temperature drops below thirty degrees Centigrade, ventricular fibrillation may occur, leading to asystole."

Michel bolted upright at that last fact.

It must be him!

He listened intently as Hauptman continued.

"The heart basically stops, but patients can be successfully resuscitated from this state with proper attention to cardiac rhythms, core temperature monitoring, and acid-base balance. Of interest: If the head and neck are fully or partially submerged, death occurs more rapidly."

Looking closer at the speaker, Michel recognized the bluish hemangioma, a birthmark at the left hairline. It was the man he had followed to the hotel yesterday afternoon...*Herr Doktor* Hans Bloch.

Martin was right. Hans had taken on a different identity. Michel scanned the room nervously to see if Martin, his worrisome nemesis, had slipped into the auditorium. He didn't see him. Michel started sweating, his heart pounding like a sledgehammer in his chest.

Feelings from the past began to overtake him, and once again, rage swept through his body. He had watched this man's treacherous experiments. Then, as now, Hans never blinked or changed facial expression when the death of his subjects was mentioned. Michel's mind raced as he clenched his hands into fists. He wanted to jump up, but remained anchored in his seat, unsure of his next move.

What should I do? How do I make this right?

After the interesting and curious introduction to his medical paper, Doctor Hauptman went on to detail his experimental studies that preceded his invention of a revolutionary new device—a cooling blanket to be used in surgery that would lower the body temperature to ninety-five degrees Fahrenheit. He said the initial experimental procedures had been carried out for the military in San Antonio and left no doubt about the safety of this new approach.

That is a lie.

The audience, now riveted, didn't seem to notice that the doctor laughed as he talked about the ease in getting volunteers for his study.

"In conclusion," Doctor Hauptman stated, "our hypothermia studies have now given us information that allows us to safely operate on complex neurosurgical, cardiac, and multiple trauma patients."

Michel's chest burned with pain, and sweat formed on his brow. He knew where these "volunteers" had come from. His distress increased with every memory now resurfacing of his time in the death camps. He waited in agony until the doctor finished discussing his paper.

During the crucial question-and-answer period, a physician approached the microphone. "Tell me, Doctor, these days, how difficult is it to get permission to carry out potentially dangerous studies on human volunteers?"

Doctor Hauptman responded, "In the usual university hospital setting, this could be a problem. But remember, we were working with, how should I say, 'willing' servicemen as volunteers."

A hushed laugh circulated in the ballroom.

Michel forced himself up from his chair and hesitantly approached the microphone in the aisle.

What should I say? Am I crazy? No, I have to do this.

He paused. An eerie silence filled the room as he spoke slowly, yet clearly, for all to hear: "I am Doctor Katz, Michel Katz. Those studies were not carried out in Texas. They were completed in Poland at a German concentration camp—Auschwitz, to be exact—some thirty years ago."

A soft murmur rushed through the audience.

"I should know…" Michel went on.

Oh my god. What am I doing…?

"I was there—as an inmate and a doctor. I did the autopsy and tissue studies on the twenty men who died after this man deliberately chilled them." He paused, his throat tightening up. "I still carry the shame and guilt for my role in these experiments—and worse, my lack of courage to try and stop them."

The hall was stunned silent. Michel stood shaking in front of the elevated stage. Finally, he realized he had nothing more to hide. The barriers he had constructed to protect himself and shield others were gone. The pressure in his chest mounting, and on the verge of collapse, he fought to stay clear and alert.

"This man is Maj0r Hans Bloch of the SS, not Jürgen Hauptman. And not only is he a liar here today, but he is a war criminal for having conducted these studies. Moreover, and more despicably, he did these and other horrific things under the guise of medical science."

Hans Bloch stood paralyzed as Michel spoke. His face reddened with fury, he jumped from the stage and charged down the aisle, crying, "Lousy Jew pig! I will finish off what we should have done thirty years ago!"

Stiletto in hand, Hans raced toward Michel…

2

October 28, 1914
Ypres, Belgium

An explosion of foul-smelling mud covered the five men cowering from the mortar round. Weeks of looking out from foul trenches at an enemy who was just as miserable as you was not the war these young men had expected. Occasionally, an artillery round came close to their bunker, making them duck for cover, but otherwise the soldiers just stood looking out, awaiting the infrequent order to leave the trench and charge the enemy. That is what "The Great War" was all about.

The filthy *Obersoldat* Gerhard Bloch sloshed through the muddy trench to await mail call with his German cohorts in the bunker. "Spetzler, Gunter, Bloch, Rausch—there is mail!"

Envelopes and parcels sailed into eager hands hoping to catch a glimpse of the life they'd left behind.

From the far corner of the command post, an excited cry was heard: "I'm a father!" shouted Gerhard. "My dream come true, a boy... His name is Hans."

Celebrating any soldier's good fortune brightened the spirits of all the men in these dismal surroundings, and Gerhard's compatriots directed a series of congratulations, back slaps, and hugs at him as he read and reread the good news from his wife. He spent the rest of the night with two close buddies drinking stolen French wine that had been saved for an occasion like this.

Gerhard Bloch's blessed luck lasted less than a fortnight. When his unit attempted to swarm the British lines, he was cut down by machinegun fire and died, along with thousands of other soldiers that day—on both sides of the war.

Following the return of Gerhard Bloch's body, family and friends gathered in Kiel, Germany for services at the First Lutheran Church. Eric Bloch was devastated by the death of his only son. Sitting quietly in church, he held his head in his hands, swaying gently back and forth in grief. Eric was inconsolable as friends approached him after the ceremony.

Garnering little attention, Gerhard's widow sat quietly in the front row holding her infant son in her arms. All eyes seemed to be drawn towards Eric, a highly respected man in the community. His shipbuilding company was one of the largest marine enterprises on the Baltic coast and he was important to the people of Kiel. In Eric's mind, great plans for his son Gerhard's future had been laid out in detail. He was to go to the university and study engineering so he could bring modern methods of manufacturing to the shipyard. Gerhard would then be in position to lead the company after his father retired. But that dream was now gone.

For a few months following the funeral, Eric was incapacitated by his deep mourning. He spoke to few friends, spending endless hours in his rocking chair, watching the boats traverse Kiel harbor. In time, he started to foster needed attention on his little grandson and began to view the boy as his own son. He became like a father to this special boy and devoted the next eighteen years of his life to preparing Hans for the life he had originally planned for Gerhard.

Eric Bloch was a serious man who was concerned about the future of his beloved Germany. More and more, he mused about the problems facing his country.

These post war years are so difficult for us. The Treaty of Versailles took away our German land, forced our Fatherland to pay reparations to the Allies and, most importantly, shattered our German pride.

Anger welled up within him as he reflected more deeply.

Our money has become worthless, and the Weimar government is weak. I see political strife present in every major city. We are desperately in need of a strong leader.

Standing at attention in front of the hall mirror, Eric Bloch stared at the image of a man who loved his country.

I want the Reich to stand up to the rest of the world... My grandson will be one of those who will lead our country out of the darkness that now envelops us all.

As the years passed, he instilled strength and pride in young Hans.

Each day, he would lecture the boy about the greatness of their homeland and instruct him in ways he could help restore it to its former glory. Hans listened intently.

When Hitler burst onto the political scene, they both grabbed onto his vision and his policies. Hans joined the forces of Hitler Youth at the earliest possible age and marched proudly with them. He collected many ribbons for his focused attitude, dress, and appearance. At a special ceremony, he was presented with an award for outstanding nationalism that had been signed by the Führer himself. Every weekend, he attended the Nazi demonstrations in Hamburg. His dedication to serving *his* Fatherland became paramount.

Gradually, Hans developed a strong sense of Aryan pride. Looking around him, he would notice the dark hair and swarthy faces of the Slavs, many with an "Oriental" appearance. Jews, in general, were distinguished by a brooding expression and were less attractive than Aryans, who were blessed with blue eyes, blond hair, and tall, handsome bodies. You could never trust the Slavs or the Jews. They would cheat and steal from you, if given the chance. At school, Hans was taught that it was the Jews who were responsible for Germany's defeat in the Great War, the hyperinflation that followed, and, sadly, the loss of national pride. After all, it was the Jews who owned and manipulated the banks, and it was their financial entanglements that had led this country down to the throes of defeat. It was also the Jews who had led the Bolshevik Revolution that now threatened the stability of the Reich. To Hans, the message was clear:

It is time to reestablish a Fatherland, firmly based on the strength of our Aryan heritage.

♦♦♦

March 12, 1934

HANS WAS JUST EIGHTEEN years old when an ambulance rushed his grandmother to Kiel University Hospital with searing abdominal pain. He paced anxiously outside the emergency room, waiting with his grandfather for updates, and was somewhat surprised when an older, obviously Jewish doctor sat down with them to explain what was wrong and what had to be done. With his large nose and deep-set eyes, there was no mistaking his race. Hans listened attentively as the doctor advised that immediate surgery was necessary for a ruptured aortic aneurysm.

He was nervous. He didn't want this doctor to operate on his family. "Is there another surgeon available, Herr Doktor Levy? We would be more comfortable with...one like us. You know...Aryan."

Staring directly into Hans's clear blue eyes, Doctor Levy said, "I am the doctor on call. If you wish to save your grandmother's life, I am her only chance at the moment."

Hans sat back in his chair and looked at his grandfather, who gave a curt nod of his chin, indicating that this doctor should proceed.

"Herr Doktor," Hans said in a steely voice, "I certainly do expect that my grandmother *will* come through this."

Doctor Levy stared back at Hans and his grandfather, but did not respond. He got up from his chair and went back to the operating suites, silently shaking his head as the door closed.

The two men sat patiently, speaking little while awaiting the surgery to finish.

Four hours later, the doctor came out wringing his surgical cap in his hands, and broke the news that Sarah Bloch's heart had stopped in the middle of the procedure. They had worked for two hours, desperately trying to resuscitate her. "I am so sorry—we tried the best we could," said Doctor Levy as he slowly walked away.

First the death of the father he had never met, and now his grandmother.

Why? Why did she have to die?

Hans tried hard to be strong, but the tears flowed down his cheeks, and he couldn't hide them. His anguish turned to rage as he tried to understand.

It had to be the doctor, that damn doctor!

Plans had been in place for Hans to attend university and study engineering, but with the death of his grandmother, his interest shifted to medicine. The following year, after taking the required course work, he entered medical school in Kiel. Yes, he would become a doctor, make his family proud, and use his Aryan superiority to replace those *incompetent Jews.*

"...Aesculapius, Hygieia, and Panacea, and I take witness to all Gods..."

3

June 22, 1940
Lyon, France

It was as if the world suddenly hushed that afternoon, and all things came to a stop. The expected noise of the city had been extinguished. Groups of people gathered outside stores where radios had been left on all day, anticipating confirmation of what they dreaded might happen.

"*La France* agrees to an armistice with Germany," the excited radio announcer was saying. "Hostilities have ended today, and peace has come!"

The crowd moved in closer.

"An agreement was signed between the governments of France and Germany at eight this morning. All prisoners will be exchanged, and troops on both sides have been ordered to halt all fighting. The specifics of the settlement will come out in the next few days."

The announcer went on to say that further statements would be forthcoming from the new government to be established in the City of Vichy. "*Vive La France!*" he signed off.

Later broadcasts went into greater detail about the "Vichy" government and their new leader, Marshal Philippe Pétain.

As if nothing had happened, the station resumed its normal Saturday programming, but the citizens in the streets remained frozen in place, as if expecting more. As the moments passed with no new announcements, a murmur arose from the crowd, growing louder, hands gesticulating in concert as voices swelled to a roar.

The cacophony interrupted Michel Katz's ponderings. Doctor Katz glanced around and watched how each face displayed a different emotion. Anger welled up in a big man next to him; perhaps he had fought in the Great War and mistakenly assumed France had won. Michel could see the pain of war on his face, his eyes tearing up as if the mustard gas had been released on him once again. Nearby, a young soldier on leave threw his head back, closed his eyes, and seemed to silently celebrate, knowing that he no longer faced death in the battlefield.

Michel turned and walked down toward the wharf, his head down, as if inspecting each stone embedded in the street. Along the way, he passed two young ladies, no more than twenty years old, who looked relieved and happy. They tittered, smiled, and hugged each other, realizing that their young men might soon come home from the war. They had no idea how their lives were about to change. Down the street, in front of the tailor's shop, men had gathered and were shouting into the air, gesturing with their hands. Like Michel, these men were Jewish and were well aware of the growing hostility Jews were facing in Germany and Poland. They had reason to be scared.

It was late afternoon when Doctor Michel Katz finished with his emergency surgery at the Hotel Dieu Hospital. He was on his way to the tram when news of the treaty was announced. Too many thoughts crossed his mind as he wondered what might happen to his family. His mind was racing uncontrollably, and he was not yet ready to return home. Rather than take the tram, he walked along the Rhone and stood on the embankment, watching the current flow and the barges slowly glide past as if nothing had changed. His eyes returned to the pavement as he drifted alone, unable to gather his conflicting thoughts. To the west, the L'Archange de Fourviere stood over the city, as it had for centuries, a protector of its souls. But it wasn't the kind of guardian the Jews of France needed now.

Michel studied the narrow cobblestone path that had been arduously laid out in a repetitive, arched pattern as it followed the river's course. He knew he should go home soon, that Anna and the children would be waiting for dinner. As he continued along the riverbank, his thoughts retraced his family's journey to France…

◆◆◆

"But, Mama, I don't want to leave and go somewhere else! All my friends are here in Vilnius."

Eight-year-old Michel's eyes filled with tears as his mother grabbed his hand and trudged down the porch stairs, pulling him into the waiting car, where he crowded into the backseat with her and his sister. As his father slipped into the passenger seat in front, Michel took one last glance at his home and buried his head in his mother's lap.

The Lithuanian economy in 1923 was depressed, and Aaron Katz had to make a difficult decision. Although his customer base, the Litvak—Lithuanian Jewish—population of Vilnius, was large, his small grocery store was faltering. Costs for foodstuffs continued to inflate at an astounding rate, and he could not keep up with his pricing. Barely breaking even, Aaron looked for a way out of his financial distress. In a local newspaper he had seen an advertisement calling for factory workers in France, with a pathway to full rights and citizenship. His wife's brother, Stan Goldfein, had just finished his medical training and had already left the country to pursue a surgical residency in France.

Even in their home city of Vilnius, anti-Semitism was rampant. The constant threat of violence and the past history of Cossack raids on outlying Jewish villages had convinced Aaron to search for a better life for himself and his family.

♦♦♦

Doctor Goldfein had been in Lyon just six months when his sister and the rest of the Katz family arrived. He quickly made arrangements for housing and directed his brother-in-law Aaron to a large metal fabricating company that was looking for workers. Excited to be in their new home, a dark cloud soon appeared over them as the Katz family encountered an unexpected form of discrimination.

The existing Jewish community in France did not seem to embrace the huge numbers of Eastern European Jews that had descended upon them during the past two decades. They were considered to be of a lower class than French Jews, and did not speak the native language. These *Yiddische* Jews from the east had little money compared to their French cousins, many of whom had climbed the local social ladders and accumulated significant wealth. Acceptance into French Jewish society was slow and awkward; only professionals seemed able to rise up and join this social stratum.

Despite these obstacles, the Katz family prospered during their early years in Lyon. Aaron worked hard and put in long hours, earning a good salary. With his savings, he was able to purchase a small home for his family, and they were soon enjoying their lives as French citizens.

Aaron's daughter, Sarah, and his son, Michel, were excellent students. Their parents expected only the best grades and continued to encourage success at school. Michel had developed an interest in science, and later medicine, as he progressed through his school years. He was a sensitive boy and spent hours helping other students who had difficulty with school. Upon starting *lycée*—high school—he volunteered at the local hospital, helping with errands and shuffling patients between tests and X-rays. Michel was well-liked and seemed genuine in his passion to help others. Whenever he was free, he would sneak into one of the observation seats overlooking an operating theater and watch, transfixed by the surgeons' ability to heal and renew people's lives. He could think of no better vocation.

Upon graduation, he was accepted into the Medical School at the University of Lyon, where he excelled. He easily passed the *concours* examinations for advancement in school and progressed through the six years of medical training. He was extremely curious about surgery, staying late into the night to observe and assist with procedures. This dedication was not lost on the surgical faculty, and Michel was invited to study as a resident in surgery upon the completion of his medical school examinations in 1936.

Among the Jewish population of Lyon, young Michel was considered a *mensch*—a good man. He seemed oblivious to racial and ethnic origin, and believed that everyone was entitled to good medical care.

Things went well for him during his residency. His thesis, "Cellular Changes in Response to Profound Hypothermia," was presented at the Meeting of the National Academy in March, 1940; he had developed a deserved reputation as an expert in this area of research.

♦♦♦

As MICHEL DRIFTED ALONG the river's edge toward his house, a new worry crossed his mind.

This peace agreement could affect my teaching position at the university… What if they place restrictions on Jewish doctors, like they did in Germany?

It was difficult to know if the French authorities would follow suit. Married just three years, he knew he had to think clearly and make decisions for an uncertain future. France's war was over, but his own might be just beginning...

Michel walked for two hours. There was no moon, the night was black, and his street was further darkened by the canopy of maple trees stretching across the pavement. It was humid, and the only light came from the oval, frosted glass lights at each street corner. This gloomy, uncomfortable time brought no solace to anyone's soul. The lace curtains on the windows facing the street filtered out any harsh light, allowing only a soft, warm glow to radiate from his home. Peering through the glass, he realized that life was all about his practice; home was only a necessary refreshing stop for the doctor whose world was centered in his operating suite.

Michel could see his wife clearing dishes from the dinner table. As he reached for the door, it seemed to swing open by itself as Anna greeted him.

There were dry tracks where tears had rolled down her face. The radio was on in the background... She had heard the news. She tried to speak but was nearly incoherent as she forced herself to say, "How was your day?"

More tears welled up in her tired eyes; she stopped trying to talk.

"The war's over... Maybe it's good." Michel tried to sound confident. "We'll be okay...I think. Remember, this is France, and we now have peace. They won't bother us."

He had lied to them both, and gently placed his arms around her. *"Je t'aime."*

Michel shivered as he struggled to understand what the next days might bring.

"...whatever, in connection with my professional practice or not..."

4

June 17, 1943
Southern France

The sudden blasting of the train's horn awoke Anna from her mid-morning slumber and the early summer heat made their compartment uncomfortable. Yet the children—three-year-old Rachel and Aaron, now five—remained fast asleep since the family had left Lyon. Anna had been taken aback by the number of people she saw traveling. Despite the war, families still crowded into trains to get away from the cities in the summer and the mountains around Grenoble provided cool relief from the pressures of rationing and sweltering heat. Glancing around the car, her eyes panned from an older couple she had met who were on their way to see their grandchild over to her husband fidgeting anxiously to her right. She'd seen Michel's hands clench when they'd left the station at Lyon and watched him brush away a tear as they stepped onto the train. Anna had never observed her husband so uneasy. The silence hung heavy between them.

They waited tensely for the first encounter with authorities, not knowing that it would come so early. A cheerful, rotund conductor knocked on their door and slid it open. *"Billets, s'il vous plaît,* tickets."

Michel produced the family's tickets and handed them to the man, who glanced curiously towards him but said nothing.

Fifteen minutes later, two gendarmes knocked on the door and slid open their compartment. "Identification, *messieurs et mesdames, immediatement, s'il vous plaît."*

Michel handed him their government-issued cards as well as a letter from Doctor Henri Deville, requesting his presence as a visiting consultant and lecturer on "Surgery and Genetics" at the Nice Institute on June 22, 1943. Stepping outside, the two men could be seen huddling, examining the documents that identified the family as Jews.

The second policeman came back into the compartment. "Doctor Katz, why is it necessary to bring the entire family with you for this lecture?"

Michel's jaw tightened as he tried to control his anger. He wanted to lash out, but as Anna touched his arm gently, he regained his composure and remembered his well-rehearsed response. "*Monsieur*, my wife is my assistant in research and she also teaches a course to Doctor Deville's aides. We were asked to come together. If you read further, it states that he is looking forward to my wife's help with his research team. It was impossible to leave the children behind. You must understand our position."

The two policemen looked at each other, then down at the sleeping children. They knew that laws established by the Vichy government restricted Jews from travel, yet this doctor seemed to have a valid professional invitation. They dropped their heads and exited the compartment, appearing defeated.

Michel sighed deeply as his pounding heart began to slow down.

That was close, but the letter had worked.

He reached into his breast pocket, pulled out a pack of Gauloises, shook it down. As one cigarette popped up, he placed it between his lips. Then he retrieved a lighter from his pocket and lit up. Inhaling deeply, he slowly exhaled like a boiler letting off steam. He glanced over at Anna, whose face had turned pale; she was nauseous with fear. The family had made it through the first crisis, but Michel knew this was just the beginning. He recalled the clear warning the mayor of Lyon had given him just three weeks earlier...

◆◆◆

May 31, 1943

IT WAS THE FLASH of light and a deafening sound that made Françoise jump up from her desk.

Surely no bombs are being dropped on Lyon?

And then, realizing it was a late spring storm passing through, she breathed a deep sigh of relief. The telephone rang.

"It is *plus important* that I see Monsieur *le Docteur* Katz *tout de suite,* as soon as possible!" railed to the man on the phone.

Only after he had identified himself as Henri Dubonnet, Mayor of Lyon, did Françoise offer him an appointment for later that afternoon. As the doctor's secretary, she recognized that in these times, it was best for him to stay on the right side of important officials. And, after all, the mayor had said it was a serious stomach malady.

Françoise walked down the hallway to Doctor Katz's office and stopped outside to gather her thoughts. Now forty years old, she had worked for other doctors before coming to this office two years ago. Doctor Katz was different—a kind, gentle man who devoted his life to his patients. She enjoyed running his office. It didn't hurt that he was attractive and in good shape, standing nearly six feet tall, with thick brown hair and bushy eyebrows. But now, as she knocked on the door, she was worried for him.

"Come in, Françoise. What is it?"

She quickly forewarned Doctor Katz of Dubonnet's visit and left, closing the door behind her.

Michel's heart was racing. The mayor knew the risks…

Why come here now?

To accommodate the wishes of their German collaborators, the new Vichy government had warned officials to avoid contact with Jewish professionals. A sense of foreboding enveloped Michel.

Could my fears be coming true?

He had hoped to get home early to Anna and see the kids before they were off to sleep, but now he knew he would be late.

It was difficult for him to listen to patients' complaints for the rest of the afternoon. Mrs. Levi, whose gallbladder had been removed three weeks prior, became nonplussed when his mind wandered off during her questions. "Doctor, you seem not to be listening," she chided. "Are you not feeling well, or have I said something to upset you?"

He managed to collect his thoughts. *"Non, non, je regrette,* please excuse me. Ask me again."

Her concerns about proper diet and activity were addressed and she left, wishing him well.

Françoise stepped out into the hallway and nodded her head. The mayor was here. From a small alcove off his examination room, Michel was able to observe Dubonnet as he left the waiting room. He noticed the mayor seemed fearful, his eyes nervously darting around the office, glancing over his shoulder as he followed Françoise down the hall. His right hand gripped his brown bowler hat, a perfect match to his dark woolen business suit. Gone was his usual air of self-importance. Françoise ushered him into the examination room.

Mayor Dubonnet was a short, balding man whose head shone from sweat dripping onto his rimless glasses, which he continually wiped with a handkerchief. The chart noted "abdominal pain" as the reason for this appointment, but he appeared to be in no physical distress.

"*Bonjour*, Your Honor, what may I do for you today?" said Doctor Katz.

"We must talk," the mayor whispered.

The room became quiet. "Please sit and be comfortable. What's on your mind?"

Michel was working hard to maintain his professional composure as the mayor took a seat and peered directly into his eyes. He spoke quietly and precisely, as if each detail was important for the doctor to understand. The story he told was unnerving, yet consistent with fears now running rampant in the Jewish community.

"My doctor friend, you must listen to me now. This is the only place I felt we could be safe from the worry of collaborators overhearing us. You must pay close attention to what I say to you and share this with no one outside your family."

Michel remembered how the former mayor, popular Édouard Herriot, had been exiled to Germany because he'd stood up against the Vichy regime and their policies. He scooted his chair closer to the mayor. "Go on. I understand."

"Klaus Barbie has just returned from Berlin, where he was reprimanded for his failure to meet his quota of Jew transports to concentration camps. As the head of the sixth division of the Lyon Gestapo, he is being ordered to double the number of transports and bring 8,200 Jews to the Drancy transit camp by October first." The mayor leaned forward intently and looked down. "Michel, understand me. Not just foreign Jews, but *all* Jews. French citizens or not, all are to be rounded up."

Michel drew a deep breath. "But this part of France, the lower two-fifths, is run by our government in Vichy and the Germans should have no say here. We may be Jews, but we are citizens of France first. We should be protected, *n'est-ce pas?*"

"The Gestapo tells us they need workers in Germany for their factories. No one here cares if they take away the Jews to do the work. Listen to me. No *real* Frenchmen are to be taken."

Michel shook his head. So rapidly things had changed. He recalled how happy his parents had been when they were allowed to become full citizens in 1927, just five years after they had arrived from Lithuania. At the ceremony, the presiding immigration official had proudly proclaimed, "We now put aside any former nationality or religious identity. We are all Frenchmen!"

"They have also asked the mayors of St. Etienne and Clermont-Ferrand to update their lists of Jews," the mayor was saying. "In fact, a group of local Frenchmen, German collaborators, have offered to help the police and Gestapo in this undertaking. They call themselves *miliciens.*"

"Tell me, Mayor Dubonnet, aren't these miliciens like the Brown Shirts of Germany—fascist bastards?"

"You are correct."

The cold, bare examination room went silent. Michel stood up, put his stethoscope in a pocket of his white coat, and brushed his hand through his thick brown hair. "So why are you telling me this now?"

"I am here because I respect you and must return a debt owed to you. I have wanted to thank you many times for saving the life of my daughter three years ago." Wiping his eyes, he continued. "Now, it is my turn to repay you. It is the very least I can do under these circumstances."

The mayor then outlined the details of the transport operation. "On June 25, 1943, just one month from now, a fully-coordinated exercise will occur at five a.m. with the participation of the local police, Gestapo, and miliciens. It will involve the roundup of Jews in Lyon, St. Etienne, and Clermont-Ferrand. This exercise is considered top secret to avoid any reaction by the public, so that no one tries to hide or escape across the borders into Switzerland or Spain."

"But, Mayor, how do you know about this if it's such a secret?" Michel asked, wanting to find a reason to not believe what he was hearing. "How did the Germans drag you into it?"

Mayor Dubonnet was now soaked in perspiration. "My good friend, the Germans have had several coordinating meetings with the police and *miliciens* to make sure this special action goes off well. They had to inform me. Three months ago, a meeting was held in Paris between the Gestapo and mayors of selected cities. They discussed the problems of the partisan resistance and 'the Jewish question.' It was a warning. They showed us movies of partisans being hanged and an early morning roundup of Jews."

Michel ran his hands through his hair again. "Please continue."

"It was horrendous. The shouted orders of the Nazis were drowned out by the screams from the people who were forced out of their homes. Children were crying as they were tossed into the backs of trucks. German shepherd guard dogs strained at their leashes and barked fiercely as the Jews were forced to march to waiting trains."

As the mayor related this series of events, he became increasingly agitated, but it was hard for Michel to discern whether his nervousness was because of the nature of the actions he was describing or fear that he would be seen in Katz's office. He kept rubbing his hands together, as if trying to rid himself of an invisible layer of concern, and his voice grew hoarse, as if his throat were closing up.

"Shall I ask Françoise to bring some water?"

"*Merci, merci beaucoup,*" he said. "It has been so hard, so devastating for me to deal with this."

Doctor Katz's secretary brought in a bottle of water and two glasses. Instead of the sharply-dressed doctor who had greeted her this morning, his shirt was now stained with sweat, his pale blue-and-black tie had gone askew, and worry lines covered his face. His hands started to shake as he poured the water and Françoise left the room unnerved.

The doctor joined the mayor in drinking the cooling water, as if to quell the parched feeling left by the news. Dubonnet looked at his physician friend. "You understand, this must be between us, or I might suffer the wrath of the Gestapo. I trust you, as a man and as the doctor who saved my little Carol." Tears welled up in his eyes. "You can now plan to save your family."

As the mayor rose suddenly and grasped Michel's hand, there was a look of terror or deep sorrow in his eyes. He quickly exited the examining room, directed by Françoise to the back door of the suite.

Alone in his office, Michel sat back quietly at his desk as he thought about his son Aaron, now five years old, and his daughter Rachel, who had just turned three. The potential horror of the Germans invading their home and transporting the family to a concentration camp weighed heavily on him. Anna Katz was a strong, supportive wife who had always backed him and his decisions, yet following the armistice with the Germans in June 1940, she had talked about fleeing France. Secretly, Michel thought she was right, yet he couldn't bear to leave his position at the university. And Michel had always placed the practice of medicine before anything else in his life. For the past three years, he, too, had feared this kind of action by the Germans and understood that his family was not immune from deportation. Nor was he unaware of the insipient anti-Semitism amongst the French, who traditionally turned a blind eye to any such hostile actions against Jews and minorities.

This time, he could not ignore the facts. He knew that he and his family had to leave Lyon, and that travel might be dangerous for them. It was time to devise a plan.

◆◆◆

THE LATE NIGHT TELEPHONE call jolted Stan Goldfein. It had been months since he had last talked with his nephew Michel.

Doctor Goldfein had been in surgical practice in Nice for nineteen years, and as head of the Department of Surgery at l'Institut de Nice, established a well-deserved reputation as the finest abdominal surgeon along the Côte d'Azur. Soon after his sister, Sophie, and her husband, Samuel Katz, had arrived in Lyon from Lithuania with their two young children, he finished his surgical training and ventured on to Nice, where he built his successful practice in a short period of time. Although Doctor Goldfein held an important position in this seaside community, few would recognize him on the street due to his unpretentious appearance. Shorter than most men, with a slender build and thinning gray hair, he walked with a slight stoop, yet moved quickly with purpose.

Stan Goldfein was a smart man who made it a point to be well- informed, and, in recent days, he'd learned much from his private connections inside the Italian government. For their small part in the defeat of France, the Italians now occupied and administered the southeastern area of the country bordering Italy, including Nice, Grenoble, and their neighboring villages. Fortunately, the inherent animosity between the Italians and French insulated Nice's Jewish population from the decrees and actions of the Vichy government and their German occupiers. Stan understood that the Italian authorities had repeatedly told the Germans that they would take care of their own Jewish problem, and that none would be transported to German camps.

"Uncle Stan," Michel asked urgently on the phone, "when may I come join you? Our lives will begin to unravel on June twenty-fifth, and I must leave here as soon as possible with Anna and the children."

Michel then related the details of the planned roundup of Jews that Henri Dubonnet had unveiled in his office that day.

Stanley Goldfein could feel his nephew's fear on the other end of the line. It was real, and he knew more than most about the true destination of the transports and what was called the "Final Solution." In fact, Michel's uncle already knew about the top secret movement of German troops to the south of France because of his relationship with Angelo Donati, an Italian Jew with much influence in Rome. "Michel, you must listen," Stan said urgently, "and pay close attention, as every detail is important. Get your things together for travel, and don't worry about your furnishings just yet. Pack your suitcases and books. Travel on the Lyon-Grenoble line and switch to the Grenoble-Valence-Nice train. Do not, I repeat, *do not*, go through Marseille, as a heavy German troop buildup is occurring as we speak and will only increase in size. There will be fewer inspections and Gestapo officers on the Lyon-Grenoble line as Grenoble is also under Italian control. I have relationships with some officials that will help you and your family when you enter the Italian occupation zone."

"But, Uncle Stan, what about my father and mother? They must leave as well!"

"Let your father know the seriousness of the situation so he can bring the rest of the family with you. When your arrangements are made, call me again on a secure line so I can contact my Italian army connections. Indeed, I will get you an invitation from my hospital to speak at a conference."

Michel squirmed anxiously in his office chair. "And, my good nephew, trust no one else. Don't talk about your plans, even with your Jewish associates, as there are scoundrels who get paid for turning in other Jews. After you arrive here, you can then make arrangements to place your goods and furnishings in storage. Have a good friend—a Christian friend—help you out with that."

There was a click, and the line went dead. Michel stared outside as he replaced the phone in its receiver and studied the lights along the river through the tall windows of the Hotel Dieu Hospital. He believed that the hospital phones were less likely to be tapped by the Gestapo than his home phone. One thing was clear—he could no longer stay in Lyon. Grasping a lighter from his desk drawer, he lit a cigarette and inhaled deeply.

As he began to think about closing his practice, a profound sadness overtook him. Many of his patients had become his friends. Yet he knew that even if he stayed, the coming action would take him away from the life he loved. He had no alternative but to protect his family.

That night, he left his office and stopped at the surgical ward to see Madame Cohen. Her recovery from a sigmoid colon resection had been slow, and he was concerned about her fevers. "*Bonsoir,* young Mrs. Cohen," he said, noting that her hair had been recently coiffed, "you look most beautiful tonight! Perhaps the Hollywood producers will be arriving at the hospital for you this evening?"

She smiled back at him. "I think it's time for you to practice your lines, Mr. Debonair Doctor." She raised herself up in the bed, grimaced with pain, and looked at Katz hopefully. "How long, do you think, before I get out of this bed?"

Michel knew things he hadn't told his patient. When he'd removed the tumor obstructing her colon, he'd found two palpable masses on her liver that turned out to be metastases related to her cancer. But rather than alarm his elderly patient about her limited life ahead, he chose to relay only optimism and get her home to her husband.

He asked her to lie flat so he could reach down and gently touch her abdomen, away from the bandages. Adjusting his stethoscope, he listened intently and looked up, smiling, "It seems like everything will be working soon. Your fever is down, and soon you will be on your way."

Mrs. Cohen gazed admiringly at Doctor Katz. "Thank you so much for all you have done. You are a wonderful doctor and a marvelous man."

As he left the room, his eyes began to well up. Turning his head away from the nursing station, he wiped the tears before they had a chance to roll down his face. Michel had not thought it would be this difficult to leave, yet it had been so much of his life—this hospital and his patients. Back in his office, he placed the phone call he had been thinking about since the mayor's visit.

"Doctor Joublanc, this is Doctor Michel Katz. Sorry to call you at home but some things of importance have come up, and I want to meet with you tomorrow morning between cases. Could you do that?" Michel listened and then continued, "Oh no, nothing like that. You're a fine surgeon, and that is why I want to see you. I may need some coverage for my patients... Yes, eleven a.m. would be great."

His last call was to his office assistant, Françoise.

"To hold him who taught me this art equally dear to me as my parents…"

5

Grenoble, France

T he rest of the four-hour train ride to Grenoble was uneventful, and the Katz family spent the day viewing the picturesque countryside, an area that the war had seemed to bypass. A sweet period of solace accompanied this portion of their trip. Grand old chateaux, verdant forests, and golden fields were their vistas. As the train approached the city, the landscape transformed into the majestic mountains that welcomed travelers into the Alps. Michel's plans had worked out well, except for one issue that dogged him. Despite his efforts to convince his parents and sister of the coming danger, they had refused to leave Lyon. Michel had gone to their home, pleading with them to join him. His father had been adamant: "We are safe. They will not deport us; we have full French citizenship. Michel, if you wish to leave, that's your choice. We are staying. No one will bother us."

"But, Father, I must tell you, a deportation action is coming—in less than a month. I know from the highest authority. All Jews—not just the immigrants—*all* Jews will be rounded up." Michel stood up and raised his voice. "You must hear me out!"

"Michel, you've always been the alarmist, the know-it-all doctor. I am older and have lived through the Cossack raids in Lithuania. I have been called 'Jew Boy' and 'Yid' and 'Christ-killer.' And I survived. Look at us, owning a home in Lyon, having our own car and a successful son like you. And your sister is just finishing college. No one, not even the Germans, will touch us."

Unable to convince them of the coming danger, Michel's eyes cast downward in defeat. He walked over to his mother and hugged her tight, as tears filled his eyes. Then, he wrapped his arms around his father and kissed him on the cheek. Leaving his parents' home, he felt a deep sense of dread that he would never see them again. Halfway down the street, he turned to go back and try one last time to persuade them, but he stopped.

Father is so hardheaded, it's no use.

Returning home to Anna and the children, he was met with another emotional challenge that allowed him, for the moment, to forget his parents' truculence.

Opening the front door he found Anna sitting at the dining room table, head down and deep in thought. Her clear blue eyes initially brightened as Michel entered the room, yet they seemed to dim as she observed the lines of concern on his face.

"Oh, Michel, I can see things didn't go well at your parents' house."

"You are right. They aren't coming with us. My father is blind to any reason to leave."

He looked at his wife's face and realized that she'd been crying alone.

Anna wiped her eyes. "This is the hardest thing for me to do, leave our home, friends, and now our family. Why? I just don't understand what the Germans want to do with us."

Michel put his arms around her shoulders and held her close. "I know I have been busy, but we can talk again tonight after the children fall asleep. Let me finish up some details concerning the trip."

He released his grip on her and headed for the desk in the family room.

Anna Katz remained seated at the table. She'd had a difficult time dealing with her thoughts after Michel told her about the mayor's visit. She had tried to talk with him about these feelings, but there had been little time, as he had been staying long hours at the hospital finishing up scheduled surgeries. There was a mixture of sadness and anger about leaving the life they had built together in Lyon, coupled with her real fear of deportation. Her quiet resentment had been building now into a fury, and she found it difficult to know to whom it should be directed. For the first time in her life, she felt the burden of being Jewish.

If only Michel's parents hadn't been so damn insistent on my conversion, the children and I might not be at risk.

Her Lutheran family had stopped attending church long ago. They had lost their religious zeal after the horrors of World War I and the unspeakable death and destruction that had descended on Europe. But Michel's parents wouldn't bless the marriage unless she agreed to raise the children in a Jewish home. Her weak religious upbringing allowed Anna room to accede to their demands and convert to Judaism, so she studied with Rabbi Silverman and even immersed herself in the purifying waters of the *mikvah*.

That rabbi must have been a prophet.

He had spoken often of the "Wandering Jew," a term resulting from the repeated persecution of Jews throughout history, and the constant need for them to search out safe havens.

♦♦♦

THE TRAIN ROLLED SLOWLY into the city proper, paralleling the Drac River, and came to a stop at the Grenoble station. The Katz family disembarked; they were to board another train for Nice in two hours.

To Michel, it looked as if the war had forgotten Grenoble. There were no German troops marching on these streets and no armored tanks or vehicles to be seen. A few Italian soldiers patrolled a city seemingly untouched by battle. People cheerfully crowded the sidewalks, chatting over wine or coffee in the many open cafés, appearing to be unaware of what was happening in the rest of Europe.

Rachel and Aaron had been penned up for so long that they rushed to get off the train as soon as the doors opened. "Children, slow down and wait for your father to collect the luggage. You must stay close!" Anna shouted, grabbing them as they reached the compartment door.

The two children gathered around their mother on the platform, waiting for Michel to arrive with a luggage cart.

After loading the suitcases onto the cart, they walked over to a café and chose a quiet table away from the crowds. A waiter appeared and they ordered coffee, milk, and rolls. Michel kept the children at the table, not allowing them to run free, which could draw attention to him and his family.

Scanning the platforms, Michel noticed a heavy police presence around the train station. In addition, there were the sordid milice in their blue berets sporting pistols at their waists while patrolling and looking for members of the resistance. These men carried the chronic scowl of malcontents, always looking for ways to increase their self-importance at the expense of others. Michel reminded the children to play quietly after they finished their snack, as he hoped to avoid the eyes of the police nearby.

The announcement of the train's departure to Valence-Nice had them quickly walking back to the platform and boarding their car. This time, the compartment was for them alone. It would take another six hours to reach their destination, and they had time to settle in and rehearse what would be said to any authority who questioned their traveling.

Looking at his fair-haired wife and children, Michel realized how easily they could pass for gentiles. As it turned out, no one asked for any papers until they had reached the outskirts of Nice.

The whole family was startled by the loud knock and the door being forcefully slid open. Rachel became scared and started to cry while Aaron clutched his mother's waist. A man in a dark suit and brown overcoat accompanied the gendarme who barged into the compartment. "May I see your papers?" said the imposing civilian with a strong German accent.

Protectively, Anna pulled both children toward her.

Michel reached slowly into his satchel, pulled out their identification papers and the letter from Doctor Deville, and then handed them to the Gestapo agent.

In a determined voice, the man in the suit spoke. "You know that travel by Jews is restricted, and you cannot enter Nice. You must come with me while I check with the Gestapo section VI in Lyon to see if they are looking for you."

Anna cried out, "No, he can't leave us."

"Not just him, but all of you."

The agent grabbed Michel's upper arm roughly, but Michel pulled away, almost knocking him down.

The train slowly entered the Nice station and came to a stop.

"Let go of me! You have the letter. Read it. I forgot. Maybe you can't—can't read."

Enraged, the French policeman restrained Michel while the German agent pummeled him with punches to his stomach and side. Michel fought back and pulled away from the gendarme, only to look up into the Luger that the Gestapo agent was pointing at his head.

"Oh Mommy, this bad man has a gun!" Aaron screamed, hiding behind his mother.

"Jew doctor, I suggest you stop." Placing the gun against Michel's head, he continued. "It wouldn't be a pretty sight for the children."

"Mrs. Katz, line up behind your husband with the children," said the gendarme.

With his hands up and the Gestapo agent behind him, Michel led his family out of the train. A small crowd had formed outside when they heard the commotion.

Anna kept the sobbing children close to her.

Desperately scanning the station, Michel spotted an Italian military officer patrolling the platform, and yelled to him. "Captain, my name is Doctor Michel Katz, and this Gestapo agent is trying to take us away. Stop him, please help us!"

Michel attempted to walk towards the Italian, but was restrained by the German. "I have a letter here, inviting me to teach at the Nice Institute, yet this agent doesn't understand."

Anna and the children were barely breathing, hanging on every word.

The Italian halted and checked his clipboard. Looking at the German and Michel, he held up his right arm and stopped the agent in his tracks. "Let go of this doctor. He is an invited guest and you have no jurisdiction here. Give me the letter he is referring to."

"But he is a Jew!" the agent roared. "His family is probably scheduled for transport to the East, and you must know that they are not allowed to travel beyond their home city."

"I don't care what your laws say. Remember, you are in the Italian Administration Zone, and you have no authority in this part of France." The officer held out his hand to the German. "Now give me the damn letter!"

Reluctantly, the Gestapo agent handed over the identification papers and the letter from Doctor Deville to the Italian, who quickly scanned the documents.

"This is not Vichy, nor is it Germany, and your racial solutions are not accepted by our government. You either release Doctor Katz, or I must place *you* under arrest."

The Italian officer stepped forward with two enlisted men on his heels and pushed the German agent and French policeman aside, releasing

Michel from the German's grasp.

The Gestapo agent's face reddened. "The German Counsel will hear about this, Captain. And Klaus Barbie will be upset. You *will* pay."

The crowd had grown larger as the Italians led the family to the safety of a small room at the back of the station.

Captain Lugano, a tall and confidant officer, apologized to Michel as he guided them inside. He sported a well-trimmed, thick black mustache and wavy dark hair. "We are in a constant battle with the Germans and Vichy French concerning the Jews here. However, you are an important guest, and we have a note from the Italian consul himself directing safe passage."

Michel began to realize…

The Italians are protecting us.

Until this moment, he had not fully understood the difference between how Jews were treated in Germany and Italy. On the surface, both Axis powers had approached the "Jewish Question" with similar laws restricting their education, business access, and ability to make a living. But to the Italians, the laws appeared to be theoretical and rhetoric only, not practiced. Michel's uncle had implied that they would be safer in Nice. The Italian-Jewish community, he said, seemed to be hindered little by "race laws" and life went on as before. It was well known that many Jews held important positions in the government and Italian Fascist party, and that the Italians lacked the ingrained anti-Semitism prevalent in much of Central and Eastern Europe.

Mussolini wanted no part of Hitler's Final Solution, and had instructed his military and diplomatic corps not to cooperate with the Germans on their Jewish policies. Little did the Jews of Nice understand why 'Il Duce,' the Italian dictator, was so important to their future salvation.

Upon leaving the back room of the station, Michel spotted a proud Stanley Goldfein sporting a victorious grin on his face. He knew what had transpired.

"...May it be granted to me to enjoy Life and the Practice of the Art,
respected by all men, in all times..."

6

Nice, France
July 1943

That summer of 1943 seemed peaceful. Michel assisted his uncle with surgical procedures at l'Institut de Nice. An apartment had been set up for his family in an upscale area of the city, just three blocks off the beach. Anna, Rachel, and Aaron enjoyed the rocky beaches of Nice while their father worked at the hospital. Non-threatening Italian soldiers patrolled in and around Nice, but the war was always in the background, and as the days passed, Doctor Katz and his family began to enjoy life along the French Rivera.

A few weeks after their arrival, the newspaper *Nice Matin* reported: "Il Duce, our leader, is deposed."

Mussolini was gone. Jews celebrated foolishly that night in the streets of this city, along with a large number of Italian expatriates who called Nice their home. But when the revelry wound down and the sun rose the next morning, the Jewish community woke up to the stark realization that they were now perhaps at even greater risk. Could it be that their merriment had been misdirected? After all, the despised dictator had actually been a friend to the Jews, having assiduously blocked the Germans from sending them to concentration camps.

"Michel, things may get bad for us," Stan said the next morning over coffee, looking more worried than his nephew had ever seen him. "This new head of state replacing Mussolini, Badoglio, may wish to stop the war and get out from under the thumb of the Germans. That would put us at risk, as the Germans would certainly move in right away to occupy the present Italian administration zone."

Beads of sweat began to form on Michel's forehead as his uncle continued.

"And the Germans have lists—lists of all Jews living in our area. They were updated last month, and our names and addresses are all recorded. We must make our plans to leave and get to Italy."

"But, Stan, how did they get the lists? I thought the Italians were our friends."

"My contact Angelo told me that Inspector General Guido Lospinoso, a high-ranking Italian police officer from Bari, was sent in early May to deal with the Germans and Vichy government regarding the 'Jewish resettlement issue.' He outlined details for detention camps in the Italian occupation zone, but the Germans correctly deduced that he represented a new form of obstruction to their plans."

Michel nodded that he understood.

"To quiet the Germans," Stan continued, "Lospinoso had agreed to allow the collection of 'Jew lists' in each prefect, but he did not consent to distribute them."

He then related his last conversation with his well-connected Italian banker friend, Angelo Donati. Donati had confided that he wanted Guido Lospinoso to withhold the lists from the Gestapo altogether, that he had strongly advised him: "Guido, you have kept the Germans away from our Jews, away from deportation, and you have frustrated the Gestapo. We know what happens to those sent to the East... So many will die. You have done all that you needed to do for the Germans. It is important that you continue to stand up for Italian sovereignty and morality involving people under our control."

But Donati had failed. "Guido Lospinoso was tired; tired of all the meetings with the Germans, the SS, Gestapo, diplomats, all pressing him to give them the lists," Stan said wearily. "He could fight no longer. The lists fell into the hands of the Gestapo."

For the first time, Michel caught a flash of panic in his uncle's eyes.

On September 8, 1943, Italy signed an armistice with the Allies. A premature announcement of this event by the Allies shocked the civilians in Nice and made the unprepared Italian troops vulnerable, as many of their battalions were immediately surrounded by the *Wehrmacht*, the German army. Italian civilians and French Jews in the Italian-administered areas of France had little time to leave and find safety in Italy. Michel watched as the peaceful community of Nice suddenly transformed into a disorganized stream of refugees packing belongings and leaving the city. But few people realized that the number permitted to cross the border was limited and required either a valid Italian passport or a visa. Thus, the Italian bureaucracy, slow and unprepared, could not keep up with the sudden upsurge in requests for visas to cross the border. Italian soldiers, too, hastened to flee France, and their retreat was also chaotic. A few units stood and fought, but they were unable to withstand the strength of the German forces. Thousands were taken prisoner; many were executed.

Without hesitation, and within twenty-four hours of their reoccupation of the former Italian Zone, the German roundup of the Jews of Nice began.

◆◆◆

September 9, 1943

"COME ON, CHILDREN. CLIMB into the truck quickly. We must go!" shouted Anna, watching through eyes welling up with sorrowful tears.

She was stricken with fear as panic escalated around her. One day, this city was calm and peaceful; now it was bursting with pandemonium. The road was filled with a bedraggled force of civilians fleeing on foot, in cars, trucks, and buses. Every vehicle was packed, and many had soldiers riding on the step boards or clinging to the backs of trucks. There were frightful sounds of gunfire coming from the western part of Nice.

The two doctors desperately needed a haven. Doctor Goldfein had been in contact with the banker Donati, who tried to get emergency immigration visas for Stan, his wife Sarah, and his nephew's family; but he was unsuccessful and had left during the night, fearing for his own life. The *miliciens* and Gestapo were anxious to arrest this Italian official, noting his previous role in frustrating their attempts to round up Jews for transport to death camps.

In a matter of forty-eight hours, the families of Stanley Goldfein, MD, and Michel Katz, MD, so respected in the community, had become refugees fleeing the Nazis, fearing for their lives and their future.

The truck cost the doctors over one thousand francs. It had belonged to the green grocer next door to the physicians' office. Michel had often watched the truck unload early in the morning as he arrived for work, wondering if he might one day need a similar vehicle if the situation turned ominous. He'd even approached the grocer, Pierre Blanc, two weeks earlier, to see if he might sell it. *"Monsieur le Docteur,* for you I could sell it, as the Germans would take it from me in any case and give me *rien du tout,"* the grocer replied.

When Badaglio took control, Michel again approached his grocer friend, who said he would let it go for "a mere thousand francs," a price he knew the doctors could afford. With no other option, the doctors paid over five times its value for the beat-up four-year-old Citroën T23.

Now, vehicles of all sorts filled the roadway behind them. Trucks belching black smoke struggled to get up the single lane into the hills north of Nice.

Michel had trouble with the gearshift and heavy clutch, grinding each change of the gears, as he had done when he first learned to drive. The regular to-and-fro lurching of the truck had the two women and children inside clinging to each other for safety as well as comfort. The children were curled up in the truck bay trying to sleep, and Anna did her best to make them comfortable. But the smell of the exhaust soon took its toll on the passengers, and the children began vomiting into a can that had been brought along for that purpose. Sarah Goldfein and Anna were frozen in fear as their husbands navigated the road towards the border. The elder surgeon, in the passenger seat, held a map in his hands, trying to determine alternate pathways, if needed.

As the road wound above the hills overlooking Monaco, the sound of a single-engine airplane flying overhead momentarily paralyzed everyone in the truck. "It's only a Luftwaffe observation plane," yelled Michel to the truck's passengers in response to the terrified screams of Sarah and Anna. But he spoke more quietly to his front seat companion: "The Germans are looking for escaping civilians; let's hope we get to the border soon."

"Your identification papers, please—all of you," the Italian soldier yelled with such force that Rachel and Aaron started to cry, and the women were visibly shaken.

They had finally made it to the border.

"No visa, no entry!" barked the sergeant in charge in faulty French.

Goldfein spoke firmly. "But *Signore*, an important official, Angelo Donati, has promised us safe passage. If we can't cross into Italy, the Germans will take us away to concentration camps. You must let us in!"

"I have my orders. You need papers, visa or Italian passport. There is no way I can let your family pass."

The soldiers kept looking past the ragged line of vehicles lined up at the crossing, as if to see if the Germans themselves were close behind.

Michel was ordered to turn around and head back into France. Along the roadside, abandoned vehicles stood empty except for a few belongings discarded by their former occupants, who had taken to the hills to enter Italy.

Doctor Goldfein had mapped out another route; retracing their path for ten kilometers, they turned up a dirt road and headed toward the border, winding along a path up the mountain no wider than a cattle trail. As they rounded an outcropping of rocks, they were met by a German patrol. Noticing the SS Sig Runes patches on their collars, Doctor Goldfein whispered, "They're Waffen SS... Let me do the talking."

He stopped the truck and eagerly approached the waiting German soldiers, speaking to them in German. "Perhaps you can help us. Our fuel is low and we have made a wrong turn trying to get to Digne-les-Bains. Do you have a map we could use?"

A young corporal seemed eager to help. Pulling a map out of its case, he started to unfold it. Just then, a serious-looking lieutenant motioned to the younger man to step aside and said, "Let me see your identification papers, please."

Soon an open car appeared from behind, two more SS officers got out.

"Doctor Michel Katz, Doctor Stanley Goldfein, Anna Katz, Sarah Goldfein, and children Rachel and Aaron. Are those your correct names?" asked the SS officer.

Doctor Goldfein answered, "Yes."

"And you are coming from Nice, correct?" he continued. Scanning the truck and its occupants, he raised his voice. "You are Jews traveling without permits?"

"Yes, everything was so, so confused, and the sounds of war scared us to the point we had to get out of the city." Stanley took a deep breath. "We were on our way to Digne-les-Bains where friends live and we could stay until the battles died down. But we got lost with all the traffic."

The SS officer pulled out a clipboard containing a sheaf of papers and started going down a list. Stanley could see the neatly typed names of people on the register, which must have been over fifty pages long. "Doctor Goldfein, Doctor Katz, you and your families are on the list of Jews to be transported to Drancy. Did you know that?" queried the German officer.

Without waiting for an answer, the officer ordered the two families to get out of their truck and directed them to a military vehicle into which they were loaded.

"It was those damn lists, those goddamn lists," mumbled Goldfein, as they now were crammed into a hot, canvas-covered truck along with ten other terrified people.

Of the 15,000 names on the list, the Gestapo was able to round up just 2,100 in the former Italian zone. Many had left earlier—some for Portugal, a few for Switzerland, and many for Italy. Others were hidden with French families who either had strong feelings against what the Germans were doing or an interest in making a great deal of money by hiding the Jews. War brings no end to greed.

The seized Jewish families from Nice and the surrounding area were brought to the high school gymnasium of the Nice Lycée, located close to the train station. They were kept under guard until enough railcars could be collected to transport them to Drancy, a French transit camp located outside Paris, where they would be interned until transferred to one of the many German concentration camps in Eastern Europe and Germany. After three days with little food and water, they were brought by buses to the rail station, where each individual was given a printed ticket designating their railcar. With enough seats for only forty passengers, eighty were assigned to each car. Twenty-six cars were loaded with Jews from the former Italian zone, and the twelve-hour trip to Drancy began.

Michel and Anna stood, allowing Rachel and Aaron to sit in the packed railcar. Crowded next to his nephew, Stanley Goldfein said, "Michel, let's keep our heads about us so we can get through this." Slipping his arm around Michel's shoulder, he added, "And, my nephew, look who is guarding the trains; it's not the Germans, but our own French 'countrymen.'"

As it turned out, the Germans could have found no better partners.

"...And that by precept, lecture and every other mode of instruction."

7

January 5, 1943
Bad Tölz, Germany

For Doctor Hans Bloch, the completion of his SS training required one last step. It was the final piece of orientation and education demanded of candidates prior to obtaining their "Paired Runes" patches, identifying them as SS officers.

The expansive grounds of Bad Tölz were beautifully framed by the Bavarian Alps, inviting the German SS candidates into the gracious world of Prussian officer heritage. The SS-VT (SS—*Verfugungstruppe*, SS Dispositional Troops), the fledgling armed branch of the SS, aimed to gather officer candidates from a much broader field than that used by the *Wehrmacht*. SS Chief Heinrich Himmler wanted his own army, answerable only to him and the Führer, truly independent of the Wehrmacht generals. Historically, the German army sought men of good aristocratic breeding for their officer corps in a tradition dating back to the vaunted armies of Prussia. The SS-VT, however, didn't limit its search to those who completed secondary school; it also offered advancement to nationalistic young men from lesser social strata and poorer educational backgrounds.

The printed description of the school at Bad Tölz stressed that it could groom men into gentlemen officers, and had designed a curriculum fulfilling that need. These SS schools were called *Junkerschulen*, or "schools for young noblemen." Perhaps this designation was true in years past, but now these faculties were used primarily to teach a kind of civility to men who grew up without the benefit of social graces.

Whatever the origins of these nationalistic men, they were suitably impressed by the grounds when they first arrived at Bad Tölz. It was in this setting that, in addition to the usual military training, table etiquette, cultural activities, and letter writing were taught. Course work also included appreciation of classical composers, with emphasis on Wagner's music, and opera. Discussion of the meaning of Hitler's book, *Mein Kampf*, and its modern practical application was also an integral part of the school's curriculum. Classes in genetics and eugenics were required for all officers.

The instructors in the humanities came from many fine German universities. It was an honor to be asked to teach at Bad Tölz; not many refused this opportunity to better their careers in the eyes of the Nazis. In addition, the recruitment of noted professors to teach the SS certainly enhanced the public's perception of this new kind of army. Without the necessity of joining the military or the SS, these professors could duly be proud of their service to the Reich.

Second to instruction in military tactics and strategy, emphasis was placed on sports achievement. Besides morning physical conditioning, the men participated in sports competitions in which team success further enhanced the standing of this military training program. Awards and recognition were given to those who excelled in track and field, swimming, and Nordic events, such as skiing. The Junker schools' *Fußball* and wrestling teams successfully competed against those of the Wehrmacht and Luftwaffe, greatly expanding the reputation of this new breed of officers. It was Himmler's grandest dream to have his forces, the SS-VT, be the true elite of the Reich and representative of the finest Aryan soldiers.

Working toward its true mission, the *SS-Junkerschule Bad Tölz* successfully lured handpicked training officers from the Wehrmacht to teach and instruct in modern weaponry. In addition, strategists from the War College at Munich regularly lectured to these young officer candidates. The school's budget seemed unlimited, as Himmler gave *carte blanche* to the Commandant, General Kraus, to secure any and all of the best military minds to instruct at the Junkerschule.

Himmler needed the best instructors to gain respect for his fledgling SS forces from the established German military leaders. Courses in gunnery tactics, leadership, military history, and combat communications were required of all candidates. The practical military training included a forty-square-kilometer course stressing action under fire, including mortar, machine gun, and 105mm howitzer range fire. A twenty-foot-deep bunker was situated in the middle of the training ground, where students could experience the effects of bombardment by various explosive weapons and simulated Allied bombing attacks. It was important to prepare these men for the stress of combat and harden them to the practical realities of war.

These young and vigorous SS officer candidates were of a special breed. Most came from the rural areas of Germany where nationalism was at its highest. The German economy in the late 1920s and early 1930s compelled the necessity of using children to work in the fields, and many teenagers dropped out of school at an early age to assist their families in planting, harvesting, and bringing the crops to market. The officers at the Junkerschule counted on the naïveté of this unsophisticated lot and filled their unfettered minds with the fascist messages that the Third Reich needed them to absorb.

◆◆◆

THE BLACK BMW BUS entered the circular drive to the school and stopped at the entrance to the administrative headquarters. It was met by two immaculately uniformed SS sergeants who opened the front and rear doors, greeting the occupants with a crisp salute. *"Heil Hitler!"*

Twenty young men were herded into a grand lobby furnished with fine leather chairs and couches. The two-story ceiling beckoned their eyes to the hand-carved woodwork surrounding a colossal spherical dome towering over the lobby. A large picture of Adolf Hitler was centered above the massive stone fireplace at the north end, and, on the opposite wall, a smaller painting of Himmler.

Doctor Hans Bloch was the last of his group to enter the lobby. Physically, he was not that different from the other candidates, albeit several years older. He stood over six feet tall, with short light brown hair, and he sported an athletic build from his many years of Fußball and gymnastics. He was a handsome man and exuded self-confidence with each step he took.

From a wealthy family, Hans was not taken with the opulent surroundings he had entered into, but he was surprised at the awe and open-mouthed reaction of his fellow officer candidates to this new ambiance. During the trip from Munich, he'd had a chance to get to know a few of his traveling companions. He had expected a more erudite group of young men, but as he grew to understand their unsophisticated origins, he noted that their glorious patriotic spirit made up for their intellectual deficits. They were young, strong, and energetic, and though he did not relish the role, he had to continuously remind them not to spit on the floor of their quarters.

Because of his previous medical education, his expected stay at Bad Tölz would be only four months, and his coursework would center on SS-VT ideology, eugenics, and military strategy. He'd been assured that other SS doctors had attended Bad Tolz and found it to be immensely important to their careers. As he studied the grand surroundings, his eyes gleamed with pride, and he could feel warmth spreading throughout his body. He was in that spiritual home of which he so often dreamed—a place where German honor was sown and reinforced; a charming mountain retreat, where the beauty and power of the Fatherland was blended and enhanced.

While sitting in the lobby, the candidates were given a short intro-ductory lecture by General Kraus, the school commander, detailing the history of this Junkerschule and the schedule of coursework. A binder was given to each man containing their class schedule and practical infor-mation about the school. They were then directed to their quarters and paired up with roommates.

Hans hoisted his duffel bag out of the bus and trudged through the deep January snow toward a big lodge to the left of the headquarters building. He was soon to meet Helmut Gunnar, his new roommate.

Once the other officer candidates recognized that Hans was a physician, he was held in some deference, and it became difficult for them to approach him. Their remoteness made no difference to Hans, as he had little in com-mon with these men. In fact, this social isolation allowed him to concentrate on his courses with a zeal he had never experienced, even at the university. He was especially drawn to Johann Schwartz, his professor in eugenics and race. His lectures were powerful, detailing the elements of Aryan suprem-acy so well that Hans could find no weakness in his carefully thought out line of reasoning. Swartz emphasized the subtle and fine differences in facial features that identified non-Aryans—the Jews, Gypsies, and Slovaks. He used science to support his views; he had numbers, statistics, and multiple studies. Most of these research papers had been written in Germany, yet there were many from the United Kingdom and even the United States. Professor Schwartz blended historical facts, anthropology, and anatomy to create his racial models. He was a master theorist.

Hans embraced the Nazi view on racial differences completely. Even as a child, he had noticed the peculiar characteristics of Jews. This race kept to itself and chose not to associate with "gentiles." Most likely, this social isolation came from the inferior feelings they harbored. Often they had anatomical oddities, like big noses, large ears, or immense, ponderous hands. They were a dark, brooding people with secrets hidden in the deep pockets of their shadowed eyes. They lacked the flawless, clean Nordic skin and clear blue eyes. A Jew's hair was often dark, curly, or tangled; in fact, many had little curls falling in front of both ears. Having seen the occasional blond, blue-eyed Jewess with light features, Hans knew she could not be a pure Jew and must have had Aryan blood in the family. *They are smart devils, those Jews,* he told himself, noting the larger number who had climbed the ladder and dominated the professions of law, medicine, and finance. Some, he admitted, had even become important industrialists, professors, and politicians. Many were leaders in the Communist party and therefore posed an immediate threat to the Reich.

At the end of coursework each week, a group of the young officer candidates hung out at the local beer hall and bonded over their favorite brews until early morning. Out of courtesy, Hans was always invited, but he would invariably decline, choosing to read and relax in the still of his quiet dormitory room. It was during these hours alone that he took time to work out his thoughts concerning his future, the war, and the new, greater Reich that would emerge once the hostilities had ceased. He would recall his grandfather telling him that he could be whatever he wished to be—that the only person who could get in his way of a successful life would be himself. Now, with those words embedded in his consciousness, Hans set his path.

General Oscar Schroeder of the Luftwaffe Institute of Experimental Science gave a captivating lecture to the candidates two weeks after Hans had arrived. The general had been invited to discuss the additional perils facing German pilots and aircrews beyond the threats from Allied planes and anti-aircraft fire. His topic, "Science and War," grabbed the attention of every man in the room as he presented statistics demonstrating that more German pilots and aircrews were lost from the elements of nature than from bullets, flak, or explosives. He went on to describe the effects on fighter pilots of high altitude, diminished oxygen, and increased gravitational or G-forces, often resulting in loss of consciousness. The last issue he discussed was the high death rate due to hypothermia of pilots who bailed out and landed in the icy waters of the North and Baltic Seas. The mortality figures indicated that more studies were urgently needed to stop this unnecessary loss of life.

Hans was fascinated by this subject. He had been looking for some area of study to help in the war effort. After the lecture was completed, he approached the lectern and nervously waited to introduce himself to the general, now talking with other students.

General Schroeder stood tall and appeared fit for a man of nearly fifty years old. His salt-and-pepper hair was cut short, and his uniform was crisp and well pressed.

"Herr General, I am *Sturmbannführer* Hans Bloch, a physician, and very interested in discussing, and possibly pursuing, the temperature-related studies you alluded to in your lecture."

"I have some time before I must leave," Schroeder smiled. Can you meet me in the main office outside the lobby in thirty minutes?"

"Yes, Herr General!"

Their meeting lasted almost one hour. General Schroeder seemed interested in the minutest details of Hans's life and education. The thoroughness of the interview took Hans aback, as he had not planned ahead, and stumbled through some of his answers. It became apparent early on that the general was interested primarily in Hans' commitment to the Reich, and only secondly in his medical skills. He asked few questions on medicine and medical care, and focused more on Hans's early life. The general inquired about the death of his father and his relationship with his grandfather. He wanted to know about his grandfather's views on The Great War and the Germany that remained after its defeat. When Hans mentioned his membership in the Hitler Youth, the general's eyes brightened. His final question to Hans was straightforward: "Why are we at war?"

Nobody had asked him that before, but to Hans, this war had always seemed predestined after The Great War, and as he answered, it was almost as if Hitler himself was speaking through him from one of his powerful speeches. "We lost more than The Great War," he began. "Millions of our finest men died, and our citizens suffered. Our money was worthless, and it took a wheelbarrow filled with Deutschmarks to buy a loaf of bread. Our forces were decimated and we couldn't protect ourselves. But, most of all, our pride was taken from us." Hans dropped his head as he took a deep breath and stared at the floor. "The Communists, the Jews, and the Slavs reduced us to a mere piece of European geography. Much of the land we called Germany was taken away from the Fatherland and given to other countries, like Poland and Czechoslovakia, as if trying to neuter our great people. This outcome was preordained at Versailles."

General Schroeder regarded Hans with deep pride and approval. This was the kind of young German that would bring supremacy back to the Fatherland. "Herr Doktor, I will strongly consider your wishes to attach you to the Luftwaffe Institute for Aviation Medicine upon the completion of your studies here. Our mission is very important to the Reich, and we need dedicated men like you to help us. But I must warn you: The significance of our undertaking is so high that methods of study will be utilized that are not customary in the civilian environment. You must be able to relax some of the ethical teachings you have learned in medicine, as we strive for a better Fatherland."

He looked intently at Hans, as if trying to extract a response to this statement.

"Herr General," Hans met his eyes head on, and did not flinch, "I understand completely what you are saying. I am a doctor, yes, but now I am a soldier for the Reich and will utilize any methods necessary to achieve our desired goals."

"You shall hear from me within one month," General Schroeder said, signaling the meeting was over.

Hans returned to his room, more convinced than ever that he could make a difference for his Fatherland. Stopping at the ornate mirror in the hallway, he stood proudly, seeing a different man than before. The clear blue eyes that stared back had found true purpose—just as his grandfather had said would happen. Little sleep came to him that night as he reveled in his good fortune.

◆◆◆

IT WAS TIME FOR a break. The weather was warming up and most of the snow had disappeared. Small shoots of plants were emerging from the ground as a salute to spring and the revival of life. Hans had continued to rebuff his associate officers' offer for Friday night trips to the *biergarten*, which bolstered the impression that he was overly stiff and self-centered. Clearly, his lack of social attentiveness to his fellow students was unfortunate and had resulted in even deeper isolation from them.

Things had been different during Hans's university days in Kiel, when he had enjoyed the light-hearted drinking and debauchery that accompanied those years. Many a night, he had awakened in an unfamiliar bed with a woman he scarcely knew, but things changed abruptly when he began to pursue his medical studies and take himself more seriously. Now, the Junkerschule year was coming to an end, and Hans felt it was time for him to celebrate with his compatriot officers. Humbly, he approached his roommate Helmut and asked if he could join them that night for beer.

sss

A SLIGHT CHILL IN the air still remained as the cocky young men entered the biergarten. The burning logs in the hearth at the far end of the drinking hall attracted Hans and his two cohorts to a small table adjacent to the fire. As they settled in, a pretty barmaid quietly approached to take their order. She was young, perhaps nineteen years old. Her blond hair was fashioned in the customary style of rural Jutland, with two perfectly matched braids enhancing her lovely face. Her bright green eyes quickly met Hans's and remained locked for a fraction of a second.

"Haven't seen you here before, Major. Is that right?" she began. Without giving him a chance to answer, she continued. "And what would you like to drink tonight?"

Hans's mind was ready to answer her first question and tripped over words as he tried to answer her second. "A good dark lager—whatever you recommend," he stammered.

She smiled knowingly, having easily broken through his stiff officer's guise. It was a slight flirtation that was not lost on his partners. The others ordered and she returned quickly, serving Hans last. The young woman brushed his hand "accidentally" when she set the glass down, and as she left, she glanced back as if inviting Hans to follow her.

The beer kept flowing, as did the men's high spirits. Raunchy ballads recalled from his rambunctious university days started pouring from Hans's lips. His Junker buddies, amused by this sudden change in deportment, raucously joined in, and the stone walls of the tavern reverberated with their disharmonious attempts at song. As the night progressed, Hans's eyes kept following the movements of the young barmaid as she glided easily among this pod of spouting men. She became ever more attentive to their table and just before midnight beckoned Hans to follow her to a quiet corner of the room.

Astonished at this lucky turn, he tried to pull his thoughts together, but before he could speak, she began. "You are different from the others who come here every night. They get lost in drink, but you don't. Their behavior is so brash, yet, aside from your sorrowful attempt at song, you seem so civilized. Perhaps I can come to understand why you are different."

Hans whispered, "Yes, yes," almost speechless as his mind reeled in response to this forward, daring young woman. "It's best I know your name for now, and later we can work on the details. I am Hans."

The girl brought her lips close to his face, "It's Giesela. Giesela Schmidt," she whispered back. "Tomorrow is my day off…perhaps we could meet?"

Eagerly agreeing, Hans arranged to see her in the early afternoon, following lunch. Returning to his table, he was met with knowing looks from his two colleagues and a warning from Helmut Gunnar. "Take it easy, old man. That young one might wear you out."

Hans soon departed and walked home alone, feeling more energized than he had in months. He sensed something more than just the swell of romance. This was a novel chance to get out of himself, to explore emotions and feel the freedom to break away from those dual fences of discipline that enveloped him: medicine and the obligations of the SS. He'd certainly known those crazy times before, when he was just a student prowling the beer halls, chasing women day and night, fighting to prove his masculinity. That ability to let loose had been pushed far back in his mind, never lost, but continually suppressed by his newfound responsibilities to the Reich.

◆◆◆

"You are even more gracious when the beer is set aside," she said the following day, "and, I must say, somewhat more handsome." They had met outside the biergarten and were walking down the street toward the bridge at the far edge of the village. Hans thought their meeting was to be simply a stroll, with no particular intention or direction. They talked of many things, yet with little depth.

Giesela seemed especially worried about the war and feared that she might never experience the romantic wonderments of youth as more men were sent to the front. She talked about her former fiancé, a tank commander, who had died in the battle of El Alamein outside of Cairo just four months previously. "I just want to meet a nice man to share some time with," she confessed.

She seemed to hurry, and her gait increased as she reached for his hand. Even though the day wasn't particularly cold, she pressed her body against his side as if she needed to warm herself.

Hans felt that familiar stirring in his groin. It was time.

Just before they reached the bridge, Giesela announced, "Well, here is where I live," pointing to a multicolored, two-story home of brick and wood set next to a roaring creek that passed under the bridge.

She explained that she was only a boarder there, and the people who owned it, the Ottermans, were wonderful to her. The couple treated her as a daughter, including setting rules for their young tenant. Visits by suitors to her room were *verboten*. She expected a kiss and a quick goodbye, but Hans had other plans. He convinced her to show him the house and perhaps get a glass of water before he returned to his quarters. Upon entering the foyer, she revealed that the owners were both at work and she'd be happy to get him a drink.

Hans was aroused. He did not want to let this interest by a beautiful young woman pass him by. When they reached the top of the stairs, he pulled Giesela close and kissed her soft lips. Responding weakly, she tried to pull back from his tight grip, but he wouldn't let go. Instead he strengthened his embrace and kissed her more passionately.

"Hans, please, we just met and you shouldn't be up here. I do like you, but not like this, so quick!" she cried. "Please let me go... I can't do this!"

But determination such as Hans's could not be quelled easily, especially by the soft whimpers of a young, delicate female. He pulled her into her room and forced her down on the bed. "Please, stop, please!"

It had been a long time since Hans had taken a woman, and he wasn't going to let this one get away. "Giesela, *mein Fräulein*, be still and enjoy this. I know you want it. I could tell last night in the tavern."

She began to fight back, trying with all her might to push Hans's weight off her, but he slapped her hard enough to open a cut on her cheek. Stunned, Giesela lay motionless for a few seconds. Then Hans ripped off her dress and blouse, and removed her underclothes. Quickly lowering his pants, he pushed himself forcefully into her as she screamed. Covering her mouth with his hand, he slapped her again as he continued to force himself mercilessly upon her. Once sated, he spread the last of his semen across her belly and wiped himself with her blouse as he backed off the bed.

Giesela immediately flexed her knees, coiled her body into a ball, and started to cry. Hans stood over her, "Now you know what a real man is like. Oh yes, you wanted me! Even my friends would vouch for that."

"Into whatever houses I enter, I will go into them for the benefit of the sick…"

8

April 15, 1944
Hamburg, Germany

The cold rain had stopped. Jürgen shivered as he pulled the blanket tighter around his shoulders and peered out the windows onto the street below. Once a beautiful *Straße*, it was now a rutted, garbage-strewn path lined with debris and waste where a row of beautiful elms once invited you to walk along them. Bombed-out buildings completed the stark landscape of downtown Hamburg. On the desk, boldly staring up at him, were the orders…orders to leave:

Herr Jürgen Hauptman: Report at Rostock to the twenty-second Medical Naval Battalion. Uniforms will be supplied and…

He couldn't look at the papers any longer. Pushing the instructions aside, he angrily flipped his surgery text closed.

Why can't they wait? Just six more months and I would be sitting for my examinations. As a fully trained doctor, I could be so much more valuable.

The corridors of the Faculty of Medicine had become increasingly empty, and many professors had supposedly left on sabbatical. The students knew better. They also understood the "transfer" of Jewish anatomy professor Herr Schwartz during their freshman year; Jürgen had seen Doctor Schwartz and his family being led to the train station by the police. Tears filled his eyes… He knew. Yet he was fearful to speak of this incident, as there were spies everywhere, even in the medical school corridors.

Why would they spy on us? The Pride of the Fatherland…medical students who will become fine doctors to bring German medicine to the world for a better mankind.

Because of the war, admission to universities had been severely restricted, and only the faculties of medicine remained open. Jürgen had been fortunate to be accepted, as most of his friends had been drafted to serve in the military, and some had died. Now, he was forced to go to war, delaying the day of graduation his parents had dreamed of. Suddenly, everything was different. His cherished hopes had been crushed by a war he couldn't understand. Whispered talk of military failures, the death of friends and the maiming of others filled the hallways of the university. Jürgen tried to extinguish his sorrow, but the tears still came. He had struggled hard to make his way this far and didn't want to disappoint his parents, but his medical degree would have to wait.

sss

Life was harsh in Hamburg in September of 1925. Illness and a depressed economy plagued the Hauptman family during those postwar years.

"Bring Jürgen warm milk and butter," Marlene shouted to nobody in particular, at least to no one visible. As if by cue, a rustling in the pantry was followed by the sound of the stove being lit, and Peter Hauptman ambled back to his bedroom where his wife was holding Jürgen. A forced wheeze brought needed attention to the tousled-hair boy, as he desperately curled himself into his mother's lap. For the past two years, the beginning of fall had been announced by the sound of her son's labored breathing; her deepest fear was that one day he would die during an asthma attack.

Tomorrow she would take Jürgen to Doctor Friedman, who would be expecting the visit. As always, the kind doctor would listen to the little boy's struggling chest and advise the same thing: "Hot milk with butter or honey. Hold the cup close so the steam washes over his face and nostrils. Keep him inside, away from the cold wind, and give him love."

The doctor would then patiently explain that asthma works itself out through childhood and the boy would be fine.

Marlene Hauptman looked tired; once the beauty of her neighborhood, little color was left in her prematurely lined face. She had two other children to tend to, and with looks of distress they meekly protested all the attention focused on little Jürgen whenever he was sick. She was at her wit's end.

The warm cup held to the young boy's face felt good, as the steam wafted up his nose to soothe his throat. He didn't particularly like the taste of the butter, but it made him breathe easier.

Peter Hauptman supported the cup as Jürgen sipped the warm remedy with a swirl of yellow on the surface. He looked down at his son with concern. The child's eyes were ringed with bluish-gray circles, which accented the paleness of his worried face. *The boy is small,* he thought, as Jürgen held out his empty cup.

He won't be a Fußball player, but he is bright, quick, and fast to learn.

Peter and Marlene were married the year after the Great War had ended and the Armistice was signed. "Too young; you're just eighteen years old," Peter's father had said when he told him of their marriage plans. But war had torn the face of Europe apart, and many of his friends and family had died. Marriage and love seemed to be the only values one could cling to.

Very quickly, a family was born. Jürgen was their first child, and within the next five years, Trudy and Max were added. Peter was a carpenter, and though there was plenty of work around, people had little money to pay him. He was lithe and a good worker, giving the impression of strength and skill despite his thin, bony frame. Inflation had made the Deutschmark almost worthless, and he had to work twelve to eighteen hours each day to make enough to feed his small family. Fortunately, he had the sound fortune of decent health, a strong back, and a good woman.

Marlene would give Peter a list of food to buy each day. She made the most of the food her husband brought home. She could make a chicken last for at least a week by first roasting it and then taking the scraps and mixing them with rice, and sometimes noodles, for additional evening meals.

Working for himself, Peter was paid in cash upon the completion of each job. His pants pockets bulged from the wads of Deutschmarks worth barely as much as the paper they were printed on. The couple had learned to buy things quickly, as the price of food, eggs, and meat might suddenly spike the following day.

The streets of Hamburg were often chaotic during these unsettling times. Various groups marched with banners extolling the virtues of their movements. Waving red flags and well organized, the Communists had the greatest following as they marched along the streets and in the parks adjoining the government offices. Peter stopped at times to watch the demonstrations, listen to the speakers, and try to understand all the politics swirling around him. The government seemed so weak and was clearly unable to control the various factions whose ideologies routinely battled one another in the streets. Still, he did notice the increasing power and numbers of those marching with Nazi flags. The strength and enthusiasm of the followers of this party frightened him.

Just let me work and leave me alone, he thought, as he tried to avoid the large crowds that increasingly filled the streets.

As Jürgen grew to be a teenager, he followed his father's advice and chose to ignore all talk of politics. Friends invited him to join the Hitler Youth, yet he declined. He found the uniforms and marching a bit silly, and he didn't like the way these boys taunted the old folks and Jewish people as they passed. Jürgen would rather spend time with his handicapped brother Max, who seemed to be ignored by his family and friends. A "Mongoloid" with facial features similar to some Asians, he was considered mentally retarded and too intellectually disabled to attend school. But Jürgen would patiently work with Max and teach him, over and over, until he actually began to read a few lines and painstakingly print individual letters of the alphabet. Each small achievement was celebrated by both boys with a piece of hard candy that Jürgen would hoard for these small victories. His parents grew justly proud of their son as he shared his time and love with his less fortunate brother. The government had offered to institutionalize Max, but Peter and Marlene decided against it. Rumors of forced euthanasia for the handicapped and retarded children frightened them.

Jürgen sought to find out as much as he could about Max's condition and he spent hours at the local library studying medical texts. As he delved deeper into the literature, he became more interested in the science of medicine and soon envisioned himself becoming a doctor. With his goal in mind, Jürgen studied long and hard at school and passed his entrance exams with high scores. His dream came true on February 2, 1938, when he received his acceptance to the University of Hamburg School of Medicine.

♦♦♦

Now, Jürgen Hauptman stood on the Hamburg train platform, looking down at his conscription papers; he was to report to Rostock today, May 12, his train departing at precisely 8:26 a.m. The trains were always on time. The war had changed most things for the worse, yet the trains were unaffected. Stations were constantly packed, mostly with uniforms, the heavy brown woolen kind worn by young men, many of them still boys with full duffels at their sides. One could see the cherubic faces without whiskers, standing tall, trying to look older, eyes darting nervously here and there.

Inside the station, there were others—mothers saying goodbye with tears, and legless young men just sitting on benches, their pants folded neatly over their shortened limbs. These men glanced up at each passerby, hoping someone would drop money into their empty pans. Off in the distance, fifty meters to the north, Jürgen spotted a group of men, women, and children waiting with valises and bags, crowded in line, standing at the very end of the platform.

But they are at the wrong place to board the train.

Just then, his train roared into the station and he looked at his watch: 8:26 a.m.—on time, as always. As the cars pulled up to the platform, he again looked to the north at the curious group of people being loaded onto slatted, wooden cars at the end of the train; not passenger cars, for they had no windows...cattle cars. He swallowed hard, turned away, and quickly entered his coach.

♦ ♦ ♦

As a slatted door was being pulled shut, a worn black shoe blocked the last few inches and a man yelled out, "Ida, I'll write you as soon as I arrive!"

A scarfed, *zoftig* lady dressed in fine clothes waiting silently on the platform waved in the direction of the closing door. *"My husband, the eternal optimist, believes he is going to a work camp to serve as their rabbi,"* she said to herself. *"May he stay safe."*

She looked away from the train so that her tears would not alarm Israel as the door closed shut. Ida Rosenberg knew better. Whispers of death from gentile friends who had traveled in the East reported that these were not work camps, but places to die, and she feared she would never again see her husband of twenty-seven years. Another train was coming for women, and it would head toward a different camp. Fearful but resigned, she wanted to cry out, but her voice seemed paralyzed. A German officer grabbed her arm roughly and led her to the holding area where the other women and children were gathered.

Israel Rosenberg was an imposing figure. Standing nearly 6'2", he was a big man who broadcasted command, but his size was not as remarkable as his other physical features. His hands were big, with prominent knuckles and wide, heavy fingers. They seemed to extend beyond his jacket cuffs, their size exaggerated by massive forearms bulging from within his sleeves. His head was symmetrically large, but kind and inviting. One could not call him handsome, for he was not; and yet, the gentle strength he radiated somehow made him attractive. Israel's coat was too small for him, making his shoulders appear even broader than they were. As he yanked his foot from the door just in time to avoid being crushed, a surreal stillness enveloped the group crowded inside the cattle car.

What is to become of us?

Slowly, each person began to claim his own space.

Must be some eighty people, Israel thought. He continued to stand, as if overseeing his flock, while the last soul lowered his body down to the straw-covered slats.

At least the hay on the floor is fresh.

Eyes beseeched the rabbi, as if to say, *"Will you sit, please? Can you explain? Can anybody explain…?"*

He joined them on the floor…and became one with them.

◆◆◆

JÜRGEN'S TRAIN SLOWED AS an announcement came over the loudspeaker. "This train is arriving at the Rostock station. Please collect all your belongings and exit your car. Our time at the station is short. You must depart quickly."

On the platform, he spotted two Wehrmacht soldiers waiting at a desk marked: "Military Arrival." He presented his identification, and his name was checked against a typewritten list.

"'Herr Hauptman'—is that correct?"

He nodded affirmatively and the soldier continued. "You are to report to the twenty-second Naval Medical Battalion, and you will find transportation in front of the station."

Jürgen didn't know what to say. *Was it "Thank you," or was he to salute and give a brisk, "Heil Hitler!"?*

Before any response could be expected, he slung his duffel bag over his shoulder and headed down the platform to the station. Glancing back at the cattle cars attached to the end of the train, he saw hands holding cups extending through the slats and heard cries of *"Wasser…wasser…"*

Jürgen recoiled unconsciously, turned, and quickly exited to seek out his bus.

9

November 16, 1942
Lodz, Poland

"*Achtung, Achtung!* All Jews line up to be listed and receive your yellow armband!" Moishe Brosky had led his wife and teenage son Martin to the small park at one end of the ghetto upon direction from the SS command. Defying the order to stand, he sat down on a bench adjacent to the line of fellow inhabitants awaiting registration with the Germans.

"Up, you lazy Jew bastard! No one sits until the process is complete!" Screamed the SS Oberleutnant Werner.

Moishe spoke as he slowly started to rise. "*Herr Leutnant*, it is my painful back. I need to rest it, believe me."

"You need to rest, scum? Faster, get up faster!"

Moishe tried to prop himself up but fell back. He pleaded with his eyes. "Please, I need help."

"Help, you ask? The poor weak Jew can't even stand by himself? Here, this might encourage you."

He fired his pistol at Moishe's right leg. Martin watched in horror as his mother ran to help his father, who lay bleeding on the pavement.

"Get away, Jew bitch, move, move!" yelled the scowling SS officer as he tried to pull Martin's mother away from his wounded father. Without hesitation, Ida Brosky lashed out with her right arm and screamed, "Why did you have to shoot him? He was getting up slowly because he is ill!"

"I told you to leave. Now!"

The blood was pumping out fast from the wound behind Moishe's knee and Beatrice, desperate to stop the flow with her hands, ignored Werner's command. With no further warning, Oberleutnant Kurt Werner put his pistol against her head and fired.

"No!" screamed Martin. "No...Mother, Mother!"

Without thinking, he ran to her side and held her bloodied head in his arms, wailing as he watched her eyes grow dim while lowering her shattered face to the ground. "Bastard!" he yelled.

With his mother's blood dripping from his arms, he started to throw himself at the officer but two German soldiers held him back.

SS officer Werner looked around and pointed his gun at the crowd: "Any more foolish heroes out there?"

Martin glanced at his father and saw the pool of blood enlarging as it continued to pump out from behind his knee.

If someone, anyone, could just put pressure on it the bleeding would stop.

"Please, sir, let me stop the bleeding, I know how, sir, please."

No one in the crowd dared move.

Werner looked at the sobbing teen and waved his pistol in his direction. The two enlisted soldiers continued to restrain him while the now frightened crowd was pushed back into line.

Martin's eyes darted wildly from side to side as he strained hard in the direction of his father as if to help him, but the two soldiers tightened their grasp on the anguished teenager's arms. With the pool of blood spreading, and the last bit of life draining out of him, Moishe lifted his left arm slowly above his chest and gazed at Martin as if to say goodbye.

Martin was sixteen. He stared at SS Leutnant Werner and seared his image and name tag into his brain. He would never forget this day.

♦♦♦

THE DEATH OF HER sister Ida and brother-in-law Moishe left Stella Rosen the only relative able to care for her orphaned nephew. Martin had never been fond of Aunt Stella. A spinster, she seemed not to understand children and had paid little attention to him while he was growing up. She preferred her quiet, uncomplicated life and passed her days reading and sewing. Stella worked for his Uncle Meyer, the tailor, and toiled hard days in his shop, only to return home to continue her sewing.

It wasn't long before Martin worked his way into the black market, acting as a delivery agent in Lodz, which was ever-expanding as a center of commerce. The war privations continued to diminish available goods and luxury items, and prized American cigarettes found their way from the Baltic Port of Gdansk to the syndicate for which Martin worked.

Jews had been banned from the public schools, and Martin chose not to attend those recently formed by inhabitants of the ghetto. While many people worked in the productive Lodz manufacturing plants, Martin followed a different path. With the tragic death of his parents had come a new independence and, in fact, he found the arrangement with his aunt to be quite comfortable. He prowled the ghetto streets during the day and sneaked out into the city at night, selling his wares and seeking ways to get back at the Germans.

◆◆◆

IN THE EARLY SUMMER of 1944, Martin became aware of a rumor that the SS was going to do a final liquidation of the Lodz Ghetto and transport the remaining thousands of Jews to concentration camps. Despite the brutal German occupation, the local population had come to feel secure over the past year, as this Jewish quarter had been providing workers for the many war-related manufacturing plants in Lodz. But the Germans had a different objective: move the Jews out of Lodz. The black market syndicate had been informed early of this future action by an opportunistic, ranking SS officer, advising them that they should be ready to loot the homes abandoned by Jews for salable items after the deportation. Martin had a different plan, and he needed to act before the ghetto liquidation date, August 7, 1944—his last chance to take revenge on the Germans.

The memory of the murder of his parents plagued him every day, and he was obsessed with finding ways to inflict pain on the bastards, but he had no access to guns or explosives. At times, he had served as a runner for the Polish resistance group, *Armia Krajowa*, or AK, camped outside the city, yet he was never trusted with their weapons. Four days before the expected liquidation of the ghetto, Martin took the well-camouflaged trail through the forest to the camp to speak with their leader, Joseph Gorlisch.

"Joseph, I have some information about the Germans that might interest you."

"My young friend, what might you know that we don't?"

From experience, Martin knew that this resistance group was not concerned about the Jews being deported or killed. Anti-Semitism had been strong among the Poles, even before the German invasion. Unwilling to share the details he knew about the planned emptying of the ghetto, Martin decided to bend the truth.

"There will be a meeting of senior SS officers in Lodz on August fifth in the downtown synagogue, where the Germans have established a lounge. I would like to kill a bunch of those murderers, especially the one lieutenant who executed my parents." Martin paused to see how Joseph would react, but the leader's face showed no emotion. "I have detailed knowledge of the back alleys and cellars of the old town near where this meeting is to take place. I could plant explosives and kill a large number of German officers; this could be done without any additional help from the Armia Krajowa." Martin took a deep breath to steady his nerves. "I just need to plant a bomb to make this happen."

Joseph sat back in thought. He was aware of a buildup of German troops in the area over the last week but lacked intelligence concerning this change.

If I let him try it and he fails, it would look like simple personal revenge and not the work of the AK. And if he succeeds, yes...we can relish in the triumph.

"Martin, I will have my men prepare a pack of explosives for you and give you instructions on its use. It may take a couple of hours; you can rest here."

Later that afternoon, Joseph sat next to Martin and handed him a backpack filled with a twenty-pound explosive charge and a detonator. "Be careful and listen closely. Set the timer to go off when they are in their morning meeting and then insert the detonator wire carefully into the charge." Pounding his fist into his hand, he admonished, "And Martin, you must vow that if you are caught, you have no affiliation with our resistance group, the AK, and received no help from us. You understand?"

"Do not worry. The blood will only be on my hands. I have prayed for this day and I won't let you down."

Throwing the pack on his shoulders, he wheeled around and headed off into the woods. As he trudged out of the forest into the fields surrounding Lodz, the weight of the pack on his shoulders felt good, giving him the sense of strength and purpose he had been looking for. As night fell, he deftly made his way back to his aunt's home, easily avoiding German patrols.

Early the next morning, Martin snuck into the synagogue before the first soldier arrived, and hid in a storage closet. Through the vents, he watched the Germans organize for their coming action. A lounge for senior officers had been established in what used to be the foyer of the ghetto's main synagogue. Studying the room closely, Martin spotted a cubicle where the prayer texts had been kept, now empty. Later that evening, he carefully exited the closet and returned to his aunt's home, finalizing his plan.

He was ready two nights before the planned liquidation. Knowing the Germans headed to the local biergarten promptly at six each evening, Martin waited until the last soldier had left and, under cover of darkness, entered the synagogue and made his way to the officers' lounge. Placing the explosive charge in the cubicle, he covered it with prayer books and led a wire along the floor just under the carpet, bringing it out through a vent on the side of the building. He would attach the detonator later.

At nine o'clock the next morning, a loud explosion was heard in the middle of Lodz at the site of the old synagogue. A dozen dead and wounded Wehrmacht officers were carried out to waiting ambulances as the astounded ghetto inhabitants shuddered at the thought of a German response. Martin blended into the throng of onlookers, inwardly smiling.

Bastards. This is just the beginning.

But his first step toward revenge had been only partially successful. As he watched the ambulances load up the wounded, he saw Leutnant Werner stopping to inspect his injured colleagues in his soot-stained uniform, uninjured.

I missed him, damn it…I missed him.

Gnashing internally, Martin slipped away from the crowd, vowing that the next time he would make sure that Werner dies, painfully.

In response to the explosion, German troops spread out into the countryside in hopes of finding the perpetrators but were unsuccessful. The following day, twenty random Jewish men and women were lined up and shot through the back of their heads. The emptying of the Lodz ghetto was pushed back two days.

Martin's revenge had turned sour. He was forced, along with thousands of other Jews, to witness these executions in a field at the edge of the ghetto. Seeing the pain on the faces of his friends and neighbors was hard for him to bear.

What have I done?

With each shot, a wail arose from the crowd and the sounds of whimpering escalated as each body fell to the ground. Martin left that field of death more determined than ever to exact true vengeance on the Germans.

Trucks with loudspeakers blaring combed the streets of the ghetto at 6:00 a.m. the next day. "All Jews, gather up your belongings and pack them for travel. Your home must be emptied by eleven this morning." Shortly after, small groups of German SS knocked on the doors of homes to reinforce the message. "This Ghetto is being liquidated. All Jews must be gone."

Twenty-five cattle cars sat ready at the train station.

It was time for Martin to leave, but go where? He could no longer feel safe, and it would be difficult to avoid the coming deportation. He had little choice; it was time to join the resistance.

The Germans had increased their perimeter force, surrounding the ghetto portion of the city in anticipation of its liquidation. They were aware that many men would leave and try to join up with the partisan forces. Martin could see heavy tanks, armored vehicles, and trucks with mounted machine guns manning the tight perimeter. What he didn't see were the stealthy patrols with dogs stationed one kilometer out of town to either intercept the few who might escape or engage the bothersome partisans who would certainly be ready to fight.

Utilizing his knowledge of the sewer systems, Martin crawled four hundred meters inside the main tunnel to where it emptied into a foul, stinking collection basin. From there, he was able to scale himself up a concrete wall away from the sewage pond and out onto the adjacent field. By doing so, he easily avoided the initial layer of troops around the ghetto. With his guard now down, he walked without fear in his wet and filthy shoes across the wheat fields towards a wooded area.

A cry of *"Halt, halt!"* took him by surprise.

Fifty meters away, four Wehrmacht soldiers had their guns trained on him. One soldier had a German shepherd straining at his leash and growling, just waiting for Martin to make a run for it. The Germans quickly surrounded him. "Your name and identification papers, now…*schnell, schnell!"* said the closest one.

Looking down at the papers, the soldier motioned to his cohort to come over, and he smiled as he pointed to the space marked: "Religion."

"Where is your yellow star, Jew boy?"

Holding his hands up to obey, Martin tried to explain that he was looking for a lost dog and asked if they would please help him. Looking at him in astonishment, the Germans laughed, as one said, "Look in the stomach of some Jew slime. You'll find your dog. The only animals you're looking for are the cowardly Polish pigs that hide from their families in the woods." He looked at his comrades. "Let's shoot him here and get on with it," he barked, holding his Luger to Martin's forehead.

The flash of memory of his parents' deaths raced through his brain, yet he tried to appear impassive.

"How long will it take this worthless Jew to shit his pants?" said the officer with a fiendish grin on his face amid grunts of approval from the soldiers.

The men smiled, but an older officer among the four was more practical. "We don't want to have to carry his dead body, so let him walk. We'll make him number one for the transport to the 'work camp.'"

They all burst into laughter.

10

A loud rap on the oaken front door shook the entire house and disrupted the early February morning for the Lissners. "Open up, this is the Gestapo! We wish to talk with Arnold and Jacob Lissner *now!*"

Tamara rushed out of her bedroom and stood at the top of the stairs next to her younger brother, Samuel.

Just thirteen years old, Tamara Lissner was scared. Her father, wrapped in his dark robe, carefully opened the door to a German officer holding papers, accompanied by a man in a brown overcoat. Without asking permission, the officer stepped into the house and said: "By order of Gestapo Unit V, you and your son Jacob are ordered to join the work battalion for Todt Industries."

He demanded that Mr. Lissner and Jacob immediately dress, gather a few toiletries, leave the house, and get into the back of the truck parked outside on the street. Her father, a big man with little patience, sneered aggressively back at the officer. He was about to speak when the German placed his right hand loosely on the pistol strapped to his waist, as if daring him to object. Jacob had come downstairs and stood behind his father.

Beatrice Lissner rushed past her daughter. "Where are you taking them?" she cried.

The officer ignored her.

"Please, sir, my husband, my son… Can you tell me where you are taking them?"

"Frau, they will be fine. There is defense work for them in Poland."

Arnold Lissner turned in silence and slowly, defiantly trudged up the staircase, looking back just once at the officer standing in front of the door.

Jacob bounded upstairs and desperately pulled his father into his room. "Dad, we can go down the back stairs and run. They won't catch us."

Arnold looked at his son in disbelief. "That would make it worse. They might arrest Tamara and Mom and take them away, instead. No, I'm sure we'll be fine and get back soon."

He failed to look directly at his son as he said these last words.

Beatrice stood at the front door, staring into space, arms crossed, ignoring the burly Gestapo agent waiting next to her. Tears had not yet formed as her face was locked in anger. She dared not blink.

Arnold rushed down to embrace his wife. No words were spoken as she held tightly onto her husband of twenty years, hoping it was not the last time their bodies would touch. Brusquely, the agent pulled Arnold away as Beatrice reached out to Jacob, only able to brush his arm lightly as the Germans pushed him outside. Once the door closed, the pent-up tears streamed down her cheeks.

Outside, Arnold and his eighteen-year-old son were loaded into the military truck and stolen away from their family's lives. Back in the living room, Beatrice collapsed on the couch.

Holding onto the rail for support, Tamara made her way down the stairs to the couch where her mother was resting. "Mom, what will happen to Dad and Jacob?"

"I don't know. You know how I tried to warn your father. He wouldn't listen. I told him that once our plant was lost, they would come and take him away."

Beatrice buried her face in her hands as tears slipped between her fingers. For three-and-a-half years, she had lived in fear of this day.

Initially, after the Germans arrived to occupy Prague in March 1939, Arnold Lissner believed the new "race laws" they imposed had no teeth and would not affect him. Orders for his plant had never been higher, and thousands of ball bearings were produced each day to aid the German war effort. Arnold and his family had been left alone—their lives had changed little. It was clear that Prague Bearings played a crucial role in the manufacture of war machinery.

His wife was not so sure.

"Why do you worry so much, Beatrice?" Arnold would say, trying to soothe her fears.

"I've heard the rumors," she replied tersely.

"Things will quiet down." Arnold's patience with her fears was growing thinner every day. "We've agonized about this since the Germans invaded. Believe me, they must act this way to show their strength and discipline, but it will ease up. They just can't ignore how valuable we are to them."

Tamara heard her parents arguing daily.

"We could leave safely now... Take the children and join my cousin Robert in Toronto," Beatrice would plead. "Just leave the business and this Nazi turmoil behind us. I am so frightened."

But it was no use. Her anguish seemed to make Arnold angry, and he would often end the argument by stalking out of the house.

With no warning, things changed quickly in November 1942. Suddenly, the German and Czech authorities were closing down businesses and manufacturing plants owned by Jews, and Arnold Lissner's Prague Bearings was requisitioned "for the Reich" and taken for a pittance—just 10 percent of its value. Now, notices were springing up daily on billboards dictating restrictions on Jews. All Jews were ordered to wear yellow stars over their hearts on their clothing. Non-Jews were restricted from shopping in stores owned by Jews. Doctors, lawyers, and other Jewish professionals were forbidden to work with or to treat non-Jews. The Lissners, once well-off, were now financially struggling. Their travel was restricted, and despair filled the household. Even though Arnold now secretly wished that he had taken his wife's advice to flee the city, it was no longer possible.

In their upscale neighborhood of Prague, the Lissner family had enjoyed a well-respected status and had a broad circle of friends. Religion wasn't an important part of the children's lives and Tamara, although Jewish, considered herself to be Czech. Her parents worked hard at their business, reaping a profit that allowed them to indulge their children with art and music lessons after school. From an early age, Tamara showed a remarkable talent for painting, Jacob became proficient on the violin, and Samuel practiced the French horn—much to the annoyance of anyone who happened to be home at the time.

It was soon clear that Tamara was exceptionally gifted, especially with oils. Her gardens and seascapes were filled with vibrant colors and realistically depicted places she had never seen. He parents encouraged her to enter competitions, and at the age of nine, in September 1939, she won first prize for a pastel of the Versailles gardens at a children's art exhibition. As her mother proudly displayed her ribbons and trophies next to the fine crystal in the curio cabinet in the parlor, Tamara dreamed of attending the Prague Institute of Art when she finished school.

But the fateful knock on the door that ripped her father and brother out of her life forecasted a cloudy future for the remaining Lissners and dashed Tamara's dreams forever. Despair settled over the family as the daily threat of deportation hung around their necks. A mask of indifference replaced the smiles that had once filled this lively household. There was stillness within this home, as one might sense inside a tomb. Despite her mother's continued encouragement, Tamara began to lose her passion for art, and when Jewish children were banned from schools, she became listless and bored.

Like the Lissners, many Jewish families had husbands, sons, and even female relatives who had been forcibly sent to the "work camps." They sought solace together. Beatrice met weekly with a close circle of friends at one of their homes to share news or the many rumors circulating in the city. But rather than comforting each other, these occasions often heightened the anxiety each woman felt as the news of increasing numbers of business closings, arrests, and deportations were shared. Beatrice also learned that several families were sending their children away from the city to the homes of gentile friends in rural areas. She knew she could not wait any longer—her children were at risk.

Samuel, ten years old, was sent to live with Nanny Freda, a Polish woman who had worked many years for the Lissner family. Freda and her husband John had moved to Prague in the early 1930s, looking for work. He had been a woodsmith, but the worldwide depression had left little work for him in Gliwice, so they moved to Czechoslovakia for its stronger economy. Nanny Freda had no children and treated the Lissner offspring as if they were her own.

Over her daughter's objections, Beatrice moved Tamara to her sister Herta's home just outside of Prague in the countryside, where she lived with her husband, a Catholic farmer. Here, Tamara was able to attend school under her aunt's name. But despite being in a safer place, this upheaval made Tamara moody and reclusive. Little joy accompanied her change.

After the children were relocated, Beatrice Lissner continued to live in her home in Prague. Working at a war-related garment factory gave her some sense of security from the round ups of Jews going on around her. Yet every morning, as she walked to the trolley, she tried to hide in the shadows, clutching her purse to her chest to cover the yellow Star of David attached to her blouse. Each day was hurtful, some more than others.

It's been more than a month and still no word from Arnold and Jacob.

In the past, the clanging of the streetcar bell near the corner where they lived had been a reassuring signal that the children were safely off to school, but now its harsh ring served only to remind her that her husband and children were gone, leaving a profound emptiness in her life.

On Friday, September 3, 1943, Beatrice was suddenly let go from her job and became one of three hundred Jews given forty-eight hours' notice to report to work in Terezin, a Jewish ghetto located just outside of Prague. As she read the papers, what little emotion still existed within her suddenly evaporated.

"I hear it's not such a bad place," she told Tamara and Herta, forcing a smile as she visited with them before she left for Terezin. "There's a job and housing waiting for me, and I have many friends who are already there. The letters I receive from cousin Ethyl tell me that things aren't horrible—it's not like the camps we've heard about," she said, pacing in nervous circles around Herta's living room. "At Terezin, you have your own apartment, and the family stays together."

As she talked, there was some hesitancy in her voice, such as a child might have when afraid to tell the truth about some misadventure. And while her words seemed reassuring, her manner wasn't. Tamara noticed that her mother's eyes strayed off to the side as she talked.

Mom doesn't even believe what she's saying.

The parting at the train station was difficult, and Tamara hugged her mother long and hard. Beatrice quickly walked down the platform and into the railcar so that her daughter would not see her emotions flowing down her cheeks. Nor did Tamara see the well-armed SS soldiers stationed inside each car.

◆ ◆ ◆

TAMARA HAD ALWAYS BEEN close with *Tante* Herta, but the wall of sadness kept her apart from her aunt. Herta understood and was patient. It took close to ten days for the years of love and trust to resurface between them. Herta tried to resurrect the good times, and the two of them would travel downtown and visit the shops still open, trying to remember the laughter they had shared before the Germans came. Still, it was difficult for the young girl to embrace life fully. She was bored with her new school and pushed her studies aside.

Being a headstrong teenager, Tamara had pleaded to accompany her mother to Terezin, yet backed off when Beatrice promised, "Stay with Herta, and I will send for you when the time is right. I'll be fine—I need you to watch out for your brother."

Tamara's fears were soothed when she received a brief letter each week from her mother mentioning only positive things about the camp, such as the evening concerts and sports activities in the park.

And it was true that the village of Terezin was more of a ghetto than a concentration camp. It had been a Czech fortress before the war, and the many apartment buildings adjacent to the old fort had been converted into a place to gather the Jews. The Germans had forced out the town's inhabitants in 1941 to make way for the influx of Jews deported from Czechoslovakia and other European countries. No more than sixty kilometers from Prague, it was an easy train trip from there.

During her excursions to downtown Prague, Tamara had begun to sense the anti-Jewish sentiment that was building in the city. Jewish shops were marked with paint and non-Jews were instructed to not frequent them. Jewish friends from her old neighborhood whispered in small groups about the latest round ups, and it was well-known that Terezin wasn't the only place they were being shipped. Names like Auschwitz, Balzac, Methuen, and Treblinka were mentioned. Everyone was scared. Tamara took time to wander alone and explore her thoughts.

The beauty of the spring with all its color contrasts now with the grayness in my life.

A bright sun attracted people to the numerous cafés scattered around the central plaza. Old men, women, and a few Czech soldiers in uniform occupied the outdoor tables, enjoying the day's warmth. It seemed that the war did not exist for them as they sat talking and enjoying a few hours of peace.

The pastoral splendor of the afternoon was sharply broken by the strident sounds of jackboots goose-stepping down Vinohradska Street. Smiles turned into grimaces, conversation stopped, and all eyes were trained on the arrogance that always accompanied these uninvited occupiers. Everyone hurried to get out of the way, and Jews, identified by their yellow stars, slid back against the buildings into the shadows. Tamara slipped inside a café and sat. Once the troops had passed, the square failed to return to its previous peacefulness; the smiles lay unused and fear was pervasive.

That night Tamara was jolted awake by the image of uniformed men forcing her into the back of a truck.

Thank God it's just a dream. I can't wait. I am scared and I must go to my mother.

♦♦♦

IN LATE MARCH OF 1944, Beatrice found it increasingly difficult to continue writing lies to Tamara about the conditions at Terezin, and was worried that her daughter was still at risk for deportation to a different camp. Suggesting that she might now want to come to Terezin, she wrote: *"It is not heaven, but they aren't killing people here. In fact, we even have schools for the children."*

Beatrice kept her other doubts to herself, asking permission of the camp authorities to have her daughter "join" her. She even altered Tamara's age from fourteen to sixteen to allow her to live with her, rather than in the children's quarters.

There was fear in Tante Herta's eyes when Tamara informed her she was leaving. "Tamara, why don't you wait for the school year to be over before you leave?" she asked, trying to sound casual, as if the girl was setting off on a holiday.

"Mom is alone, and I am becoming frightened. There are more German troops in the streets, and many of our old neighbors and friends are being sent away."

"This is a passing phase," said Herta. "The Germans will soon begin to treat us as they did before, and things will return to normal."

Tamara had heard these same words from her father before he was taken away. It was as if she could sense the unspoken anguish in her mother's request.

♦♦♦

THE SUNDAY MORNING TRAIN to Terezin was full. Despite Tamara's objections, Tante Herta had insisted on helping to pack her things. Most people at the station carried suitcases and bags as if planning for a long stay.

They aren't just going for a visit, she mused.

It was a short train ride and the packed coach remained deathly silent. The presence of SS soldiers at the end of the car muted any conversation. Tamara recognized two girls from her old school seated next to her, yet no one spoke.

The sky was darkening amid distant rolls of thunder as the train pulled up to the station. Beatrice had written that she would meet her daughter in the camp, rather than at the train depot. Little did Tamara know that the ghetto inhabitants weren't allowed to leave the town. Upon exiting the train, the passengers had to walk one kilometer to Terezin.

Rain began to fall as she carried her bags in the direction of the old fortress, which looked much cheerier than she had imagined. The roads had recently been swept, and the approach to the town was indeed delightful with flowered gardens on each side of the entrance to the main courtyard. More flowers spilled out of baskets hanging from windows on the south approach to the little city. Soldiers guarded these entrances, but traffic flowed easily through them.

Tamara asked directions from a courteous Wehrmacht soldier who directed her to a park-like area where she immediately spotted her mother and ran and hugged her as if she were seven years old again. "Mom," she whispered, "I'm here… It's okay."

Tears mixed with rain rolled onto her young shoulder.

When she finally looked up at her mother's face, she saw a mixture of sadness and joy. As if trying to smile through a face that had forgotten how, the older woman was sending a guarded message. "Come up to our apartment; let's get out of the rain," she said quietly.

Arm in arm, the two entered an old stone building and walked up rickety stairs to a landing that opened onto a narrow, exposed hallway that extended the length of the building. Paint was peeling off the old block walls, and the floor was made of unstained wooden planks. There were ten doors off the hall leading to individual rooms. At the end of the hall and behind a door, a single toilet stood with a washbasin beside it. The stench that greeted Tamara as she passed it was an unpleasant combination of mustiness, urine, and shit.

They entered the third door on the left, and Tamara was stunned.

I would never have thought…

The room, maybe four meters square, was bare except for a straw mattress on the floor, with her mother's clothes folded neatly to one side of it. A small wooden table, maybe one meter in size, was in the corner. A single light bulb hung perilously from the ceiling with a note in German at the wall switch: *"Lights off except for the hours of seven to nine p.m."*

There was a small window over the bed with a view of the attractive city center.

Such a contrast…beautiful gardens serving as cover for the cheerless existence inside reserved just for us Jews.

Tamara remained quiet.

Beatrice must have read her daughter's thoughts. "Tamara, these quarters are a bit crowded but, trust me, we have a better room than most people here. Sometimes two families are squeezed into a room this size."

She pointed out the narrow window toward an ancient two-story stone building. "And the men are crowded into those barracks across the way."

Tamara had expected better. Her mother's letters always spoke of the openness and beauty of Terezin. She seemed happy in her words, and the girl had believed them. What she didn't know was that all letters out of the camp were read and censored. They had to be less than thirty words and those who complained often were sent elsewhere—to Auschwitz. Also, Beatrice had been unable to reveal that in order for her to keep this room, her daughter would have to join her. Otherwise, she would be forced to share with another family. "Mother, you couldn't tell me how bad it was, could you?" Tamara sobbed.

Sheepishly, Beatrice wrapped her arms around Tamara and pulled her close. "You must speak quietly—we cannot complain. Had I told you the truth, my sweet Tamara, I might never have seen you again. You would not have come."

Tamara cast her eyes downward as her mother talked. "I know you. I worried so, with all the rumors you hear, that you'd be sent off to one of those…death camps."

Tears flowed as mother and daughter grieved quietly in the cold, dark apartment. They both knew that the drops that fell to the floor were for their family, probably never to be together again.

They spent the night lying together and talking. Beatrice told Tamara about her work sewing uniforms and talked about the ladies she worked with. She asked about Samuel and some of the friends left behind. Tamara told her that Nanny Freda had Samuel enrolled in the Catholic school, where few questions were asked. She had shared their mother's letters with him whenever she visited, and he understood that it was too risky for Mom to send letters directly to him from Terezin.

"Freda says that often he cries and asks for you."

As the words fell out of her mouth, Tamara wished that she hadn't spoken. She could hear her mother trying to contain her emotions.

Long after Beatrice drifted off to sleep, Tamara lay awake listening to the strange sounds of her new home. The scurrying in the attic was probably rats, and the sounds of sleeping people came from all directions through the thin walls. Finally, after she had labeled every sound, she fell asleep.

The following day, Beatrice directed Tamara to a camp school that existed without the knowledge or approval of the Germans, providing a useful escape for the children from the miserable surroundings. Tamara quickly made friends with other teenagers and learned much about ghetto life. She was shown the back alleys and corridors that would keep her from having to pass the German guards and lower her face.

There was a great deal of activity during the first week after she arrived. The newly-planted flowerbeds, clean streets, and throngs of people outdoors were reminiscent of the center of many old European cities. Each evening, music was performed in the park, promoting a semblance of civility. This happy, optimistic, outside activity contrasted with the dank quarters to which the captives returned at the end of the day.

Tamara realized what was happening. The camp had been preparing for a visit by the Dutch Red Cross as the Germans attempted to show the world how well it treated its Jews. Just three weeks after she arrived, a large group of well-dressed civilians toured the camp and its recreational facilities, yet avoided visiting the living quarters of the inhabitants.

They didn't bring them upstairs to see how we really live. They didn't show them that there is no heat, no hot water, and barely any electricity during the evenings.

The German camp officials put on quite a show, with the ghetto orchestra performing as the tour passed by. As the Red Cross officials departed, much like a chameleon, the camp reverted to its original colors.

Smiles on the faces of camp guards disappeared with the last of the guests. Flowers seem to wilt as if no one cared any longer, and barbed wire reappeared around the central park. It was so transparent to Tamara.

That was just a show—smoke and mirrors; a kind of reassurance to a world that does not seem to care.

11

September 14, 1943
Drancy, France

"Oh, Michel, they've taken the children from me... Stop them!" cried Anna.

They had just stepped off the train from Nice when a policeman directed the children to a corner of the platform. Michel broke out of the line and grabbed hold of the female guard who was ushering his children away.

"Stop, I say! These are my children, Rachel and Aaron! What are you doing with them?"

"Monsieur, at Drancy, the children are cared for in a common nursery and children's unit where their needs can be better met than in the dark, small adult quarters," said the matronly-looking woman.

Michel motioned for Anna to come over as the guard continued, "We have play areas and plentiful food and milk for the children. Trust me, they will be better off."

Anna knelt down and reached out to Rachel and Aaron as they rushed to their mother's side.

"Parents can visit each afternoon and enjoy them," said the smiling guard, while gently pulling the children away.

"Just allow us a few minutes?" asked Michel. "Anna, it'll be okay. The children need to give you a hug before they go."

While holding back her tears, Anna embraced both children together. She reminded each one to mind their manners and get along with the other children. As soon as she let go of them, Anna felt as if her heart had been torn from her chest. She felt a silent wail course through her bones as she watched them disappear behind the drab concrete building in front of them.

Anna turned back around and appeared dizzy; her face had gone ashen as her knees buckled and she collapsed into her husband's arms.

Michel laid Anna down on a bench. In a few seconds, she regained consciousness and looked up at him. "The children...are they okay?"

"I think they'll be better off; I hear the quarters they have for us are truly nasty."

There had been little conversation during the fourteen-hour train ride to Drancy punctuated by multiple stops allowing troop trains to pass. Thoughts of what lay ahead remained unspoken. Windows were propped open, but the warm September air brought little relief to the crowded masses of people. There was seating enough for only half of the men, women, and children being transported to their uncertain future. A limited amount of water was passed around and shared by each family. Motion sickness overwhelmed a few of the children, who were moved close to the windows and encouraged to hang their heads out while vomiting. The persistent crying of babies added to the tortuous atmosphere and to the helplessness of their parents. French police, not Germans, were placed at the ends of each car so that no Jew could escape.

Stanley Goldfein passed the time trying to make eye contact with the gendarmes, his countrymen, but they looked away—perhaps out of shame.

The detention center was located in the town of Drancy, a Parisian suburb some ten kilometers northeast of the city. It was never intended to be used for this purpose. Built in 1933 as a public housing project, it won architectural awards for its progressive style, yet due to the deep economic depression in France, sadly, it was never occupied as housing. Following the German occupation of France, the project ended up as a police barracks. Only later was it converted into a detention center for Jews, homosexuals, Gypsies, and others labeled as "undesirables." In truth, it was nothing more than a way station for people destined for Auschwitz and other concentration camps.

The individual family quarters were dark, and soiled mats of straw served as mattresses. Planned for short stays, the authorities spent no effort in making anyone comfortable, piling more than seven thousand people into a complex that was designed to house only seven hundred.

Management of Drancy was taken over by the Germans from the French in July 1943. Alois Brunner directed the camp and was responsible for the transport of inmates out of Drancy to Auschwitz and, to a lesser extent, other camps.

Michel and Anna settled into their drab existence and found ways to occupy their time while waiting for transfer to a "work camp." He chose to volunteer his services in the small clinic located on the fourth floor of this massive U-shaped building and organized other recently transported physicians to assist him in seeing patients. Anna volunteered her time in the children's quarters.

It didn't take Michel and his colleagues long to identify and isolate a single typhus case. In less than two weeks, Michel had convinced the Germans to institute a rat removal program, thereby averting a typhus epidemic. Michel's quick action did not go unnoticed, and Commandant Brunner openly thanked him for his efforts. Seizing a chance to keep his family safe from the "death camps," Michel quickly made an appointment to speak with Brunner immediately after the typhus threat had been eliminated.

"Sir," he addressed the chief officer, "I thank you for seeing me on this short notice." Keeping his head down and feigning deference, he continued. "We have just been advised that my family and I are on the transport list to Auschwitz next week. I don't think I can transfer my experience here in typhus prevention to an encampment of that size." Michel paused and lowered his voice. "Might there be somewhere else where my expertise could be better used?"

Alois Brunner well understood what Michel was asking. Rising from his seat he put his arm on the doctor's shoulder. "Doctor Katz, everyone here owes you a favor for preventing a typhus epidemic. I will now change that list and send you and your family to Terezin, instead—believe me, a far better place to go."

A slow smile worked its way across Michel's face as he thanked the commandant and left quickly to tell Anna the good news.

Three days later, Anna gladly reclaimed Rachel and Aaron from the children's unit and packed up for their next destination.

sss

On October 3, 1943, Michel, Anna, Aaron, and Rachel Katz arrived at Terezin, while Stanley and Sarah Goldfein were sent to Revel, Estonia, to work in a slave labor camp. They were never to be heard from again.

Michel and his family were treated a bit more deferentially than the others Jews; doctors seemed to always get that special respect. While the other passengers had to ride in cars designed for cattle, the Katz family was given real seats for the two-day rail journey to Terezin. Still, there was little joy in this trip. Sensing their parents' apprehension, the children remained almost mute during the ride, shifting their focus to the landscape outside their window.

Although the Jews were not considered true "prisoners," SS troops surrounded their train prior to departure, and armed soldiers seemed to reappear out of nowhere each time the train stopped. Michel tried to quell his wife's fears when the SS jumped out at the first stop, jesting, "Look, our German friends are surrounding the train to protect us!"

His attempts at humor felt feeble and increased his helplessness. There was no need for Anna to respond as the look she gave her husband spanned a thousand words. Her strong inner senses were acute, and no amount of joking could distract her from what was truly happening or the terror of the unknown life ahead.

Most fortresses in Europe had been designed to keep invading forces out; this was not true of Terezin. The gates were opened wide as if to welcome visitors in, much as a spider might invite unsuspecting prey into its web. It was that element of entrapment that was most significant to those who passed through. Embraced by deceiving arms, the new invitees were physically captured in a town reserved for the vulnerable, restricted only to Jews.

Reinhardt Heydrich, the former Gestapo head and governor of Czech Bohemia and Moravia, wanted a place to show officials of governments and relief organizations, such as the Red Cross, how well he treated displaced Jews. World opinion seemed to matter to the Germans, so the world would be told that the war effort required civilians to move to areas where labor was needed for manufacturing plants. Citing the hostility directed at Jews in their native countries, it was deemed best "to move them to a place of safety where they also could serve the Reich."

In reality, Heydrich had been placed in charge of the Final Solution to the Jewish problem. Hitler wanted a Germany and Europe to be *Judenfrei*—free of Jews—and he chose to deport them to concentration camps throughout Germany and Eastern Europe. But Heydrich was assassinated in 1942, before his "accomplishment" at Terezin could be appreciated.

Upon arrival at Terezin, Michel was given "upgraded quarters"—two rooms and a small kitchen. His family was allowed to stay together, rather than have Rachel and Aaron housed in separate children's quarters. There were four small beds with straw mattresses, two in each room; one thin sheet covered each mattress, and a single blanket was draped over the bed. Shelves were located in a closet for their clothes. A small, round table and four basic wooden chairs sat next to the kitchen area. Threadbare white curtains draped the single front window giving a small semblance of privacy to their new home. The walls were dirty and in need of new paint, and the wooden floor creaked with each step anyone took in the adjacent living quarters. The Katzes's apartment faced the center court with an outside hallway running along the front of the building. Common toilets were found on every floor.

Taking in a deep breath, Anna studied her new home hopefully. "Maybe we can find a small rug for the front room to warm it up a bit. Even some inexpensive prints on the wall might make it more comfortable. Beyond that, I don't know."

She became quiet and laid her head on Michel's shoulder; her tears fell softly, muffled into his broad chest, safely unnoticed by the children.

Mindful of Anna's anguish, Michel knew they needed time alone. "Rachel, Aaron," he called out, "why don't you go out in the hall, explore our building, and come back with a report?" He pulled his tearful wife closer as he closed the door behind them. "Anna, we are safe here and all will be fine. You heard the SS officer speak as we were led off the train. We are among the fortunate ones and have been given more comforts than the others. This is the 'model' ghetto, remember?"

"Michel," she retorted, pulling away, "we've listened to the same stories—the ones we heard in Drancy and those from others on the train; they talked about the camps, the killings, and the rumors of a gas chamber. You know, as I do, that they burned the bodies—Michel, they burned them to hide what they were doing! We both know there has to be some truth in all of this."

Standing up, Michel walked to the window and pulled the curtain aside. He didn't want to respond just then, but he knew what she was saying. He could not forget or deny what he had learned from the Italian banker, Angelo Donati, whom he had met with his uncle in Nice. Donati had shown them a secret memo from the Italian government and translated it for them:

"Reliable sources have interviewed two Jews who claim to be escapees from Auschwitz. These men maintain that there is systematic killing of Jews at Auschwitz-Birkenau, just outside of Krakow. Five gas chambers and perhaps six large crematoriums exist at this concentration camp. Those unable to work are directed from the trains to the chambers where they are murdered with gas. This includes women and children."

The memo went on to confirm rumors of similar death camps from other sources, yet none of these reports were as detailed as this one about Auschwitz. He had not shared this information with Anna, recognizing her fragility.

Wrapping his arms around his tearful wife, he spoke softly with confidence. "We are safe. Remember, I'm a doctor."

Michel was assigned to a small medical clinic adjacent to the town square. Within two days of arriving, he was seeing patients each day, often extending late into the night.

♦♦♦

A JEWISH COUNCIL OF Elders, or *Judenrat*, existed at Terezin to tend to the smaller details of community living and to create the lists of Jews who would be available for transport to a work camp away from Terezin. This Judenrat was formed under the auspices of the Camp Commandant so that Jews would deal with their own matters, shifting responsibility away from the Germans. Stronger members of the community were chosen by their captors to serve on the Council. Working under a supposed doctrine of objectivity, their major function was in determining who would fill the German demands for transport to Auschwitz and other "labor" camps. By putting the distasteful chore on the Jews themselves, the Nazis hoped to diffuse the angst associated with these "selections." This was a difficult job for these men, dealing with the obvious pain their decisions caused as well as the temptations presented to them. Bribes were offered—women tried to exchange sex for delisting, nothing was held sacred in the face of likely death.

Michel understood this mechanism of human nature. Although his altruistic spirit encompassed the concept of fairness, he sensed his own ideals changing with each passing day. After a few weeks at Terezin, his former empathetic nature took the first small steps toward evolving into that person who took care of his own *by whatever means necessary*. Not that he was less of a doctor in his clinic—no, that did not change. But he began more and more to dissociate himself from his patients' concerns. The more Michel began to understand the true destination of the transports, the more a fissure started to form in his capacity for compassion, and he began to realize that he could never be the same again.

Man should not be so selfless as to not try anything possible to save himself.

Michel noticed that the Terezin population remained quite stable, with little change in the apparent census of the ghetto. The "apartments" were kept full, and at times, families waited outside in the square for days before their rooms became available. The emptying of these living quarters coincided with the sound of the train whistle as it departed to the East.

A certain "pecking order" existed at Terezin. At the top were members of the Judenrat, whose decisions affected the status of the other ghetto inhabitants. Doctors were held in high esteem and, in many ways, were protected by the council. Other professionals—lawyers, architects, engineers and the like held out hope that the elevated status of their former life might exempt them from transport to "other camps," but they were wrong. Anyone who made demands or requested special treatment by the Judenrat soon ended up on the list for transport. It was only human nature… Get rid of those who complained to make the Council's life easier.

Michel recognized that his family was not immune to these risks. There was no assurance that they could avoid being chosen for transport out of Terezin. He thought they might be treated differently because of his profession, but he accepted that nothing in these times was certain. Families were often separated; the wife and children were sent off while the husband was left back at Terezin to work. Michel was well aware that a call for medical professionals had been made in the past to serve at other camps.

I must be careful, we are still vulnerable.

◆◆◆

WITHIN FOUR WEEKS, MICHEL had established his surgical practice and had modified an empty examination room into a minor surgery suite. He saw patients in his clinic each day and performed surgery on Tuesday and Thursday afternoons. His mind remained occupied while working, and he enjoyed the sense of power and control he experienced while doing his surgical cases. His success in bringing elective surgery to Terezin was appreciated by his colleagues as well as by the members of the Judenrat. He had done much to ingratiate himself with the community and Council without appearing overly assertive.

Michel also encouraged the Germans to expand their pest control program to eliminate the growing rat population. There had been one typhus epidemic before he arrived, and he felt additional precautions should be instituted. Lice lived in the fur of the ever-present rats and carried the *rickettsia typhi* to humans, resulting in a 50 percent death rate among those people infected with the disease.

The Germans carried out extensive de-lousing programs on the new ghetto inhabitants soon after they entered the camp. They had their hair shorn close, and showers were given on the day each family arrived. Convinced that rats contributed to the problem, the Germans initiated a program of extermination by gassing the attics and basements where rats congregated. The same pesticide they used to kill rats they later used on humans: Zyklon B.

Michel paid strict attention to the timing of the transports headed east as he continued to fear for his family's future. The lists were posted one day prior to the actual move, and it was difficult, almost impossible, to remove a name once it had been listed. This undercurrent of fear plagued everyone at Terezin.

It was in the evenings that Michel and Anna found time together, once the children were asleep. One night, just two weeks after their arrival at Terezin, they had just begun to talk when the sound of the train whistle interrupted their special time. A transport was leaving for Auschwitz. Anna started to cry, obsessed with her fear of being sent away. "More going to that camp, that death camp. Oh, Michel, I am so scared for us."

"I know, and I must do something."

He stood up and walked about the apartment running his fingers through his thick hair. "I will find a way to get in front of a Council member and talk with someone soon."

Needing to change the subject, he sat down at the kitchen table.

"I am frustrated and my clinic is busy, and there are many who need care, but there is just one operating room. I cannot schedule any more surgeries for this week." He looked at Anna. "Work going any better?"

"I don't know, Michel, work is work." She looked away as if she didn't want to talk about it. "It's just an old garment factory, and many women sit at tables sewing army uniforms together. The other women are nice, but we have a hard time talking, as they are from all over Europe. We speak a multitude of languages, but best communicate in what little Yiddish each of us knows. There is a nice Czech lady next to me, Beatrice, who is looking forward to her daughter coming here next week." Anna paused, as if trying to find something to say. "Aaron and Rachel seem to be getting along at the school, but it's difficult for them, as classes are taught in different languages—German, French, or Czech."

"At least, for the time being, they are safe," he said softly, his mind racing out of control.

I must find a way to keep us from being sent to the death camp.

♦♦♦

TWO WEEKS LATER, THE head of the Judenrat, Harry Meyer, came to his office for care.

"Mr. Meyer, how are you today?"

Michel gave his full attention to this last patient of the day.

"Doctor, there has been some bleeding from my rectum."

Harry Meyer went on to talk about his symptoms in great detail. Michel sat back and listened, patiently hearing the complaints, forcing himself to feign interest as the poor gentleman went on and on about his bowel habits.

This is it, Michel. This is your chance. Take it.

Harry Meyer had been a member of the Judenrat for more than a year and he was responsible for making up the lists for transport to the "work" camps. Consequently, he was often deluged with people who wanted to find ways to keep from being sent away. Michel was now in a position to ask for help, but he knew he had to be careful with his approach.

After completing his exam, Michel invited his patient back into his office. "Your problem is bleeding hemorrhoids, Mr. Meyer, and I believe we can take care of them here."

"Does that mean surgery, Doctor Katz?" asked the worried middle-aged man.

"A simple procedure, my friend. I can arrange for it to be done quite soon, as there is a cancellation next week on Thursday, November eighteenth. My nurse will give you the instructions. It should not be a problem."

"Thank you, my good doctor. If there is anything I can do…"

Michel didn't give him time to finish. "Yes, there is, one other thing… My wife—she worries so, you understand."

As Meyer left the office, he thanked Doctor Katz profusely and said, "I know you are very concerned about the transports, but don't be. I will watch out for your family."

Michel forced himself to make eye contact in spite of the fact that his profound relief brought tears to his eyes. "Thank you," was all he could say.

See, Michel? It's going to be okay.

♦♦♦

HANUKKAH WAS A TIME of gifts for the children, but there was little to buy in Terezin. The camp store handled only basic needs, and no one was allowed to venture outside the camp to peruse the stores. As the cold of December approached, the quiet despair of the inmates tamped down any hope of celebration. Selections for the transports continued despite the holidays, in sync with the almost robotic train schedule pursued by their German hosts.

Even though Meyer had promised to protect his family, Michel still nervously reviewed the transport lists each time they were posted. As his eyes swept over the last few names on the list, he would sigh with relief. But on a dark day in mid-January 1944, his heart nearly stopped when he saw the names of Anna, Rachel, and Aaron Katz on the list, scheduled to depart on the eighteenth of the month.

Michel sat alone in his clinic office, shaking and staring at the empty wall facing him. It was just eight weeks ago that Harry Meyer had assured him that his family would remain safe. He was furious with Meyer and also with himself.

How could I have been so naïve?

He angrily marched into Meyer's office. "You lied to me! You practically promised that they were not to be sent away!"

Meyer straightened his tie and sat back in his chair, assuming an air of importance. "You know, Doctor Katz, we must provide certain numbers for our German hosts. They make serious demands on me to fulfill their needs."

"But you just praised my work here and offered to protect us from transport to Auschwitz. What changed?"

Meyer couldn't tell him the truth—that he had pulled the Fisher family off the list in exchange for a gold wristwatch. Casually, he pulled his shirt cuff down to hide his new jewelry. Having anticipated such an outburst from Michel, he began to share his alternate plan.

"Doctor Katz, I believe we might have a better solution, if you are willing." The tiny glimmer of hope in Michel's eyes gave him the signal he needed to continue. "I can exchange their names for yours. You know they need more doctors at Auschwitz. It's a large camp with too much sickness. I'm sure the addition of your name would satisfy the Germans."

Michel sat back and closed his eyes for several seconds.

I promised—whatever it takes to keep them safe.

Internally, he struggled deeply as he recalled his conversations in Nice with Donati about the gas chambers and the ovens.

But, what about me? Would I survive? Could the family survive without me here? And how will I tell Anna?

Michel swallowed hard. "Go ahead, you may change the list, but I must know, and you must promise, that you will protect them from transport in the future. Give me your solemn word as a man, as a Jew. I need to know!"

"You have my word."

Michel left quickly to work out Meyer's proposal in the solitude of his own mind. Knowing Anna would be inconsolable, he chose to keep his thoughts quiet while he contemplated the changes ahead. He walked around the deserted central square, now isolated with barbed wire, as he wrestled with the decision he had just made.

The trains seemed always to be a one-way passage; Michel recalled no one coming back from Auschwitz. Over the three months he had been at Terezin, several physicians had left to serve at the large group of camps comprising Auschwitz-Birkenau, and he had heard little from them, aside from the postcards that arrived for their families. The brief notes on the cards expressed the fine and fair treatment the doctors were receiving. Of course, Michel knew full well that all correspondence was censored, so the news did not necessarily indicate the reality of their existence. He had no way of knowing what Auschwitz was like.

I have to find out from someone who has been there.

Michel had developed a reasonably amicable relationship with a Sergeant Sontag, who he had treated for an infected finger two weeks prior. The German military physician had been on leave, and Michel was asked to take care of this emergency, despite the supposed ban on Jews treating non-Jews. Michel believed he could talk with him about Auschwitz. He tracked down the sergeant at his guard post.

"*Guten Morgan, Herr Unterfeldwebel.* I wonder if I might talk with you for a few minutes...?"

"Anytime, my doctor friend. What can I do for you?" Sontag answered.

Michel told him about the offer Meyer had made to him. Sontag motioned for Michel to step closer, and took a few moments before he answered quietly. "You must understand what those camps are about, Doctor Katz. First of all, I have not been there, but I hear that the men and women are worked hard, often to their death, and disease is sometimes rampant in their quarters."

He paused again, not wanting to venture further, as he hoped Michel understood the unspoken message.

But the doctor seemed oblivious to Sontag's pause as a warning. "Well, it must be true that they do need more doctors to, say, fight disease and keep the workers strong."

"*Ja,*" Sontag nodded, "that is true."

Deep inside, Michel had desperate thoughts he dared not speak aloud to Sontag. He wanted to ask about the rumors of gas chambers and crematoriums and wholesale killings of people—of Jews. Yet he did not question Sontag further, as he clung to his belief that a horror of this magnitude could not be happening. The stories and rumors had to be exaggerations of one or two events, he was sure. Michel thanked the soldier for his time and returned to his clinic.

That night, he spent time in deep thought before returning to his apartment. He wondered whether he could do this—leave his family and go to Auschwitz.

Is this about their safety, or is it about me?

Michel's head pounded as he wrestled with all the conflicting thoughts that ricocheted back and forth.

Will the children really be safe without me here? Can Meyer be trusted to keep his word this time?

Tears flowed in the tiny apartment later that night when Michel told Anna and the children he would be leaving. After reassuring Rachel and Aaron that it would not be long before he returned, the parents finally put their tearful children to bed. Michel and Anna stepped outside and hugged each other as never before.

It was a few minutes before Anna finally allowed her pent-up emotions to erupt. "I don't know if I can do this!" she exclaimed. "Without you, I feel naked, unprotected. I need you more now than ever before!"

"I know, *ma chère*, it will be hard. I cannot deny this. But please believe me, you will be protected here with the children. Meyer has given me his word."

Anna hung her head as Michel continued. "Whatever hardship I have to deal with at Auschwitz, I can handle knowing that you and the children are safe. There, I am needed. I can help our less fortunate people. It is for the best, and you will be safe."

Stepping back, Anna studied Michel. She had always known her husband to be a confident, strong man. But tonight she saw something new in his eyes—she saw he was beaten. His work and passion for others had saved him at Terezin by being the doctor who cared. But now, when she looked at him, he cast his eyes to the side. She knew her own beseeching actions must have been pulling hard at her husband's heart. How she loved this good, good man, and how he strived to protect his family and give to others. She knew all too well that little sleep would come to both of them that night, and perhaps for many nights to come. She would set him free, assuage his guilt, and trust that his decision was right.

Meyer will keep his promise. The children and I will be safe. Michel will find some small happiness in helping others. We'll be together again someday, and it will all be okay.

A train whistle broke the silence.

"...and will abstain from any voluntary act of mischief or corruption."

12

January 20, 1944
Auschwitz, Poland

I t seemed incongruous.

I hear music, how bizarre...

The train slowed and stopped at the siding; the sign announced Auschwitz. As the doors clanged open, Michel stepped out into the chaos.

Amidst the cacophony of hundreds of new inmates filling a rail yard, there was, in fact, an orchestra of sorts comprised of camp inmates welcoming the transported Jews to their new life. Perhaps the Germans thought they could somehow disguise the horrors of the camp that would soon be obvious. Other sounds masked the symphony—barking dogs, Nazis yelling, and people crying.

A cheerless, gray-clouded sky melded with the thin layer of snow that dressed the camp and its buildings. Scanning the flat, treeless landscape, Michel noticed endless rows of identical buildings, similar to horse barns, spread across the grounds. Barbed wire surrounded this large, dismal space with guard towers evenly distributed along the periphery of the immense complex. Certain barracks were fenced off and isolated from the rest. Warning signs, *"Achtung, gefahr—elektrizitat,"* were posted along the perimeter wires indicating the danger of electrocution if touched. Groups of inmates in gray-and-white striped outfits and hats could be seen walking in lines or working at construction sites.

Physicians were separated from the rest of the deportees and ordered to line up, gather whatever equipment they brought with them, and follow an SS officer. The physicians showered, were deloused, and then were given the typical striped woolen uniforms and caps. Michel picked up his bags and marched along with the somber group of twenty-five doctors.

He checked his watch; it was 5:00 p.m., and it would be dark soon. At the far end of the camp, black smoke was escaping from several chimneys along with a foul scent he couldn't readily identify.

Could it be...?

The doctors were led to a red brick building located in Auschwitz I, the oldest section of the concentration camp complex. "These are your barracks," said the accompanying SS soldier. "The clinic and housing for the sick is located close by, just down the road. One of the physicians inside will provide the necessary details concerning your duties. I'm sure you will be quite comfortable here."

He brusquely turned and walked away, sporting a wry smile on his face.

Upon entering the building, the muted voice of Doctor Abraham Levy greeted the physicians. "*Willkommen,* doktors. Hippocrates would be proud. Pick a bed, rest up, and we'll orient you after...dinner. Oh, yes, you'll need to share your bed with someone." Beds were stacked three high, with a stained, straw mattress for padding, covered by a single threadbare blanket. There were, perhaps, sixty beds in the barracks.

As Michel stood shivering in the cold, dank room, inmate doctors started returning from work; they did not acknowledge the new arrivals, and few spoke at all, even to each other. Their thin, drawn faces spoke volumes.

Sitting on the edge of a bed, his face buried in his hands, Michel was suddenly accosted by a harsh German voice. "You're on my bed—move, find your own! There is another who I share this with."

Michel moved to get up, but was restrained by a hand on his shoulder. "I'm so sorry, please forgive my anger—you will soon understand. I am Aaron, Aaron Bernstein, and you must be one of the new people."

"Yes," said Michel, "I am Michel Katz. Our train arrived this afternoon."

Sitting down close to Michel, Aaron clasped his hands loosely together on his lap, slowly shaking his head. He spoke in a low voice. "Tell me, where are you from?"

"France, Lyon originally, but moved to Nice where we were rounded up after the Italian surrender. The Nazis sent us to Drancy, and then to

Terezin. My family is still there." Michel hesitated, then continued. "And what about you?"

"Berlin, where I was a professor at the university. Sent here with my family last October." Looking out the window, eyes glistening as he stared at the smoke pouring from smokestacks, "They're all gone, gassed... burned to ashes."

Michel slumped forward, bowed his head, and closed his eyes.

And I heard all this before but never really listened. I didn't believe my uncle, I thought it was Allied propaganda; the guard at Terezin tried to tell me, but I stopped him because I did not want to know. Rumors, I said, just rumors. And that's why people were placed in two lines when we arrived; one had mostly women and children, plus a few old people; they were destined to die. No highly educated society could act like this. And Meyer, on the Judenrat at Terezin, he knew all this. He lied once when my family was put on the list to Auschwitz; I should not have believed him then. No, he won't protect them now. And I thought myself so smart to come here, saving them.

Aaron put his arms around Michel's shoulders. "Dinner will arrive soon. They'll place the kettle next to the stove..."

Michel was one of six doctors assigned as a unit to the infirmary attached to the French camp. Shortly, they were presented with a schedule of coverage for the bed patients, as well as for the clinic. The SS staff offered veiled encouragement, reminding them of their responsibility to care for their countrymen. Their unit was told to establish a plan to care for the Jewish transports from France. It was stressed that medical care was important to the health of the camp and the availability of workers for the defense plants in the area. Specifically, the authorities were concerned about typhus epidemics that had devastated other concentration camps. Tuberculosis, typhoid fever, and other infectious diseases were also of significant concern.

Despite the miserable surroundings, the plan of care initially sounded reasonable. Yet shortly, it became apparent that there were no medicines, no supplies, and too much overcrowding to effectively treat or, for that matter, prevent any disease processes. Straw mattresses in the infirmary were shared by a minimum of two inmates per bed, often three. Running water was limited to a single sink at the far end of the barracks, next to the latrines, and the infirmary also housed its share of flies, cockroaches, and the occasional rat.

The newly arrived doctors met repeatedly with Eduard Wirths, the SS physician overseeing their group, to request what they needed to care for ill inmates, but these meetings never seemed to produce results. Initially, Wirths listened and made excuses for the lack of food and medicines, but as their requests persisted, he seemed annoyed. "The first priority is to care for our soldiers; then we can treat the inmates and prisoners here," he said curtly.

"How can we expect to get someone healthy on only four hundred calories a day?" complained Michel one morning to Wirths. "The diet has few vitamins, no fat, and very little nutritional value."

Wirths stared directly at Michel and said nothing. Michel lowered his head; he understood. After that, the doctors were careful not to incur the wrath of the SS doctors with demands the Germans obviously had no intention of meeting. The responsibilities they had spoken of upon the physicians' arrival were, in fact, only a ruse. Besides keeping the inmates on a starvation diet, the camp medicines and supplies were almost non-existent.

Every inmate eventually developed chronic, watery stools accompanied by episodes of cramps. After a few weeks, if someone did obtain food with significant protein value, he had to be careful, as his body would often rebel, and explosive diarrhea followed. Inmates were forced to stand outside for long hours each day, even in the cold of winter, while the barracks population was counted. This resulted in many deaths from pneumonia. Bruising, sores, and non-healing trivial wounds, such as scratches, often led to overwhelming cellulitis, systemic infection, and death. There were few supplies available to treat these wounds. Sulfa powder and iodine were in short supply, and bandages were nonexistent except for the few paper dressings doled out in insufficient quantities. The doctors suffered along with the other internees, but to a lesser extent, as they were not subject to the same cold and unbearable working environments.

Early on, each of the physicians tried to work to their former medical standards, with accurate diagnoses and detailed notes. This quickly became problematic when they realized that once a diagnosis of typhus or tuberculosis was made, the entire barracks could be sent to the gas chambers and cremated as a means of stopping its spread. The physicians soon became wiser, substituting lesser diagnoses to avoid this kind of dire response by the Germans.

Michel's feelings mirrored those of the other doctors in his infirmary. They felt powerless in their inability to treat even the most common health problems that arose among the inmates, having virtually nothing with which to treat disease—despite empty promises from their SS colleagues that "medicine would be coming soon."

To allow my "doctor" self to fall so perilously low and be unable to effect change is beyond my comprehension. Why, my God, why did I come here?

It became clear to the inmate doctors that the camps harbored an industry of death. The lines that had formed at the rail station had two destinations: barracks or the gas chambers. Those sent to the gas chambers had no numbers tattooed on their arm; they were not counted. They were told only that they were going to showers. That was a lie.

He thought back to his past, which had been filled with a series of expected educational triumphs beginning with his graduation from the lycée with highest honors. He later completed the University of Lyon School of Medicine at the top of his class. Awards, recognition, and faculty praise graced his professional life; three years of residency and several published research papers culminated in his appointment as assistant professor of surgery at the medical school. Michel's world of medicine was, in fact, like his operating suite: he was respected and he was in command. He hungered to restore that feeling of competency, but that was difficult to find at Auschwitz. Mired in frustration, his sense of helplessness was increasing by the day.

♦♦♦

IT WAS AN AFTERNOON Michel Katz could never forget. *SS Doktor* Josef Mengele visited the infirmary and introduced himself to the six inmate physicians assigned there. Mengele had initially been seen only in his role as the "selection doctor" when the trains unloaded, dividing the new inmates into those able to work and those fated to die in the gas chambers. Yet soon, the clinic physicians recognized that he was head of the SS experimental medicine group and was familiar with and responsible for the human studies ongoing at the camps. Mengele's reputation made the inmate physicians wary; he could be remarkably friendly and civil one moment yet turn into a murderous child killer the next.

Standing with an air of absolute authority, Mengele was a strikingly handsome man with dark hair and penetrating brown eyes who seemed to demand submission from anyone in his presence. Today, he was strongly encouraging the clinic physicians to visit the pathology laboratory and observe Doctor Miklos Nyiszli. The inmate doctors welcomed the break and eagerly followed Mengele to Crematorium II, where Doctor Nyiszli worked in an adjacent laboratory, performing autopsies for the head physician and other SS doctors engaged in human experimentation.

Doctor Nyiszli had visited the doctors' clinic briefly the previous month and introduced himself to the new physicians. He'd surreptitiously brought along small amounts of medicines and dressings for their patients, supplies usually designated for the care of the SS soldiers. Michel recognized it as a feeble gesture to overcome the scarcities they were facing to treat the inmates. He kept his eyes on the floor, trying to hide his contempt for this Jewish doctor who voluntarily helped the Germans.

There were ongoing rumors of Nyiszli's participation in the experiments performed by Mengele and the other Nazi doctors. He had been a prominent Hungarian pathologist who was transported to Auschwitz in May 1944 with ten thousand other Hungarian Jews. When his train arrived, Mengele pulled him directly from the lines and easily convinced him that his talents could best be used by continuing to practice his specialty—forensic pathology. Because of his perceived importance to the SS physicians' experiments, he was soon separated from the other Hungarian Jews in his transport and was rarely free to mingle with the other physicians in the camp.

It was known that the doctor spent day and night in a modern autopsy facility that had been constructed in the same building that housed Crematorium II. Doctor Nyiszli was assigned to this laboratory where sleeping quarters were provided, further restricting his need to mix with other prisoners. In addition to doing autopsies and assisting in the various studies, he was given the responsibility of caring for the *Sonderkommandos,* inmates who worked in the gas chambers and crematoriums.

This "laboratory" where Nyiszli worked was a source of pride for Mengele, and he visited the facility at least once daily. From time to time, other SS physicians would come to view an autopsy on a subject involved in their studies. This well-equipped "Facility of the Dead," as Michel called it, clashed harshly with the reality of the hellish scenes occurring daily in the infirmary and the barracks.

Little is done for our living inmates, and yet here there is an abundance of supplies for the dead ones.

These and other thoughts crossed Michel's mind as the group of Jewish physicians arrived at the lab with Mengele.

"Gentlemen, Doctors," Mengele began, "let me introduce you once again to the noted pathologist, Doctor Miklos Nyiszli from Budapest. He has been quite obliging here in helping us identify the diseases that are killing many of our camp inmates."

Michel wanted to spit on the floor.

"From time to time, I call on Doctor Nyiszli to examine some of those volunteer inmates who have unaccountably expired during one of our studies, and he has mentioned to me that there might be other doctors like yourselves who would be interested in assisting in our research."

Looking around the room, Michel noticed that the doctors' faces appeared impassive. No one appeared ready to step forward.

I see deep fear in their eyes; they want to stay invisible.

"Today, we have a special case," Mengele continued, "a young Jewess who died unexpectedly during one of our studies. And we need Doctor Nyiszli's expertise to determine the cause of death. Please, Doctor Nyiszli."

The short, bespectacled man of about forty-five years walked to the head of the autopsy slab. He wore, not inmate garb, but woolen slacks, a pressed white shirt, tie, and a white smock. There was little sign of his being a prisoner. He might have been a few pounds underweight, but he had a spry step and kept his head up, not looking at the ground as the others had learned to do. His hair was thinning and gray and his eyes appeared sad. At the most, five foot six, he was a small man who exhibited the confidence of an academic professor.

Doctor Nyiszli waited quietly while Mengele finished his presentation. "This woman was well until three days ago, when she started to complain of pelvic pain accompanied by fever, chills, and sweating. Her temperature was forty-one and a half degrees Centigrade, and she exhibited a rapid, threadlike pulse. She died suddenly at eleven this morning."

Mengele looked at each of the six doctors, his dark eyes boring into them. "This inmate had been in the fertility study barracks and was part of the contraceptive study, yet had received no injections or treatments. Because she passed so quickly, no blood was taken for testing." He walked over to the body, stood there, and crossed his arms on his chest. "Are there any questions?"

Michel could see that two or three doctors looked ready to speak, but something they saw in Mengele constrained them. He was staring directly at each man, one by one, as if daring the Jewish physicians to say something. But all remained quiet. This presentation was superficial compared to those they had attended in the past, and it lacked the thoroughness one would expect when discussing a case with other physicians. They refused to venture, even cautiously, into this unfamiliar territory. Taking the silence as an affirmation, Mengele nodded towards Nyiszli, prompting him to speak.

"We start here," Nyiszli began, "at the suprasternal notch." He pointed to the hollow just above the breastbone. "And we end here at the pubis."

With a surgical blade, he sliced deeply through the skin from top to bottom, as cleanly as a gladiator might disembowel an enemy. A sticky, mucous-like fluid started to ooze out of the abdominal cavity, and the room was quickly permeated with the stench of dead tissue.

The visiting physicians had attended autopsies in medical school, but had never seen anything quite as foul as this. They tried hard not to react to the overwhelming smell, or to the rivers of pus pouring out of the incision, and they offered little response.

Specimens for culture were taken, and the liver, spleen, and kidneys grossly examined. The stomach was then inspected externally, palpated down to the beginning of the small intestine. With his fingers on either side of the intestine, Doctor Nyiszli slid it through his hand all the way down to its intersection with the colon, pointing out the ileo-cecal junction. He similarly "ran through" the large bowel down to the rectum. The entire stomach and the large and small intestines were then excised as one from the body, laid out on the sink counter, and washed by an assistant.

Doctor Nyiszli kept a running commentary for his guests as he completed the autopsy in a systematic manner. Michel struggled to keep his thoughts to himself.

Horrid! The smell...this place...that poor woman...

Mengele stood back and coolly watched with his arms crossed.

Nyiszli went back to the corpse and examined the contents of the pelvis. The uterus was swollen, discolored, and engorged. Both ovaries were bathed in pus, and the uterus was covered with yellow-green, sticky ooze.

Nyiszli reached down and felt something hard in the cervix. He removed the uterus with a knife as far down as he could, still keeping the ovaries intact. As he moved to lay down the organs, his audience stifled a collective gasp as a round, black, rubberized cap, about five centimeters wide and one centimeter deep, fell into the pelvis from the vaginal vault. Mengele noticed it, too. Quickly donning gloves, he retrieved the object from the dead woman and wrapped it in a towel.

"Oh, you now know about one of my secret studies," Mengele said with a self-conscious laugh. "We are developing a birth control device to contain the birth rate of undesirable populations. Once implanted over the cervical cap, it can be left there indefinitely."

His usually pale face seemed to blush in embarrassment as he wheeled around and abruptly exited the laboratory. The assembled physicians remained silent. Even with Mengele gone, no one spoke.

Michel well understood what had happened. Permanently blocking the opening into the uterus through the cervix with any foreign mechanical device could only lead to this outcome. The backed-up blood and normal secretions in the uterus make for a perfect culture medium, triggering the subsequent pelvic infection and peritonitis.

Demonstrating his professionalism, Doctor Nyiszli continued to complete the autopsy and inspect the rest of the body. He noted to the assembled physicians that appropriate slides of the tissue would be made and cultures taken to help determine the cause of death. At a later date, however, the autopsy report would read only, "Cause of death: peritonitis."

It was a somber group of doctors that slowly made their way back to the barracks. Not a sound was uttered. Looks of disgust were poorly concealed, even with their heads bowed down towards the earth.

Only after lights were out did conversation slowly begin to rise out of the silence, and the physicians' personal feelings swept to the surface. Everyone held their thoughts and listened as a voice, anonymous in the dark, whispered; "We live and die with our Jewish brethren while that Hungarian butcher becomes the lap dog of Mengele and the other demented SS torturers. Look at him, dressed as if he's ready for a stroll in downtown Budapest, clean and well-fed. And he does their bidding, that bastard."

Murmurs of agreement crisscrossed the room as another voice lashed out. "It is beyond belief that he thinks and acts as if he is truly practicing medicine. And then has the nerve to lecture us! May God have no mercy on his soul when his use is over and he is discarded! Besides temporary comforts, what can he really think he is gaining by working with the Nazis?"

Michel became troubled as he lay in the dark. He, too, felt only loathing for Nyiszli. Yet he wondered why this renowned doctor would do this and suffer, so obviously, the abject criticism of his peers?

♦♦♦

IT HAD BEEN TWO months since Michel had received any word from Anna. He would awaken each morning at two, and be unable to return to sleep as he repeatedly questioned his decision to leave them. Terezin was a resort compared to this hell.

- *Did I make the right choice? Was there anything else I could have done to keep them safe?*

His last meeting with Meyer played for the hundredth time in his mind.

How could I not have seen through that bastard?

Michel often had dreams of holding Anna and each of his children close in his arms. He relished these times, as images of his family flashed by—alive, happy, and away from this hellhole in which they had become trapped. And it wasn't long before he started to fall into a pit of depression. He cried alone in his bunk, quietly, with tears wetting the thin mattress where his face would lie. Silent sobs in the night stayed with him until he felt as if he were drowning himself to sleep.

The sadness that enveloped him seemed to increase each day as the trains unloaded more Jews. The new transports all endured the same ritual, as Mengele scanned each one, brusquely assigning him or her to work or to proceed directly to the gas chambers. He would raise his arm and point to one of the two lines in front of him. Line up to the right, death now; line up to the left, death slowly...day by day.

Michel recalled the conversations that had continued well into the night in his barracks after the visit to Nyiszli. As he listened to the hatred unleashed in the dark, his mind raced out of control. Had Nyiszli cut a deal to save his life and his family in exchange for practicing his specialty in the camps?

One night after visiting the Hungarian's lab, Michel woke up screaming, alarming his entire barracks. The dream was vivid, almost real. He was peering out his barracks window, watching the soldiers unload the next round of inmates, when he saw his wife and children jump out of the rail-car, lining up to be selected. "Anna! Rachel! Aaron!" he yelled through the window. "Run! Get away from them! Don't get in that line!"

He pounded on the window, trying to get their attention, screaming at the top of his lungs until he woke himself up—his thin blanket soaked in sweat.

It was time to talk with Mengele.

◆◆◆

"So you were a professor of surgery at the University in Lyon—why didn't you tell me sooner?" Mengele said almost warmly, seating himself at his desk. Without giving Michel time to answer, he peppered him with questions. "What were your areas of study?"

Michel looked down at the floor, perplexed by so much interest.

"What was the subject of your thesis?" Mengele closed the file he was looking at and stared directly at Michel. His dark, emotionless eyes trans-fixed him for a moment.

"I was involved in a study on cold thermal injury, but the war inter-fered with funding for my follow-up research," he answered.

He then went on to relate a list of studies he'd authored dealing with various aspects of general surgery and modestly mentioned his position as Director of Research Studies at the Lyon Institute of Surgery.

Mengele leaned forward, giving Michel his full attention. "Tell me more, Doctor Katz, especially about your cold studies."

"We utilized adult New Zealand rabbits and did a timed immersion study in cold water baths at zero degrees Centigrade. Vital signs, including pulse, rectal temperature, and respiratory rate were recorded. The rabbits were subject to re-warming, both rapid and slow, and anatomical changes were noted." Michel looked up to see if Mengele was listening. "The animals were sacrificed at intervals of two, four, and six weeks, and the histology of the major organs was studied."

"So Doctor Katz, let me know a little about your family, and how you ended up here at Auschwitz," said Mengele, in a low, comforting tone, his lips twisting into a smile.

The question strangely reassured Michel, and he recounted his move to Nice, emphasizing his desire to work with his uncle. He was truthful with Mengele about the roundup, incarceration in Drancy, and the rail trip to Terezin. He spoke of his concern for his wife and children and his ongoing worry about their welfare.

When he finished, the SS physician put his hands behind his head, leaned back, and stared at the ceiling for a few seconds, and then spoke. "If you agree to work with our research group, I could get information about your family for you and perhaps even allow full correspondence sent back to them."

Mengele smiled as he saw Michel's face and eyes light up. He pushed back from his desk, rose slowly, and walked about his office, apparently deep in thought; then he opened a file cabinet and pulled out several folders.

While the SS physician perused this material at his desk, Michel had a chance to look around the room and notice the extreme orderliness of the desk and files.

There are no loose papers anywhere.

The desktop was bare except for a marble pen and inkwell set engraved with Mengele's full name and a swastika alongside a photograph of the doctor and his wife. On the back wall, a full-faced Heinrich Himmler, the SS chief, took command over the room. Impressive diplomas from Munich University, Vienna University, and the University of Frankfurt hung on the sidewall. These were flanked by certificates admitting Mengele into the SS and his Nazi party membership. The endless rows of camp barracks occupied the view from two windows to the left of Mengele's desk. To the right of the entry door stood a bookcase spanning the entire wall, crammed with German medical texts.

It seemed as if an eternity had passed as Michel waited for the head physician to speak again. He hadn't been invited to sit down, nor did he expect it.

"Doctor Katz," Mengele said suddenly, breaking into his thoughts, "We have a need for someone familiar with surgical pathology and research protocols to aid us in our studies. The staff has fallen behind in our anatomical and pathological examinations, and we would like to finalize at least three projects so that I may forward the results to Berlin in a timely manner. In addition, a Doktor Hans Bloch is arriving here within a few weeks to complete his cold immersion study—your area of research, yes?"

Michel affirmed with a nod of his head.

"I do understand your very natural concerns for your family's welfare," Mengele continued tenderly. "You must understand—it would be in your best interest to voluntarily participate in our research programs." Mengele paused for several seconds, looking out the window. "I can assure you their health will be attended to at Terezin and frequent communications will be maintained between you and your family."

This second reference to his family by Mengele encouraged Michel. Whatever doubts he harbored concerning the "science" being practiced by the SS physicians disappeared as he began to think of his family's well-being. Yet, deep inside, questions of right and wrong echoed through his soul as words summoned from the Hippocratic Oath came back to him...

Primum non nocere... First, do no harm.

Michel looked at Mengele, trying to contain his emotions. "Doctor Mengele, thank you for this opportunity. I would be honored to assist in any way I can."

No time was wasted. Arrangements were made for Michel to meet with Doctors Mengele and Nyiszli in the autopsy facility the very next day.

♦♦♦

INITIALLY, THE JOB WAS stimulating. He worked alongside Nyiszli, doing postmortem exams and slide preparation, and started to feel the stirrings of renewed purpose. The Hungarian doctor was a bright man, and Michel learned a tremendous amount about various disease patterns, their respective organ changes, and histology. His duties also involved helping other SS physicians in research design, and his days were now spent somewhat enjoyably doing investigations in a clean, warm laboratory. Yet, at night, he returned to the barracks and the realities of concentration camp life. The other doctors in his barracks had stopped talking with him shortly after he began helping Nyiszli.

After his work assignment began, Michel's food rations improved, and while at the laboratory, clean clothes were provided for him. Nyiszli even let him shower in his room, but the Hungarian still maintained a boundary of separation from Michel. It was made very clear that a personal relationship could never develop.

Most of Michel's work involved doing autopsies on thin, debilitated souls who had died during one of the SS doctors' experiments. It seemed that many of the sickest had been chosen for the malaria inoculation study and, once infected, few lasted more than three or four weeks. Michel could justify his activities in the laboratory as being for the benefit of the inmates and scientific advancement. He rarely let his mind rest on the poor individuals who had died during the experiments or the twisted logic responsible for their demise.

One month later, a room adjacent to Crematorium III was remodeled into an additional laboratory for research studies. Not as fancy as Nyiszli's facility, it still had an autopsy table and metal counters on which to do the experimental work. Mengele reassigned Michel to this new facility, and a small room in the back soon became his bedroom. Michel thanked Doctor Nyiszli for all of his instruction and moved his work into the new space. Despite working so close to the horrors of the gas chambers and crematoriums, he was soon able to focus on his work and block out the harsh realities surrounding him.

In addition to his research duties, Michel was now responsible for the health of the Sonderkommandos. These inmates, usually young and strong men, were assigned to work twelve weeks at one of the six crematoriums at Auschwitz-Birkenau. Their job included removing the dead after they were gassed and bringing them up to the furnaces to be cremated. At the end of their rotation, they too were sent to the gas chambers or shot behind a crematorium. Himmler wanted no witnesses.

Michel began to realize that he, too, was now a witness.

13

February 18, 1944
Auschwitz

Your persona died well before you were murdered. Martin knew this; he would fight for his life.

It was inevitable, death. To some, it came when they forcibly removed you from your own home and placed you in the ghetto. For others, demise followed the forced march out of the squalid tenements to the train. Death of your soul commenced once the doors of the cattle car were slammed shut and locked. And if you lasted that long, upon entry to the camp, you became an invisible being—faceless, nameless, and without spirit. Any personal identity you once had was stripped from the living corpse you had become. The years of developing your own persona, your own style, were summarily erased and taken from you. There was no individuality; that wasn't allowed. You were identified only by the number tattooed on your left forearm. For their masters, the SS and filthy Kapos, it was so much easier to do those horrible things to nameless inmates.

Martin Brosky was number "42321."

"Move quickly," yelled the stern-faced guard as he slid open the doors, allowing the crowded masses of people to crawl out or jump down from the foul-smelling railcar, unfit even for the cattle it had been built to haul. Pointing to a pile of luggage and boxes, he commanded, "Leave your bags and belongings there and line up here!"

The barking jaws of the camp's German shepherds encouraged the frightened Jews to comply with the orders. Families were separated right away. Males were sent to one line, females and children formed another. The stridency of sounds combined with the chaos of hurried souls left many of the captured unfortunates dazed and confused with terror.

Martin jumped from his railcar and looked about, trying to assess the situation. His many years combing the streets of Lodz had given him a wisdom and perspective not taught in school. The killing of his parents had further hardened him beyond his years. At the far side of the rail yard he saw groups of men working in striped clothing, digging trenches and moving stone. Most were thin and bedraggled souls who walked slowly, constantly looking down. Guards with rifles prodded these prisoners on, sometimes beating them savagely with the butts of their weapons.

That will not be my fate.

Standing amid all this bedlam was a man stationed at the head of the line. Clean and handsome in his neatly-pressed SS uniform, the man Martin would come to recognize as Josef Mengele, MD, seemed to be the conductor of this operation, directing the flow of people, at his whim, to live or to die.

"All healthcare workers—line up here!"

Martin moved quickly toward the voice. Thirty to forty men and a few women answered the call, and a large line formed quickly in front of the doctor. Each person then was quickly barraged with a series of questions about his or her skills. Mengele wrote their qualifications on a lined sheet next to their names. Martin listened closely as the others explained their experience to the SS doctor. Eventually, he was called up, and with his head lowered in expected deference, he convinced Mengele he was an experienced pathology assistant who would be happy and honored to provide his services to the camp. He noted Mengele's raised eyebrow at one point during his interview and was relieved when the doctor nodded for him to move back into the line of doctors and nurses.

I've made the right steps so far... Just stay alert and stay in the shadows.

He looked over at the other two lines of human freight that had formed, wondering about their fate. What he didn't know was that the lucky ones were led to a shower, while the rest were marched into a room that only *looked* like a shower.

As if bathing animals to get rid of vermin, soap and disinfectant were given to Martin and others deemed lucky enough to work for the Reich. Little did they know that this was the last shower they would take for many months, unless they were transferred to another camp. Each person's hair was shorn close like a sheep's, and the hair collected was to be used in some way for the war effort. Coarse, striped gray-white camp wear was given to each inmate. The new arrivals were unaware that these garments had already accompanied someone else to his death.

Following entry into the camp, each person became sexless, without gender or, even worse, without spirit. Female breasts would soon, in time, wither to nothing. Skin would become tattooed with dirt and filth that would eventually be removed by the ovens. Gaits would become alike—a kind of aimless shuffle marked by the common, scratchy sounds of the wooden clogs worn by each prisoner. Knees were lifted with such difficulty that shoes often dragged along the gravelly earth. Whatever cadence or mannerism that had differentiated one person from another was quickly lost.

The SS guards and Kapos could not see an inmate as a person. It was much easier to lash out at the number "06789" and go on to the next one without guilt. To bring any human emotion into the barracks would be upsetting to many—even the tormentors had trouble dealing with that. Hiding behind a mask of sternness, they found relief in their rooms after work through alcohol binges, blurring any remembrance of that day's activities. It was simple and easy to assuage their personal and collective guilt under the guise of drunkenness. And they would awake the next day, not refreshed, but rekindled again to continue their jobs of humiliating the inmates, while elevating their own selves.

As a prisoner, all of life's dreams are erased once you enter the railroad cattle car and later unload at the camp. If you have ever exhibited any caring or gentleness to others, it soon passes. Just hours after your arrival, the concept of fairness and sharing taught to you by your parents becomes foreign and unimportant. Your spirit of independence becomes moot, replaced by a dependence on your captors for any need. A scrap of moldy bread crust becomes your greatest focus. You beg for permission from the Kapos to let you enter the latrine to relieve your crampy, watery bowels. No one is smiling; there are no signs of joy. To show any hint of happiness would be inappropriate and a sure sign of mental illness to your tormentors, who are looking for any excuse to send you to the gas chamber.

One by one, your former personal needs are reduced, replaced by the craving for food. Even the pain produced by beatings from the guards or SS is bearable when compared to the ever-present gnawing of hunger churning in your stomach. As an inmate, you would rush like a starving dog to get any scraps of food tossed your way.

Shame...what's that? You smell bad, but so does everyone...so who cares? And the worst thing that happens—you forget to care. Your wife, son, or daughter is away in another camp, and it's best to assume they are dead; to hope that they are alive takes too much from you, and there's little emotion or sentiment left to spare. You cannot recognize friends in camp, they all look the same; you can't seem to think about others as before. Your name, like theirs, has been replaced by a tattoo on your forearm.

There is no sense in worrying about the future; life has been reduced to the next day, the next hour, the next meal.

◆◆◆

MARTIN AND THE CAPTURED healthcare workers were marched to a dingy barracks, once a horse barn—block twenty four. It seemed better than the others, as there was a wooden floor and a stove at the end. Beds were stacked three high, and dirty straw served as a mattress. Three were expected to sleep in one bed. At the far end of the room was a separate area, a series of holes cut out of boards, maybe twenty, that served as latrines; the stench was horrible that first day, yet quite soon, one could not smell it at all.

A man standing at the door wearing the coarse stripes of a prisoner yelled, *"Achtung, Achtung!"* He announced, "I am your Kapo, and I am in charge of this barracks. Anything you want must go through me. If you must use the latrine, you ask. To eat, you ask. If the bed is bad, I can't help you, but you can ask. You speak when I let you; you sleep when I say so. You get up at four a.m. for roll call and march off to work. I strongly advise that you always appear for roll call, no matter how you might feel. Those that don't will be left behind and may be taken over there..."

He pointed to the smokestacks belching black smoke and fire.

The room became ghostly quiet; even the coughs and grunts were suspended. Everyone looked at this person in the garb of an inmate, telling them how they should live and how they might die. He was a man of about forty years and wore the badge identifying him as a criminal, not as a Jew. Compared to the other inmates, he looked too healthy. His shoulders were broad and arms muscular—hardly the look of a starving individual. He carried a perpetual scowl on his pock-marked face, as if he were ready to strike someone at any time.

The others looked to Martin to say something, who, at six foot two, was the only one close enough to this man in size to challenge him. After the Kapo had stepped out of the barracks, one young man, Moshe, spoke everyone's thoughts aloud. "What can we do? How do we live in this pest-hole? This place is *Scheisse.*"

Others joined in, and a general commotion arose as fear and pain overtook the men. They were all beaten down from the rail trip, but Martin could not get over the cool, emotionless way that Mengele had guided the life or death selection process. It was beyond any man's reason that such tragedy could occur. The children, old women, and even babies had gone to the other line.

I know what will happen to them.

"Listen closely, as we must not talk long." Martin jumped on the closest bed to grab everyone's attention. "They call this a work camp, and it is for those healthy enough to work." Despite his young age, he stood tall and calm among the fearful group and spoke in the manner of a man wise beyond his years. "We are selected to work, the others were not, and I fear they have been led off to their deaths."

For a few seconds, the room became quiet. Most of the men had tears streaming down their faces as they thought of their families that were taken away. Only soft sobbing was heard as Martin listened and watched the other men grieve. He remained silent, wishing not to interrupt the river of emotions flowing past him. He did not have to fear for a wife, child, or parent being killed—he had none. But he was now a point of clarity among the confused and frightened men. "The only way any of us will survive is to work, share our food, and help one another. If we look out only for ourselves, we will lose, and probably die. We can help each other stay alive in this camp until the war ends. That should be our goal."

Just as Martin finished talking, the Kapo stormed back in, screaming, "You'll speak when I let you! Now be silent! Tomorrow, we'll line up outside the barracks and we will be counted. It is an important day for all of you. You will be given your tattooed numbers."

As each miserable day blended into the next, Martin was grateful to be alive. He began exploring conditions around the camp and couldn't hide his growing disgust for the Nazis. His one set of rough, striped pants and shirt became as foul as his skin and hair, and he soon noticed that some of the men needed a rope to tie around their waists, as their diminishing waist offered little support for their pants. If one looked too healthy or failed to lose weight as the rest did, he fell under suspicion for sneaking additional food. The Kapos had their favorites, of course, and at times would slip them extra rations.

Arnold Kahn was assigned to keep track of days and marked each day off on the back wall of the barracks. Within a short period, however, he stopped counting. Time became unimportant to each of the inmates as the pain of hunger gnawed at them. Saturday, Monday, or Friday didn't mean a thing; each day was the same. There were no Sabbath services; they were given no holidays. They worked every day of the week, walking the three miles to the munitions plant and back. No, days were not meaningful to anyone.

Martin used his well-earned skills as a trader and negotiator in the streets of Lodz to ensure his survival, and soon began to gain the respect of his Kapo and guards. He never feigned illness so he could take a day off work and go to the infirmary. In fact, he appeared helpful to many of the others and tried to elevate their spirits with his actions. From time to time, the Kapo would give him the ration of someone who had died or left for the infirmary, and he often shared it with others. Better than the rest, Martin seemed to understand the importance of relationships, even with those as detestable as the Kapos and SS guards.

Although more comfortable in camp than most of the inmates, he had one thing on his mind: Escape. The vision of his father slowly bleeding to death next to his murdered mother resounded through his head several times a day.

I should have done something at that moment, but I didn't, so I must, someday, find a way. And now, with so many being killed by these bastards every day, I will find that time for vengeance. I swear.

♦♦♦

WHILE THE REST OF his barrack mates marched off to produce munitions for the Reich, Martin was reassigned to the experimental laboratory housed in Crematorium III. This came as no surprise to him—he knew he had impressed Mengele with his made-up "work history" at Lodz infirmary and the ghetto hospital.

He was told to report to Sergeant Fürst, the guard in charge of the Sonderkommandos, the inmates who worked the gas chambers. Martin kept his head lowered as he approached the sergeant standing outside the doorway to the building. "I am Inmate 42321," he announced, holding out his left arm with his tattoo visible. "I am ordered to report to the research laboratory upstairs."

"*Ja*," replied the guard. "We were told. Climb up those stairs and you will find the laboratory."

Respectfully backing away, Martin hastened up the steps and knocked softly on the wooden door.

A response came from inside: "Come in. The door is unlocked."

A man wearing a white doctor's coat was standing by his desk looking over one of Mengele's reports from his ongoing study on twins. He glanced briefly in Martin's direction, then finished reviewing the page in his hand before he spoke.

Martin studied him. Underneath the clean white coat, he was wearing striped inmate clothes and stood nearly six feet tall. His hair was short, but not shorn like all the other inmates. Much like the Kapos, he looked reasonably fed and didn't exhibit the same pallor as the other prisoners. But what fascinated Martin were his shoes: full leather, lace-up oxfords in perfect condition.

"Herr...Doktor," Martin stumbled over his words. "I am Inmate 42321 and have been assigned to work up here in the laboratory."

"Please, you may use your name with me. I am Doctor Katz, Michel Katz. Please sit down."

Michel tried to put this confused-looking young man at ease.

"I am Martin Brosky," he said.

Michel explained that he too was a Jew, a physician who had been deported like the rest. As he talked about the work he was performing in the laboratory, he saw Martin's shoulders relax. It seemed that this boy was relieved to know this doctor was an inmate like himself.

"Martin," Michel said, assuming a more professional tone, "What we do here is important work, and I am grateful to have your assistance. Now please sit down and tell me about yourself and your training."

As Martin began to speak, Michel thought about this new intrusion into his life sitting across from him. Even though the laboratory could use more staff, he used his analytical skills to calculate what effect the addition of another person might have on his now well-controlled existence.

Physically, Martin was a good-looking boy with a strong build and decent manner. He was no more than eighteen years old and appeared much healthier than most inmates. The story Martin related told a few more truths than deceptions. His transport had arrived February 18 with the last of the Jewish population of Lodz. The ghetto, once holding sixty thousand people, had been liquidated. He told Doctor Katz how the Germans had killed both his parents when he was fourteen and how, before his family was arrested, he'd been attending Lodz Polytechnic Institute, where he'd learned laboratory skills and could perform most any blood test. He had also assisted with autopsies on numerous occasions while working in the Jewish hospital in the ghetto.

Michel found this extensive work history unusual for such a young man. "Tell me, Martin, how do you do a Haematoxylin and Eosin preparation?"

The boy looked away, avoiding the doctor's eyes; it was clear that he had no answer. After a few more technical questions, it was obvious to Michel that he was lying about his "medical" training.

Inside, Michel began to fume. His face reddening, he tried to control his emotions. "Martin, it's apparent that you've never had medical assistant training and have little experience, if any. I don't know how you fooled Doctor Mengele, but my ethics dictate that I should turn you in. What we do here is important to science, and to our inmates as well, and I can't accept anyone into my lab who tries to deceive me."

Martin kept his eyes focused on the floor.

Slowly, Michel began to pace the room as if trying to understand this turn of events.

If I expose him, he'll be gassed. Can I live with that?

He glanced at Martin and his heart softened as he saw him look down to hide the tears that were forming.

He is just a boy.

"Doctor, sir, I know I can learn and be valuable to you in the laboratory… Trust me, please!" he pleaded.

Michel shot him another glance and continued to pace. He sensed that this boy was different from the rest. He may have lied to save himself, but there was no crime in that. Perhaps he would have done the same.

Brosky is resourceful and bright, and could easily be trained.

"All right," Katz said, laying a hand on the boy's shoulder, "I'll give you a chance. There's a lot to learn here, and I have confidence you will apply yourself. I understand that your options are certainly limited."

Martin took a deep breath, obviously relieved. His self-effacing skills had worked just now, as they had in the past.

However, this Doctor Katz takes himself seriously and believes he is doing important medical research in the midst of this cesspool.

Martin knew what he had to do. He had worked too hard on the streets of Lodz to pander to some fool of a doctor who talked about ethics. Yes, ethics in the midst of this death factory.

"But should I trespass and violate my oath, may the reverse be my lot."

14

July 12, 1944
Auschwitz

The characteristic sound of Mengele's heavy footsteps leading up the stairway alerted Michel. He was worried, knowing that SS physician Hans Bloch had just arrived at Auschwitz and would be coming to see the laboratory and meet him. Bloch had been told that a "doctor-prisoner" would help him with his experiments.

How was Mengele going to introduce him? Was it *"Herr Doktor,* I would like you to meet my associate"? Or was it "inmate"? How would it go? To see a Jew looking much like a professor, in a white doctor's smock in the midst of all that surrounded him, must be incomprehensible to someone like Bloch. Yet Mengele, with his aura and status, most certainly would have explained Michel's position and his importance in helping with experimental studies.

Michel had been told that Major Hans Bloch had come from the Dachau Concentration Camp to Auschwitz to continue his work in cold immersion and would need more healthy male volunteers to complete his study. He hoped Mengele had briefed him on Michel's research experience and previous experimental studies.

"Allow me," said Mengele, as he held the door open. "This is the dissection room I was telling you about, and here is Doctor Michel Katz, a surgeon who is now a research specialist."

As if he had rehearsed his response, Doctor Bloch acknowledged the inmate doctor with a slight tilt of his head. It was understood that there would be no contact, no handshake. His displeasure was apparent in the very slight narrowing of his eyes, as if trying to understand what this Jew doctor could be doing here.

Michel stayed quiet, having learned to speak only when Mengele allowed him to do so. Mengele continued to walk the major around the room and show him specimens from the various studies that were underway.

Doctor Bloch carried himself more like a military officer than a doctor. Impeccably dressed, his tall leather boots were shined to a high gloss and his pant creases were knife-sharp. The twin SS death head patches designating concentration camp service were displayed on his collar. Obviously fit, he stood close to six feet tall with broad shoulders and large hands, and upon removing his cap revealed closely-cropped blond hair. He was a handsome man whose only flaw was a bluish birthmark on the left temple at the hairline. Looking toward Michel, he spoke slowly and directly, "Herr Doktor Mengele, may I speak with your...Jew doktor?"

Mengele nodded affirmatively. In a contemptuous voice, Bloch said, "Katz, to get started on my studies, I need two open tanks, perhaps four hundred liters, and an ice machine. I understand you have a copy of the protocol we studied at Dachau, correct? I suggest you reread it so no errors are made." Before Michel could respond, the SS physician continued, "I also need some space to work." He eyed Michel's desk. "Yes, maybe here."

The only response Michel could muster was a submissive, "Yes, Herr Major. Whatever you might need, I will do my best to help."

Mengele was standing in back of Bloch, watching Michel's deference in silence.

"Perhaps tomorrow I will be back and we can get started."

Their task finished, the two SS doctors walked toward the door together. As they left, Michel overheard Mengele telling Bloch about the Hungarian transports arriving the following week.

The quick visit was unsettling to Michel. He looked around his room trying to envision sharing his laboratory with such an arrogant SS doctor.

He can't stand me...or is it just Jews in general?

Sitting down at his desk, he closed his eyes and wondered what new weight would be placed upon him. The brief period of civility that he had enjoyed in the midst of this death camp would fade as Sturmbannführer Hans Bloch entered his life.

◆◆◆

BLOCH WAS NOW THE SS officer in charge of Michel's laboratory, as well as responsible for overseeing the efficiency of the gas chambers and crematoriums. Although he supervised those activities, he had little day-to-day interaction with the Sonderkommandos assigned to work in the gas chambers. The daily task of managing these inmates, the gas chambers, and the ovens was left to the noncommissioned SS guards.

Upon his arrival, Hans had been briefed on the camps and the various functions they served. He learned that Auschwitz was not one facility, but several sub-camps, all incorporated under the name Auschwitz-Birkenau. These sites provided slave labor for the Monowitz work camp operations near Auschwitz. The earliest industrial facility was the IG Farben Enterprise, housing the Buna-Werke complex that made synthetic rubber. The Krupp armament factories and the Siemens-Schuckert Bobrek complex were added later.

Together, the Auschwitz-Birkenau camps provided a labor pool for the war effort, a place for medical experimentation and, above all, an extermination center to implement Hitler's plan to make Europe *Judenfrei*. Because of the sensitivity and political implications of these functions, it was necessary to have dedicated SS officers in charge of these activities. Men of lesser determination or commitment had little stomach for the implementation of the Final Solution—the plan to exterminate every Jew in Europe, which the Germans tried to hide from the rest of the world. This secret operation rested squarely on the shoulders of the SS leaders.

During his first week at Auschwitz, this policy was hammered home to Hans. Discussion of the camps' activities was not allowed. The existence of the gas chambers was to be concealed and not shared with anyone outside of the camps. Although well-known to the inmates, no mention of gas chambers was to be made by the SS to anyone. No small
, commerce, or trading was allowed between SS and inmates, and physical intimacy was *verboten*. Every SS member had the right to discipline camp inmates at any time for any perceived infraction.

The week of orientation also included a review of racial theory and eugenics. To Hans, this was redundant—it was well-encased in his memory and beliefs. Yet it was necessary to retrain most of the other SS officers, as the task before them demanded total allegiance to the Reich and a full understanding of the need to cleanse the world of Jews and other "undesirables" who inhabited Europe.

The laboratory was a mixed blessing for Hans. It was well-equipped, and the machines and glassware were adequate for his studies, but he was not pleased about having to work with Jews: Doctor Katz and his assistant, Martin. When Hans walked around the room, he did his best to avoid touching either man. He longed to have the space to himself, but Mengele had made this arrangement, and there was no way he could contradict his orders.

For Hans's study, Michel directed the male inmates to sit in a tub filled with water at thirty-five degrees Fahrenheit while he monitored their vital signs, pulse, blood pressure, and respiratory rate. Most often, he had Martin hold the person down in the tank for the required period of time—a minimum of thirty minutes. While the victim was forced to tolerate the frigid water, Hans Bloch often stood next to the tank, hands on hips, as if daring the poor man to climb out.

"Jew doctor," he would yell, "if this man jumps out, either you or your Jew assistant must take his place."

A few inmates struggled at first, and Michel tried to soothe them by whispering in their ear as he counted out the minutes of this painful process. But if a subject did try to get out of the tank, he would be shoved roughly back in. His piercing cries would be ignored until the poor soul passed out in the water.

And if problems did arise, either with control of the inmate or an inmate's demise, Michel would soon incur the SS doctor's wrath. Grabbing him by the collar, Hans would backhand his face with his gloved hand, cutting his lip or bruising an eye.

Michel was emotionally spent after each subject was studied. He could not allow Hans to see the personal pain he suffered. As each afternoon's session was completed and Bloch departed, Michel would sink onto his bed and curl up in pain, trying to wrap himself in an invisible, protective cocoon. But it was merely a temporary escape. He would not allow the images of inmates experiencing that terrifying, burning sensation—the fire of freezing—to affect him.

As each day passed, many men suffered. But the more Michel distanced himself from his emotions, the more he began to believe in his own heartlessness and, worse, that he was becoming just like the SS doctors he despised.

◆◆◆

AFTER SEVERAL MONTHS, THE cold immersion investigation was nearing completion. Even though uncomfortable with his assistants, this study had worked out to Hans's satisfaction. And it was time to get rid of Martin.

"You! Jew!" he shouted as he entered the laboratory the next day. "Do you not remove your hat when I come in?"

Martin quickly grabbed his coarse, striped hat and held it to his side. He looked down as Hans continued to speak.

"Do you not respect me, you dirty Jew bastard? I've noticed that smirk of yours." Hans pulled out a Luger from his holster, pointed it at Martin's head, and continued.

"You have things too soft up here and have forgotten respect. I should shoot you now, but that would be too quick."

Martin's eyes darted around the laboratory looking for something that could be used as a weapon.

I could've disarmed him, but I would certainly die in the end. No, I will wait for a better time, a better place to make Hans Bloch pay. I am a patient man.

Hans continued. "There is little need for your assistance up here any longer," he said with a sneer, returning the gun to his holster. "You need a taste of evolving death to help erode your Jew soul. You shall join the Sonderkommandos in the gas chambers and crematoriums, and help with the bodies."

Martin remained silent as Bloch raised his voice to a small thunder.

"Do you understand, Jew slime? Do you?"

Though Martin was visibly shaking on the outside, he felt a growing, internal rage as he restrained his desire to lash out. "Yes, Herr Doktor, I understand."

Michel watched from a corner of the room, recognizing that this was the same fury Hans unleashed at him from time to time. Since he was sitting slightly in back of Hans and to his left, the SS man could not see the fear in his eyes. It wouldn't be long before he, too, would be considered excess baggage. Fortunately, Mengele continued to rely on him for some of the autopsies, and that had "protected" Michel from other SS such as Hans—so far.

Within hours, Martin had transferred his meager belongings from his barracks to the large attic above the crematorium where the Sonderkommandos were housed. He was greeted by male inmates dressed in civilian clothing, sitting around a long table filled with food and many varieties of wine. It was like waking up in a dream: breads, candies, and various food dishes were spread out like a banquet for the Sonderkommandos to eat. *Unbelievable!*

Men were smoking cigarettes and playing cards, and only a few looked up to acknowledge his entry.

"There's an empty bunk down the way, friend, if you wish. Put your things there," said a healthy-looking man in his twenties, glancing up from his card game. "You may also partake of the wondrous goods brought to us in suitcases from the recent Hungarian arrivals—who won't be needing them any longer."

Martin made his way down the row of bunks to one that appeared unoccupied. He must have looked as confused as he felt. The man who had spoken left his card game to approach him. "We heard you were coming... What's your name? They call me Jacques."

"I am Martin Brosky," he answered, "and I was assigned to work with Doctor Katz in his laboratory."

"He's like us, men," said Jacques, to anyone listening, "he works with the dead, too!"

A roar of laughter came from the group around the table.

That morning, Michel had filled Martin in on the function of the Sonderkommando group and their duties. The majority of the men worked twelve-hour shifts, taking the dead from the gas chambers to the crematorium and incinerating the bodies. Others were involved with sorting clothes, removing gold from teeth, and gathering hair from the recently gassed bodies. The abundance of food, drink, and other items came from the baggage of those led to the gas chambers. The men here lived a different life, filled with excesses that had belonged to the dead.

He was now part of the twelfth Sonderkommando group. The others had been selected for this assignment because of their youth and strength, but there was one detail Michel had chosen to leave out. The news would have to come from the men themselves. After each Sonderkommando group had worked twelve weeks, they were taken out and shot. The SS believed that they could hide the truth of this death factory by killing all associated with their machines of death, and Michel knew that it was only a matter of time before Martin learned his fate.

It was Michel who had direct responsibility for the health of this group of men, and he was given medicines that only the SS enjoyed in order to keep this group free of disease. He would visit the sick daily and get them well as fast as possible so that the death factory could continue to function "productively and efficiently."

But one fact stood out and was evident in everyone's mind: once you entered this house of death, you left only as ashes.

15

August 1, 1944
Auschwitz

During the first two months of his assignment to the laboratory, Michel became acquainted with each of the studies being carried out at the camp. Initially, he was responsible for performing autopsies on the inmates who had died during the experimental periods or were purposefully killed for pathological study. At each autopsy, the SS physician engaged in that particular research was present and took notes. Michel kept a secret journal of the studies done, tracking both the SS doctor involved and the results of the postmortem studies. Doctor Carl Clauberg was interested in sterilization techniques and injected formalin into the testicles of men and into the ovaries of women. Doctor Helmuth Vetter, an SS captain, infected Jewish inmates with typhus for his pharmaceutical studies to test anti-infective agents. A study involving differing eye color (heterochromia) in twins was carried out by Doctor Mengele. Each of these children was killed with a phenol injection to the heart and postmortem examinations were performed, including enucleation of the eyes.

Initially, Michel performed autopsies, paying little attention to the moral issues involved and turning a blind eye to the tragedies occurring in the camps on a daily basis—the beatings, degradation, and suffering. After all, he had been allowed to live and practice his profession. SS doctors often asked for his advice on statistical analysis and study protocol.

My actions may, one day, come back to haunt me.

He regularly examined the dead at the autopsy table and relished his role as a doctor. It was here, in his lab, that he allowed himself to double as both trained physician and inmate. As he performed his professional duties, he would curiously forget why he was there. His role as an inmate diminished in his eyes as he became separate from the realities of the harsh barracks. The overriding strength of his self-image, the omniscient healer, allowed him to see his personal value above mortal humans, and certainly well beyond that of the unfortunate inmates. During the day, he had the power; yet, at night, alone, a sense of personal despair prevailed.

As I grasp the scalpel and incise deep from the sternum to the pubis, I am the expert, the doctor doing what I am trained to do. This is to save my family...

But as the weeks passed, doubts about his judgment began to arise. Michel had made the decision to come to Auschwitz and he had chosen to approach Mengele. This was not the same boy who had studied so hard to become a doctor; nor was it the sensitive, compassionate student who was concerned for the sick. He had indeed changed: his face had hardened and lines of concern stretched across his forehead. Yet these creases reflected worry about himself, not others. As these painful thoughts rose nearer to the surface of his consciousness he began his self-examination.

Have I done this to save myself?

As he stared at his aging image, he knew that the person in the mirror who gazed back was not experiencing the cramping abdominal pain and diarrhea that wracked the inmates each day. Nor was he shamed by the Kapo, who would not allow prisoners to use the latrine hole, but choose instead to watch the tortured shamefully discharge their watery stool on fetid legs. And he was not forced to watch daily beatings by the sadistic guards and the SS while standing for hours outside the barracks in the cold, awaiting an accurate roll call. "I can do nothing for them—nothing!" he shouted at the arrogant image in the mirror.

I am totally impotent to effect change.

Mengele had strongly discouraged any of the study doctors from leaving their laboratory. Whether it was fear that they would reveal their secretive studies or that the other killing places, the slow death houses or barracks, would be shown to them, Michel didn't know. He had always assumed that the camp's living quarters housed those able to work; and perhaps, at one time they did.

◆◆◆

THE JOURNEY TO AUSCHWITZ deeply tested Rabbi Israel Rosenberg's faith as the cattle cars slowly made their way to Auschwitz in June 1944. At rabbinical school, he and the other young students had been taught that their faith was carried within them; the external vestments—the *yarmulke,* the *tallit,* and *tefillin*—are worn as respect to God, yet were not important when compared to their internal relationship to Him and his people. Sunlight peeked through the spaces between the wooden rafters on the railcar ceiling. As Israel studied the others trapped in this cattle car with him, he sensed more than fear. He saw men who didn't fight back to protect their family or themselves and were now despondent. Their lagging spirit was reflected in the absence of meaningful conversation amongst themselves. The rabbi knew that he would need to step up and work to renew hope in these men once they arrived at their journey's end.

The train ride seemed endless. No information about their destination was announced, and the ride continued for seven days—a forced existence, a passage to the unknown. Israel found reasonable excuses in his own mind for the delays; troop train priorities, repair stops, and air raid sirens forced the interminable stops. A bucket of thin soup was brought in each day in exchange for the bucket of waste utilized by all the men. Each dipped his cup in the wretched pot of greasy broth, a poor reprieve from the incessant hunger and the undeniable and unmistakable odor of common waste.

That miserable stench filled the crowded car. The dry hay had turned wet and caused the floor to be slippery. As each day passed, hope faded as every man realized his fate was sealed.

A screech of the train whistle, a sudden crashing sound with the opening of the railcar door, and shouts and orders from their new masters ended the trip for those still alive.

Upon his arrival at the camp, all external signs of the rabbi's faith were stripped from him. There was no yamulke on this shaved head, no tallit to cover the striped garment of the camps, and the string that held up his trousers was certainly not tefillin. There would be no Sabbath services, no open prayers, and no holiday services. None of these were allowed. They could not be Jews; their traditions could no longer be visible. Yet they were here because of who they were. It made no sense.

It was up to each rabbi to keep those Jewish hearts alive and beating in each of the men in his barracks so that they all might survive and remain undefeated by the animals who had captured the Jews. The rabbis could not let their people forget who they were. In the quiet of the darkened barracks, each Friday night a silent group found their way to prayer, heard only by each other in hushed whispers.

♦♦♦

OCCASIONALLY, MICHEL WAS ASKED by the clinic doctors to provide a surgical consultation. He first met Rabbi Rosenberg in September 1944, when examining him for a non-healing sore on this right lower leg.

"Rabbi, I believe you have a basal cell cancer, a relatively benign lesion that can be removed at any time. Unfortunately, we have no surgical facilities here, but this can wait to be removed, as it won't grow quickly or spread to other areas of the body."

"Thank you, Doctor Katz. I haven't seen you at the clinic before. Have you just arrived?"

"No, Rabbi, I've been here nine months… I don't normally work in the clinic."

The rabbi eyed him cautiously, wanting to ask him more, but held back.

Michel felt reluctance, but knew he had to explain. "I do pathological studies and autopsies in a laboratory over there…"

He pointed to Crematorium III, averting his eyes as he spoke.

"Hmmm, you must be quite busy, you know—with so much death." The rabbi seemed to understand.

"I am. Very busy, but it's hard. Maybe we can speak again." Michel started to walk out but stopped at the door. "I'll come back in two weeks to re-examine your leg. Yes, that would be a good time."

A single guard accompanied Michel back to his building. Sitting at a counter, he plunged deep into thought.

I need to share my angst with someone.

Michel found his voice with Rabbi Rosenberg.

Three weeks later, he asked the rabbi for help with a Sonderkommando whose actions upset his bunkmates. He was deeply concerned about Stephen Borowsky, who worked in Crematorium III and had begun to exhibit a kind of paranoia that was frightening to his fellow inmates. "They will kill us, kill us all, when we are used up here!" he would burst out with no warning. "We will burn; we, too, will burn as we descend into this new hell!"

Maybe, if he had said it just once, the others would have let it pass. But over and over, he sang the same refrain. It buzzed inside the heads of the inmates; they all knew that Stephen's predictions were not the fiction of a demented mind. But because his work value was still great, the Germans hesitated to send him back to the barracks and inevitable death. Having no psychiatrists available, Michel called upon Rabbi Rosenberg to speak with Borowsky in the hope that he could stop his paranoia from infecting the other men.

The rabbi took Stephen aside and quietly counseled him. Although he knew the man's claims were not unfounded, he did his best to reassure him and quell his fears so that he could find some semblance of peace. Michel was at the other end of the room and did not know exactly what had been said, but it was clear that after talking with the rabbi, Stephen believed he might be spared.

"It would be a mistake to confirm this man's rants to the others destined to die," the rabbi explained, taking Michel aside. "To leave hope behind would certainly hasten the death of the soul before the body. And all they may now have left to cherish is their individual spirit. We must not let the Germans take that away from us."

After leaving the attic where the Sonderkommandos lived, Michel bid the rabbi follow him upstairs to his laboratory to talk for a few minutes. Sitting down with him, Michel opened up about his growing personal pain to his new confidant. The longer he carried out Mengele's orders, he confessed, the more he writhed inside, silently and tortuously. His nights had been sleepless and he feared he was losing his mind.

"Rabbi, I can't carry on... These doctors, these SS, are madmen doing unspeakable things to people. Each and every day I must bear witness, and I feel my own sanity is at stake. Yesterday, four children died. I have been forced to do so many painful autopsies. At first I fell prey to Mengele's empty promises to protect my family at Terezin, yet, I have heard nothing from them. These experiments on inmates are not based on science but on poorly substantiated theories held by certain SS doctors. They are all just butchers."

The rabbi stood and faced Michel and gently placed his large, gnarled hands on the shaken doctor's shoulders, "To survive, we all will do things that we may not be proud of. It is so very important that we stay aware and understand what we are doing, even if it is wrong. Just now I broke a covenant with God by lying to that poor man with the hope of helping him restore some sanity. If we do make it out of this death camp, we can and will someday make peace with ourselves and with the God who loves us all."

As the rabbi was hustled by a guard down the outside steps and back to his barracks, Michel followed them out the door and searched the sky, looking to God for some indication of personal salvation. He wanted to believe the rabbi's words, but it seemed that the acrid scent of burnt flesh in the smoke billowing out of the chimneys obscured any hope he might find for himself. He wondered if he deserved to live while others around him continued to die. Ideas of death at his own hand found their way to his consciousness, and he allowed himself the luxury of that dark embrace in his mind.

I don't know if I can go on like this.

16

September 1, 1944
Terezin

The parade of Red Cross visitors was over and Terezin, the "model" ghetto, returned to its previous state. The soccer games had stopped and the nighttime reverie and music came to an end. Transports, which had been discontinued while the visitors toured, resumed, and scores of cattle cars packed the railway station several hundred meters from the entrance to the village of Terezin.

Perhaps this reversion to the camp's true colors was in tune with the symphony of seasonal change. Summer had gone, and the flowers began to die, as if no one cared if they lived or not. As the nights became cool and even quieter, the sound of rail engines and train horns dominated the senses. The reality of the human cattle cars was resounding.

Word spread from the camp's Jewish Council that female workers were needed in "defense plants" to the east. Each day, a new list was sent to the Nazi officials containing names of those the Council deemed best for the new assignments.

Oh, no! We're next.

Tamara saw the transport list and immediately sought out her mother at the apartment. Beatrice saw the tears in her daughter's eyes and jumped up from her chair.

"My baby, what's wrong?"

"Mama, Council has put us on the list to go east. We leave tomorrow."

Beatrice sat stunned for a moment before speaking.

"Are you sure?

"The list was only of women and children—no men. Mom, can you talk to the Judenrat?"

"They won't listen, believe me. I have nothing—nothing to offer them."

Trying to be strong, Beatrice put her arms around her daughter, as she understood what was to be their true destination. They had only been told that the transports headed 'East,' yet it was known that 'East' meant Auschwitz. Recently, the trains had been leaving every two or three days, and she felt pain each time a train whistle announced a departure.

The rumors of the death camps instilled paralyzing fear within the residents of Terezin. However, the Council officially listed "work in factories" as the reason for the transports.

Beatrice got up and paced around the dimly lit quarters, her eyes fixed on the floor. She felt helpless. "Let's get on with it—we must get ready."

The sense of doom thickened as they packed their clothes in the apartment.

♦♦♦

"LINE UP AND HOLD onto your belongings!" yelled the SS guard, as Tamara, her mother, and the others were forced along the wall in double file, waiting to be loaded onto the railcars. Most women had a child or two with them, which perplexed Tamara.

Who will care for the children while the women work?

The same guards, who had been civil when the Red Cross came through, now barked at them, using vile words like "Jew bitch" or "Jew slime."

Beatrice was well prepared, having gathered bread and butter in preparation for the trip. Concerned about revealing her own anxiety to Tamara, she remained overly quiet, knowing that, if she spoke, her daughter could easily read the torment building up inside her.

I dread this is the end, but I dare not tell Tamara... Dear God, just let me hold her close for one last day.

After climbing up into the cattle car, the two sheltered themselves together in one of the corners on the straw-covered floor. Fear constricted Tamara's chest as the doors were locked shut. Packed like animals, she and her mother huddled close for warmth, awaiting their next destination.

IT WAS STRANGE. QUIET, *yet warm—not what she had anticipated in death.*

Tamara had expected to feel none of the sensations one would have when alive. There was a searing soreness in her throat, and her head was throbbing. She was breathing fast, as if trying to get more air into her body. Reaching up, she felt her forehead, warm and slightly damp. It surprised her to find real flesh.

Does one dream in death? No, not possible. There should be no substance, no person, just nothing.

She turned and her neck moved with her. Everything was blurry, yet there was light coming from what appeared to be a closed door to her right. She was in a bed with covers over her. No one else was present. A strange bandage attached to a tube dripping fluid into a needle was wrapped around her right arm.

I am not dead.

Tamara tried to look around, but everything seemed to spin, forcing her to lie there, motionless, and fall back asleep.

Awakening again, the horrors replayed in her mind as the agony of the chamber reverberated within her being. It was late and dark, and the women had been standing in line for what seemed like hours. The cold October chill had greeted them once the doors of the cattle car were opened, but they all agreed it was better to be cold than stay in that putrid, foul car they had been packed in for two days.

The guards had let them keep their coats, yet all of their bags and suitcases were taken away. A few women were pulled out of line and selected to go off in a different direction. Tamara, her mother, and the others were loaded onto trucks. Beatrice was aghast.

We're going to the showers to be de-loused? How horrid and insulting to assume that I have foul insects burrowed in my hair! As if I am a wretched child from a poorhouse?

Mother and daughter passed many male prisoners as they moved through the camp. Some of them were shoveling; others were moving rocks in wheelbarrows. They all seemed to look alike with their striped, ill-fitting outfits and matching caps. Each one was so thin and weak-looking. No conversation could be heard among them, and those they passed did not look up while the truck full of women and children rolled by. Tamara's mother stood next to her, stoically looking ahead, trying not to upset her daughter as she contemplated their fate.

The truck unloaded its human cargo.

"Take off your clothes and hang them on the hooks. Tie your shoes together, so you might find them when you are finished," ordered the guard.

Night had come, and it was dark outside.

They were led into a large room, maybe eight by ten meters, with showerheads on the wall. Beatrice held her daughter close so that they wouldn't lose each other. The floor was wet, as if another group must have recently been there. Her mother tried to distract her from the strange blue stain on the floor.

Suddenly, the doors clanged shut… A murmur grew into a fearful cacophony, and then the lights went out. Screams and cries filled the room as many seemed to know what was happening. Tamara heard the sound of pebbles being dropped, as pellets rained from the ceiling and hit the floor. The pellets started to turn to gas and gave off an almond-like odor. Some people close to the gas dropped right away. The vapors seemed to stay low, so people climbed on top and over each other, as if reaching the ceiling would give them safety.

Beatrice pushed Tamara down into a corner onto her knees. People fell around her and on her, essentially sealing the young woman off from the room. She smelled and tasted the gas and coughed harshly until she passed out… She couldn't fight her impending death.

♦♦♦

"Okay, quickly, you men, get ready to pick up these dead Jews and take them to the ovens," cried the pimply-faced, SS enlisted man, cradling his automatic weapon in his arms. "Go, scum, now! There is a line of thousands waiting for their shower." He laughed, hoping his fellow guards caught his humor.

After several minutes, the doors opened. The guards donned gas masks, but the Sonderkommandos entered the room without protection. Climbing over the piles of bodies, Martin began pulling the dead out of the room and stacking them on carts to go to the crematorium above. The carts were sent up on an elevator, where other inmates placed the bodies in front of the ovens.

"Martin," yelled the guard, "I think we've finished, but go down and check the chamber to see if it is cleared."

Crossing the room, he came across a young girl, maybe fourteen, huddled on her hands and knees in a corner and hidden in the shadows. He reached down to lift her and almost dropped her when he heard a cough.

He looked more closely at her face and saw her eyes open briefly, then close heavily. He checked her neck and found the slow timbre of her pulse.

How did she survive this?

He glanced around quickly. The guards were all gone.

What am I going to do with her?

The Sonderkommandos had left as well; the chamber was empty except for him and the weakened child.

Pulling her as if she was one of the dead, his hands under her shoulders, he slid her heels along the floor towards the cart. Stopping, he looked around and noticed that the SS enlisted man was not there.

Should I save her? No one knows...

Instead of loading this young girl with the other bodies, he carefully cradled her in his arms and carried her, as quietly as he could, up the outside stairs to Michel's laboratory. Halfway up, he halted and hugged close to the wall as he heard voices below.

"Heinrich, do you have a light?"

A spark, a small flame... "Yes, Bloch. It's late for you to be out."

"Just leaving the laboratory, checking on some data," Bloch responded. "Now home for a little rest, some wine."

Martin stayed paralyzed for the next thirty seconds as Bloch walked away.

Opening the door to the laboratory, he entered. "Doctor Katz! Doctor Katz, get up! I have a young girl here, alive and breathing. Somehow she didn't die from the gas!" Martin spoke with urgency, yet made sure to keep his voice low so the Sonderkommandos in the attic above wouldn't hear. "Hurry, please, she needs your help!"

Michel, brushing away tears, stumbled out of his quarters. Seeing the young figure in Martin's arms, he moved into action. "Are you sure she is alive? No one, *no one* could survive the gas! Put her down on the table."

"Yes!" answered Martin. "She was curled up in a corner, in a pocket, covered with other bodies." He gently laid her down. "That must have somehow protected her from the fumes."

Michel wheeled over a tank of oxygen and placed a mask over the girl's face, letting the cool, life-giving gas fill her lungs. As the oxygen was inhaled, she started coughing. Each hacking movement seemed painful to her irritated throat as she thrashed about. Michel placed an intravenous needle in her arm, infusing sodium chloride solution into her antecubital vein. With the fluids running, the two men covered her small body with as many blankets as they could find. Michel took her blood pressure and pulse. He hovered a few more moments, making certain that she was out of danger before stepping back.

Pacing around the room, he tried to sort out his thoughts. Just ten minutes ago, he had been on the brink, beginning to formulate a plan to take his own life.. Now, any thought or plan to end it all, along with his part in this madness, would have to wait.

This young girl may not survive without my help. Michel, you are first and foremost a doctor. Forget yourself. You must save this girl.

"I believe she will be all right, Martin. Carry her to my room and be careful about the IV." Michel looked at the young man before he picked her up, "We must not let anyone know she is here—no one, not even the other Sonderkommandos."

With a slight nod of his head, Martin silently assented. He carefully lifted the girl and walked down a narrow hall to a small room filled with a single bed. He had wondered where Doctor Katz slept, knowing that the doctor rarely left the crematorium building. He placed her gently on Michel's mattress and suspended the intravenous solution from a hook on the wall as Michel entered the room.

Michel placed his hands on Martin's shoulders. "This girl is alive and here now because you found her. Both of us could easily be killed for saving and hiding her. You do understand? The Germans want no witnesses to survive."

Martin nodded again. He now knew that Sonderkommandos were changed every twelve weeks and every one of them was killed. His fate would come. The first job of the new group was to carry the bodies of the previous undertakers into the ovens. He would make it to those ovens even sooner were the girl to be found and his part in her survival discovered.

Glancing down at the girl lying motionless on the bed, he realized that since she had come directly from the trains, she had not been counted and would not be missed. He looked up at Michel and asked, "What do we do with her now?"

Michel sat silently on a corner of the bed holding his head with his hands, as if its weight had become a great burden. "She is now my concern. You must get back to your group before you are missed."

Michel studied the sleeping girl even closer. She was just a child, perhaps thirteen or fourteen, with fine chestnut-colored hair. Her innocent face was clear and smooth, and long brown lashes adorned her resting eyes. She was thin, no more than thirty-eight kilograms, a child just beginning to develop into a young woman. Although she was slight, she had yet to suffer starvation, as evidenced by the normal color and texture of her skin. She was just a waif, a still-pure soul, in an instant almost lost to the world, left to become his charge—and perhaps his saving grace.

And I was ready to end it all.

Staring down at her forced him to think about his daughter Rachel, now four years old. He pictured her face, smiling, as he would tuck her into bed, holding her dear "Bunny." The sound of "Daddy, I love you!" played in his mind like a familiar melody, while a mixture of loss and guilt overwhelmed him. He had no communication with his family, outside of a postcard three months ago. He looked forward to any mail, yet it was a mixed blessing when none arrived; any reminder of their separation was simply too painful.

They are in a safer place, he assured himself.

◆◆◆

THE LIGHT STREAMING THROUGH the open door awakened Tamara yet again, and a man in a white coat—a doctor—walked toward her and sat on the bed. The girl attempted to talk, but her throat was sore and raspy, and no words came.

Looking kindly at her face, he spoke in German: "My name is Doctor Katz. You did not die in the gas. You were spared—a lucky young lady. No one else has ever survived that room. Now," he smiled, "I have to figure out what to do with you."

He appeared caring, and his warmth seemed genuine. His German was mixed with a French accent. At first, she thought he must be one of the German doctors, to be dressed as he was.

But why would he be so nice if he were trying to kill me?

She couldn't understand.

"How are you feeling?"

She understood enough German to answer him. With her scratchy voice and school-learned German, she said, "My name is Tamara Lissner. I am Czech. I feel dizzy. My stomach is sick, and I ache all over. Where am I, and who are you?"

She was worried that she might have sounded rude, but he seemed to not notice. The doctor talked to her for maybe an hour and told her he was French and also forced to come to the camps because he was Jewish. He explained what had happened to her and the rest of the people in the chamber.

"My mother...she was with me...is she...?"

Tears filled her swollen eyes. Tamara knew.

For a few seconds, he looked down at her, lost in thought. Then he clasped her hand in his. "Tamara, I have to hide you from everyone here at the camp. If they find out that you survived, you'll be in grave danger. I'm just not sure how I'm going to manage it yet."

She watched him walk out of the room, but it wasn't long before he returned, appearing satisfied.

I trust him, he knows what to do.

He had found an opening in the closet ceiling leading to an attic space. It was located adjacent to the Sonderkommandos' quarters, but separated by a wall. Tamara was worried at first.

How can I stand to be alone in that small space every day? *When will I be able to come out?*

"It's okay," he told her. "You only have to stay up there during the day. As soon as I close my laboratory at night, you can come down and we can talk."

He tried to smile as she wiped away a tear, but he had no words to soothe her. "Tonight, you'll stay down here. Put on these camp clothes."

The next morning, Michel awoke early to check on his new patient, taking her blood pressure and pulse. "My little friend, how are you feeling?"

Bleary-eyed, but awake, she answered right away, "I feel somewhat better, except for my sore throat." Pointing to the ceiling, she continued, "I guess it's time to go up there."

"Right. Let's get you settled now, before anyone comes." Removing her IV needle, he hoisted her up into her hideaway, where she would spend her days while Doctor Katz and the German doctors continued their studies. She had to stay absolutely still and not move around when anyone was present in the laboratory below. At night, he kept his word and allowed her to come down and sleep on the floor in his room. Pushing his bed to the side, he made a space on the floor for her, cushioned with a pad and blankets.

At first, the days went by slowly, but soon weeks had passed. The German doctors were at the laboratory every day, working on their experiments and observing autopsies. Oftentimes, waiting for their studies or autopsies to be completed, they would wander about as if bored, looking into cabinets and opening doors. Fortunately for Tamara, the attic opening went unnoticed.

Doctor Katz and the girl ate together in the morning and evening and spent long hours talking about their pasts, especially their families. They spoke about Terezin, Tamara's mother's work as a seamstress, and the school there. They had both been at that camp at the same time, but in different buildings.

I wonder if she knew my family…

Although tempted, he feared to ask.

Tamara described the painful details of how she and her mother were rounded up in Prague and shipped to Auschwitz. She listened with tears as Michel told her about his sorrowful journey. Wise for her years, she could sense the depth of Doctor Katz's grief and what appeared to be the absence of his will to live. She felt concern for her new friend and savior, and quietly prayed she would somehow be able to help him.

From her position over the laboratory, she could hear the incredible details of the experiments carried out by the German doctors. She discovered a small crack in the ceiling near an exhaust vent that allowed her to peer down into the room and observe much of the activities below. Sometimes she scribbled down notes on paper the doctor had given her so she could ask him questions later. She kept those notes as a kind of journal or diary and started to sketch what she observed with a pencil.

Tamara was shocked and mystified by what she witnessed. One horrible day she watched as Doctor Katz was preparing to perform an autopsy on a young, dark-haired child, maybe seven years old. Mengele had explained beforehand that he needed to study fresh tissue on this girl, who he'd inoculated with tuberculosis.

But she is still alive, what are they doing to her? Oh no!

Mengele was sticking a long needle into the girl's chest, and her screams pierced the room.

I can't look.

It was now quiet, except for the doctors talking.

She is not moving… She's dead. I think I may throw up. No, I must be quiet. Oh God! Doctor Katz cut into her chest…

I can't watch anymore…

◆ ◆ ◆

TAMARA WELCOMED EACH NIGHT that passed, as it allowed her to savor the victory of having eluded death that day. One after another, each day she survived meant she was closer to winning the war against her captors. Night was when she talked with her new friend. Michel quickly became more than a doctor; the pair was bonded not only by a shared fear of being discovered, but by a growing fondness and mutual understanding.

Their conversations were always conducted in hushed tones so that the Sonderkommandos couldn't hear them. "Tamara, you cannot trust anyone here—no one; no inmate, no German—maybe not even me." He stared down at the floor, remembering the doubts he had about himself and his own motivations for coming to Auschwitz. "The quest for survival is so great that anyone might give up another for his or her own survival."

Tamara wrote in her journal: *Maybe I was too young then to grasp things of this nature. As time passed, I saw things that no adolescent should ever be exposed to.*

Michel continued to explore Tamara's past, as she did his. Long hours were spent talking deep into the night, as Tamara lay on the floor next to his bed. The Germans required all lights to be off at eight, so it was into the darkness that their life stories were told. On her seventh night in the camp, she described how she had started painting as a young child, impressing everyone with her talent. She recalled how she had enjoyed using vivid colors while concentrating on landscapes, gardens, and seashores—many places she had never seen.

"But my passion to set up my easel and paint seemed to stop when they took my father and brother away. My mom tried to encourage me, but I just couldn't do it anymore, and then she was gone too… I felt abandoned. My bright memories had dulled to shades of gray."

Michel sat up and looked at Tamara, who lay curled on the floor. "The time seemed to pass slowly after Mom left," she said softly, fighting back tears. "My aunt tried to rekindle my spirit and hunger for art, but it had all vanished and I could only doodle with pencils and charcoal. She encouraged me to sketch the beautiful city of Prague again, yet it did not come out the same. With my family gone, life's colors disappeared, and I was sad."

As Tamara continued to speak, Michel seemed strangely unresponsive. She feared that her story had become wearisome and that he had lost interest in her tale. "Doctor Katz, are you sleeping?" she whispered.

"No, Tamara. It's just that I understand." She could hear him refusing to let the tears flow. "I loved being a doctor, taking care of people, and making them well. And now, I feel like I am living in those shades of gray you were talking about."

Something told Tamara to stay silent.

"abstain...from the seduction of females or males, or freemen and slaves."

17

September 29, 1944
Auschwitz

The pleasing sounds of violins spilled out from the open doorway as Hans Bloch approached Doctor Mengele's residence. Crossing the threshold, he was greeted by a young woman smiling shyly and dressed neatly in a maid's uniform. There were several young ladies serving hors d'oeuvres and drinks to the twenty officers present. Hans had heard rumors that some high-ranking SS officers had taken attractive Jewesses as servants and cooks, but of course, there could not be intimate relations between Germans and Jews, no matter what your status was. It was verboten.

Feigning graciousness, he took the wine glass offered by the young lady and continued across the room towards Doctor Mengele, who was beckoning him.

"Thank you for coming, Herr Doktor Bloch. I have wanted to gather all our medical colleagues together in a refined setting, much like we were accustomed to before the war started."

Alongside Mengele was Eduard Wirths, the chief medical officer at Auschwitz, who quickly brought Hans into the conversation. "Doctor Bloch, I have heard that you are an expert in research protocol. I have been having some difficulty with my statistical analysis and hoped that you, with your experience, could give me some direction."

Doctor Wirths stated that his study on cervical carcinoma was concluding. He had researched the effect of caustic agents applied to the cer-

vix. Cervical excisions had been performed on ninety-one treated inmates but, microscopically, just one carcinoma-in-situ and thirty-five with dysplastic changes were found.

"Do you have a control group or previous study to compare it with, so that a 'paired-test' can be done?" Hans asked. His question seemed to confound Doctor Wirths, who had not considered the need to compare his findings with another group. To ease his concern, Hans quickly added, "Why don't you break down your study group racially, or by age, so that some valid numbers can be reported? Perhaps you could send your data over to my office and I could subject it to statistical testing?"

Doctor Wirths seemed delighted and held his glass high, offering Hans a toast. "To Doctor Bloch, may your research skills help save the Reich!"

The conversation turned to the war and the recent battles with the Allies in Belgium. "The Americans will now know what it's like to fight on our ground," offered Wirths. "Our Panzers will destroy their Detroit-made American tanks and march through their forces like butter."

Just then, Mengele offered another toast: "To our V-2 rockets now raining down on London. May they inject everlasting fear into the British!"

A soft murmur of agreement emanated from the group; no one chose to bring up the rampant rumors of failure on both the Eastern and Western fronts that Wehrmacht radio had intentionally ignored.

Excusing himself, Hans walked over to the hors d'oeuvres table where an ample supply of *foie gras*, herring, and cheese were displayed amid pine branches, multicolored leaves, and other decorations celebrating the coming fall season. Having not seen such delicacies in over two years, he quickly filled a plate and headed off to a corner of the room to enjoy this small feast.

Despite the suffering surrounding him, Mengele had made himself comfortable here. The front room was large and had ample windows facing north and south. His home stood just at the north end of the camp, and looking through a south-facing window, the massive expanse of Auschwitz-Birkenau was visible. Further to the southwest, a well-tended farm with even rows of wheat filled the window. He had brought along some fine furnishings and paintings to warm the house. If one were to close his eyes, the polite talk of small groups, punctuated by the friendly clinking of crystal, would create the illusion of a soirée in Berlin, Munich, or Hamburg.

It seemed bizarre, Hans thought, as his eyes scanned the room—these men enjoying themselves with such luxuries in the midst of war, while just beyond the gates, masses of miserable humanity lay starving. But, for the most part, it was merely wretched Jews that filled the barracks—the same people who had brought forth the downfall of Germany and Europe. It was *their* bankers and financiers who had engineered the defeat of the Kaiser's army in the Great War, forcing the German people into a prolonged economic depression.

Only after Germany makes Europe "Judenrein," cleansed of Jews, and defeats the Allies, will the world recover from the devastation the Jews have caused.

The wine enhanced Hans's appreciation of the lessons he had learned and filled his chest with pride in the righteous cause of his people.

An excellent meal of roast duck and braised potatoes and broccoli was served with steaming fresh, hot bread. Wondrous smells emanated from the kitchen, partially masking the ever-present, acrid odor escaping the camp's chimneys. As the meal was finished and the wine took effect, some minor flirtations with the Jew maids could be observed.

The gathering continued late into the evening, and the prisoner string quartet enjoyed this period of temporary civility as they played for their masters. The wine continued to flow, allowing many of the SS to release their inhibitions and slip into various levels of drunkenness.

"A toast to the Reich!" roared Doctor Clauberg, as all glasses were held high and touched each other.

"Heil Hitler!" added Mengele to more clinking. "And to our newly-arrived guests from Hungary, who have brought forth such fine foods and beautiful glassware, we salute you! Unfortunately, you will never enjoy these things again where you're going."

The group roared with laughter as Mengele nodded in the direction of Crematorium III.

Hans noticed the fair-haired Jew maid rearranging the hors d'oeuvres and slyly looking in his direction.

Ah, I could enjoy that little Jewess.

As his eyes connected with this surprisingly attractive young lady, she looked away, embarrassed that she was caught flirting. Mengele saw the exchange and quickly intervened. "Myra, Herr Doktor was looking for the restroom. Could you show him the way?"

She knowingly smiled and led Hans to the back of the house. All pronouncements and feigned disgust with Jewry became moot as the bathroom door closed and Myra expertly fell to her knees, unzipped his pants, and pulled out his excited member. She teased, licked, and sucked, while watching this grand SS officer grovel and moan. Before she could finish, Hans brashly pulled Myra up, ripped off her clothes, and, bending her over, entered her from the rear as she cried out in pain. As he finished, he pushed the maid down, pulled up his pants up, straightened his uniform and reentered the party as if nothing had happened. In the morning, he would blame it on the wine.

Hans felt uplifted as he left the party.

Yes, perhaps it is good to socialize again and drink with colleagues.

It was 2:00 a.m. as his abdominal discomfort began to act up again. His pain had started three years ago, but bicarbonate of soda seemed to manage his symptoms. He noticed the bright lights shining from watchtowers, as their beams systematically scrutinized the grounds. The sky was clear and dark. There was no moon, but Mars and Jupiter stood high in the south while the Milky Way and its millions of stars dusted the central sky. He briskly walked through the cool, fall air toward his room. The only sounds to disturb the night were those of his shoes on the crushed rock surface.

"To consider dear to me…"

18

October 1, 1944
Auschwitz

"Y ou're late!" barked Michel. "I've been waiting over two hours for you to come and move these bodies to the crematorium. Hans is quite anxious for us to finish the other two autopsies."

Martin looked around, somewhat crazed. "Fuck Hans. They were short one person in the head count and we stood outside in the cold for three hours. They finally found old Leo Schwartz dead. The old, deranged bastard had fallen off the latrine bench, hitting his head, and nobody saw him."

Martin paced in circles in the lab, rubbing the back of his neck while muttering to himself, and spoke little to Michel that morning. The midday soup was brought up to the Sonderkommando quarters, and he went to fetch lunch for the two of them. They quickly finished the thin tasteless broth, and then Martin gently touched Michel's shoulder, silently motioning him to a corner of the room. He put a finger to his lips, and pointed up towards the attic where Tamara was hidden.

"We must speak. I've made my decision. It's time," he whispered.

"I thought you put the idea of escape aside. You said the danger to those of us who remained would be too great if you were found missing," said Katz.

"I have found a way to make it work," Martin replied confidently.

He went on to explain in detail what was going to take place. Michel had heard rumors of an "event" happening, but knew nothing more. "On October sixth, the Sonderkommandos at Crematorium IV will set off a

1 4 2

series of explosions with dynamite smuggled in by two women working at the Monowitz munitions factory. This will be followed by detonations in Crematorium II. Munitions will be placed at strategic weight-bearing walls to bring down the building, gas chambers and ovens—all of it."

Michel sat paralyzed, his mouth open, listening.

"A breakout will be attempted through the north gate at the same time, while the SS rush to the crematoriums. The guys have a few guns, and some will make it out. We know most of us will die."

"But, but... How does that help *you?*" stammered Michel.

"I plan to take one of the dead men waiting to be cremated and stencil my number on his forearm. I will dress him in the clothes of a Sonder-kommando and place him in an area of the building where he will appear to have been killed by the explosion. The SS will be so riled, they will not check beyond the number. You report me missing, and the Germans find the body."

"But why go through all that trouble of changing identities if your chance of escape is so small?" Michel was struggling.

Why would he take such a risk?

"Because I won't leave the camp then. I will stay—and you will hide me."

"Are you telling me *I* will help...?" Michel flared back at Martin. "At *my* peril?"

He fought to keep his voice down.

Martin took in a deep breath. "You are *already* at risk. Besides hiding the girl, I worked up here, and the SS will then connect you to the plan... I swear that, if you hide me, I will never, ever link you or the girl to this business. But for now, you must help me."

Michel was angry and wanted to lash out at Martin, but he couldn't. Instead, he stood at the window and gazed through the barbed wire where hundreds of inmates toiled, repairing a road leading into the camp.

I can't blame him... Who knows when we will be freed?

His mind was spinning.

This could be the end.

"Go on, let me hear the rest."

"At six p.m. on Friday, I will take one of your finished autopsy bod-ies to Crematorium II to be burned. Fortunately, there is always a mass of gassed people piled up ready for the ovens. The body on my cart shall be exchanged for one on the pile and I will hide behind the stacked wood next to the bodies as I dress the poor soul in our civilian garb. I will quickly stencil in my number on to his left forearm and cover the corpse with wood. Avoiding the Sonderkommandos working there, I will return to the laboratory, and you will hide me."

Michel swallowed hard crossing his arms across his chest.

"Explosions will occur exactly thirty minutes later, and the remaining Sonderkommandos will make a break for the gate, Martin continued. "The sounds of the blasts should confuse the guards enough to allow some of that group to make it out."

Michel sat down, weighted heavily by information he felt he should never have known, fully aware that death was certain if he was linked in any way to this plot. Already, he had chosen to save and hide Tamara; that was, in itself, enough to get him executed. *Now this.*

Martin just stood there with his scowling, reddened face, staring at Michel.

♦♦♦

October 6, 1944

His day had come.

Martin knew his plan was tenuous, as it depended on the timing of others for the detonations to work. Bringing the body on the two-wheeled cart to the elevators outside the gas chamber was easy; it was normal for him to be there. The lazy SS guard gave him a malevolent look, spitting into the hallway before announcing: "Another Jew to heaven, or whatever you people call it. It's always good to lighten the load, or at least thin the herd."

While he unloaded the body into the elevator, Martin looked down.

You will be the first bastard—just the first.

He ran up the stairs to meet the elevator, as if to finish delivering the body for the fires. The ghoulish pile of naked cadavers was off to his left, and Martin studied the dead lying there before finding one reasonably similar in age and coloring to himself. He pulled it behind the tiny hill of death next to the woodpile. Quickly, he dressed the body with the civilian clothing worn by the Sonderkommandos and took out his charcoal pencil to stencil "42321" on the dead man's left forearm. He was just going to drag the body into position close to one of the ovens where crumbling bricks would fall onto it, when suddenly a large explosion shook the building.

Schiesse! Too soon!

He bolted for the stairs.

"*Halt!*" yelled the SS guard, with his Luger drawn, as he ran up the steps towards him.

Martin immediately ran back upstairs and hid just beyond the landing as the guard approached. Deftly, like a natural assassin, he crashed a brick down on to the back of the guard's neck, easily dropping him to the floor. Picking up the brick, he came down on the face and skull of the German again and again, stopping only after another explosion rattled the building.

Oh, no! Is the building coming down?

He picked up the guard's Luger, tucked it into his waistband and ran downstairs, looking to escape back to the laboratory through the chaos.

♦♦♦

SECRETLY, MICHEL HAD HOPED that Martin's plan would not work. That way, the inmate revolt wouldn't involve him. He was wrong.

Just after the explosions, the sound of gunfire erupted and Martin charged through the door. His eyes were wide, his clothes rumpled, and blood was sprayed across his face and neck. He spoke harshly and uncontrolled. "You must hide me *now*—in the attic, with the girl!"

Huddled in the attic, Tamara was terrified. The building shook with each detonation, and wild shooting was occurring outside. Peering down through the grate on the ceiling, she watched Martin screaming his demands to Michel, and cringed at what might happen next.

"Hurry, you must protect me," he yelled, his face contorted, tears rolling off his cheeks.

Martin had the Luger in his hand waving it back and forth impatiently. She could see that Michel was reluctant, but now he was opening the closet that led to the attic and he was boosting Martin up into her space.

Ten minutes passed and sounds of gunfire and men yelling were coming from the building next door as a dozen trucks arrived and unloaded

Wehrmacht troops. Martin was itching to go downstairs and join the fighting, but he forced himself to close the hatch to the attic door. Within minutes, the thuds of boots climbing steps rocked the building, and shouts of "Out! Out!" filled the laboratory as Doctor Katz was led forcibly down the stairs.

Tamara looked outside through the vent facing the yard. The Sonderkommandos had been rounded up, along with Doctor Katz and three other doctors; At least seventy men were lying face down on the cement in the adjacent courtyard, pistols pointed at their heads.

Just then, Mengele's car rolled up. He jumped out and screamed over the noise, "Let the doctors go! They have important things to do! They have no dealings with this revolt."

Michel, Nyislizi, and one other doctor were led away, spared from the ensuing slaughter. Seconds later, those on the ground were killed with shots to their heads. Michel wearily climbed the steps and was barely able to open the door before he collapsed into a chair. As he entered, Tamara watched him from above.

He is so pale and listless.

After a while, as if speaking to no one, yet talking to the two of them above, she heard Michel murmur, "I was just a few centimeters away from death. And now, here I am...still."

"All that may come to my knowledge...I will keep secret and never reveal."

19

Tamara
Auschwitz

The strange, shadowed light that came in from the south-facing vents gave Tamara perhaps seven hours of light with which to sketch with the pencils Michel had given her. There could be no lights in the attic—no candles, nothing that would indicate anyone was living there. Although physically constricting, her attic retreat allowed her to continue her passion. But when Martin was hoisted up, everything changed.

Before this wild man invaded my life, I felt free to draw the images around me and pass each day in anticipation of my next inspiration. Now, I feel smothered.

She had overheard the conversation when Martin held Doctor Katz hostage to his escape plan. Soon after, she saw her protector begin to change. Day by day, he became more nervous when the SS doctors arrived to review their studies. He developed a twitch in his right eye and often fell asleep at his desk. The slightest sound in the building made him wipe sweat off his brow.

It was difficult to accept another person into the small attic space. This had become her safe place.

And now it has to be shared with a man who has placed us all in danger.

Yet there was nothing she could do but remain quiet, and speak to Martin as little as possible. Tamara had paid slight attention to Martin working in the laboratory prior to his conversation about escape. She did not remember him as the man who brought her up from the gas chambers until Doctor Katz told her the story. Yet his boorish behavior made it difficult for her to feel any gratitude for his actions in saving her.

One night, as she lay on the straw mattress next to Katz's bed, she boldly spoke up in the dark and cautioned Michel. "Doctor Katz, that man is frightening, and he is interested only in himself. He wouldn't care if we were all sacrificed so that he might escape."

Doctor Katz whispered so low that she strained to hear him, "Yes, you are right, child. He has brought peril close to us, and we must be careful. It is best that we not talk about this anymore."

After the revolt of the Sonderkommandos, Doctor Katz became even more distant. His narrow escape from death and the pressure of hiding two people in the attic added yet another burden to his already anxious existence. Tamara continued to come down at night and sleep on the floor, but they didn't talk as they had before. She was hungry for his wisdom, but Michel had clammed up. And it crushed her.

Martin, too, noticed that Doctor Katz had changed and how little he talked, even to Tamara. He felt the girl's increasing loneliness and barraged her with questions about her life, some quite personal. But she refused to engage him. He tried to fill that void for her, but she firmly closed the door on his attempts.

"You must remember," he said in frustration one day, "that I am the one who found you in the gas chamber!"

He tried to lie close, rub his body against her, but she would scoot away. *I wonder if it's about the doctor.*

His frustration growing, he began to taunt her. "Do you sleep with Doctor Katz each night when you leave the attic?"

Tamara could barely respond, her voice heavy as she clenched her fists. "No! He is a friend, and we talk. We talk of things, many things, until I fall asleep on the floor."

"Don't be so upset. I thought…it was just natural that you might…"

"You're such an ass! Keep your miserable thoughts to yourself," she whispered and curled up protectively.

Her drawings changed, too. She sketched Doctor Katz with heavy lines in his face depicting stress and grief. Her drawings portrayed an empty camp, as if everyone else were dead.

When Martin talked of escape, Tamara brightened up. She became enthused and strongly encouraged him to follow through on his plan.

I could be alone again.

Michel, too, could only pray that Martin would soon leave. His nights became increasingly long as he lay awake, unable to sleep, besieged by a veritable torrent of stress and fear.

The quiet of the night was broken only by the sounds of the sleeping child lying next to his bed.

20

November 15, 1944
Auschwitz

The ashes were removed daily from the back of the crematoriums. Small, spring-loaded, forged-iron covers on the backside of the building gave access to each of the ovens inside. With the use of shovels and rakes, the ashes and unburned, bony shards were removed by inmates each night and later loaded onto a truck for the daily ritual of dumping the remains of thousands of souls into the Vistula river—a mile away from the camp. This truck was one of the few regular vehicles in and out of the camp at night.

Since the revolt of October 6, the guard patrol had been doubled to prevent another violent rebellion. But on November 10, the SS reverted to the routine existing prior to the escape attempt, and the guards resumed a more relaxed approach to their jobs. Perhaps even the Germans were aware that the war would be over soon.

Martin had planned his escape in minute detail and was ready to move ahead. Wearing civilian clothes underneath his inmate garb, he had fifteen minutes between patrols to leave the building and hide in the shadows to avoid the searchlights. The military trucks would be loaded with ash remains at 5:00 p.m., just as dusk fell. A tarp would be placed over the ashes to keep the contents hidden and protected from the wind.

He easily could have stayed in the attic until liberation. He'd been listed as dead; no one was looking for him, and he had a relatively safe existence in the cramped space above the laboratory. But his desire to escape went beyond his personal safety. The vision of the execution of his parents ran continuously in his head, as did his vow to avenge their deaths. He would hunt down the lieutenant who had murdered them and kill him slowly, remembering how his father had died. It was his dream to bring a partisan force back into Auschwitz and line up the murderous SS and Kapos, killing them deliberately, one by one.

At 9:45 p.m., he sneaked out of the attic and tiptoed quietly down the back stairs. Staying close to the crematorium walls, he made his way to where the truck was parked and climbed under the left side. The vehicle's high clearance enabled Martin to wedge his thin body into a space between the rear axle and spars that supported the gas tank. He had come prepared with rags in case he needed to tie himself to the underside to further avoid detection. In his jacket was the Luger he had taken from the SS guard he'd killed in the uprising. His face blackened with ashes from the ovens, he curled himself up in a ball, hidden by the immense springs visible from the side of the BMW truck. It helped that he had accompanied the trucks before and shoveled the remains into the river on two occasions. The trucks always left for the river at 10:00 p.m. and returned at eleven.

"Jew pigs! Into the back of the truck!" growled the driver.

Two Sonderkommandos immediately jumped onto the truck, their feet dangling off the back end. The second guard rode along on the right running board with his automatic weapon in hand, keeping his eyes trained on the two inmates in back. When the truck stopped at the gate, Martin became rigid as lights were shone under the truck from the right side. He dared not breathe as the nonchalant guard finished the search and appeared to wobble as he walked back to open the gate.

"Siegfried," yelled Volker, the man on the running board. "A little too much *Schnapps* tonight?"

"*Ja, mein* good friend, tonight and last night, and the one before. It's my lifeblood in this hellhole."

"Me too," said Volker, patting the square bulge in his pants pocket.

The truck lurched ahead, bouncing along the rutted, muddy road to the river. One of the potholes was deep enough to slam into Martin's back as he pulled himself tight to the undersurface, wincing in pain, unable to cry out. He continued clinging to the spars, his hands numb and ready to give out, not moving a muscle as the truck bumped to a stop.

"Swine, out now and let's get this over with!" yelled Volker as he reached into his pocket, unscrewed his flask, and took a swig of his courage.

The two inmates jumped down and grabbed their shovels, as the pair of guards assumed their positions, rifles in hand, observing the ghastly process of fouling the river with little interest.

The truck was parked next to a spot bare of branches with little brush along the roadside, its right side facing the river, allowing the ashes to be shoveled directly into the water. One guard stood at the front of the vehicle, the other at the back near the disposal spot. Both men faced the water about five meters away, where dense foliage grew up to the edge of the road. Martin knew the guards were far too lazy to walk around to the other side of the truck.

Waiting for just the right moment, he listened to their idle conversation as he studied the adjacent roadside. To his horror, little vegetation was present where he planned to hide.

"It will be good to get home," said Siegfried at the front of the truck, referring to the scheduled Christmas leave. "But the family always asks about work and the war, and I must lie to my children. They think I'm killing Russians at the front." Volker chortled. "But even worse, you let someone else kill, and you just hide their ashes."

Gingerly, Martin let himself down to the ground while he looked around to see exactly where the guards stood. Finding a rock the size of an orange within reach, he grabbed it and flung the stone under the truck into the river. The splash made both inmates and guards look in that direction while Martin made his move. Hugging the ground closely, he crawled on his elbows, dragging his body flat along the dirt until he reached the edge of the road, then made his way into the bordering brush. He lay there still, barely breathing. Seeing the side of his left shoe uncovered, he quickly moved it off the dirt road under a branch. The scratching sound caused one of the guards to look in his direction, and he froze.

"Siegfried, forget it—just another creature," yelled the other guard. "It's nothing, now let's get back."

The guards assured each other that it was probably just a small animal creating the noises. The inmates finished their task and were ordered back into the truck. The vehicle started up and swung around slowly, headlights blazing along the bushes as it headed back to camp. If anyone with a sharp eye had been paying attention, he would have spotted Martin lying face down, without the benefit of leaf cover, under the void branches of winter.

Oh God, please don't let them see me.

As the truck blindly rolled past, the drunken voices of the guards singing "Lili Marlene" became the hymn Martin would remember as he pursued his plan of revenge.

"And I will do no harm or injustice to them..."

21

December 21, 1944
Auschwitz

The distant sounds of Christmas carols wafted out from the camp's offices, carrying fond memories of past holiday times. As a youngster in Vilna, Michel envied the gentile children and their celebrations. There were so many presents, parties and good spirits evident in his little village. He often asked his father if he could visit his friends' homes during Christmas, but the response was always the same: "That's their holiday, and we have ours. We do not believe what the *goyim* believe, so we cannot celebrate with them. Besides, we have Chanukah."

Michel's children had always asked the same question of him this time of year. They were invited to the Christmas parties in Lyon, and unlike his own father, Michel allowed them to go. Anna, though she'd converted to Judaism, missed the joys of her childhood Christmases and believed that the children should celebrate with their gentile neighbors.

He'd heard no word from his family in six months. The failed revolt, hiding Martin, and his final escape had temporarily replaced his worries about them. Chilling thoughts again now coursed his mind each night as he tried his best to fall asleep.

Surely, Mengele would let me know if they were moved from Terezin. He gave his word. I would give anything to see them again.

♦♦♦

TAMARA WATCHED SILENTLY AS Michel reached into a drawer by the desk and pulled out what appeared to be a diary. Gently placed between the pages was a photograph. "This is my family: Anna, Aaron and Rachel."

Leaning forward to look at the picture, a wave of nausea struck Tamara. *It is them! This lovely mother and her two sweet children were in the train next to me!*

She remembered them clearly because she was so moved by their affection for each other and how the mother's soft singing had soothed even her. Tamara had stayed close to them as they were herded off the train together and marched toward the "showers."

Oh, no! The showers, the gas!

She opened her mouth to speak, but stopped. "Doctor Katz, I must sit down."

He extended his arm and led her to his bed.

"What's wrong, Tamara? Are you feeling ill?"

"No, Doctor Katz," she lied. Many conflicting emotions coursed through her at once, and her mind became confused.

Does he need to know the truth? How could he react but with heartbreak? No, I can't let him know... I can never forget the lines, nor the sounds of those two children crying as they waited: "Mommy, why? Why do we need a shower? Why, Mommy?"

Tamara forced a smile as she ran her right hand through her hair. "I just reacted, that's all. I know how much you worry about your family. They are so very beautiful. It moves me to see them so."

♦♦♦

THE RUSSIANS WERE COMING, and the crematoriums were scheduled for destruction. Michel's laboratory was moved on November 30 to a building adjacent to the camp administration offices. He was disappointed, as the room was much smaller than what he had become used to, and it had an unfinished wood floor. There were just a few storage cabinets and little in the way of working surfaces, but as he inspected the quarters, he was relieved to find an attic space where Tamara could hide safely. He had the Sonderkommandos transfer his autopsy slab to the new site.

That night, dressed as a male inmate, Tamara walked with Michel carrying boxes towards the new laboratory after the other helpers had left.

Michel squinted as a searchlight from a tower illuminated Tamara walking down the stairs from Crematorium III.

"Halt, I say! Halt!" yelled a guard standing in front of the gas chamber. Michel stopped and instructed Tamara to put down her boxes. "Katz, who is this inmate? I haven't seen him before."

Thinking quickly, Michel approached the guard. "Sergeant Schultz, I should have checked with you. This inmate is one of Herr Doktor Bloch's subjects for cold immersion. The study just finished, and I needed some help in moving, you do understand. His Kapo will meet us at the new laboratory and escort him to the barracks. We had to finish quickly as, you know, the crematoriums are being deactivated."

Backing away, the guard left to assume his position at the double doors to the gas chamber. It was just a few days later that a series of explosive charges went off in the remaining four buildings housing the gas chambers and crematoriums.

At first, Michel thought the camp was under attack from the Russians and became hopeful. A series of detonations began under Crematorium I, followed by Numbers III, IV, and V. He heard the crashing sounds as they collapsed, one by one, but the timing of each explosion allowed him to conclude that they were not under attack. Multiple explosions occurred at each building, and they crashed into a pile of bricks, forming a disordered mausoleum that would hide and seal forever the fate of millions of Europe's Jews.

Hearing the explosions, Michel could almost visualize the dust ascending from each site and imagined the various souls rising up, freed at last from their graves of fire.

Almost poetry... No, no, that couldn't be... Those words are wrong. This was not poetry, nor was it poetic justice. Never could those two words ever be used for this place! These buildings are brought down by fear alone—the fear of discovery... fear of being recognized as the monsters these bastards know they have become. Yes, it was clear to me. The all-powerful SS was trying to cover their tracks by destroying these structures, but the truth would remain. These swaths of hate, murder, and rot were etched not into things or places, but scarred into man; not only these men, but mankind itself.

As silence hung in the air after the final explosion, an uneasy thought rattled Michel's mind:

Monsters... Have I become one of them?

♦♦♦

MOUNTAINS OF RUBBLE WERE all that remained of the buildings housing the gas chambers and crematoriums, and a work crew of inmates carted off the stone and wood. It was dumped into an area just to the north of Crematorium V—the same area where common burial pits had been dug for those not cremated. A large fire was roaring to one side of the open area and building debris was fed into the inferno, as if to extinguish any and everything, including all memory of the lives that had passed through this death factory. The fire burned for three consecutive days and spilled a different sort of ash over the camp. It was almost a pleasant odor, compared to the usual smells emanating from the incinerated flesh of the murdered. At night, the glow continued, as inmates worked to rid the camp of debris. Time was short. The Russians were on their doorstep.

The camp was a buzz. Inmates who had spoken little before were gathered in groups, in spite of and in full view of their guards. As if a steel veil had been lifted, the poor unwashed skeletons started to speak and point with their hands toward the east. A spark of hope became the sustenance that kept them going, replacing the pain of hunger in their wasted bodies.

♦♦♦

NEW YEAR'S DAY, 1945, was filled with optimism for Tamara, as the sounds of war were clearly heard off to the east and the Russians grew near… Liberation was certain to follow. But anticipating freedom was more complex than she expected, as she looked back at the evolution of her feelings for Doctor Katz. He was much like a father, protective and loving, as one would love a child. And that is what she was, at fifteen, simply a child. Yet during these months with him, she had matured many years beyond her age. He had no one else to talk with and confided thoughts and emotions a father might not share with his child.

Not long after Martin's exit, Doctor Katz began to talk again, and the two grew closer. Martin's surly presence had depressed the doctor, and his departure was greeted with a kind of shared relief. Now Michel spoke honestly of his fears about Anna and the children and his stupid—and possibly selfish—decision to leave his family, trusting that Meyer and Mengele

157

would protect them. As she listened, she knew that she would not, *must not*, tell him that his family had been on the train with her. The more he revealed his struggle and guilt, the more she saw how it could destroy him. In her young wisdom, she recognized that he had been on the verge of suicide just before she entered his life.

"Tamara," he said one evening, with tears in his eyes, "I must find my family, and I truly believe they are still at Terezin. Everything there was good when I left; there were schools, sports fields, music, and art. I am convinced they must be okay."

Michel shifted his eyes to the side as he talked; he didn't believe what he was saying.

Tamara took a deep breath and gathered her courage as the nausea swept through her again. "Doctor Katz, I must tell you that after the Dutch Red Cross finished their inspection in May 1944, many things changed. All sounds of music stopped and the children didn't play on the soccer field anymore. The schools continued to be operated secretly by the ghetto inhabitants. The Germans even closed some of the factories where the people worked."

Tamara broke into a cold sweat as she saw Michel's anxiety increase.

"Do you believe that they were moved?" he asked.

"I wish I knew... I wish I had met your family," she lied, avoiding his eyes. "And even if I had, you know, it was so confusing... Trains coming and going each day. Who knows which families might have been transported?"

She stood up and walked a few steps away from Michel, trying to gather her thoughts and hide her tears.

I do see them sitting in the corner of the cattle car, all bunched up, trying to keep warm. His wife, Anna, has each child wrapped in her arms as if she is holding onto them forever. She is singing French children's songs in the softest, sweetest voice I have ever heard. "Au claire de la lune, mon ami Pierrot, prête-moi ta plume, pour écrire un mot; ma chandelle est morte, je n'ai plus de feu, ouvrez-moi ta porte, pour l'amour de Dieu." Both children are sleeping and at peace. As the railcar doors are violently opened, everyone becomes startled and the children are crying. We all jump out and are forced to stand in lines, and then put into trucks. We head towards the building with the chimneys. The children keep close to their mothers as they are led to the "showers." It is this memory that I will forever bury in my soul, never to be told to Doctor Katz.

◆◆◆

WATCHING FROM A PEEPHOLE in the new attic Tamara found it increasingly difficult to understand how Michel could work on these inmates side by side with the SS doctors each day without exhibiting some human emotion. One night she gathered her courage. "Doctor Katz, this is hard for me to ask, but how can you appear so calm when you are experimenting on these unfortunate people?"

Michel stared at the ceiling. This question stalked him each night as he tried to fall asleep and was there each morning as he awakened. He dreaded it, whether it screamed in his head or came from outside. Now Tamara's words jolted him, forcing him to find a response. His head began to pound.

Just what am I doing? This isn't medicine, it is not science... It is torture, it is murder... We can deceive others, non-doctors, but not ourselves. Am I really doing this to save my family...? It's all wrong. I am saving myself. Day in, day out, I give advice to the SS doctors in their experiments, as if it is science they are engaged in. I can't fool myself any longer. They are murderers, and I assist them.

He gazed down at his feet like a stubborn child, refusing to answer. When he finally looked up, he was expressionless; there was no emotion, as if his face were a mask. "I cannot answer your question now, yet someday, when we are free of the camps, I hope to be able to do so."

The very next night, he confided details of a young boy, sixteen years old, who had died during Hans Bloch's study on hypothermia. Michel had been furious at Hans for this boy's death, especially after Hans forced him to submerge the boy to the base of his skull. They already knew that submerging the body this deep in the chilled tank was fatal in other subjects, yet that didn't stop Hans. On another day, Michel was seething again. Hans had told him he was lowering the age of his subjects to twelve to increase the numbers in his study. Michel knew that these youngsters would have to die to satisfy Hans' morbid desire for more tissue samples.

A confrontation ensued between Hans and Michel. Michel, for the first time, was able to summon some courage and question Hans. "The physiologic and tissue responses of children are different than adults," he burst out.

Bloch put his hand on his holstered gun and stared at Michel. "Jew doctor, you shall never again question me in that manner—should you wish to live."

◆◆◆

DESPITE MICHEL'S DEEPENING DEPRESSION, his nightly talks with Tamara now included a bit of optimism. The specter of liberation was on the horizon, as it seemed certain the Russians would storm the camp any day. Yet it was with mixed emotions that Tamara looked forward to freedom. She knew that Michel would leave and search for his family and that she would return to Prague, leaving her with an emptiness in her heart that would be hard to fill. And who of her family might be alive to greet her?

22

November 16, 1944
Outside of Krakow, Poland

Martin lay motionless in the brush for two hours. A sense of relief filled him as he relished the joy of freedom. He could feel his face relaxing into a smile, something he hadn't done in months. Enjoying it, he rested peacefully and looked upward at the dark, cold sky, knowing he was liberated. Free at last—and ready to make those Nazis pay for their crimes.

Noting the truck had passed a farmhouse on its way to the river, he wanted to avoid any action that might disturb a dog or farm animal. He rose slowly, looking along the waterway for any boats or barge traffic. German troops were patrolling the countryside, expecting the Russians to attack this area at any moment. Martin had understood what he had to do to be safe and complete his journey. He had obtained a map of Eastern Europe from a suitcase belonging to a recently gassed Hungarian and had carefully plotted his trek to Lodz.

The night was moonless and the deepening darkness comforted Martin, now in civilian clothes, as he started to move along the road toward Lodz, where he hoped to meet up with the Polish resistance unit he had worked with prior to his capture.

There was little roadside vegetation in which he could hide as he made his way north. Only a few corn stalks were still present, too few to provide enough cover should German troops come into view. Martin planned to do most of his travel under the cover of night and rest during the day. Gripping the handle of the Luger shoved under his belt, he felt a sense of security that had been missing for so long. He had to be careful and could not trust the civilians, as he was aware of the inherent hatred of Jews prevalent among the Poles.

Estimating it would take four days to get to Lodz, Martin had packed enough bread for, maybe, two days. He would have to forage for anything else he needed during the journey.

On the second night, he came upon a farmhouse that appeared abandoned; no light shone from the windows, and he heard and sensed no sign of activity. The rickety back door easily gave way as he shoved hard with his shoulder. Slowly and cautiously, he made his way to the small kitchen. But as he was opening cabinet doors, he felt the cold steel of a rifle placed against his neck and heard a shout in Polish that paralyzed him. "Hands up or I shoot you dead, right now! Hands up, you hear?"

Martin did as the man commanded without turning around. Standing very still, he said, "I am sorry. I have been so long without food, and I didn't think there was anyone here."

"Did you think that you could just break into my house, steal my food, and scare us half to death? I should just shoot you now!" yelled the man, jamming the rifle into Martin's back.

Martin took a deep breath. "Please, sir, I beg you. Your house looked empty. I don't want to scare or hurt anybody. I just need food. My name is Martin Brosky and the Russians bombed our village, Zagorze. I had to leave for fear they would come and get me. I was so frightened. All my family is dead."

This apparently struck the right chord, as the man immediately put down his rifle and sat at the table, seemingly exhausted. He asked Martin to turn around and said, "My name is Georg Pulaski. We are so nervous here. I have to be careful."

Martin saw a man of maybe forty years, but aged well beyond. His face was drawn and his clothes hung limply, as though he had lost a great deal of weight. He appeared little different from some of the men at Auschwitz. A gray sadness enveloped this man's person, as if all his life's energy had been sucked out of him.

Pointing to the cabinet that Martin had opened, he said, "You may have any scraps you can find in there. Little is left. Maybe there are a few scattered grains of rice and a couple of rotten potatoes, but that's all. Our bread is gone, and we have no fuel to bake with. As you can see, there is no electricity, either."

Georg led Martin into the front room. Dawn was just breaking, with light coming from the two small front windows, and Martin was able to see, huddled in a corner, a woman and a child of about eight years. Only their faces were visible. The rest of their bodies were wrapped in a blanket, shielding them from the cold. Both bore that same exhausted appearance as Georg.

"Klara, Oskar, don't be afraid...it's all right... He won't try to hurt us," said Georg. "This is Martin from Zagorze. It was bombed, and he has had no food for days."

Martin did his best to appear civil and tilted his head as if to acknowledge them. "I am so sorry if I frightened you. Is there anything I can do to pay for this food? I have no money, but I can work."

Klara shivered as she spoke. "Yes, yes—we are so cold, and there is something you can do for us. Georg was trying to strip off some of the wood planks from the barn to burn for heat, but he didn't have tools and wasn't strong enough. Georg won't ask, but I will. Could you help him now? I am so worried about our son."

"Yes," said Martin, "anything you need."

"Thank you," said Klara, her teeth chattering.

For the next two hours, the two men toiled together, pulling and ripping boards from the partially destroyed barn and piling the wood next to the house. Klara quickly started a fire in the wood stove and the house seemed to heat up magically, putting a smile on everyone's face.

While sitting around the stove, the family told their story of hardship. Apparently, the initial push by the Germans through Poland had concentrated on the cities and the Polish military bases. Farms like the Pulaskis were not bothered at the outset of the war. At first, food supplies for the German Wehrmacht were plentiful, and they did not trouble the farmers for grain and corn. A few officers did come by to determine whether any Jews were living in their homes and left satisfied there were none. As the war raged to the east in 1943, German food supplies dwindled and more troops stopped at their home. At first, they demanded only food, but later the Pulaskis were forced to house officers for brief periods of time.

Hearing their plight at the hands of the Germans stunned Martin. "Georg, Klara, how did you endure people taking over your home, taking your food?"

Klara spoke first. "It was horrible, simply miserable. Many nights we were forced out of the house as the endless line of soldiers passed us. I was so concerned when Oskar got sick with a high fever and cough. We nearly lost him."

"Each day, an extended stream of trucks, tanks, and cannons filled the road going east," said Georg. "It was an especially cold winter last year, and we were asked to house more troops for greater periods of time. Believe me, they were bastards."

Martin's eyes remained fixed on Georg and didn't blink while he listened.

"These men became very anxious and threatening, demanding more of our food stocks to take with them to the front," Georg continued. "We were told that the German supply convoys were stalled by the weather and couldn't deliver food in sufficient quantities to the troops." George glanced at Klara and reached for her hand. "Our greater problems started as the troops began returning to the west. It was obvious that many of the Wehrmacht forces were in disarray, with broken-down equipment and clothing that did not appear warm enough for the weather they had to withstand. Their disciplined troops had turned into an almost maniacal force, stopping at our farm, angrily demanding food and shelter."

As he listened, Martin reached down and patted the gun tucked into his waistband. "We almost had to leave," Georg said, squeezing Klara's hand. "I tried to satisfy them with shelter in the barn, but that wasn't good enough for Hitler's army. There was many a cold night we had to sleep on straw out in the barn in the bitter cold."

Georg became more animated when he talked about the Russians, who would soon pass through Poland. Stories of Russian soldiers raping and killing as they advanced frightened the Pulaskis even more than the Germans. It was no secret that Germany was losing the war, and it was just a matter of time until the Russians arrived. It was Georg's hope that by making the house appear abandoned, they might be left alone.

"That is true; there was no sign of life here when I opened the door," said Martin. He expanded on his original story about leaving his village. "The Russians bombed and strafed the civilian homes as the Germans moved out."

Klara shuddered at these words and looked up at Martin, who added, "Russian or German bastards—not much difference."

The Pulaskis accepted Martin's story without question and offered to let him stay with them until he could return home.

◆◆◆

THE RELATIVE SAFETY WITH this Polish family gave Martin time to plan his next step. He hoped to join up with the Polish resistance outside of Lodz, and was well acquainted with their leaders. He didn't know if they had disbanded, but believed that they were his best chance to get the revenge he longed for since the death of his family.

But there were problems to solve first. He had neither an identification card nor any way of attaining one. He had no transportation, and could not count on being able to walk the distance to Lodz in the freezing weather. He could only rely on himself, his instincts for survival, and his pistol. For now, he was safe, with a roof over his head and people who believed his story.

For two weeks, Martin helped Georg with several projects, including fixing the roof leaks, gathering enough wood to stave off the winter cold, and scouring the adjoining potato field for spuds overlooked during the fall harvest. The family of three was quite happy to have him there and made a makeshift sleeping area on the floor of their son's bedroom. Oskar enjoyed listening to Martin's nightly stories about his exploits as a youngster.

In his quiet time, Martin had explored ideas that would most safely and easily get him to his destination. He could hitch a ride with a supply truck going north, but he saw few trucks on the road. Besides, any driver could insist on seeing his identification, and the military often accompanied these trucks. He even thought of hijacking some vehicle but that, too, seemed risky.

Two days later, a hard knock on the front door awakened everyone from their slumber. Martin jumped up. He had been asleep less than an hour.

Who could that be?

Another solid rap, this time forceful enough to shake the windows. Georg ran into the room and whispered to Martin, "Get out, go to the barn, and cover yourself with straw… They are Germans."

Martin didn't question him but instead grabbed his blanket and exited the back door just as Georg was opening the front one.

"*Guten Nacht!*" said the officer. "By order of the Reich, we are commandeering your house for my fellow officer and me for the night. I am *Kapitän* Spetzler and this is my aide, *Leutnant* Sondheim. We will leave in the morning."

Both officers entered and stood there, surveying the room. Oskar peeked out from his door. Instead of the crisp look of typical German officers, their uniforms were dirty and torn. Each looked as if he hadn't bathed in weeks, and dirt and fatigue etched their faces. The second German pushed Georg aside and stumbled into his bedroom. A loud shriek emanated from the room, and Klara ran out with great fear in her eyes.

Georg moved to defend his wife, when the first officer calmly explained, "The lieutenant is harmless, just tired. I would suggest that you, your wife, and son move some blankets into the barn and stay there tonight. You needn't worry."

Martin heard Klara's cry and was ready, gun in hand, to jump to the family's defense. But just then he saw them marching out of the house holding blankets to join him in the barn, and he shoved the gun back under his waistband.

It's going to be easier than I thought.

Under his blanket, on the frozen straw, Martin lay face up, listening to the sounds of the family sleeping. Little noise came from the fields; only the wind was heard playing a melody as it whistled through the rafters. He could see the officers' sedan parked to the side of the house.

Perfect!

It was time.

Grasping the Luger tightly in his right hand, he silently walked the twenty-five meters to the back door of the house and stealthily entered. He carefully walked through the kitchen into the front room, where he found the captain asleep on the couch and snoring loudly. Looking into the bedroom, he could see the other German's stomach rise and fall in time to his sleeping grunts.

Martin knew he had to be quick and efficient. Wrapping the pistol in a pillow to mute the sound, he entered the bedroom and shot the officer in the back of the head. Just as quickly, he headed into the front room and was surprised by the captain reaching for his gun next to the couch. Martin fired his Luger. It jammed. He lashed out at the German, striking his temple with the pistol, knocking him to his side. The officer's weapon was now pointed at Martin, who quickly responded with a kick, knocking the gun away. Martin struck his pistol again and again to the man's head, stopping only when the officer's eyes stared blindly at the ceiling and he was sure that he was dead.

Martin stood paralyzed. A strange sense of power coursed through his body, the same feeling he'd had when he'd killed at Auschwitz. His heart was thumping in his chest, and clarity of purpose overcame him as he peered down at the lifeless body beneath him.

I can do this... I can kill Germans with my hands.

His mind shifted to the future.

Sizing up his two victims, he took the uniform from the captain, who was close to his size, and put it on. The officer's identification was in the right front pocket. Boots, hat, wallet, watch, he took them all, then dragged both bodies outside and loaded them into the trunk of the Mercedes sedan they had arrived in. He would dump them somewhere eventually. But for now, he had to get away.

Prior to leaving, he walked back to the barn to inform his hosts that their German guests had decided to leave unexpectedly early. "Don't be concerned if you come across a little bloodstain," he added.

He explained that he would be leaving to drop the officers off "somewhere."

"We understand," said Georg with a sly smile. Klara wrapped Martin in her arms and silently said goodbye.

♦♦♦

IT WAS NOW THE first of December, and the road towards Lodz was covered with a fine layer of snow and ice. The identification card in his pocket read: "Kapitän Erik Spetzler, second armored division." There was no way that Martin could pass for the blond-haired, blue-eyed officer who appeared on the card. He knew he would have to show it at every checkpoint along the road, and he could easily be detained if someone challenged his identity. Taking the card out if its sleeve, he dropped it onto the muddy water outside the car and rubbed it with dirt until the photograph was nearly removed and only the name was distinguishable.

Searching the vehicle, Martin found a pouch with two sets of papers ordering both officers to Germany, where they were to prepare their artillery division for the defense of Berlin. Not wanting to explain the absence of Leutnant Sondheim, he started a small fire, burning the lieutenant's papers and other unnecessary documents he found inside the car. A worn, brown leather case contained detailed maps, which he then used to plan his route and find a place to dispose of the bodies. Assuming his new identity, Martin was ready and pressed on towards Lodz.

He encountered his first checkpoint after ten kilometers.

Too soon!

With a crisp salute, the soldier manning the gate said, "Halt! Sir, please show me your papers."

Martin handed over his card in its sleeve and the man peered hard at it. "Sir, what happened here? I can hardly make out your name, let alone anything else on this card."

Sporting a childish grin, Martin appeared forthcoming. "I had to dive into a puddle during an air raid while outside of Kiev and everything got wet. Just look at my uniform; there were no washing facilities on the front."

The guard, now laughing, started to walk around and inspect the car. He opened the right side back door and checked under the seats. Martin held his breath until the soldier reappeared on his left. He still had the bodies in the trunk.

Hoping to distract the guard, Martin pulled out a pack of cigarettes. "Sergeant, would you like a smoke?"

"Ja Kapitän, danke," as he placed a cigarette in his lips, stopping his inspection. Coming around to the front, he raised the gate and signaled Martin to pass. Looking back, he could see the guard lighting his cigarette and telling his cohort about the sloppy kapitän who really looked like schiesse.

♦♦♦

AFTER ANOTHER TEN KILOMETERS, Martin turned off the highway onto a dirt road paralleling a stream. He travelled for two kilometers to a bend in the road well out of sight of the main roadway and dumped the bodies into the deep brush along the water's edge, covering them with snow. Martin turned the car around and started back toward the highway, but stopped. A column of trucks loaded with troops could be seen heading west. He waited until they passed. After an hour, he reentered the roadway toward Lodz.

Ten hours later, he arrived at the city. The only light visible was the flashlight held by the soldier waving him through. The customary blackout had continued for fear of Russian bombers. He stopped alongside the road and waited; dawn was breaking, and the colorful sky contrasted with this now dark, lifeless city in which he had grown up. He had passed the last checkpoint, again without difficulty. Each guard he encountered heard his story and waved him on without question, grateful for the moment of comic relief.

Martin wanted to visit his old home and try to recall the life he'd had before the Germans came. Parking the sedan in a military lot, he closed his eyes and drifted off until the light of the day awakened him. With a yawn, he left the car and headed toward his old neighborhood.

He watched the faces of the people he passed as he walked along the street. Wearing the German officer's uniform was uncomfortable, yet gave him a strange sense of power that he had never experienced before.

Yes, thought Martin, *making people respect and fear you is quite satisfying.*

Most civilians looked down and shied away as they encountered him on the street. He didn't recognize anyone; all the Jews were gone. Most, he assumed, were now dead.

He turned onto Bracha Street and stood looking up at his old house. Tears welled up as he gazed at the two-story structure, now sadly falling apart, its shutters dangling and front windows smashed. He recalled the wonderful times with his family before the Germans came and forced every Jew to live in the ghetto. As he peeked inside through the window, he imagined his mother in the parlor, waiting for him to come home from school. He tried the front door. It opened easily, and he peered inside. Piles of trash, broken tables and chairs littered the living room and hallway amidst the smell of feces. Martin stopped.

I have seen enough.

Wracked with despair, he could not step any further inside. He closed the door and headed back through the city.

As he came to Balucki Square, the place where his parents had been murdered, a deep fury replaced the tears. He gripped his fists tight enough to cut his palms with his fingernails, stifling an overwhelming need to fight something or someone. Gnashing his teeth, he knew in that moment he could kill any German soldier with his bare hands.

He went back to retrieve the canvas bag containing his clothes. Having been careful so far, he knew it was best to keep wearing the uniform; it allowed him to move around freely until he could come into contact with those he was seeking.

Martin had last visited the AK Resistance camp to obtain explosives just prior to being captured. The site was located in the woods, just six kilometers outside of town. No roads came near it, and it was purposefully difficult to find. He was confident that this camp still existed, as it was well hidden, and few operations were done in Lodz proper, but rather to the north and east of the city.

It was now easy for him to stroll across the fields whose perimeters were guarded by dogs and soldiers. Unlike eight months ago, when he was captured, the dogs didn't strain at their leashes. They seemed to recognize the uniform.

"It is a bit cool, yet it is December and more snow is bound to fall." Martin greeted a guard as he passed. "Would you have a light, *mein soldat?*"

He bent forward with his cigarette dangling from his lips, and the young private lit it for him. Martin smiled his thanks, and went on his way. He trudged along beyond the field into the woods, where a well-worn path was visible. Walking down this trail, he veered off to the left at about one kilometer and came across the crashing stream he remembered from his childhood. He climbed up the hill to the east alongside of the rushing water to a point where a man might try to cross by stepping on submerged rocks. Martin recognized danger; he knew that if someone dared try to cross here, he would likely slip on the loose rocks and fall into the cold stream.

Further up, beyond a large boulder, he spotted the familiar crossing point that wasn't visible from the trail—a place that required one to scale up a smooth block of granite to get across. Martin changed out of his officer's uniform, hid the clothing, and made his way onto the rock and over to the other side.

A narrow path wound its way up the hill toward another set of large boulders and an old mining cave. Martin knew this area well, having visited it often when delivering black market supplies to the Resistance. Taking a large stone from the ground, he tapped out his name in Morse code on the large rock that blocked the eastern opening of the cave. The boulder seemed to roll back slowly, revealing two men, both holding rifles pointed at him. Martin didn't recognize either one.

"Your name again, your business here," yelled the shorter one.

"I am Martin and I'm here to see Tadeusz, Stefan Tadeusz. You must be new here as, up to eight months ago, I delivered goods to the camp."

Hesitantly, the other guard said, "Follow us."

Beyond the tunnel, a shallow canyon stretched below, covered by dense pine trees spreading their limbs so that the ground was hidden. A faint wisp of smoke flowed up between the pine-covered branches. The area was ringed with tall, rock-covered hills. So steep were the rock walls that no one could expect to climb in or out of this camp. Under this protective umbrella of trees, a working space of perhaps one-kilometer square existed.

Martin made his way down into the site, accompanied by the two unsmiling men. There were thirty men sitting at tables and logs, many cleaning their weapons. Instinctively, they all looked up as Martin arrived, and their eyes all said the same thing:

Strangers are never welcome.

Just then, an excited voice boomed from the cook tent. "Ah, Martin! You are back! Welcome! We thought you had been killed by those rotten SS."

A big hairy arm was thrown around Martin's shoulders and he was violently hugged. Stefan Tadeusz, his former partner in black market dealings, was truly happy to see him. With Stefan's hearty greeting, the wariness of the AK resistance fighters was lifted. Most of them did not know him; there had been turnover since Martin last visited the camp, and new men had joined while others had died. When they found out he had escaped from Auschwitz, they wanted to know everything. Martin spoke late into the night, grateful for an attentive audience as he shared his recent experiences of horror.

Most had heard rumors of what went on at the camps, and these stories alone had fueled their passion against the Germans. Yet many wondered if these were just tales fabricated by the Allied forces to rile them against the Nazis. Hearing first-hand about Auschwitz from Martin was different—the stories suddenly became real. The gas chambers did exist, and millions of people had been incinerated. More than a few men didn't sleep well that night.

Stefan explained what recent actions the group had taken and held up a new, different weapon. "We have come up with a pretty good submachine gun. We make them here. What do you think?"

He handed the gun to Martin, who examined the weapon in his hands. It had a short barrel, and was lighter than any rifle he had ever held, and its magazine held thirty-two bullets. "Can I try it over there?" he asked.

"Oh, no!" Stefan said quickly and shook his head. "Can't fire guns here. Too many German patrols." He took the gun back from Martin. He placed it carefully on the table and ran a cloth up and down the barrel. Eyeing his old friend, he sat down and leaned back, crossing his arms across his chest.

"So, Martin, what brings you back to this bad place? Old scores you'd like to settle?" Stefan smiled; he knew exactly what Martin had in mind.

Martin got up and slowly walked around the campfire. The sight of these men fighting the Germans excited him. He wanted to join them, to take some revenge, but he had even greater plans. He wanted to find the SS lieutenant who had killed his father and mother, and capture and torture those damn Nazi doctors who had caused so much suffering and death. Yet, these were but dreams of revenge and wisps of imagination; he needed a solid partisan group to work with.

He turned to Stefan. "I've heard that the Brits have agreed to put together a Jewish force on the front. Is that true?"

"You are correct, my friend. I have friends who know about this unit. In fact, the British SOE, the Special Operations Executive attached to us—Mark—is expected to parachute in next week with supplies and new strategies to deal with the retreating Germans. I will get you together."

Martin smiled. "Thank you, I need to speak with him. I have a job to finish."

"With purity and with holiness I will pass my life and practice my art…"

23

December 1944
Rostock–Potsdam, Germany

The twenty-second Navel Medical Battalion was moving out of Rostock to somewhere near Berlin. That's all Jürgen Hauptman knew. He had arrived just seven months ago at the height of enemy attacks, yet now the war had slowed; it had been more than one month since the last Allied bombs had fallen on this port city. Some civilians had started to return, yet the streets remained mostly empty. The port was so badly damaged that ships had to anchor deep in the harbor and transfer supplies and people by smaller craft.

The naval medical clinic had escaped the bombs, as it had been placed in a safe area one kilometer from the harbor and next to an elementary school. Once a bustling medical center, it now saw few patients, as most fighting units had been transferred to the east. The officers and doctors who worked there had taken great pride in their facility and received special accolades from Berlin Headquarters for their care.

Now, it was over. The announcement came at a hastily called meeting after lunch. The surgeons were told to delay their afternoon surgeries for an important session with the hospital commandant, Herr Major Brownweiser. These "meetings" had been occurring regularly, once a week, and each dull session usually addressed the need to conserve supplies. Standing at the front of the room, the hospital commandant positioned himself in a military stance, feet apart, trying to look important. With hands clasped behind his back, he appeared uncomfortable. Some weighty issue had obviously come up.

Herr Major was a bit of a man, maybe five foot four and one hundred thirty pounds. He sported a thin mustache, very English-like, and had brown-gray, thinning hair combed straight back. His uniform looked in need of pressing, while his body might have benefited from a good scrubbing. Brownweiser was kind to Jürgen, but had become somewhat morose over the past week. He seemed to know that things on the front were getting worse.

Before the war, Herr Major had been a general practitioner outside of Nuremberg in the small village of Wolframs Eschenbach, a romantic old enclave surrounded by a stone wall, where many of the original buildings dated back to the 1600s. They had been tediously maintained, giving the villagers the comfort of history. An arch guarded by a statue of a soldier standing above a fountain formed the northern entrance to the village. Sharply-gabled houses of brick and wood, each brightly colored, framed the cobbled street, and the hand-set cobblestones produced a curving, whirled pattern that continued up to the main square.

Herr Doctor Brownweiser had a comfortable practice there, taking care of adults and children and delivering babies. He mistakenly thought he was too old and important to his village to be taken by the army.

Why should the Reich ask me, a man in his fifties, to rejoin the war, after all I have been through?"

He had served Germany as a physician during the Great War, rising to the rank of captain, with immense pride in his service to his country. Yet never again did he want to hear the moans of the wounded or see the faces of the dead, as he had each day of the Great War. He had been stationed just outside Verdun and had seen the collapse of the German lines as he treated the scores of injured and dead at his field hospital. Upon receiving a relatively minor shrapnel injury due to a misdirected German mortar, he was evacuated home, just in time for the armistice to be signed.

Politics had never been important to Herr Major. Following World War I, he and his village were left alone by the battles between the various factions and *Freikorps* that plagued Germany during this bitter period of dissension. The political battles brought on by the success of the Nazis over the next two decades scarcely affected his little township. Even after Hitler's war started, the small, rural villages and towns in central Germany were isolated from the shifting political landscape and, to some extent, from the privations of war. The only evidence of change was the absence of young men on the streets of the village. Being self-sufficient for food, the daily reminders of war were centered on gasoline rations and the Reich's radio reports of victories.

But as the war dragged on, daily accounts of injury and death did not escape Wolframs Eschenbach. The enemy planes flew high over the countryside surrounding the village, yet no warning leaflets ever fell from the sky on the town. Doctor Brownweiser certainly preferred to be in this forgotten part of the country.

While his city's physician colleagues rushed to join the Nazi party and apply for vacant university appointments previously held by Jews, Herr Major was satisfied to practice as he had for the last twenty years. He truly believed that, as a veteran, he was untouchable. But he was wrong. On October 15, 1942, Major Bruno Brownweiser was called to serve the Reich and ordered to report to the German Naval base in Rostock. There were no celebrations as he packed up to leave for the city over 670 kilometers away on the Baltic coast. Hannah, his wife of twenty-six years, stood silently on the railway platform wiping tears from her eyes, as she had done once before in June of 1916, shortly after their marriage.

◆◆◆

JÜRGEN HAD BEEN ASSIGNED to the medical clinic at Rostock, caring for soldiers and seamen with minor health problems. He was somewhat disappointed to see only two patients the first day at work. Over the next few weeks, his patient volume increased, but he was seeing few war injuries— just the infrequent venereal diseased patient or some maladjusted sailor looking for an excuse to not go back to his ship.

I was pulled out of medical school just prior to my examinations to do this?

Three weeks after arriving, he approached Major Brownweiser. "Herr Major, I have too much free time. Is there anything else I can do medically, here or in the city, to stay busy?" he asked.

The major stopped and thought for a moment. "Yes, Jürgen there is a place—a children's orphanage, Kinderhaus on Fahrberg Straße, that has been asking for a doctor. Would you like that?"

Jürgen's eyes lit up.

"You could hold morning clinic here and go there in the afternoons. I'm sure they would be happy to see you."

"Thank you, sir, I might like that!"

Jürgen found his way to the orphanage and was surprised that it was a facility for crippled children. It was run by a group of nuns dedicated to the sick. Knocking on the old wooden front door, he was greeted by Sister Candace. "Doctor, I must see your identification, as we are careful what government officials we allow in. In time, you will understand. "

He handed over his military card, and after carefully looking him up and down, she invited him in. "We must be watchful," she apologized. "Sometimes the Gestapo sends over people to try and move our children, but we know what they want to do with them."

Jürgen understood; he recalled the warnings he had received about letting his brother out in public alone. Crippled children were known to disappear.

He was given a brief tour of the dormitory and saw medical condi tions he had only read about. There were children with heads as large as a soccer ball, with eyes disappearing back into their face: hydrocephalus. In addition, he saw children with cerebral palsy, polio, and spina bifida. As the sister walked him about the room, he mentally planned to review the charts of each and every child, and come up with a treatment plan to im-prove their conditions.

The sister appeared surprised by Jürgen's intense interest and sat down to map out a schedule with him to begin the next day. "We are so happy to see you, Doctor Hauptman. Nobody else seems to care."

"Sister, I'm not a doctor yet, but thank you. At home, I helped my younger, disabled brother before I was drafted; I would like to work with these poor children."

Jürgen returned to his medical unit with a spring in his step that had been absent since he left Hamburg.

◆◆◆

HERR MAJOR STARTED THE meeting, grasping a sheaf of papers. Jürgen and the assembled doctors, nurses, and aides quieted down to hear him speak.

"Today, December 19, 1944, the following orders have been delivered to me from headquarters in Berlin: 'Doctors, Nurses, and Medical Personnel: It has been ordered that the twenty-second Naval Hospital unit move from Rostock to Potsdam, where troops of the Reich are guarding Berlin from the Russian forces.'" Taking a deep breath, Herr Major Brownweiser read on. "'Within two days, you shall have packed up your equipment and transported yourselves to Potsdam. A building at town center has been reserved for our clinic and hospital.'" Lifting his eyes from the orders, he added, "The port authorities and Wehrmacht forces have their own medical personnel, and we are not needed here in Rostock any longer. Four trucks have been provided for transport. Please begin your packing tonight." He glanced around the room. "Any questions?" No one spoke. "I wish to leave Thursday morning."

He slowly walked toward the door of the conference room, head lowered as if his unwanted duty had been completed.

Silence filled the room. Jürgen would not have expected Herr Major to acquiesce so easily without comment or complaint. As his eyes followed Brownweiser, he noticed two men in dark gray overcoats sitting at the very back of the room. Gestapo, for sure, he surmised when he saw the men quietly leave the room, apparently satisfied that Herr Major had carried out his instructions.

Jürgen had heard about the Gestapo and their controlling tactics, but this was his first exposure to them. There had been frequent stories of officers and troops deserting to avoid service on the eastern front. As a warning to others, three bodies in Wehrmacht uniforms had been left at the square in Rostock dangling from a tree; all had been captured by the Gestapo and hanged there the prior week. Despite these warnings, desertions continued to be rampant, as news of the war from the BBC made defeat seem inevitable.

Other BBC broadcasts had alarmed the population. Reports of Russian success on the eastern front alarmed the few still left in Rostock. Hearing stories from returning soldiers about rape, torture, and other brutal behavior by the Russian troops scared the civilians. Two large transport ships were sitting in Rostock harbor, loading up with anyone who had the 10,000 DM for passage to Denmark. Gestapo and SS troops guarded the wharves and checked the identification papers of anyone trying to board the vessels.

Jürgen made his way back to Kinderhaus that evening to give the news to Sister Candace. In the few months since he had come to the institution, the spirit of the children and the morale of the sisters had sharply improved. For the first time in years, someone had taken a true interest in the health of these poor children. Sister greeted Jürgen with tears in her eyes.

"My young doctor friend, it meant so much to see you working with us and examining each child as if you cared. No one has done that. And now I cry, not just for the children, but also for you and what may happen to you on your journey east. Please be careful."

As he made his way back to the medical base, Jürgen was also close to weeping. He began to understand the burden of being a physician and the difficulty of walking away from his patients. But he brushed these thoughts aside. It was getting late and he had to help prepare for the move.

Back at the clinic, he aggressively threw himself into packing up supplies, trying to push away the memories of the children he would never see again. The single anesthetic machine was placed in a large crate with several gray cans of ether and chloroform strapped next to it. Surgical instruments were carefully wrapped in muslin and placed in stainless steel trays. Two operating tables and a good supply of towels and white sheets were also added to the crate. Cotton and catgut sutures of all sizes, #3-0 to 5, were stored along with reusable cotton sponges. The operating room lights were dismantled and put into cardboard boxes. A box of antiseptics, including tincture of iodine, alcohol, hydrogen peroxide, and Merthiolate were placed in a container with newspaper wrapped around each bottle. The pharmacist boxed and labeled the limited supply of narcotics and a greatly diminished amount of penicillin and sulfa. A strange variety of uncommon medicines were also on hand, but of little use in war injuries.

He carried out an assortment of crutches, stretchers, and wooden splints along with a limited amount of cotton dressings and placed them in the trucks. There was just one carton of plaster of Paris, yet it would be of little use, as the clinic had run out of wrapping gauze two weeks earlier.

Two days later, Herr Major appeared wistful as he strode for the last time through each room in the clinic and hospital. Dabbing at a tear from his right eye, he locked the front door and walked to the waiting trucks.

Jürgen jumped into the rear of the first Mercedes truck along with three nurses and two medics sitting on two rows of wooden benches facing each other. The physicians rode up front with the driver in the covered cab. It was bitterly cold. The canvas cover of the truck bed allowed little protection from the cold December weather, and the men and women were bundled in multiple layers of clothing and blankets. Herr Major and Captain Drucker, the unit's surgeon, were up front in the second truck. Two additional trucks carrying supplies and equipment completed the convoy.

The ride would have taken ten hours two years earlier, but Jürgen and the other soldiers now were expecting two days. Lines of trucks, carts and wagons going west, in the opposite direction, stretched out for many kilometers on the other side of the road. Much of the route had been bombed out, and detours around destroyed bridges seemed to appear every ten kilometers. One couldn't have planned a more miserable, uncomfortable ride, with ruts and potholes tossing the soldiers around in the back of the trucks. The belching exhaust of synthetic fuel seeped up into the canvassed truck bed while the motor lunged and coughed, much like a patient in the last stages of tuberculosis. The motley group in the truck bed yelled insults and profanity at the driver to little avail, more to vent their own fear than to affect his performance. Despite the discomfort, most of the medical team dozed into the night, leaning against one another.

Jürgen was jerked awake by the sound of thunder or explosions in the distance, to the north. It looked to be a thunderstorm, yet the flashes were not lightning.

Look, over there; bombs are falling.

The driver, noting danger, pulled to a stop five kilometers outside of Oranienburg, a city under aerial attack. All four trucks sat on the side of the road and the doctors climbed out of the truck beds, gathering to watch the explosions in the distance.

Herr Major was the first to speak. "Be aware, all of you, that this level of bombing is happening all over Germany. Such horror…" He paused.

"Shouldn't we go there for the injured?" asked Captain Drucker.

Herr Major, his hands linked behind his back, paced next to the trucks. "We can approach the city when the bombing is through, but we can't stay. Our orders require us to be in Potsdam tomorrow."

The sky was filled with flashes and the air was bursting with repetitive booming sounds erupting like a never-ending thunderclap. And the light from each blast melded together with the flash of the next, as giant flames leapt up all around the central city. Jürgen shivered as he watched infernos embrace one another until the industrial area was a mighty conflagration expanding outward. Bombs stopped falling, and the Allied planes were heard returning to the west. They jumped back into the trucks.

The small medical convoy continued on its way towards the city center. Jürgen and his colleagues had never seen anything as ferocious as this. Phosphorous bombs, bursting yellow and green, coated the buildings with a burning liquid, flowing down walls, sealing doors and air raid shelters shut. A lava-like stream of unquenchable fire engulfed everything it touched.

This is a living hell!

Their truck edged a bit further, cautiously, yet seemed to be pushed by the wind toward the conflagration. Jürgen had read about firestorms, but could never have anticipated what he was experiencing. The trucks stopped on a hill two blocks from the city center and they all stepped out. Strong gusts of cool air came rushing in from all directions, replacing the superheated exhaust of the fires that pushed upwards. The winds were powerful enough to toss streetcars and buses around.

It looks like a child's play set being blown across the backyard.

Trees toppled and crashed down on abandoned vehicles in the street. The wind became more punishing, blowing over them towards the city as the fierce gale sucked all sorts of wood, paper, and boxes into the blaze. These vicious gusts turned into a strange and powerful howling racket as the intensity of the firestorm increased. Jürgen watched as fire trucks stood by helplessly, feebly spraying water only upon the buildings some distance away from the greatest rage of fire.

There were people running away from the buildings, terrorized by it all. Jürgen watched one young woman emerge from a basement with her coat in flames. His heart sank.

What can I do?

He observed in horror as she fell to one knee, tried to rise, and fell again. Her screams pierced the cacophony of the firestorm. Sounds of buildings crashing down, windows bursting from the heat, and muffled cries for help filled the air.

Herr Major stood in front of his group and had to yell over the sounds of the storm. "We must now go. There is nothing we can do for them here and there is a line of ambulances waiting for the fires to burn out so they can enter and take the injured to hospitals close by."

Reluctantly, the clinic staff returned to their trucks. They could only look at each other—all struck mute in awe. Never had any of them witnessed an event so powerful.

None of those poor people could have survived.

The bomb shelters had turned into giant ovens and everyone would die. The medical personnel sat quietly. There were no words. Jürgen and his unit continued down the highway towards Hennigsdorf, six kilometers away, where they stopped and stayed the night.

Most of the men slept, but fitfully. As dawn broke, there was an endless line of people, carts, and animals exiting the city. They were awakened as their trucks started up and moved out to bring the medical unit back into the decimated city. Driving against the flow of the refugees, the trucks spewed their noxious smoke and reentered the city center, now a smoking pyre. Fires were still burning and smoldering in many of the buildings, turning the area into a dirty white haze smelling of burned paper, sulfur, and human flesh.

It is surreal—there are naked bodies, their clothes burned off, littering the streets. Some corpses have literally melted into the road where the asphalt has turned liquid in the eighteen hundred-degree heat. I see dead bodies clinging to iron bars of basement windows, as if they had been caged in a zoo, desperately seeking release.

A fire truck lay abandoned, burned out, its windows smashed through, a victim of the inferno it had come to quell. There were no children to be seen. A few women wandered the streets aimlessly, looking into buildings, peering at the dead, searching for husbands, brothers, and sons. Later, news reports claimed that over twenty thousand civilians had died in the bombing and firestorm.

Jürgen was transfixed by what he'd just seen. He could not imagine the experiences of horror and pain of those who lived in that city. Seeking apparent safety in the underground train stations, thousands had died as the oxygen was sucked out of the tunnels and replaced with black smoke. Heavy air pressure had surged into basements, bursting lungs and eardrums. People had been advised to keep their mouths open when the bombs were dropping to prevent ear pain, but nothing would relieve the pressure if they got caught into a direct strike: their knees would get weak, their bodies felt light, and a sucking sensation would quickly follow as the pressure tried to equalize. Some sought refuge in shelters, many others in home basements. In both, people huddled together like animals in a storm. Yet these underground shelters afforded little protection, as many dead were found charred, almost unrecognizable as human.

This catastrophe transformed Jürgen's whole countenance.

I feel my face has become an unhappy mask; I can't raise the corners of my mouth upward. It is the power of violence that paralyzed my face; my inner feelings are numbed and frozen into this same grim expression.

The memory of this horror would be tattooed into his spirit for the rest of his life. Soon to be a physician, this staggering trauma weighed heavily upon him.

"There is little we can do to help them now," said the major. "The fire brigade and ambulance crews know what to do, and we need to move on."

He had his orders.

When they got to the outskirts of Berlin, his unit was directed by the Wehrmacht police to drive south of the city to avoid Allied bombers. The suburban factories in Wannsee had been totally destroyed, but fortunately much of the war industry had been moved to the countryside two years earlier. Albert Speer, Hitler's choice to head war manufacturing, had done an admirable job of saving much of German industry by dismantling plants and moving them to rural locations.

Jürgen wondered if the Red Cross insignia painted on the canvas tops of their trucks would protect them or just make an excellent target for the Allied bombsights. He knew they were heading into the center of conflict and danger, and an element of fear enveloped him. Sitting in the back of the truck, he sensed the others with him had similar feelings, as they remained eerily quiet. Dodging potholes and bomb craters, they arrived at Potsdam, completing their journey from Rostock, as predicted, in just over two days.

Somehow, Potsdam had miraculously escaped the wrath of war. Maybe because it was away from the industrial areas, it had been of no interest to the British or American bombers. But few civilians were evident. Most had left, joining the endless swarm of refugees fleeing west.

At the corner of Friederickstraße and Rhinestraße, a two-story building stood empty. It was soon to be the home of this naval medical battalion. Up until then, it had been serving as a minor dispensary, awaiting arrival of the clinic medical team. Some soldiers milled about outside the front door, the only sign of life in their otherwise forsaken surroundings.

Inside, a young medic was wrapping a leg with paper bandages. The front receiving room was dark and devoid of any color, housing only a single examination table and a small wooden desk and chair. The windows allowed little light, as they were covered with blackout paper. One bare bulb hung alone from the ceiling above the desk. Beyond this front room "clinic" there was a darkened hallway, again lit by a single bulb, leading to a series of small office rooms. Jürgen noted the absence of wash basins, other than the sink in the bathroom at the end of the corridor.

Herr Major exited his truck and peered into his new surroundings; he walked slowly through the front room, barely responding to the "Heil Hitler" salute given by a young medic. He was deep in thought, trying to envision this series of ramshackle offices as a clinic and operative suites. The accompanying surgeons, Captain Drucker and Lieutenant Wolffe, followed him with a similar downcast expression.

The major spoke. "Doctor Wolffe, please find Sergeant Stern and bring him here. Have him hold off on unloading the supplies, as we've got some work to do to turn this place into a medical facility."

As the sergeant and the other medical support personnel came in, they gathered around Herr Major. "As you can see," he began, "this place is as close to a hospital as a barn would be. We need to clean it up, take out all the trash and broken furniture. Those cracked windows need to be sealed off and the furnace inspected, turned on, or whatever else can be done. We will see no injured soldiers until then. Contact the base CO at his headquarters and see about getting a plumber up here to install sinks outside those two rooms down the hall. And Herr Doktor Hauptman I want you to take charge of the dispensary. Unload the clinic supplies and get ready to handle minor problems."

Jürgen felt his face relax into a smile.

He called me: "Doktor."

"You'll start in the morning. Bring your duffel packs and personal items upstairs; those offices will serve as our barracks."

While the major was issuing orders, the sounds of remote artillery were heard. Twenty, maybe thirty miles away, the *thump, thump* of howitzers kept a steady beat to the east. Several truckloads of soldiers passed by, headed toward the front. Cherubic faces without beards peered out through the canvas in the back of the trucks. Boys no older than fifteen or sixteen had suddenly become soldiers, thrown into the lion's den of war.

It had been posted that anyone born before 1929 should come forward to defend the Reich. These weren't the dedicated Hitler youth who had chosen the path of SS righteousness; these were German youth, many with no desire to fight, lifted from whatever innocence in their lives that still survived. Thrown into battle unprepared as boys, they were to live or die as men. Jürgen wondered how soon it would be before he would see some of these children arrive back on stretchers.

◆◆◆

THEY HAD BEEN IN Potsdam five days. For twenty-four hours, the operating rooms had been going continuously as a steady stream of casualties was delivered. The fighting had been horrendous, with home militia and teenage Wehrmacht viciously defending the lines just fifty miles east of Berlin. The Soviet onslaught had been nonstop, with their big guns raining closer and closer to the clinic. Despite the optimism of some of the commanders at the front, the increased flow of wounded soldiers, and now young boys, demoralized everyone. For the first time, Soviet fighters were seen flying over the city and strafing anyone on the streets. People looked for Luftwaffe protection, but no planes were seen to engage the Soviet aircraft.

The sounds of a screaming Soviet Air Force fighter rolling over Friederickstraße caused all those in the clinic to dive for cover. The plane was firing its machine guns and cannon at anything along the road. Outside, several people were down and others were running. Grabbing a stretcher, Jürgen and the medics ran to a soldier whose supply truck had been strafed with bullets through the windscreen. Blood was pouring from his neck, flowing down and covering the left side of his jacket. Jürgen applied pressure with a compress to stem the venous flow from the internal jugular vein. The injured man was lifted onto a stretcher and carried toward the clinic. Then, just like a messenger from hell, that same fighter came from the opposite direction, its guns blazing and tracers streaming. It damaged the front wall of the clinic and struck down everyone on the street. The buildings across from the clinic burst into one big wall of flame.

"...According to the law of medicine, but to none others..."

24

January 4, 1945
Berlin

Hans was tired from the long train ride from Auschwitz to Berlin. That night, after checking in at the visiting SS officers' quarters, he had stopped at a local tavern, surprised it was still open. The bar was tended by an old man, perhaps seventy-five years of age, who talked constantly and showed little restraint in voicing his feelings.

"Say, Doktor, did you hear about the weekly executions of high-ranking German officers that occur on the Führer's orders? They hang the bodies just out there, in front of my bar, to scare others from questioning the Führer's plans."

Hans swallowed hard and remained silent; he didn't want to encourage any further conversation. "And I see them," the man continued, "officers like yourself, fleeing in staff cars, just like rats—scared shitless."

Hans left shortly after his first drink and returned to his room.

I can't dwell on defeat.

Besides, it was time to get ready for the next day.

Luftwaffe headquarters had been moved to a set of bombproof offices three stories underground. At the time Hitler's expanded Chancellery quarters were built, Wehrmacht and Luftwaffe officials lobbied hard and were given a similar deep, protected shelter to continue work if aerial attacks did strike Berlin. The effectiveness of this planning paid off when, during the daring British bombing of the city on August 4, 1940, the Wehrmacht headquarters suffered no damage.

The main offices of the Luftwaffe Medical experimental programs had previously been situated in Munich on Blumenstraße, but all records and necessary personnel were moved north to Berlin in November 1944, where the final defense of Germany was being prepared. Six feet of steel-reinforced concrete protected this series of bunkers from any bombs the Americans or British might drop.

The next morning, Hans approached the Luftwaffe headquarters and noted that the top two levels of the four-story structure had been heavily damaged by the air raids. He entered.

"What can I do for you, Herr Doktor?" asked the sentry, as he studied the insignias on Hans' lapel and the identification card he handed him.

"I am here to meet with *Generaloberstabsarzt* Oskar Schroeder. He is expecting me, as I have important information for him."

The sentry directed Hans to a passage leading down three flights of stairs to a dimly lit hallway. Here, another SS guard took his identification card, compared it with his face, and opened a heavy metal door.

The usually confident Hans was quite nervous; this was his first opportunity to share his experimental data directly with the Chief of Staff of the Inspectorate of the Medical Service of the Luftwaffe *(Chef de Stabes, Inspekteur des Luftwaffe-Sanitätswesen)*. Hans had last seen Doctor Schroeder eighteen months ago, when he'd presided at a general meeting of officers involved in experimental studies for the Luftwaffe, and seized the opportunity to propose his study to this committee. His research plan was approved, and a modest sum of twenty-five hundred Deutschmarks was authorized for his research program.

Because of his interest in the effects of body cooling, he was initially assigned to the Rascher group at the Dachau Concentration Camp to study healthy male inmates. Doctor Rascher had ongoing studies of different aspects of cold immersion in place prior to his arrival, so Hans was able to insert his own protocol quite comfortably.

Hans's study grant had called for sixty subjects and focused on the relative merits of different fabrics in maintaining the body's core temperature. The experiments involved inducing hypothermia in male subjects by immersing them in tanks filled with water and ice. But as his first year at Dachau drew to an end, he had completed studies on only twenty subjects.

The reasons for his failure were multiple. First, the camp commandant, Sturmbannführer Martin Gottfried Weiss, had daily work quotas required for war-related factories and needed healthy males to fulfill them. In addition, certain prisoners, specifically clergymen, were not allowed to be subjects in experimental studies. Third, by the time the Jews arrived at the camp, many were weakened and half-dead from their train ride. The rest of the inmate population was on the verge of starvation and ill with chronic dysentery. To find suitable candidates for his study he had to select from hundreds of recent transports and, to make matters worse, he was in competition with the munitions factories. They, too, needed able-bodied men. A series of memos had already been exchanged through Rascher and the camp commandant outlining the difficulty in obtaining subjects. SS Chief Heinrich Himmler ultimately intervened, noting the value of these experimental studies. Orders were quickly dispatched to release more working male inmates to the physicians.

Hans filed a preliminary report on May 10, 1944, ten months after his cold immersion investigations began. It included an addendum that his project be continued at a larger camp, where more healthy "specimens" would be available. His request was approved, and Hans was assigned to the Auschwitz Concentration Camp, just outside Krakow, Poland, where he arrived on July 12, 1944. In the ensuing six months, he was able to study an additional forty healthy males and gather enough data to complete his original study. He had not expected a significant death rate, yet he lost 30 percent of his subjects far too soon, all dying within twenty-four hours of the first immersion episode in five-degree Centigrade water. It wasn't until his twelfth subject expired that he noted that immersion of the head and neck appeared to be more commonly associated with early demise. At this point, he altered his protocol. He had his assistant control the head and neck to keep those parts outside of the immersion.

In his report, Hans detailed the above information, as well as the conditions under which he worked. Besides SS physicians, there were inmates—Jew physicians, who had been made available to help in pathological studies. Doctor Miklos Nyiszli, a Hungarian pathologist, performed postmortem studies on Hans's dead subjects, and this encouraged Hans to expand his experimental approach. Tissue slides could easily demonstrate organ damage secondary to cold, and could provide even more value to the original study. Another inmate physician, Michel Katz, assisted with his study protocol.

By November 1944, the additional forty males had been studied and the data recorded. Dutifully, Hans prepared two reports for the Luftwaffe: "The Effects of Cold Immersion, Noting Insulating Properties of Natural and Synthetic Fabrics on Core Temperature" and "Viscous Changes in Response to Rapid Cooling in Humans."

He pointed out that his original grant proposal dealt only with measurements of vital signs during immersion of his subjects in freezing water while the later studies were done on those that died during the process. Hans soon recognized the additional value of the postmortem observations and the pathologic changes in various organs that occurred. He was fully confident that this expansion of his study would result in accolades from his superiors and the recognition he deserved.

He sent his completed report to Doctor Schroeder, who curtly responded: "Thank you for your information, Doctor Bloch. We will review it and report back to you."

Having heard no response for four weeks, Hans feared his project had not made a significant impression. Now, with the Auschwitz camps on the verge of closing, it was the perfect time to present his data directly. He wrote a second letter to General Schroeder saying that he would like to spend a few minutes presenting his results. Anxiously checked the mail daily, he hoped to get a positive response. Finally, a letter arrived December 30, inviting Hans to Berlin to discuss his results.

He approached the general's office with trepidation. "Enter, Herr Doktor," a strong voice boomed in response to Hans's single rap on the door. Hans crisply marched in and stood in front of General Schroeder's desk. The older man made no effort to rise and greet him. He appeared extremely tired and thinner than Hans remembered him, and his hair was graying, with equal recession along each side of his forehead. His eyes appeared sunken and hollow, and his collar hung loosely around a bird-like neck.

The general had the Hypothermia Project file open on his desk, and it appeared as if he had been reviewing the data.

"Heil Hitler!" Hans announced, raising his right arm as he had done a thousand times before. The general responded weakly with a matching salute, yet without the same enthusiasm.

"Thank you for giving me this time with you, General. My train arrived last night. I know that you must be occupied with many more important things than listening to me discuss our progress," said Hans.

"No, no, Doctor Bloch, your work was most important, at one time, and I must see what you have found," replied the general without conviction. "It's a shame this study wasn't finished sooner. It would have been vital to apply your findings to our pilots. Of course, even with fewer missions, we may still lose some planes over the Baltic and North Seas, and many will still die of hypothermia while they await rescue. Please go on—tell me about the project."

He was nervous, and found his mind drifting back to his first piano recital as a child in front of an audience and the butterflies that accompanied it.

Hans launched into a concise, yet complete, presentation of his data on cold immersion, but almost immediately he saw the general's interest begin to wane. At intervals, he would nod his head forward, indicating that he continued to be engaged, but not to the extent Hans had anticipated. Hans's delivery took no longer than twenty minutes, yet it seemed like a lifetime as he struggled to complete his report. The general's attention seemed to increase sharply when he reported on the postmortem studies on his subjects. Yet he posed no questions. Sensing Schroeder's distraction, Hans skipped over some of the minutiae in an effort to end his talk as quickly as possible.

Schroeder sat quietly for a long three minutes and then spoke. "Your report expands the findings that Doctor Rascher has described at Dachau. Doctor Bloch, at one time this information would have been of immense value to the Reich and would have certainly saved many of our aircrews." Then Schroeder became suddenly serious and asked sternly, "Tell me, Doktor, was it really necessary to sacrifice so many subjects?"

Hans was not ready for such a question and tried to look confident as he delivered his response. "Sir, we had the opportunity to study some early subjects who died unexpectedly, and found useful changes in tissue under the microscope. I thought you might find that area of the project… interesting."

The general looked away at that remark. Leaning back, he removed his rimless glasses and rubbed his eyes. He stared down at his desk and then up at Hans.

"The war will be over in just a few months. The Reich has lost. Look around us... There is rubble, despair, and most of the civilians have left. Those who remain live like rats coming out between air raids, scouring the streets for food, gathering wood to burn, and stealing clothes from those who have died. It is not just Berlin; almost every major city in Germany has massive destruction such as this. I know I shouldn't be talking like this to you; others might call it defeatist, treason. But I have seen the devastation with my own eyes as I have flown to various airbases throughout the Fatherland and personally viewed this demolition of our cities. We have fighter planes, some bombers, and many inexperienced pilots, but we have little fuel to fly them. A few fighters based near Berlin will help in defending this city. No more bombers and crew will be lost over the Baltic or North Sea; no planes are flying there. We will have no fighters lost over the English Channel; our bases are gone in the rest of Europe. What the Chancellery will not admit is that this war is over."

Hans had not expected this admission. His hands started to sweat and a pulsation began in his right temple. Being isolated in Auschwitz for so long had taken him away from the war. When colleagues had mentioned BBC reports of Allied successes, he took it with the same lack of conviction that he felt when he heard the Wehrmacht radio announcements. But failure, absolute loss, was never in his mind. Perhaps he was so wrapped up in his own world of medicine and experiments that he had no idea how bad things had become. Yes, the Soviets had advanced to Poland, but the briefings and reports had emphasized the strength of the reserve and home front forces.

Positive productivity reports on armament production, synthetic fuel stores, and military hardware had been disseminated monthly to the officers at Auschwitz. Despite some losses, the Wehrmacht had done well at the Battle of the Bulge, emphasizing the reserve strength of the infantry and Panzer divisions. And while he might have expected the war to end with less conquest than Hitler had promised, he never anticipated total defeat.

But if we lose the war, what happens to me?

"General, this study may have significant benefits other than to our pilots." Hans tried to sound confident. "I can see the day when either heating or cooling patients may be beneficial in their treatment. Might I go to Kiel and discuss my findings with Professor Holzlohner at the University?"

"Doctor Bloch, if you must go, you have my permission to travel to Kiel. But be careful, as the British and Americans will soon overrun the U-boat base there."

General Schroeder stood up, signaling the meeting was over. "I will place this report in my files. Others may not understand what we have tried to do here for the Reich, our brave soldiers and pilots. They will not recognize that these men from the camps did volunteer for your study. If they were not part of a study, they would certainly face death, either directly through the gas chambers, or slowly through starvation and illness. We saved them, yes, for a while, and someone should thank us. Our adversaries may see it differently—experimenting on inmates, even killing some directly. The Soviets and the Americans might consider you and me criminals... I can't predict exactly what will happen to us. But you must understand that I will probably destroy any studies done at the concentration camps once the end is near. And, Doctor Bloch, I would certainly burn your second, unauthorized study—the postmortem exams and histological specimens—as soon as possible; I believe you understand. Take care, and good luck."

The words "once the end is near" hung in the air just long enough for Hans to feel their impact. For the first time, concern for his life after the war enveloped him. He knew that his Luftwaffe Medical Services and SS credentials would be chains that followed him and his work at Auschwitz and activities as an SS physician would certainly attract the postwar investigations to come. Hans had hoped to hear a more optimistic forecast from General Schroeder, one that included the promise of newer weapons or even words of a negotiated armistice.

Yet even now, rumors were spreading that Hitler might be pushed aside and Reich generals would meet with the English and Americans, especially to halt the Soviets and their intent to occupy all of Eastern Europe. Meanwhile, Hitler had chosen to conceal himself in his bunker and force his troops to fight to the end, no matter what the reality might be. His own secret spy system kept him apprised of dissenting voices so that they might be quashed before significant opposition to him materialized.

Hans walked past the Luftwaffe building and headed west down Lindenstraße. It was time to plan for the war's end and his future. Authorized travel to Kiel certainly now masked his true intention to avoid possible postwar prosecution for his activities at the camps. While listening to General

Schroeder, he had begun to formulate his own image of postwar Germany as a montage of an occupied, defeated Fatherland raced through his mind. Beyond the obvious visual damage and civilian disruption, there would be ruin to the very fabric of German society. The victors and the restive populace would look for someone to blame for this war and its carnage, and SS officers would be prime targets. It was time for him to go home; he needed to formulate a plan.

The offices of the SS were within two blocks of the Luftwaffe building, and Hans walked quickly feeling the January chill on his face. Every building he passed had some evidence of bomb damage; over 50 percent of the windows were broken in each structure he saw. Women crouched in stairwells in shoddy clothes, begging to anyone who passed for food, clothing, or money. Occasionally, one would approach Hans as if to silently offer herself to him for anything he could give her.

To what level has the wholesome German woman and mother fallen?

He turned right on Friedrichstraße and continued towards the headquarters of the SS. The front entrance was impressive; to the right of the heavy, carved wooden door stood a lion. An SS sentry stood to the left side and looked at Hans's identification card before allowing him in. He walked down a dim hallway and entered the offices of Major Karl Genzken and presented his papers to Leutnant Salzberg, the adjutant.

"What can we do for you, Doctor Bloch?" said the lieutenant.

Without hesitation, Hans answered, "I have just come from the work camp, Auschwitz, which is closing down. I was attached to the Luftwaffe Department of Experimental Studies as a medical officer stationed in Auschwitz. My grant and studies have been completed. I have presented the results of my experiments to General Schroeder, who wants me to discuss this with Doktor Holzlohner in Kiel. Since I am on administrative leave, I would like to travel to Kiel and see my family, as well."

"You are not with the group of SS officers that are meeting here, are you?" asked the lieutenant.

"No... I am alone."

He asked Hans to take a seat for a moment so that he might review his papers. Returning with file in hand, he glanced through it, noting no areas of concern. "I will prepare your orders right away," volunteered the young officer.

Within twenty minutes, Hans was on his way with orders in hand, giving him passage to the western part of the country and his home city, Kiel. He was directed to the SS transport office, offered up his papers, and inquired as to any transportation heading in that direction. The sergeant reviewed his train schedule and informed Hans that few, if any, trains were headed west. The war effort required the tracks to remain open for easterly traffic of materials and troops. He did say, however, that there was an SS staff car headed in the direction of Kiel, to Lübeck, where certain high-ranking individuals were to board a ship to Sweden. "If there is space in the car, would that accommodate your needs?"

Hans answered with a grateful, "Yes."

The young soldier disappeared for a few minutes, returning with an additional sheaf of orders and instructions to show up in front of the building at eight the following morning.

♦♦♦

It was a Friday afternoon in Berlin. Soldiers and staff were leaving their offices to go home or to their barracks. Most everyone on the streets was in uniform. The electric trolleys were still running, carrying just a few people. The life, vitality, and spirit of the Berlin Hans had known most of his life had all but disappeared.

Posted next to the train stop was a placard noting the performance of the Berlin Philharmonic, January 5—that same night. Hans stared at it. He couldn't quite comprehend that the orchestra would still be performing. The concert would be at the old Opera House at 6:00 p.m., with tickets available at the door. His watch said 5:30, and he could walk there in fifteen minutes. Perhaps, he would catch a glimpse of the old, civilized society he once knew.

He sat fifteen rows from the stage. Looking around, most of the patrons were in uniform, officers from all branches, including the SS. A smattering of civilians, a few older men and many women, made up the rest of the audience. Sitting up front was Heinrich Himmler, surrounded by a protective cordon of SS. The orchestra members were dressed in tuxedos. Even the women musicians wore men's clothing, down to the black cummerbund. The formality was a reprieve, a sharp contrast to the disintegration of the city and its functions that was the reality outside the concert hall doors. The program featured Wagner's *Lohengrin*. Hitler's love for anything Wagner often dictated the conductor's choice of music for a performance.

The concert was timed to end prior to the usual onset of English bombing raids; tonight, it would be over by nine, giving everyone a chance to return to their homes, and later to their shelters. For the first time in three years, Hans relaxed to the point of falling asleep ten minutes into the first piece. Refreshed at the end, he walked quickly to his assigned quarters to get ready for bed, and later, most probably, a trip to the subterranean shelter beneath the SS headquarters.

As he entered the officers' lodgings, the lone sentry was sitting at his desk listening to *Drahtfunk* cable radio. This ingenious device was produced in Germany to be attached to home radios and give early warning of bomb attacks. The attachment gave off a steady tick-tock, tick-tock sound, an assurance of no incursions. But as soon as an enemy bomber crossed into the Reich, the sound changed and became an alarming ping-ping-ping noise. At regular intervals, an announcer would interrupt a program, advising the location of the bombers, the type, and the direction in which they were headed. In some civilian neighborhoods, people would take turns monitoring the radio; there was always someone on "Drahtfunk duty."

City dwellers often resorted to wearing "all-purpose" clothing. This allowed them to jump out of bed and go directly to the shelters without need to change. Because the attacks occurred close to eleven at night, people got into the habit of eating in the late afternoon and going to bed much earlier than was their custom.

As the populace of Berlin could not count on electrical power, gas delivery, or adequate water being available each day, they filled their bathtubs with water and cooked food while gas and electricity was running. Then they stored food and water for those days without utilities, counting on ice deliveries to keep their food from spoiling. To keep morale up, the authorities increased the rations of meat, lard, and butter in areas under recurrent bombardment.

◆◆◆

HANS SAT IN THE lobby of the officers' quarters prior to retiring, reading the day's newspaper. At 9:30 p.m., he heard the Drahtfunk sound change to the dreaded ping-ping. The radio announced that a formation of one hundred British B-17s had crossed the border at Trier, bypassed Wiesbaden and Frankfurt, and was headed northeast towards Leipzig and Halle, in the direction of Berlin. The announcer estimated that they would be over Leipzig at 11:00 p.m. and reach Berlin by 11:30 p.m.

The radio broadcasters were not known for their accuracy in determining exact time of bombardment, so Hans went to his room, changed to fatigues, and packed his bag, fully prepared for a morning trip to the shelter at whatever time it came. He lay down and waited for the piercing screech of the air raid sirens. He even managed to fall asleep, but was abruptly awakened by the sirens and simultaneous knocks on his door by the sentry alerting the officers to the raid. Grabbing his pillow and blanket, he followed the signs and arrows directing him to the underground shelter for the SS.

While on his way down the stairs, he recalled the regular bombing that had occurred near Auschwitz. In August 1944, bombing of the Monowitz synthetic oil plant started to occur every other day. Even though the concentration camp was not targeted, the SS were forced to go to shelters with each alert, once or twice a week. The only time damage was done to the camp was when a stray bomb blew up a railroad siding just outside of Birkenau. He sometimes wondered why the gas chambers and crematoriums weren't bombed, but concluded they had little military value to the enemy. It certainly wasn't a matter of avoiding injury to the inmates; hundreds of inmate laborers had been killed when the Farber plant suffered damage from an air raid.

Comfortable sofas, chairs, and cots were arranged in the large lounge for those wishing to sleep. A table laden with fruit, baked goods, and coffee stood next to a counter loaded with a generous supply of reading material. This shelter had been built to be self-sufficient. A separate generator guaranteed electricity when service was interrupted. Several five-gallon containers of water were stored in a room where a small pantry held a large supply of canned vegetables and meats in reserve. Two relatively large inlet fans drew air from the outside, from opposite sides of the building, providing a background hollow noise of air moving through two vents.

When Hans entered, there were perhaps ten to twelve officers in the room. He didn't recognize any of these men. Two of them occupied an office in the far corner of the lounge, with one speaking into a telephone, flailing his arms in an agitated fashion. Hans could see him only from the back, but he imagined it could be Himmler.

At the opposite end of the lounge, a serious group of six officers sat around a table filled with maps. Casually strolling, Hans noticed that the officers were studying a large map of South America.

Strange, really strange… Why would they be interested in a place so far away?

He was tempted to stop and find out what they were talking about but stopped short when large thumps could be felt above the shelter. A louder concussion seemed to come from just above, followed by a shower of dust that was sucked into the inlets and spread into the lounge. The smell of smoke and oil quickly filled the room, resulting in a rash of coughing among the officers. Further concussions shook the shelter coincident with the muffled sounds of exploding bombs for the next twenty minutes. When the smoke tried to enter the lounge from under the single door entry, an officer ran to stuff towels under the door to complete a seal. Still, the vents continued to fill the lounge with light dust and some smoke, but mostly fresh air. The attack ended forty minutes later, with an 'all clear' signal following close behind.

The upper two floors of the SS offices had been severely damaged. A small fire had started just under the roof, but the fire brigade had arrived quickly and was scaling ladders onto the upper floors. The officers' quarters were untouched, and Hans and the other SS officers returned to their rooms, each man visibly shaken by the closeness of the explosions. Back in his bed, Hans had trouble falling asleep as the sounds of the attack reverberated in his head.

"In purity and according to divine law..."

25

January 6, 1945
Berlin to Potsdam

At 7:00 a.m., there was a wake-up rap on the door to his room, as he had requested. He showered, cleaned up, and shaved, getting ready for his trip. As he looked at his face in the mirror, Hans saw the stress lines that were forming in his forehead and the shadows that had started to appear beneath his eyes. His blond hair was now tinged with gray.

Ahh, an interesting sheen I hadn't noticed; more professorial in appearance.

The Mercedes sedan was parked outside of the SS headquarters with a soldier sitting behind the wheel, the engine idling. A thin sheet of snow had covered the street during the night, lightly frosting the broken streetscape, somehow muting all that was torn apart during the preceding night's attack. Hans spoke to the driver and handed him his papers.

Two officers arrived, and Hans quickly raised his right arm. "Heil Hitler," he saluted smartly, introducing himself. He did not recognize these men, but they identified themselves as General Conrad Ravenscroft and Colonel Karl Gunter. Three large document bags were carried with them into the car and held tightly by the officers; duffel bags were placed in the rear boot. Once the gear had been stowed, Hans was invited into the back seat, and the black staff car roared away down Friedrichstraße towards the southern highway, in the direction of Potsdam.

The sergeant spoke. "To the north, most of the roads are badly damaged and bridges are out. We're less likely to come under aerial attack if we head out of Berlin in this direction, towards Potsdam."

Traffic was light going west. A few military trucks were heading in the same direction; all of them empty, none carrying soldiers. As Hans looked around, he saw an increasing pedestrian stream—some pulling wagons or pushing carts with chests, suitcases, and other articles piled high. The exodus consisted of mostly women and old men; they had gathered what belongings they had as they tried to survive the dual conflict of bombs and deprivation. Interestingly, there were no animals to be seen and no horses pulling wagons.

A series of bomb craters and broken concrete marked the devastation on the roads leading through the Charlottenburg-Wilmersdorf area of southern Berlin. What used to be a collection of industrial buildings that housed furniture manufacturing, metal foundries, and wire works, now appeared more like a ramshackle dump of deflated structures. There were piles of stone and corrugated iron bent into a thousand shapes. Hastily made fences surrounded the destroyed plants, yet they could not prevent the determined access of those in need of wood for fires and metal for shelter. The superficial dusting of snow perhaps made the visible destruction a bit more tolerable to one's eye.

Maybe a grand snow could hide all this from view and, for a few days, cover up this folly.

On the left side of the road, a chemical plant lay in ruins with 160-liter drums haphazardly scattered about, as if struck by a giant bowling ball. Two large smokestacks had toppled over, crossing each other in an X-pattern, an inviting site for a British bombardier to practice his art. Several tanker cars on the siding had also turned over and spilled their contents into what had become a multicolored toxic lake encompassing the entire railroad yard.

From time to time, the car was stopped to allow approaching military vehicles to pass, and the road was often reduced to one lane. The government always repaired roads quickly following attacks; it had been a point of pride that the Office of Transportation could fill holes and make passable any road within four hours. Now, with mounting damage, a repair often took days or was not done at all; there was so little labor available.

Looking out the side window, Hans saw crews of foreign laborers working alongside the roadway. These men looked familiar, with their drawn faces, foul clothing, and emaciated bodies.

I feel like I'm back at the camps.

The inmate garments—cheap cotton fabric with alternating gray and white stripes—was common to all the concentration camps. A crew of six was working on a series of gaps in the pavement produced by recent bomb attacks. Two men struggled with pickaxes, chopping down on the pavement and removing loose asphalt. Two others with shovels cleared out the rubble, emptying their loads on the side of the road. A mound of sand had been dumped by the roadside and other laborers used it to fill highway defects. As recently as six months ago, it would have been filled with asphalt, but the supply of petroleum had diminished, a necessary ingredient of this paving material.

Two uniformed soldiers stood guard, leaning on their rifles, trying to appear important. When the staff car approached, they became animated, as if awakened from their stupor, and began prodding the work crew with their insults and rifle butts.

◆◆◆

BEING JUNIOR TO THE officers, Hans waited for one of them to initiate conversation. It would have been impolite for him to begin. After ten minutes, General Ravenscroft turned in his seat, regarding Hans warmly, and asked, "Herr Doktor, what mission brings you to the West?"

"I must report to the University Clinic at Kiel and Herr Professor Holzlohner concerning my most recent studies."

"Very interesting, Herr Doktor," offered the general. "Maybe you could enlighten us unpolished military types about what you were doing, and what your studies have found. It's a long drive, and it's time we improved on our intellectual and scientific knowledge. You can be our mentor for the road."

Hans was excited to have an audience and readily began his discourse, simplifying some of the medical terms as he described the studies. As he spoke, he stressed the practical basis for his work and how it would save Luftwaffe lives. During his discussion, no one raised the obvious issue—the specter of the virtual dissolution of the most powerful air force in Europe. Colonel Gunter was most interested in the subjects of the studies. "Herr Doktor, did you just use Jews as your subjects, or...were there Gypsies, prisoners of war, or captured American pilots, perhaps?"

"Auschwitz-Birkenau consisted of Jews from all over Europe," Hans replied. "There were some Poles, Gypsies, and Soviets, but mostly Jews from Poland. We had little access to prisoners of war, although they would have made the best subjects."

He went on to talk about the difficulty in the selection process and the competition with the manufacturing plants for the healthiest and best men.

Although both the general and the colonel had been familiar with several of the camps earlier in the war, they were surprised when Hans spoke about the typhus and typhoid epidemics and the rampant starvation present among the internees.

General Ravenscroft mentioned the success of Albert Speer and the Todt organization in bringing "foreign workers" to German factories, and was dismayed to hear about the loss of valuable labor in the camps due to starvation and disease. These men seemed to understand the complexities of subject selection, the needs for the labor force, and the poor condition of male concentration camp inmates. The exchange was precise, with little rancor. It was professional and lacked the emotionalism common in other settings when Jews were mentioned.

Little was discussed as to the destination of the other officers. Hans learned only that they were both from the Ministry of Armaments. If during the conversation any mention was made of their travel, the general coolly avoided further discussion by stressing the importance of this mission to Germany's future.

They had been on the road for two hours. Entering Potsdam from the north, they exited Highway 115, driving to the center of the city. Streams of refugees were moving west along the road, as if Potsdam offered some kind of safe haven from the war.

Whatever semblance of peacefulness existed was suddenly destroyed by a single twin-engine Soviet MIG-5 (Mikoyen-Gurevich DES 200) strafing the road with 50mm cannons. Those on foot dove for the ditch on the right shoulder. Hans's driver veered sharply to the left, heading their vehicle into an abandoned warehouse yard. Seeing an open bay in the building close to the road, he drove in to hide his vehicle, knowing that the Soviet pilot would be flying back looking for them—a certain trophy.

Three minutes passed. *I hear a motor...it's coming back.* The high-pitched whine turned into a murderous roar as the plane returned. The clatter of the .50-caliber bullets bouncing off the pavement was accompanied by screams of injury, as the ditch provided little protection from the vengeful fighter pilot. Hans looked back and watched several civilian women drape themselves protectively over their children. Although he could not see the airplane, he could hear the MIG-5 flying along the road toward the town's center with both cannons blasting almost continuously.

"They have spent their ammunition and they have gone back," the colonel muttered. "It is safe to proceed." As if he didn't quite believe it, the driver slowly backed out of the bay and cautiously proceeded toward the center of Potsdam.

Blocking the roadway was an overturned military truck, and lying beside it were two dead soldiers on stretchers. On the south side of the street, the glass front of a building housing a military treatment unit was shattered. At its entrance, two medics and a young doctor lay massively injured and bleeding heavily. Hans jumped out of the car without thinking and attended to the injured. Large, gaping wounds in the right chest of the first medic bled profusely from the pulmonary artery; it was only a brief moment after Hans bent down to help that the victim stopped breathing and he realized there was nothing he could do. The second medic had the left side of his skull blown away; the only signs of life were the terminal respirations; those, too, ended within seconds of the staff car's arrival.

The last injured man appeared conscious. Although seriously wounded, he spoke to Hans and identified himself as a medical student from Hamburg. A large open wound in the mid-abdomen exposed his small intestine. Profuse bleeding welled up from deep within the belly cavity. Suspecting an injury to the vena cava, Hans wrapped a sheet around the midsection and applied as much pressure as he could, trying to slow the massive venous ooze. A bag of emergency supplies was lying next to the injured medic. Hans started an intravenous line and normal saline was infused as fast as the line would allow. Jürgen Hauptman would live for another fifteen minutes before succumbing, and Hans, in that short time period, would learn enough about this unfortunate dying student to create a new future for himself.

Hans developed tears as he watched the young man slowly die. He rested his lifeless head on a makeshift pillow, and then reached into Hauptman's wallet and removed his military identification card. It read: "Jürgen

Hauptman, age twenty-four, senior medical student, the University of Hamburg; temporarily assigned as preceptor, the 28th Naval Medical Battalion." Hans dutifully returned the wallet, having surreptitiously slipped the ID card into his own pocket. He left the rest of the contents undisturbed.

One man's death, another's freedom.

"Will I carry out my life and my art..."

26

January 21, 1945
Auschwitz

Mengele's booming voice startled Michel from his mid-afternoon lethargy brought on by the monotony of recalculating statistics. "Please, Doctor Katz, I would appreciate some help in completing this work, as the final treatise is lacking only the microscopic descriptions."

He badly wanted to finish his paper on twin studies and he clearly needed Michel's assistance. Doctor Nyiszli had left Auschwitz with thousands of other inmates on a forced march to concentration camps in the West prior to finishing the work for Mengele. The camp doctor's gruff voice sounded almost whining; he had never asked for anything from him with such humility.

Michel didn't have much time to dwell on the answer, as the SS physician stood impatiently in front of him with his hands on his hips, waiting. Michel, too, had wanted to leave the camp on foot with the rest of the inmates, but his problem was Tamara. Since she was not yet able to leave her hiding spot, he had to stay.

For three weeks, it had been quiet at the camp. The transports had stopped; there were no more gassings. The last train filled with Jews had been delivered to Auschwitz eight weeks earlier in November 1944. The final Sonderkommando group had been dispatched shortly thereafter with gunshots to the back of their heads. After that mass execution, the guards and Kapos seemed to know the end was near, and eased up on their punishing behavior. Rumors had spread quickly that the SS was preparing to empty the camp.

Twenty railcars had been deposited at the Auschwitz rail yards, and prisoners had been loaded onto half of them. The unfortunate inmates stayed locked inside, suffering in the January cold with no food. With the pounding of Russian heavy artillery to the east, an order to leave the camps was dispatched, yet these cars sat on the tracks for three days until locomotives arrived. The remaining guards ignored the cries of the prisoners. Even after the cars left the station, many inmates did not reach their destination alive, frozen to death in their cramped tombs.

The greatest number of inmates, however, had been pushed out of camp several days earlier on foot, with Doctor Nyiszli among them. As many as sixty-five thousand people were forced to march along the road going west, carrying their few belongings and forming a trail of death three miles long. Roughly divided into nationalities, each group had its cadre of SS guards to keep the inmates moving.

The first group had left the camp on January 18, 1945, and the massive on-foot evacuation continued daily, with thousands of inmates dying of exposure and starvation as they were pushed to march toward the camps in the West. They were to board trains assembled fifty kilometers away, and be taken to concentration camps in Germany.

Only a few thousand prisoners remained at Auschwitz, including those important to the maintenance of the buildings and others who stored and guarded the stolen items in the warehouse. The camp infirmaries were full of the dying, but there were no medicines or bandages, and most inmate doctors avoided making rounds in their assigned sick wards; there was nothing more they could do for the patients. Many of the ill could not communicate in more than weak whispers and mumbling gibberish, anyway. Yet, a few physicians walked through these barracks each day with kind words or encouragement, knowing, however, that these poor souls would not make it out alive. Soon they would join the daily stack of ten to twenty corpses laid outside each night to await pickup by the death wagons the following morning.

♦♦♦

January 22

THREE DAYS LATER, ACTIVITY at the camp had slowed to a standstill, and few guards remained. A frosting of snow covered the ground and seemed to add to the quiet now embracing Auschwitz. Michel had finished the slides for Mengele, and they were packed away with other study materials in the back of an ambulance. Early on the evening of the twenty-third, a convoy of three ambulances departed towards Dresden, and Mengele must have left with them, as he was never seen again. The Russian guns in the distance continued to boom unanswered, edging closer every day. Lines of Wehrmacht trucks and equipment going west passed by the camp, driven by what appeared to be teenage boys—fear etched in their faces.

January 25

ONE OF THE FINAL shipments to the camp before the Germans fled consisted of a score of red and white paint cans. Tamara watched the Germans paint the canvas tarps of Wehrmacht trucks white with a red cross on the top in an apparent effort to mimic ambulances and avoid the diving fighters of the Russian Air force. Now, as the Soviet troops closed in, the remaining guards and SS officers dashed out of their quarters, throwing their duffel bags into these bogus emergency vehicles, oblivious to the silent cheers of the inmates as they passed out of this hell.

They're scattering like scared rats whose nests have been destroyed, she thought.

As the last of the SS departed, Michel brought Tamara out of the laboratory and into the camp. Walking down the outside stairs on his arm, it felt as if her personal cage had been let open and she was allowed to spread her wings again. For so long she had only been able to observe the camp through a narrow vent in the attic on one side of the building, but now she could see the entire grounds as the barracks stretched endlessly in both directions. And she could watch as the survivors sensed their first taste of freedom.

A change had occurred in those left in the camp. The anticipation of imminent freedom was expressed in different ways by those barely alive enough to appreciate its meaning. Nevertheless, there were some men and women who still had the capacity to shed tears. Others, sitting on the ground, attempted to stand and hobble toward the main gate to show that they, too, understood and were ready for their liberation. Many could manage but one or two steps before they slowly sank to the ground again. But, in a brash blending of multiple languages, "Goodbye, bastards!" filled the air as the fleeing Germans made their exit.

Tamara peered into one of the infirmary barracks. Here were the forgotten souls crowded into beds, so weakened that they could not come out to witness the departure of their murderers. Most of them would not survive the next few days as they lay on their foul mats of filthy straw. These men did not communicate. They lay awkwardly with their knees flexed up to their chins and eyes receded into dark sockets. Scabs and non-healing ulcers covered the exposed areas of their arms and legs. It was quiet, except for the occasional sound of gibberish or moaning coming from somewhere inside the room. Tamara stood mute in the doorway.

It saddens me…these sick people will never know the joy of liberation.

As she and Michel walked around the expanse of Auschwitz-Birkenau, he spent time explaining the layout of the camp to her. The gates and barbed wire separating the individual camps were now open, left unlocked by the fleeing guards. The French camp lay in the distance and a few inmates could be seen packing up. Closer were the barracks of the Hungarian and Polish inmates, now almost empty, save for a few survivors sitting stoically on the ground. The Gypsy camp to the west had been exterminated on September 28, 1944; it now stood abandoned, having become a mausoleum containing only memories of this vibrant group. The inmates seemed to have withstood the atrocities better than most, only to be marched to the gas chambers like the millions who had gone before them. Michel pointed out the open gate to the women's camp adjacent to the area where the camp orchestra played during daily roll call.

Tamara surveyed the internees now free.

They just stand there, as if paralyzed. I expected them to rush out of the gates, away from this horrible place, and enjoy their new liberty. I, too, wish I could run out, but to where?

Outside the complex, a similar yet different kind of despair existed. That same day, two of the stronger young men had walked out of camp and traveled four kilometers to the IG Farber complex at Monowitz, looking for food or anything of value; they returned empty-handed, having searched every abandoned building and home in the village. The last of the factories, the Monowitz synthetic rubber plant had been evacuated after the Allied bombing of August 20, 1944. No life lingered there, either; not one person was sighted. The remaining plant overseers had vanished quickly, joining the lines of refugees and inmates marching west.

Everyone had expected the Russians to enter just after the murderers fled; they had all looked so forward to liberation. Yet the grounds at Auschwitz-Birkenau lay silent for forty-eight hours after the last of the SS guards had departed. It was clear to Tamara and Michel that it was best to stay put for now. Winter had not yet started to fade and the nights were still cold enough to require heat. Yet, there was none. After the Germans had exploded the remaining crematoriums, they had shut off the utilities to the barracks. On that first night of freedom, several hundred more people died.

The camp inmates plundered the near-empty camp stores for food and drink, but found very little. What they did scavenge, they kept for themselves, huddling in corners and clutching stale bread. A few good people gathered up what food they could carry and went to the infirmary, distributing the meager rations to those who could still eat. Although they were relieved to be free from their captors, the liberated mostly sat and waited.

♦♦♦

RABBI ROSENBERG WAS IN the first group of thousands forced to march out on January 19 and they had been traveling on foot for six days towards the Buchenwald Concentration Camp. Soon, they were told, they would board a train at Wodzislaw to finish the last hundred miles of the journey. It had been three days since they had been given anything of substance to eat, and the rabbi was suffering as much from watching his people starve as from the hunger that screamed from his own belly.

Even that foul soup with the one piece of potato would be welcome right now.

They hadn't seen the discolored water that passed for "soup" since they had marched from the camp, and the gnawing sensation in the rabbi's gut was beyond his worst day of hunger. There was an unrelenting cramp, boring like a knife straight through to the back of his abdomen.

How long can I last?

As he forced his body to keep up with the others, the rabbi kept thinking about Michel. He had tried to get him to join the march out of Auschwitz by stressing the importance of doctors being available for the inmates along the route. He knew it could be an opportunity for Katz to reclaim his identity as a physician and remember the joy of helping those who truly needed his skilled care. To the rabbi's disappointment, Michel said he could not go, claiming he had unfinished obligations in his laboratory.

Men continued to fall to the ground during the long days of walking. Noting the extreme hunger, at dusk, the SS guards spread their lines of inmates out to allow them to plunder through barren fields, looking for remnants of potatoes. They searched fields, houses, and barns for anything that might ease their burden of hunger, but retreating peasants and the military before them had stripped the soil and structures clean of everything that could feed them or offer them warmth.

On that first day, they marched for thirteen hours. The rabbi's old friend Ruben had fallen back in the line and was now out of sight.

I fear he has collapsed and can't get up. The SS will shoot anyone who falls. I should go back and look for him, but...

At sundown of the first night, the guards directed their group of three hundred into a partially destroyed factory building. The roof was gone and the cold, dark January sky beyond the open ceiling was their canvas to look at as they huddled close together for warmth and sleep. The quarter-moon faintly illuminated the inside of the building that appeared to have been a clothing factory before it was destroyed. The jumble created by the fallen timbers, overturned tables, and machinery provided accommodating, protective spaces in which many could lie down. Even though the cement floor was cold, the rabbi easily fell asleep with the one blanket he had carried from the camp and the rags he wore for clothing.

The shrill but familiar sound of guards blowing their whistles startled them awake. Everyone was expected to line up outside, as they had each morning for months, so that a count could be made. And this morning, like all the previous ones, not everyone arose. As if still fast asleep, Arnold Herzog lay curled on his side, his eyes closed peacefully—he appeared to be frozen. The march resumed and many hundreds, unable to walk further, would die with a gunshot to the head. It would take three more days to get to the train station where they were crowded in like cattle for a single day's trip to the Buchenwald Concentration Camp.

Their arrival at Buchenwald was not greeted with fanfare; instead, the pitiful prisoners at that camp looked at them with dismay. As they were led into the decontamination showers, Rosenberg heard an inmate mumbling, "Why do they bring in more people when they can't even feed us?"

◆◆◆

April 11, 1945

THE RABBI AWOKE HEARING a commotion at the camp entrance, and a few shots were fired as guards ran from a tank bearing down on the gates. He looked up to see soldiers—American soldiers—marching into the camp. Rosenberg felt himself lifted onto a stretcher, as one pair of gentle hands covered him with a blanket while another offered him a cup of water—*clean* water. For the first time in three years, a smile formed on the rabbi's face. By the grace of God, he had survived.

"...according to my ability and my judgment and never do harm to anyone."

27

January 27, 1945
Auschwitz

Tamara had a difficult time sleeping that night, anticipating the Russian arrival as artillery shells continued to detonate just outside the camp boundaries. The remaining inmates celebrated each shell burst as the explosions raised dust and smoke into air already befouled with the smell of dead bodies. Noting no return fire, the Red Army's guns fell silent at midnight. The next morning, Tamara stood outside keeping a watch on the open main gate when she heard the sound of tanks coming up the road.

Oh, by the grace of God! I see them, a line of trucks and tanks filling the road. So many...

She watched as the first truck passed through the gate and stopped. The soldiers were dressed in white winter camouflage outfits with brown fur hats.

What will they think? The dead are stacked in front, piled up outside each barrack, creating a sight that most of these soldiers will never forget; nor do they understand exactly what ring of hell they are entering.

Two soldiers emerged from the truck to take a closer look. As the driver approached the fly-infested pile of twisted bodies, he became overwhelmed by the stench of death and the images in front of him. He retched violently, turning to the side so that the newly freed could not see the agony in his face as he heaved over and over, and then slowly walked back to the truck. Several more trucks arrived, but as the young soldiers grasped the horror, they hung back, struggling to regain their composure before approaching the inmates.

Tamara tried to talk with one of the soldiers, but he backed away.

They're staring at us as if we are freaks in a circus show, using the language barrier as an excuse to not speak to us.

Many inmates were sobbing, while others stoically stared back; a few approached the Russians, who, as if by reflex, stepped away. Medical personnel and interpreters arrived, trying to make sense of what they saw and to decide what they should do first.

♦ ♦ ♦

AFTER THE GERMANS HAD fled, Tamara spent hours roaming the camps. But as she walked along the crushed gravel, she continued to feel enslaved as she searched for the meaning of "freedom." Strangely, it seemed like just a word, like any other word in the dictionary. "Freedom" meant that physically she could go—and yet there was no food and shelter out there to go *to*.

We may have been freed from the Germans, but freed to go where?

Despite the fanfare of liberation, the inmates were still captive in their dismal surroundings. Clearly, the Soviets were not prepared to care for so many people in such dire condition. The cry of the liberated was for food to fill their ravaged stomachs. To their credit, the Russians gave liberally of their rations, and the survivors ate heartily, like starved animals might.

The survivors are gorging themselves.

But, just as soon as their frail intestines received the protein-rich rations, many of them suffered cramps as their bowels rebelled, and they shuffled off to the closest latrine. Others in the camp, whether by luck or discretion, filled themselves with the starchy food they'd been used to, such as bread and potatoes, and suffered fewer ill effects. In fact, these staples were most favored by the survivors. Although somewhat weak and thin, Michel and Tamara had not suffered the same depth of starvation as the others did. The sight of the former inmates filling their stomachs uplifted Michel, yet he knew there could be a downside to so much new food. Earlier, Michel had explained to Tamara about what he'd seen on the autopsy table; the small and large intestines of the prisoners were but paper-thin envelopes, having lost most of their digestive function from prolonged starvation, and could no longer handle a variety of foods.

It took some time for the Russian medical teams to recognize the cause of this widespread digestive intolerance. Having had so little protein in their diet, the non-functional intestines rebelled and contracted, hastening the indigestible food through the bowels. Michel also pointed out that a sudden increase in protein absorption could result in cirrhosis of the liver and lead to death by hepatic failure. He advised the Russian and Red Cross doctors of this problem.

Michel and Tamara stayed in his laboratory while the other survivors were moved into the SS barracks. Within a matter of days, the majority of Russian troops had moved on to pursue the retreating Reich soldiers, leaving the camp to be served by medical and clerical personnel alone. A few representatives from the International Red Cross arrived with some meager supplies, including blankets, clothing, and shoes.

When a radio was brought into the camp, the former internees listened continuously to the BBC war news. The German Army station persisted in false claims of victories on the eastern front as the Wehrmacht fell back to defend their homeland.

As the war had not yet ceased, it was still too dangerous to leave Auschwitz. It took several weeks for a sense of safety and relief to be felt by those still captive. Yet other issues evolved. It wasn't long before that comfort of discipline, of order, gave way to the anarchy of emancipation and the confusion that accompanied the start of their new lives.

◆◆◆

March 1, 1945

MICHEL STOOD IN THE center of the near-deserted camp feeling alone and exposed, as all physical barriers had been removed from around him. He watched as the remaining survivors embraced their newfound freedom. There were no guards to ask if they could eat or shit; no one forced them to line up and stand in the cold each morning. But going from harsh structure and discipline to endless days of waiting carried its own toll for those who just wanted to leave as the war continued to rage near the camp. Some just sat and stared, unable to move.

Those left in camp combed the warehouses for clothing, stripping off the foul, striped garments that had come to identify their lives. Wading through mountains of clothing taken from those led to their death, it was easy to find warm pants and sweaters to fend off the last few weeks of winter. Yet the clean, mismatched outfits felt strange; they almost missed the feeling of that coarse, stained fabric camp garb they had so come to despise.

The wind shifted, bringing the smells of the fields that were pleasant and overwhelming, fruity and fresh, but unfamiliar. It wasn't that Michel missed the stench of unwashed bodies or burnt hair and flesh, but those were the odors to which he had become accustomed.

The eerie quiet, broken only by the sound of newly returned robins and cardinals, was unnerving. Missing was the constant clanging of gates closing, the heavy footsteps of jackboots, and the strident voices of SS guards barking their orders and demanding that the weak and miserable do some inane task they had devised. Michel had longed for liberation, thinking that one day he would wake up, walk out of the camp, and be free. But he was soon to find out that there was a penalty to pay for achieving freedom, a cost that was far too dear to acknowledge. He could try and forget all that had happened at Auschwitz…but Auschwitz would not forget him.

Having lived and worked in the laboratory situated above the gas chambers, never would he forget the cries of the collective deceived as their lungs filled with Zyklon B gas and they scrambled over each other, climbing toward the ceiling, instinctively believing they could escape the poisonous fumes.

He knew he was lucky. Most around him had died. Each Sonderkommando group had been summarily shot when their twelve-week term of service was over. Other prisoners fortunate enough to have jobs inside, such as removing the gold from the teeth of the corpses, cutting hair from the dead, or arranging and storing the clothing were also executed because they knew too much. Even amid sounds of gunfire to the east announcing the imminent arrival of the Russian victors, the SS had continued to take scores of people out to the execution wall and shoot them.

I'LL LOOK TO THE *time when I find a way to forget*.

♦♦♦

As MICHEL VENTURED OUT of his laboratory, it was clear that his personal status had changed. That sense of importance attached to being a doctor seemed not to matter to anyone anymore. And his protector, Mengele, had vanished just before the camp had been emptied.

Having little to do, he volunteered to help the Russians in the infirmary, but was greeted with icy-cold stares from the surviving doctors. The fact that Doctor Katz escaped the miseries that had affected everyone else was not lost on the other physicians in the camp. He had not stared at his own death each day, as they had. His clothes were clean, and he weighed just twenty pounds less than when he had first arrived—in contrast to the others who had lost three times that weight. He wasn't a walking skeleton with that ghostly, gaunt look and those telltale retracted eyes. It was obvious to Michel that he had become a pariah.

Initially, he secluded himself in his laboratory and watched from his window as the liberators began organizing the survivors, but after a few days, he left his room, hoping to enjoy his new freedom. He tried to walk among the others and talk with them, but they turned their heads in disgust and said nothing.

As he walked past a barracks, he recognized a woman from Drancy that he and Anna had befriended before they were sent to Terezin. "Madame Levy, it's good to see you! And your family… Do you know…?"

The look she gave Michel pierced his heart as if a knife had been thrust through it. What she said was even more painful—so unforgettable that the words were seared forever into his soul.

"Monsieur le Docteur, you left us in our misery. You cannot know how the rest of us have suffered. Yes, you shall live. But the walls of Hell will certainly surround you during the rest of your life on earth. Look at you, clean, well-fed—all because you served that monster of evil, Mengele. You saved yourself by opening up the bellies and chests of Jews and others for that devil's horrible studies. I can never know if my children were seized by that madman, but no, Doctor, they do not live; and I will mourn them and all the children who were butchered by Mengele and the monster assassin's Jew assistant."

As Michel turned to walk away, she screamed, "Stop! Do not leave! You must listen. You, Monsieur, cannot now or ever again claim to be a Jew and must never again dare sit in a synagogue. You have forfeited that privilege, just as you have forfeited the right to ask about my family!"

She turned to amble off, but looked back over her shoulder and spit down into the dirt at Michel's feet before she walked away.

THERE WAS NOTHING HE could say or do. It was as if the liberation of others meant the beginning of imprisonment for his soul.

◆◆◆

TAMARA OFFERED HER HELP to the Russians and worked at the clinic offices through April. She was surprised by the clumsiness of the bureaucracy that was set up to administer aid to the displaced persons now trapped in Auschwitz. Bundles of warm clothing and blankets were distributed despite the spring weather. The food brought in by the Red Cross was served from the same large kettles as before and was not much different from that provided by the Germans; only the quantity was increased. Distribution of Red Cross parcels was sporadic and uncertain, adding to the frustration of the many thousands still unable to go home. The world had been ready to liberate them, but most countries were not prepared for their return.

What has taken these organizations so long to help? Why didn't these people look for us years ago? Did anyone really give a damn about the Jews? Are we so feared by our former friends and neighbors? Are they actually worried that a hoard of Jews might come back and take their measly jobs away? Yes, we are free. But the price of liberation is higher than anyone could have imagined.

◆◆◆

EACH DAY, MICHEL'S LONGING to leave the camp increased. He wanted to be gone from Auschwitz and all its horrible memories. He wanted no more fingers shaken in his face, pointing him out as "Mengele's boy" or "the Jew doctor who cut up other Jews" so that the Nazi doctors might peer inside the dead corpses. To have his own people treat him as an outcast, resented and shunned, was painful. It was time to go.

When Tamara looked at Michel, she saw that his confident manner had disappeared. He now was a broken man, not the solid doctor who had once saved people's lives.

I remember those first evenings, as I sat and listened to Doctor Katz describe his surgical practice in Lyon. He seemed so confident, so smart. I asked him what it was like, being a doctor and having people depend on you. He was somewhat subdued and didn't wish to sound important, but I could tell he was certainly proud of his skills. He did describe one incident in Lyon where he had come across an accident victim on his way home—a young girl of twelve, struck by a car. A group of people was just looking at her as she lay on the street, not breathing.

Bending down, he breathed into her mouth, compressed her chest, and started her heart beating again. He accompanied her in the ambulance to his hospital, Hotel Dieu, where fluids were given before she was taken to the operating room where he removed her ruptured spleen. He had saved a life, and her father, the mayor of Lyon, was eternally grateful.

On those fearful nights, whispering so the Sonderkommandos above would not hear, Michel had talked about the long hours in the hospital and his concern for the patients he'd left behind.

Yet, now, things have changed. The veil of his profession no longer shelters him. Now this man stands naked before the world.

It seemed to Tamara that as Michel ventured out, away from the protection of his profession, another part of him—the man inside the doctor—had disappeared.

"Even upon those suffering from stones..."

28

July 2, 1946
Atlantic Crossing

Heavy swells broke over the rails on the starboard side of the bow, sending a salty mist back onto the mid-deck of the ship. Several death camp survivors braved the pounding seas on deck, freeing themselves from the airless cabins in steerage and the painful sounds and smells of passengers retching from an epidemic of seasickness. July is supposed to be warm, yet the North Atlantic continued to deliver its ruthless cold storms, making this final passage yet another difficult step toward freedom.

Michel Katz had boarded the Riksgransen at the port of Rotterdam on June 29, 1946. It was an ungainly ship with more rust than paint covering its sides, looking very much like the wartime freighter it had been. Indeed, it had belonged to the Johanssen Freight Line out of Malmo, Sweden, and had been modified for passenger travel shortly after the war's end. This conversion had required removing all its cranes and lifting equipment and subsequently transforming its immense holds into rows of small cabins separated by narrow hallways. The Swedes had seized the opportunity at the end of the war to convert unused cargo vessels into passenger ships. Being neutral during the conflict had left the Swedish government and the country's industrialists with large cash and gold reserves from sales to both sides and, when the war ended, an opportunity to expand their riches. There seemed to be an endless demand from refugees and Displaced Persons (DPs) for overseas passage, and the many shipping firms based out of Stockholm quickly increased their passenger fleets to fulfill this need.

♦♦♦

DURING THE MONTHS SHE was hidden in the attic and protected by Michel, Tamara had fallen in love with him. Her fantasies included returning to Czechoslovakia with the handsome doctor and, someday, marriage. Being young and naïve, she thought that the presumed death of his family would make this a possibility. It seemed much like a fairy tale—the strong prince coming to the rescue of the princess in distress. Yet, realistically, she wanted to get back to Prague to take care of her younger brother and find her father and older brother. Her romantic dreams would have to be put on hold.

The remaining days became increasingly stressful for Michel and Tamara, as they were anxious to leave. What they needed were papers identifying them as DPs, which would allow for easier travel and the right to meals and lodging along the way. Earlier, Michel had identified the Russian private responsible for creating the paperwork and found that a pack of cigarettes, still considered valuable camp currency, was all it took to get documents for him and Tamara processed quickly.

Prague and the concentration camp at Terezin were not to be liberated until May 9, 1945, one day after the surrender of the German forces. Having received word that rail traffic to Prague had been reinstated by the Soviets, Tamara was desperate to get home—yet her concern for Michel made her hesitant to leave.

Michel sensed her anguish, and took her aside. "There is little sense for you to remain here when your thoughts are with your family. You've lost your mother. It's time to find the rest of your family again. You must go. Don't worry about me."

"But Doctor Katz, I can't just leave you like this! Things are still not stable here and I want to make sure you are all right. Even now, you brood for several hours each day, just lying on your bed. I worry about you so."

What will happen when he learns the truth about his family... Oh God, should I tell him?

"Don't trouble yourself...I will be fine." His eyes drifted away from Tamara. "They tell me that Terezin will be stabilized and ready for visitors in less than two weeks, and I can leave and look for my family then. Putting his arms around her shoulders, he looked into her eyes, saddened with tears.

218

"Tamara, just take care of yourself. Get back home and begin your life anew. I have your address, and we'll be in contact. I promise."

Tamara turned away to hide the tears running down her cheeks as she contemplated what the future might hold.

Might this be the last time I see Michel? I look at him more than as a man who saved my life; I do think I love him. Will he really write? And will he think of me?

Three days later, Tamara stood on the platform with Michel, waiting to board the train. "I will miss you." She looked up at him as tears spilled off her cheeks. "I do not know if I ever thanked you for all you did, saving me after the gas chamber. And I will always...always remember you."

Michel wrapped his arms around Tamara and held her for what seemed like an eternity. "I should thank *you*," he stammered. "I..." He stared at the ground, then looked up and met her eyes. "You didn't know. I was ready to kill myself before you arrived. You gave me purpose to live... I am grateful. You gave me life."

Not ready for that admission, she understood. She reached up to kiss his cheek and Michel held her. Both had tears in their eyes as she entered the passenger car.

♦♦♦

THE FINAL WEEKS AFTER liberation passed slowly for Michel as he spent his days helping in the infirmary and treating the ill with newly arrived medications and dressings. By spending so many hours in the clinic, he hoped to assuage some of the guilt he carried. The Russians appreciated his devotion and had been hoping that he would stay longer, as he was so desperately needed. Yet, some of the former inmates were still wary of him, and there was little Michel could say or do to change their views.

The Russians recognized that there were a few select men like Michel in good physical condition, and they stood out as curiosities in contrast to the majority of survivors. The Soviets had many questions about the camp and sat down with Michel shortly after a command post was established. They were interested primarily in what he knew about the fate of Russian POWs. He also was questioned about the camp, the SS command, the crematoriums, and the many dead that had been left in grotesque piles. Michel answered their many questions and provided the names of Germans responsible for the horror the Russians had inherited. He carefully steered away from any discussion of human experimentation.

Michel received word that rail traffic to Terezin through Prague would start sometime in mid-May, but with Europe so damaged from the war, he knew the risks of travel. His documents allowed him to use the railroad and get food and shelter at DP camps, but he was otherwise on his own. Although eager to leave Auschwitz, he was fearful of what he might find when he arrived at his former camp, as every dark scenario coursed through his mind. Yet it was time—time to search for his family. The absence of any communication from them added to the mounting anxiety that had weighed heavily on him since liberation.

Anna's letters had stopped three months after Michel had made his decision to help Mengele. In an earlier letter, she had described her job in a clothing factory and related that Aaron and Rachel were attending a "school" taught by the ghetto inhabitants themselves. There were no gas chambers there, and they lived in relative safety. The last note he had received suggested that they had "chosen" to eat less and share their food with the many other inhabitants in need, and that the children had a "good" appetite. The same letter mentioned the possibility that she would be moved again in October to work at a munitions plant in the eastern part of Germany. Anna didn't say what would happen to the children. He received this final communication on September 21, six weeks after it was written. Michel had replied with letters of his own but received no answer from his wife.

Michel had inquired of Mengele if he was aware of this plan to move female inmates out of Terezin for munitions work, and the SS doctor had promised to contact the commandant there. Several days later, he approached Mengele again, who impatiently responded that he had heard nothing and blamed the poor communication on the nearby battles with the Soviets. As before, he was certain that his personal interest in Michel's family would prevent their transport out of Terezin. With these assurances, Michel believed that his family would be safe and waiting for him when the war ended.

◆◆◆

ON MAY 21, MICHEL was given passage to Terezin by train. He traveled in a regular passenger car, so different from the cattle car that had brought him to Auschwitz. But the trip was interrupted several times due to the extensive damage that had been sustained by the rail lines during the war.

The Terezin rail station brought back painful memories of his arrival there in October 1943. Entering the town, he observed that the clean, almost resort-like appearance of the camp had vanished. The planters with flowers were gone; the wooden trim on the buildings had all but disappeared, most likely burned for fuel. The once orderly streets were now strewn with refuse, and the rough furnishings of the inmates' quarters were scattered about. Soviet soldiers lazily guarded the camp entrance.

The International Red Cross had set up offices in the old commandant's suite. There was a small knot of twenty refugees searching through multiple printed lists attached to an elongated bulletin board outside the offices. The twenty thousand names listed were those of the surviving inmates still located at this camp, now referred to as a Displaced Persons facility. The names were sorted by nationality, and listed alphabetically. Framing the lists were notes pinned to the board by loved ones asking for any information concerning members of their family. Michel elbowed his way forward, jostling with the many others hoping to view the lists. After searching for over an hour, he could not find the names of his son, his daughter, or his wife.

After pinning his own notes to the board in French and German, he stepped back and cupped his head in his hands—physically and emotionally depleted. Silently, he walked away, turning north up the town's main street. Passing by a Christian chapel, he stopped just outside its entrance. A quiet despair engulfed him, and he hunkered down on the side of the road, propping his face in his bony right hand. He dwelt on the missing names of his loved ones—playing each possible scenario of his family's plight over and over in his mind until it felt ready to explode.

A white wooden sign marked "Infirmary" was posted on a building to the right—the same building that housed the clinic where he had worked. *Perhaps someone there might remember.*

He entered the clinic and approached the familiar offices, knocking on the first door he encountered. Doctor Elias, a Czech physician interned since June, swung open the door. "May I help you?" he asked curtly in German.

Michel was gracious and introduced himself as a physician who had worked at the clinic. "I am looking for my family—my wife Anna and my two children."

The Czech motioned to Michel to come in and sit.

Doctor Elias sat back, deep in thought for a moment, then thumbed through a stack of papers containing people's names. "I recall meeting Anna on a few occasions, but have not seen her since September of last year."

He sat quietly, as if waiting for Michel to question him further. Michel did have a question on his lips, but feared asking it, expecting the doctor to relate more details on his own. An awkward moment passed as Doctor Elias fumbled with his stethoscope, gazed at the floor and looked away, averting Michel's insistent stare. "There were a large number of women and children transported to the east," he said carefully, "perhaps on the twenty-seventh or twenty-eighth of September."

He kept his eyes directed downward as he tried mercifully not to erase any possible shred of hope. "I was in the clinic when they were lined up to march the two kilometers to the railroad siding, and was surprised that this transport included just women and children." He paused. "Later that day, I found out the destination was…" He paused and looked away. "… Auschwitz."

Michel stood up. Stone-faced and silent, there was nothing he could say. Leaving the office, he turned down a deserted hallway. If there had been any hope left within him, it was yanked out with such force and pain that he collapsed on the floor, as if there was nothing left to keep him standing. He didn't pass out, but he wished that he could. In that one instant, his spared life had transformed into a living hell. No longer a gift of hope and renewal, it was like a heavy weight around his neck. From now on, it would serve to remind him of what he had become, and everything that he had lost.

He had no idea how long he lay on the cold floor, but somehow, whether minutes or hours later, he rose shakily to his feet. Exiting the building into the cold night air, he looked skyward without focus, as if to find an answer written somewhere above.

◆◆◆

THE OCEAN CROSSING SMOOTHED out after the first three days. Sunny skies greeted the voyagers each morning, and the air became good and fresh. A few of the newly freed tried to exercise by walking around the deck. A strange sight indeed, these pale, skinny men in mismatched clothes moving about the ship like marching birds. As painful as the recurrent cramping of their thigh or calf muscles was, it also felt good. This was only self-inflicted discomfort, no longer the result of torture at the hands of others who wanted them dead.

A rabbi held Shabbat services in the dining hall, but Michel didn't attend. *I cannot go there... I have become unclean. Each morning I attempt to cleanse what is left of my remaining soul with the natural breezes that come off the foredeck. The ocean winds may pass over my skin, but cannot penetrate deeply enough to heal the torn substance of my heart. I cannot find anything to remove the eternal stain on my person, a veritable tattoo that marks this man's infidelity to his Jewish heritage.*

◆◆◆

DURING THE REMAINING MONTHS of 1945 into Spring 1946, Michel traveled from one DP camp to another, scouring every posted list of Displaced Persons. He was desperate to find some word of his wife and children as well as his parents. But this futile quest had left him feeling even more alone than ever, his weakened spirit dying a thousand more deaths as each remaining sliver of hope led to an invariable dead end. Although he could not bring himself to give up, the fear that his family had disappeared within the ashen smoke outside his Auschwitz laboratory window was growing into an unspeakable horror that he could not control.

After leaving Terezin, Michel tried to find a train to Lyon, hoping that perhaps Anna, Rachel, and Aaron had returned home. But the rail transportation was chaotic and poorly scheduled. Although his DP card allowed for unlimited travel, it was almost impossible to find the right train, since miles of tracks had been destroyed, forcing him to spend many hours sleeping on benches at rail stations. His personal odyssey was frustrating: one DP camp after another, bringing him no closer to his family than when he'd started. At one point in Belgium in October 1945, too many nights of cold exposure and poor shelter caused him to be hospitalized with pneumonia. As soon as he was released, with train service becoming more reliable, he made his way toward Lyon.

Arriving there in November 1945, Michel went straight to his old house, trying to keep his fear in check, but expecting the worst. He stopped short at what he saw. His home, the heart of his family, his refuge, had been violated beyond imagination.

Every window was shattered and the word *"Juif"* had been scrawled across the front wall. An order of expropriation was nailed onto the front door: "By order of the CGQJ *(Commissariat General aux Questions Juives)* this residence has been placed in trust for the *Gouvernement de France.*"

The non-functioning entry door was hanging by one corner hinge. All the carpeting had been removed, the sinks and toilets had been torn out, and the kitchen had no oven range or cabinets. Debris was scattered purposefully, as if defacing all who had lived there before and denigrating the dreams and hopes he once held for his family. The words: "Juives, Communists" were painted coarsely over the living room walls in red.

Walking from room to room, Michel could visualize his wife and children at home—an image from what seemed like just a short time ago. He peered into each bedroom as if expecting to find his son and daughter asleep in their beds. The empty kitchen was bereft of the warm smells and sounds he associated with his wife's cooking. Tears flowed continuously down his cheeks as he faced the reality that this vacant home mirrored his present and future life. The tight wrap that held his emotions could no longer contain his pain, yet a silent wail pierced his heart—a wail too deep to find its voice.

Memories tugged at him each time he stepped into a room. Walking up the stairs to the second floor, he recalled how Aaron would bounce a ball down to him.

"Daddy, catch this!"

Rachel's dolls always sat in a corner of the upstairs hall.

"This is their room, Daddy."

And as he walked into the bedroom, he imagined his Anna, lovely in her nightgown, waiting in bed for him, inviting him to make love. He stood in the hall, imagining all these things until his knees crumbled, and he lowered himself to the floor sobbing.

Forcing himself to rise, he wiped his tears with his sleeve and ventured out to the backyard. He'd hidden important documents there before the family fled, ahead of the Germans and miliciens. Finding an old shovel, he dug into the far corner of a garden plot, overrun by weeds, where he discovered the small wooden chest he had buried. It contained copies of his medical diplomas, residency certification, and other papers. Their home deed, insurance policies, and bank account information were all still there. Clutching the box, he reentered the house.

Michel sat on the floor of the kitchen for a long while, trying to find some small morsel of meaning to his life. The fond memories he had of this house had been torn and scraped off the walls and floors. There was nothing left for him here at his home, but his parents... Could they possibly have survived?

My parents may be back, safe.

But walking two blocks to his parents' house, only brought more sadness when he found that it, too, was empty and defiled. He was now sure that they had all been killed—every one of them.

Michel realized he was now alone in the world, and as he walked back to his house, each step seemed heavier than the last. Strangely, he did not suffer the pain as he had at Terezin. Once your heart has been ripped from your body, it cannot easily be restored. Whatever feelings had been kept alive in his soul were now gone, and reliving this agony filled him with numbness. As he looked over the papers dealing with his life and family, he felt tempted to throw them all away, to become invisible to the world.

Over the next week, Michel attempted to contact friends and family who might still be in Lyon; he found no one. The Catholic family who had stored his goods and furnishings had moved away, leaving no forwarding address.

The burden he bore now felt too great to deal with, and he was overwhelmed by these additional barriers placed before him. Someday, he reassured himself, he would return and track down the rest of his things, but for now, it might be best to put his previous life behind him. Searching the DP camps, poring through Red Cross lists, and finally arriving at his old home had convinced him—all was lost. There was nothing left for him in France or Europe. It was time to leave and start anew. He found no joy in freedom—no place to call home.

Yet he still had to depend on others. A once proud doctor, he had no money and was forced to rely on aid organizations for food and clothing. Wherever he found himself, he carried the unmistakable yoke of survival.

It was the acceptance letter from the hospital in Montreal that offered an opportunity to restart his life.

Canada could be my salvation.

◆ ◆ ◆

THE RESPONSE WAS WRITTEN in French, and began…

Dear Doctor Katz,

The application committee at the Jewish Hospital of Montreal is pleased to offer you a position as a second-year resident in general surgery. We acknowledge your previous training and experience in Europe, but note that the provincial laws of Quebec require two years of post-medical school education in Canada, the US, or Britain to gain licensure. In addition, noting the time you have been removed from clinical practice, it would make medical sense for additional training in surgery…

Clearly, the committee was avoiding any references to his camp experience, and that was fine with Michel. This could be his first step toward physical freedom.

◆ ◆ ◆

THE SOUND OF THE ship's horns signaled the end of the journey. It was July 12, 1946, and he had arrived at the Port of Montreal. Crewmembers lowered the gangplank, and soon a line of people shuffled off the boat as hopeful souls scanned those waiting on the dock for familiar faces. But many, like Michel, had no one to greet them.

"...but will leave this to be done by men who are practitioners of this..."

29

January 6, 1945
Potsdam, Germany

The twin engine Soviet MIG-5 fighter did not return to again strafe Potsdam, easing the fears of the German officers waiting impatiently in the staff car outside the military medical dispensary. Hans continued to help the remaining doctors with the severely injured. Pleading national interest, General Ravenscroft insisted that Hans halt his resuscitative efforts and get back in the car as soon as possible. After one hour of assisting the injured, Hans regretfully left the chaotic trauma scene and reentered the classic 1935 Mercedes sedan, which rapidly pulled away from Potsdam and headed towards Lübeck.

Hans had been helping resuscitate a young soldier whose arm was badly injured at the shoulder. Massive bleeding, probably from the axillary vein and artery, could only be controlled with pressure. Using only his hands, he pushed on the paper bandages and helped stem the loss of blood until intravenous saline and plasma could be instilled and replace the lost blood volume. Once the patient's blood pressure had stabilized to 85/50, he was wheeled into the operating suite. Only then did Hans allow himself to leave the still frenzied scene and get in the back seat of the waiting Mercedes, deep in thought. It troubled him to leave, as it had been a long time since his medical skills were required.

For a while, I felt good—like I was a doctor again, caring for people who needed me. Isn't that why I went into medicine? The war, yes—the war changes all things.

They turned on to the A24 autobahn and entered into the sparse traffic headed towards Hamburg, about 275 kilometers to the west.

As Hans viewed the once grand roadway, he mused about what it was like the first time he drove on it.

I was young, maybe twenty-one, and we drove fast along the finished portions of this true marvel of German engineering.

The classic old roadways had been too narrow and wouldn't allow two cars to pass at once. Vehicles of all types had to wind their way around these streets through the small cities and villages, and traffic was often slowed to a standstill by horse-drawn carts mingling with the local flow of trucks.

The autobahns had radically changed travel. Adolf Hitler had started a program to build two North-South and East-West links in Germany, as he recognized the propaganda value of a high-speed road system and its immediate military and employment implications. The first of these was *Reichsautobahnen*, which opened in 1935 between Frankfurt and Darmstadt. Over twenty-one hundred kilometers of roadway comprising the autobahn network was completed by 1945. The Reichsautobahn connecting Hamburg and Berlin was built in 1940 and had narrow medians, no shoulders, and cobblestone ramps and waysides.

RAF bombers had repeatedly attacked this important link from the capital to the western part of Germany. Viewing the roadway was now painful for Hans, as this once superb highway was now marked with multiple repair sites. Patches of black asphalt spotted the smooth surface, as if imprinting blemishes on the purity and sanctity of the Reich itself. Along the cobbled waysides, broken-down Wehrmacht trucks and buses awaited towing to their shops.

So different now, our beautiful Fatherland, destroyed.

All sorts of debris lay scattered throughout the normally spotless roadside shoulders, as if order didn't matter to anyone anymore. A thin blanket of snow covered the fields on either side of the highway. Against the side of the road, mounds of dirty, blackened snow lay in regular piles. Coming from the west was an endless line of trucks filled with troops and equipment, hurrying to join the battles just east of Berlin.

For Hans, the staff car's Drahtfunk radio contributed a sleep-inducing, constant background noise, announcing a temporary lull in bombing attacks. The gray-white overcast sky served as a protective blanket from the

Allied air forces, which preferred open skies through which to pummel the now defenseless German cities.

The somber view outside the car would not allow Hans to nap. As he gazed out, he saw the countryside had changed in other ways, too. The once beautifully manicured fields had been left untended. Ghosts of corn and barley crops stood in silence, dead and brown, uncared for—in keeping with everything else in view. Among the rolling hills, bomb craters interrupted the rows of abandoned crops, adding a greater sense of despair to the land, once so rich. The great stores of grain usually positioned alongside the barns were not present; the farmhouses that had been filled with family life looked deserted. Little light came through their windows, although some human figures could be detected, milling in and around the houses. Two older men were scavenging wood from an overturned cart along the roadside, dragging it toward one of the farmhouses to use for heat. With fierceness foreign to the gentle farmers, these men used crowbars, hammers, and rods to pry apart the lumber from its frame. No oil, no coal, little electricity...

Where has this war taken us?

As the monotony of his road trip was broken by the many tragedies of war visible from the autobahn, Hans ruminated about what his future might hold. The war would be over in a matter of weeks—perhaps a few months. Most certainly, he would be detained and interned in a POW camp. If he tried to flee and hide, he would still be at risk, as checkpoints and roadblocks would be looking for SS such as himself.

Records... Oh, the need for records would surely be his downfall. There would be interrogations, long and tough, with questions about the concentration camps and all the deaths—and what duties he had performed there. He feared that the real value of his scientific studies would be overlooked and not appreciated.

The interrogators won't understand. No, they must find scapegoats for all that went on in the camps.

He was certain that the Allies would look for those responsible, those Nazis who had brought this country to ruin—those Nazis who had caused so many to die, especially the Jews. "A relentless hunt for those responsible..."

Self-righteous American and British zealots will search for Nazis, the SS, and the Waffen SS. Ordinary Germans will end up denouncing the Nazis to somehow assuage their personal guilt for staying quiet all these years.

The same people who so proudly marched, cheered, and celebrated Hitler would now condemn him. And soon the world would see that the Germans who fashioned themselves as the true patriots, those who stood up at rallies and screamed "Heil Hitler" as loudly as he had done, would come to lay blame.

They will wipe their own souls free of responsibility and point their fingers at the others and me.

Hans knew it would happen. He could hear it all. The German voices excusing themselves to the conquering Allied troops with feigned ignorance.

We didn't know! Nobody told us about the camps and the killings of Jews and Gypsies. Had we known, we would have stopped it.

Not that the burned flesh odor of crematoriums just stopped at the fences in cities such as Dachau, Mauthausen, or Natzweiler-Struthof. Not that the civilian tradesmen, the plumbers, or the electricians ever saw anything when making calls to one of the camps. And the common man, he never participated in the slaughter of the Jews. Not as ordinary camp guards, not as uneducated members of the "Special Police Units"—no, they did nothing to the Jews.

People talked, perhaps in whispers, and they knew—yes, they knew about the death camps and yet they voiced not a single complaint.

Feeble excuses, all of them.

Their silence through this period was deafening, as their mantra droned on—"A better Germany, a cleansed Germany"—until the end came and the melody abruptly changed. "We didn't know. How would we allow such a thing to happen in our Germany?"

And the cloak of responsibility would easily slide off their shoulders.

♦ ♦ ♦

HANS NOTED THAT THE German officers had planned well for the trip to the port of Lübeck. Four twenty-liter containers of fuel had been strapped to the back of the car; there was very little chance that any of the military depots along the way would have extra fuel at this point in the war. And there would not be any stores or restaurants open, as food supplies had been meager and most of the available produce and livestock had been shipped east for the Russian campaign. The SS kitchen had supplied the officers with two large rolls of cheese, several loaves of bread, and multiple tins of sardines and canned meat for their trip north.

Very little conversation was exchanged between Hans and the others. He volunteered little beyond what he had explained earlier about his experimental work. They chose not to ask further questions about his studies, either out of medical ignorance or a desire not to be involved.

From the small talk in the front seat, Hans could only surmise that these high-ranking SS were carrying important documents and technology to be taken out of Germany and placed on a vessel bound for a safe port. Beyond that, he knew nothing else.

The relative quiet during the remainder of the trip allowed Hans to reflect on the gripping events that had occurred in Potsdam. He'd regained that sense of being a doctor again and caring for the injured. It upset him to be pulled away so soon from the frightening scene when he knew he could make a difference and help save lives. Watching that poor medical student die in front of him did tug at his heart, yet his compassion was limited, having seen so many die. Hans reached into his front shirt pocket and pulled out the student's identification: Jürgen Hauptman, University of Hamburg School of Medicine. Perhaps this was his ticket to freedom. He had a plan.

They arrived in Lübeck late in the evening and proceeded directly to the docks. Hans could see three additional groups of SS officers milling about the wharf area. When the car stopped, the officers briskly bid him adieu and walked directly to the dock. Two enlisted SS soldiers unloaded the bags and boxes from the Mercedes and stood silently, waiting for further instructions.

General Ravenscroft walked back to Hans and quietly addressed him. "Herr Doktor, I enjoyed traveling with you, but we must part. Now we ask that you continue your trip with haste, as our assignment must be completed in absolute secrecy—you must understand."

The general pointed in the direction of a truck that had recently been unloaded and had been ordered to transport Hans to Kiel, now just seventy-six kilometers to the northwest. Hans would never know what happened that night in Lübeck, nor did he care. Right now, his self-interest and future freedom dominated his thoughts.

The ride to Kiel brought back pleasant childhood memories as the route took him through Hamburg. He recalled the frequent auto excursions with his grandfather, as they drove the winding, one-lane road to Hamburg from their home in Kiel. This trip took just an hour and a half, short enough to avoid fights between Hans and his cousin, Johann. The low, marsh-like fields out of Kiel gave way to a series of bridges over canals and the River Elbe. Their usual destination was the park next to the Alster Lakes in downtown Hamburg, an area lined with beautiful homes and exquisite gardens that enhanced the lakes' perimeters. With a picnic basket and blanket, the family often lunched along the edge of Inner Alster Lake. The boys played Fußball until their grandfather stood up to go home; a sign that always saddened them. For years after that, Hans often visited Hamburg with friends and enjoyed the excitement this international port city had to offer.

Such an excellent city to get lost in!

But as his truck passed north of the destroyed city, Hans realized,

This is not the same Hamburg I remember.

30

Kiel, Germany

The highly disciplined German mind demanded detailed records in every aspect of civilian and military life. In 1944, all SS personnel files were safely stored in a basement bunker in Berlin. These files contained important minutiae of salary, pension, and family benefits, and they were to be protected at all cost. But with certain defeat just a few weeks away, there were other files that Himmler ordered destroyed that included details of transports and statistics from the various concentration camps. These were burned in large piles outside SS headquarters.

When the booming artillery of the Soviets and continued Allied bombing heralded the impending collapse of Berlin in early 1945, the SS loaded up their personnel files into trucks for a journey west. Local citizens watched as the senior officers in the once-vaunted SS scrambled out of their headquarters into trucks heading west ahead of the Soviets. These papers were successfully transported to Hamburg, where the British and Americans would ultimately retrieve most all of them.

Along with the fleeing SS and Reich officials, a line of trucks, carts, and bicycles crowded the roadways. The German citizens feared the terror that would accompany the arrival of the Soviets as stories of rape, murder, and beatings by vengeful Soviet soldiers circulated the populace.

◆◆◆

Hans was now aware that he couldn't risk being seen on the streets of Kiel, as many neighbors recognized his SS history. As a young man, he had proudly worn his swastika armband during the weekly marches of the Hitler youth. In fact, to the dismay of many of his family and friends, the party had become overly important in his life, and his preaching had been intolerable.

Surely, the Americans would come looking for him after they found the SS files. Germans reluctantly faced a dilemma: They needed to preserve personnel information for pensions, etc., but Hans's file could incriminate both the government and the people in those files. And even before that were to happen, he was convinced that someone would turn him in.

Hans was still an officer in the SS. His orders had allowed him to visit Kiel on leave, and he was expected to report to the command center on arrival. The war was all but lost, yet Hans still felt a responsibility to the SS and his country.

He hitched a ride to SS headquarters, situated close to Kiel harbor. On arriving, he noticed a general commotion outside the building. Secretaries and SS officials were dumping boxes of files, papers, and documents into a raging bonfire.

Amid the smoke and turmoil, he located the officer in charge, Colonel Horst Swartz, a burly, no-nonsense Bavarian who was visibly sweating through his black coat.

"Colonel Swartz, I am Hans Bloch, a physician stationed at a camp no longer being used in the East. I am here on personal leave. Here are my papers."

The colonel paused and looked directly into Hans's eyes, then shook his head incredulously. Without reaching for Hans's documents, he said, "Major, I suggest you look around here. We are leaving, as our enemy is arriving at any moment. If you wish to help, step inside, and move boxes outside. If you wish to save yourself, I suggest you find a way to get out of Kiel, and perhaps out of Germany. *Now!*"

Hans was stunned.

Another admission of failure.

German Army radio had continued to marshal support among the civilians to protect the front along with their homes. Stories of the vaunted German jet fighter and the new, almost invisible, Schnorkel U-Boat filled the airwaves. Yet here, the SS colonel was leaving and covering his trail—and perhaps his excesses—with the help of a burning pyre. Hans started to walk towards the headquarters offices, but at the last minute turned away and headed down toward the docks. His stomach began to ache—again.

◆◆◆

THE SWEDES HAD BEEN considered "business" friends of the Germans during the war. Staying neutral, they had been able to sell raw materials to both the Axis and the Allied powers. Iron ore, so vital to the Fatherland, was shipped from the great mines in Kiruna across the cold, northern landscape of Sweden to Narvig harbor for loading onto ships bound for the Reich. To this end, Sweden had become a kind of pariah among the Scandinavian nations. The ongoing supply of iron served as a lightning rod for hate by the besieged Norwegians, who had suffered so greatly at the hands of the conquering Germans.

Frantic residents of Kiel and Hamburg were booking passage to Stockholm on hastily arranged transports across the Baltic Sea. It was an avenue of escape, especially for those at risk for capture as war criminals by the Allies. Posted on a message board at the Kiel Yacht Club was a notice:

Passage to Stockholm aboard the Rheingold
March 12, 1945—3000 DM
Board here for transport to the ship.

Hans had set aside most of his salary, planning for the future. At Auschwitz, except for cigarettes and the occasional black market wine, there was little need for spending his hoard. As it became more obvious that the war would be lost, he further protected his funds, hiding his Deutschmarks in the back of a locked file cabinet at Auschwitz and in a trunk at home when he visited on leave. Recognizing that these bills could be worthless at war's end, he would now spend them to secure his future and leave Germany. But first, he had to return home.

Realizing that neighbors would be alerted by the sight of a military truck stopping at his house, Hans had the truck drop him off one kilometer from his street. He walked slowly up a hill until he reached the family home; the only light visible at his house came from candles on the dining room table. Eerily quiet, it was not the homecoming he had dreamed of.

His mother screamed with joy as he came through the door. She threw her arms around him and started to cry. "Oh, my dear Hans, it's been such a struggle. I am so glad to see you safe!"

It had been weeks since he had sent her a letter, and he knew she would be worried. Holding her tight to warm her, he asked, "Mother, why is it so cold, so dark here?"

"We have had no electricity for three days," she answered. "The power plant has so little coal. The authorities say they need the blackout to avoid the bombers, and they've shut off our power. Yet the bombs keep falling. We know better. They have no fuel to run the plant."

"And Grandfather, how is he?"

"Hans, you must know, he sits in front of the living room window all day and looks out. He barely talks. I am so worried for him."

Walking into the adjacent parlor, Hans saw the elderly man in his worn, favorite chair, feet up on an ottoman. He was seated in front of the large, front glass window facing the harbor and the few remaining sailboats at anchor. He looked tired, older than Hans remembered. Hearing footsteps, the old man slowly turned toward the sound. Recognizing his grandson, he smiled faintly and signaled for Hans to approach him.

"Come closer," his grandfather said weakly, "I must see your face, Hans."

Hans reached out and hugged him. "Grandfather, I am back from the war. I am home."

Taking a couple of seconds to look him over, the elder Bloch said, "Your face has grown old, that spark of youth is gone. You have suffered. I can see it."

"It has been a long trip, Grandpa. I'm just tired, but okay."

Studying him up and down, the old man continued. "Sometimes, the things we must do can age us, Hans, and I am concerned about you." Shifting in his chair, he stared at his grandson. "I think I understand from your letters what stresses you must have endured at the camps. We now hear about all the deaths there, people starved and worked to death. And gas chambers—it is all so frightening. I know you thought it was for the best, your experiments and all."

"Let's not dwell on the war; it's good just to be home."

"But I am afraid. The neighbors have been talking about you and the others who joined the SS. Now, they are hearing for the first time stories of the concentration camps. Our old friends barely speak to us anymore, and this has been especially hard on your mother." He paused and wiped a tear from his eye. "No, you should not be seen outside. Someone will turn you in. You know, the British are closing in on Hamburg, and next will be Kiel."

Hans turned away...

I'm not even welcome at home.

His mother had been preparing the evening meal and called out to the two men in the parlor. "Dinner will be ready in five minutes."

A strong, fishy odor filled the kitchen as she warmed up some day-old fish and potatoes. Hans walked in and she planted a kiss on his cheek, wiping away her tears as she went back to cooking the meager meal.

"Mother," he began, "have you seen Josef lately?"

"Well, yes, he comes here once a week with some supplies for us. He's been good to us, Hans, bringing in special food we can't get. I expect him tomorrow."

"Good, I need him to help me."

Little was said during dinner, and afterwards Hans and his grandfather retired to the front room. He had often spent hours there, listening to the wisdom of the old man, and quietly hoped to hear some now.

"Hans, you know well that I have always supported a greater Reich," his grandfather began, "a reborn Deutschland whose pride has been restored. We both worked hard to make that happen. Yet now that dream is lost." He rose slowly and looked down at his grandson. "I see little hope for Germany, and less hope for us Germans. You must try to leave Germany, as it is not safe; you must look out for yourself."

As always, Hans knew he was right.

◆◆◆

JOSEF AND HANS HAD been close friends while growing up. Attending the same primary and high schools, they were inseparable and had planned to join the military together. Unfortunately, Josef was rejected for service due to a deformity in his arm related to a fractured elbow at age six when he fell out of a tree. Hans felt bad, as he had dared Josef to climb the tree that day.

Unable to join the service, Josef tapped his ability to live by his wits and, in his mind, aided the war effort by becoming a kind of "expeditor." He could find anything for anybody, whether legal or from the black market, and he had made friends with many Swedish boat captains who delivered valuable, rationed items to war-torn Germany. Josef had also maintained connections with important officials in Hamburg and the University, and he was a prime source of food and supplies to satisfy their needs. That's why Hans turned to him now for the execution of his plan.

"Josef," an excited Hans greeted his friend as he stepped through the front door. "It's so good to see you!"

"And you too, old man," said Josef, eyeing the SS uniform and the death-head pins on Hans's collar. "Tell me, what have you been doing these last four years?"

"My friend, there is much I must keep quiet about, but suffice it to say, I spent time doing medical research for the Reich. I was posted at Dachau first, and later at the Auschwitz-Birkenau concentration camps."

Josef held up his hands as if telling Hans to stop. "I have no need to know; I understand. I had an easier time staying here in Hamburg, dodging British and American bombs and trying to make a living selling whatever I could. I had promised to watch after your mom when you left, so here I am."

Putting his arm around his old friend, Hans led him into the parlor. "Thank you for all the help you gave the family. But now, we must talk." Taking a deep breath, he paused and whispered, "Can you obtain the layout of the Hamburg University Medical College and the dean's office?"

◆◆◆

HANS KEPT TO HIMSELF in Kiel for the next three weeks, rarely venturing outdoors as he laid plans for his journey to safety. Searching his closet, he retrieved civilian clothes that had not been worn for three years. Even when he'd returned home on leave, he'd worn his uniform everywhere—a true source of pride. Now, trying on the brown woolen slacks he'd last worn in medical school, he pulled the belt tight and cinched it one eyelet beyond the usual hook.

I must have lost a few pounds.

Opening his wallet, he removed any papers that might identify him as an SS officer.

Lifting the top of the chest at the foot of his bed, he neatly folded his uniforms and placed them inside. Closing the heavy lid, he hoped to lock out the existence of Major Hans Bloch forever.

He was able to hitch a ride with a truck out of Kiel to the A7 Autobahn. On the road to Hamburg, Hans was overwhelmed by the devastation. As they approached the port, it looked like one half of the city was destroyed, as if a giant hand had reached down and swept away all the houses, factories, and trees. The port structures were twisted and torn, most of their support lying in the harbor waters beneath. Several sunken ships and barges were visible, some at port and some in the center of the river. One destroyer was keeled over on its side with its bow sticking up, essentially blocking the channel. A grain barge, half unloaded, was partially sunk adjacent to the damaged pier. Up the channel, a transport ship was loading, clear of the damaged destroyer. Multiple small boats could be seen tied up next to it with civilians desperately trying to get on board.

Fires burned and smoldered to the south of town from the continual British bombing in the evenings. Further up the channel, a U-boat bobbed on the surface, the target of a recent attack—its conning tower now a twisted mass of black metal. Very little activity could be detected at the port. A sense of revulsion swept over him.

This beautiful harbor is now reduced to rubble.

The truck discharged him at the Alster Lakes. The exquisite homes that bordered the lakes stood damaged from repetitive bombings; every home had been affected, and most had no windows left intact. The newly homeless had pulled off what remained of wood trim on the houses to provide heat for themselves. He could see the blackened remains of the once-delicate woodwork above the windows and door arches. Piles of bricks, debris, and waste littered the adjacent streets. The latticework that had guided the growth of the flowering plants had been ripped out. Manicured front gardens had been replaced with craters and soot. It appeared as though someone had harvested the beautiful trees with fire and explosions. In contrast, the two lakes, though devoid of life, remained eerily pristine— the deep blue colors of his childhood memory. It seemed as if they alone remained untouched by war.

It was spring and the grass in the park had just started to turn green, yet it looked as if no one would care for it. Hans walked past the spot where his family had picnicked on Sundays and gazed out at the lake. There were no swans; the ducks had long ago become meals for the once-affluent residents. The beautiful path along the lakeshore was strewn with all sorts of rubbish.

Distant artillery sounds startled him back to the present. Looking past the smoke rising south of the harbor, Hans decided he was right to head back toward Rostock and escape to Sweden, but not before he completed his final preparations for his new life. And he knew just where to find Josef.

◆◆◆

THE WHARF DISTRICT WAS a short walk from the lakes, and Hans easily found his old friend in a small office at the southeast corner of the heavily damaged harbor warehouse complex, the Speicherstadt. An excited Josef emerged from his "office" and wrapped his arms around Hans. "I was able to get the plans you needed."

"Thank you! I'd like to use them tonight," Hans replied. "But first, let's catch up," he said, tossing his valise on the floor.

With the ravaged harbor as their backdrop, the two old friends went on to talk for several hours about the war, their families, and what the future might hold for them. Josef had been surprised to see Hans at this crucial time in the war. Having taken up residence in an abandoned, partially destroyed harbormaster's office and, despite the destruction of the city and lack of services, Josef continued to run out a relatively lucrative black market business, salvaging stores and equipment from bombed out warehouses and damaged ships.

The two friends decided it was best to complete their task during the nightly air raids carried out by the British Mosquito bombers, as the citizens hid in shelters. Josef was confident that the University Medical School would not be a target.

The two men waited until dark when Josef wheeled out two bicycles from the back of his office. "Here," he said, "we can quickly and quietly get to the University."

"Josef, you don't know how important this is to me."

"I know it's not for national security. Can you give me a hint about what you are up to?"

"No, but I can tell you this. It may save my life."

◆◆◆

Dust—everywhere, dust. A shadowy figure brushed the wall as an irregular row of bricks toppled into the courtyard of the medical school buildings. Distant and near sounds of artillery rounds concussed the ground, filling the air with more dust, adding to the ever-present brown fog.

"Hans," a whispered shout was heard. "Hans, come here! I think I've found it."

The figure of a man silently darted across the rubble-strewn street and jumped behind a wall adjacent to the University of Hamburg administration building. Hans tried to answer, but emitted only a hoarse cough, his voice stifled by the irritating dust. Josef looked up to see if his partner had heard.

There were no lights in the administration building, no lights in the street. They had peddled through an eerie mausoleum of a city blackened almost completely, save for a few flashes of light from exploding bombs in the distance. The city had gone four days without power. Thunderstorms without clouds, raining only dust. Hans and Josef laid their bicycles down.

"Josef, come in. You have the flashlight and the tools?" Hans asked as he entered the building.

There had once been a door, but it was gone, along with the frame. All of it had been ripped out. Their light illuminated a small hallway strewn with debris—books and the remains of chairs that had been aimlessly thrown about. Josef carefully reached into his coat pocket and pulled out a neatly folded paper. He scanned the crude sketch, a floor plan of the school offices.

Ah, I see the hallway here; this works.

He walked and measured with his steps: seven meters down the hall, a stairway to the right, fourteen steps down to the first level, turn to the left, walk five meters to a reinforced door. Hans joined him, and slowly they headed for the stairwell. Picking their way down the corridor with care, they descended the stairs, using the light held by Josef. Hans balanced against the wall, as there was no handrail to hold onto.

With Josef following, they spotted the door that was circled in the plans. It was metal, but Josef had brought along a prying bar, just in case. They noticed that some of the wood molding had been removed as if someone had tried unsuccessfully to enter. As they forced the bar into the lock, the two men's heavy black boots simultaneously crashed into the door, and it opened.

It was as if the war had stopped beyond the steel door. Everything was in order, albeit dust-covered. The flashlight beam lit up a heavy oaken desk on the right, commanding the room. A comfortable black leather chair played host to the desk and the room, as if to welcome its new visitors. To the left were three matching wooden file cabinets. The wall behind the desk held several artistically-framed diplomas; the largest in the center read: "Franz Schondheim, MD; University of Heidelberg; 1918."

Both men exchanged knowing glances. They had arrived.

As if he had rehearsed it, Hans moved to the locked file cabinets, pulled a screw driver from his pocket and pried open the drawer marked A-L, revealing a series of identical folders with neatly-typed labels: Goetz, Happner, Hauck, Hauptman... He opened the file: Hauptman, Jürgen. The vision of this dead medical student, lying lifeless on the street in Potsdam, unnerved him. He could still hear the terrifying sound of the Russian warplane roaring down the street, its bullets clattering off the pavement.

There were multiple letters, notations, and grading sheets in the file, along with an application to medical school. Deftly, he unfolded the application, removed the picture and replaced it with one of himself. The file was put back, the drawer closed. Josef quickly opened the third cabinet to the right, pulled out a file marked "Diplomas" and removed a blank document. Reaching deep into the back of the cabinet, he found several marking stamps, including one imprinted: "Seal of the University of Hamburg School of Medicine."

On the desk, there was correspondence signed by the Dean, Herr Doktor Schondheim. With the mastery of an artist, by flashlight, Josef issued a diploma to Jürgen Hauptman, MD; dated April 20, 1945. He expertly forged the signature of Doctor Schondheim, applied the Seal of the University of Hamburg School of Medicine, and stamped it with an imprint of the swastika. His task completed, Josef replaced the files in their original locations, as if nothing had been disturbed. Hans clutched the diploma protectively under his arm, as he and his accomplice left the building and pedaled quietly into the night back to Josef's quarters.

Sinking into the tattered leather couch Hans eyed his old friend, and smiled. He reached for the valise he'd tossed on the floor earlier, and handed it to Josef. "Open it—it's for you."

Gingerly opening the clasp, Josef stared at over twenty thousand Deutschmarks. "I can't take this; you'll need it, I'm sure."

"You have been watching over my family," Hans began, "and I know you will continue during these trying times. I'll keep enough for passage to Sweden, but I fear the money will be worthless outside Germany." Handing the money over to Joseph, he added. "I trust you, my friend, to do the right thing."

Tucking the documents into his valise, a smiling Hans headed towards the Alster lakes to hitch a ride back to Kiel.

"...abstain from whatever is deleterious and mischievous..."

31

May 15, 1945
Hamburg, Germany

"Halt!" barked the British sergeant as he held up his right hand in front of the control gate, ordering Hans to stop.

Hans swung off his bicycle, gently placed it down at his feet, and reached for his wallet and papers.

"Let me have a look at your identification," said the soldier in passable German. The Englishman examined the papers and then looked Hans over, as if trying to match the description on the documents with the person in front of him.

Hans hoped to cross into Sweden and join the last of the SS officers who had shed their uniforms and paid off mercenary Dane boat captains with Reich gold to get them across to Malmo. But by the time he had tried to leave Germany, the British had quarantined the Baltic, and all ships were now boarded and inspected. He had studied the possibility of going overland to Denmark, but the borders were under Allied control. Fearful on leaving his home, he had spent the last two months indoors and rarely ventured out. The British were now knocking on doors and actively looking for SS officers. It was time to leave Kiel. He hoped to hook up with Josef, who knew Hamburg well enough to allow him to become invisible in this large city.

An anxious column of people filled the roadway for at least two kilometers leading up to the checkpoint. They had lined up to cross the only undamaged bridge over the River Elbe into central Hamburg. Carts, bicycles, and a few automobiles were entwined with this watershed of humanity trying to reenter their city after the bombings had so forcefully chased them out. But the city that remained was unrecognizable to its returning inhabitants; half the buildings within view of the crossing were either destroyed or severely damaged. Even those with intact walls and undamaged windows had been thoroughly ravaged inside by those seeking shelter and warmth. Wood had been torn from paneling, doors, doorframes, and cabinets. Those who stayed after the bombings and firestorms had been forced into scavenging what they could to survive.

The announcement of the surrender on May 8 did little to quell the despair carried by each German. These victims had lost more than the war; they had no food, little shelter, and no heat. Lives had been disrupted and families dispersed. Children who had been sent away from the city remained in the country, separated from their families. Proud women had been forced to beg or offer their bodies for the smallest bite of food. Uncounted minions of the Reich, nameless soldiers, had been killed or wounded—the rest captured and placed in prisoner-of-war camps. Families awaited word of their sons and husbands, fearing capture or death at the hands of the Russians.

The stories could be read in the faces of those in the queue. Premature lines of aging marked the gaunt faces of those trying to go home. Every woman's head was covered with a scarf. They had little water to wash and style their hair. No one looked up unless asked; their eyes remained downcast as the line slowly shuffled toward the control gate.

Fortunately, it was the English who had held the area around Hamburg; the German forces had surrendered to the British without resistance on May 3. A strong push by the British and American troops into Lübeck, Hamburg, and Kiel had secured this area to be part of the Western occupation zone, keeping it out of Soviet hands. Now English soldiers patrolled the streets of this strategic port city.

The soldiers controlling the bridge entry were firm, but not harsh; orders to "Pass" or "Stay" were spoken in halting German, as each person was stopped and their identification cards examined. Hans took a deep breath as he approached the gate on his bike.

The British sergeant on duty glanced at Hans's papers, and then studied his face. "Come with me, sir," he ordered, motioning toward a roadside building that had once been a petrol station.

Sitting at an unadorned desk was a young lieutenant engaged in reviewing a stack of documents. The checkpoint sergeant handed Hans's identification papers to the officer with a slight nod, saluted, and left to return to his post.

Blond and fair-skinned with bright blue eyes, the lieutenant had barely enough beard to need shaving.

Quite Nordic looking, almost German. Perhaps he is just out of the university.

The man appeared quite fit, as if he had not yet faced battle. He spoke German without hesitating. "Doctor Hauptman, your papers say that you're not yet a doctor, but still a medical student. Is that correct?"

"Yes, of course. I just finished my examinations in March, even as the war was going so badly," Hans answered with a confidence he did not feel.

He reached into his satchel, recovered his diploma, and handed it to the officer. "These papers say that you are twenty-two years old, but you look much older. And they state that you have no identifying marks."

Shuddering internally, Hans studied his interrogator.

While this officer is young, he's keenly perceptive in a way that belies his youth. In fact, minute by minute, he's becoming more of a threat.

"Sir," Hans began, "I swear, the troubles of the last few months have taken their toll on me."

He went on about how the privations of war and the constant attacks had stolen his youth. As he talked, he realized the Englishman was scrutinizing his face, specifically the birthmark on his left temple.

Damn it. Why didn't I cover that up?

It had not occurred to him earlier that his hairline had receded and the mark was clearly more visible. He held his breath again as the lieutenant looked him squarely in the eyes. "It is your eyes that belie you, Doktor Hauptman. A person's age is easily read in their eyes. You must be at least thirty years old," he continued in German, "and I believe you are not this person you say you are."

He stared at Hans, his gaze unblinking, fixated on his left temple. "'Doctor Hauptman,' or whatever your name is, can you enlighten me?"

Hans winced inside, struggling to remain outwardly poised. "Lieutenant, please take a better look at me. The war has been difficult, we were often without food, and I had to deal with so many horrible injuries that I aged beyond my years."

Now his heart was racing and he started to sweat. He fought to control the response of his autonomic nervous system but couldn't. The lieutenant's clear eyes were still fixed on him, closely observing his reaction, watching his fears come to the fore. It was time for a better story.

He had anticipated trouble over the ten-year age difference, but had not found a way to overcome it on paper. The national identification papers he'd recovered from the fatally injured medical student, Jürgen Hauptman, specifically addressed eye color, hair color, height and weight, which he matched. But they also included the date of birth, place of birth, and home address. A skillful forger might have been able to change the date, but in his hurry to find passage to Sweden, there had been no time to ask his friend Josef to alter these facts. Predicting difficulties with the documents, he had developed an alternative strategy. Leaning forward in his chair, he cupped his chin in his hand, as if deep in thought.

There would be no way to justify his professional activities at the concentration camp to the Allies. To the Luftwaffe, he had been important, an asset to the war effort, but to his enemies, he would be detested as one who had shamefully tortured prisoners while starving them to death. Even though he didn't light the fires to the furnaces, they would see him holding the match. Now, everyone who worked in the camps would be seen as responsible and would undoubtedly share in the guilt and the consequences. If his guise as a medical student didn't work, Hans would need a better plan to escape the wrath that would certainly be brought upon him by the victors.

And he had one—built around extensive, damning information he'd gathered on his SS physician colleagues and their "experimental studies"—a plan carefully rehearsed and to be set in motion should that difficult moment arrive. He had it all: where each camp doctor was from, what his interests were, and most importantly, what experiments they participated in at Auschwitz-Birkenau. This list of SS physicians and their programs was safely stored back at his mother's home. At the outset, he had gathered this data for future academic use, but it soon struck him that should the unthinkable happen and the Fatherland go down in defeat, he could use it to save his life.

In an effort to both ingratiate himself with the other SS physicians and gather more information, he had offered to prepare and type their studies in a format suitable for scientific journals. Little did they realize that his outstanding support would become their future demise. As part of his "preparation" for these journals, he was able to obtain each physician's home address for later correspondence between the doctor and the medical editors. Hans prepared the papers in triplicate, keeping one copy in his personal files. He knew he possessed an important commodity that could one day be his ticket out of confinement and punishment.

Now was the moment to implement this contingency plan. Hans knew that rather than spar with this lowly officer for his freedom, he must change direction and trigger his Plan B.

In fact, this young officer will pass me directly through to the intelligence community.

Looking straight at the lieutenant, Hans broke the heavy silence. "Sir, rather than going back and forth with you over the issue of my background, I must now tell you that I was a physician working in the concentration camps. Furthermore, I *may* have information relative to the human experimentation carried out at Auschwitz, which *may* be of interest to the British Secret Service or the American OSS. If there is someone here who is concerned with such matters, I would like to talk with him."

The words were barely out of his mouth when the British officer turned and reached for the phone to call his captain. Not able to hear any of the conversation, Hans finally exhaled as he watched the young lieutenant write down a series of numbers and instructions.

Two MPs appeared, and Hans was swiftly driven two kilometers to a former police facility now surrounded with barbed wire, where he joined a large group of German soldiers milling about. Some were in Wehrmacht uniforms, others in civilian clothes, yet he saw none in SS attire. Many were talking quietly in small groups. He kept to himself and spoke with no one. Shortly, he was taken into a makeshift examining room where a young enlisted man took his pulse, blood pressure, and respiratory rate. A physician followed, and a full physical examination was performed after which Hans was allowed to put his clothes back on and sit quietly awaiting whatever would happen next. In a few minutes, the same soldier escorted him to another office and asked him to sit down opposite a massive desk, the only item of significance in this bare, cold office. Stacked rows of files covered the entire desktop. A black leather-backed desk chair sat empty facing Hans. A short time later, an officer entered, sat at the desk and peered directly at Hans.

"Herr Doktor Hauptman, or whatever your name might be, I am an American, Colonel Max Fisher of the OSS. I understand you wish to talk with someone of authority."

Swallowing hard, and silently rehearsing his story, Hans stood up straight and saluted the officer. "Doctor Hans Bloch, of the twenty-first Medical Battalion SS. I am your prisoner and expect to be treated under the protections and accords of the Geneva Convention. I have already told the other officers all that is necessary under international law."

Hans studied his adversary. He was about forty-five, short and squat, less than five foot eight with a receding forehead topped with salt-and-pepper hair. He wore a bushy mustache, neatly trimmed, and seemed to enjoy touching it with his fingertips. His eyes were alert and bored into Hans, carefully watching him as he recited his name, rank, and serial number. The colonel waited patiently, expecting Hans to say more.

"The war is over," Hans began slowly, "and I have no desire to relive this agony we have all gone through. Whatever I can do to help make all of this come to an end, I will do. I will assist in any way, but I do expect a certain level of consideration from you."

The colonel nodded, as if he understood.

Okay, I'll trust that he will recall what I have said about "consideration" and confirm his support later on.

Taking a deep breath, Hans began delivering the carefully constructed script that he hoped would lead to his freedom. "If you please, Herr Colonel, forgive my poor English. It's been too long since I studied at Oxford, and I have spoken it so infrequently since then."

A brief flash of warmth crossed the American officer's face when Hans mentioned his time in England. He looked as if he wanted to probe about his time there, but instead, he smiled slightly, encouraging Hans to continue.

The story Hans told for the next four hours was mostly true, especially about his family and childhood. Born and raised in nearby Kiel, he knew Hamburg well and was able to identify points of interest, such as the picturesque harbor that existed before the war. Hans expanded his real Oxford experience—a single summer course—to two years of pre-medical training, hoping to create some kind of cultural bond with the American agent. The colonel, in kind, spoke of his visit to Berlin as a student. Hans sensed that the Allied officer was also looking for some form of connection by inflating his experience in Germany.

Looking at his SS captive, Colonel Fisher found himself warming up to the nervous young man.

This guy doesn't appear to be a criminal.

Still, both men were on guard, playing the game cautiously, though the stakes were highest for Hans. Seeing the colonel smile, a wave of relief swept through his body.

This is a game I can win.

There was certain information that had to be stated clearly and accurately, as Hans knew that German military and SS data could easily be verified. And he realized that the more personally credible he became, the better chance he had to make his strategy work. He spoke nostalgically of his journey to become a physician, fondly relating how his grandfather had encouraged him to pursue medicine, and talking about the father he never knew since he was killed in the Great War.

Hans then recited his education from kindergarten through medical school. He again mentioned studying at Oxford but did not specify the dates. He told how, after graduation, he'd developed a fascination with research and talked about some of the early papers he'd published before the war started. He reflected on the importance of becoming SS, to himself and his family, and the honor he wished to restore to the memory of his father and to his beloved Germany.

The colonel listened attentively and took copious notes, jotting down every date mentioned. Hans's words came more slowly as fatigue and hunger weighed upon him, and, noting his weariness, the colonel suggested they stop their discussion and resume in the morning. He also advised Hans that he was going to verify some of the information he had given him.

Hans was placed alone in a cell and a soldier's packaged meal was delivered to him. He had never been locked up before but, surprisingly, it felt reassuring to be isolated.

It is better to be alone. No Germans to question my motives.

Sparse, with no furniture, the room had only a cot. This outpost appeared to have been one of the Hamburg police jails located just outside of the central city. The privacy and quiet gave him time to better prepare for the next meeting with the American agent. He looked up to see a small, narrow horizontal window protected with bars at the top of the outside wall. Standing on his cot, he gazed out at the city he once knew, and the canal nearby. For the first time in years, his eyes began to tear as he recognized that, if his plan were to be successful, he would have to leave his beloved country, most likely forever.

He began to organize his thoughts into chapters. Within each segment, he would bring forth some small fact that would pique the colonel's interest and tease him into looking ahead to the next session. *Write the book, keep the reader interested, and make him a part of it.*

Early the next morning, the polite young soldier from the previous evening unlocked the cell door and led Hans back to the same office as before. The colonel, already there and reviewing his notes, looked up as Hans entered the room. "Please sit down, Doctor, we have much to talk about," he said in a somewhat cheerful tone. "I was able to confirm that the authorities' records from Kiel were intact and are in our custody at this time. And we were able to review your SS file." He looked at Hans, expecting some facial response, but Hans remained stoic. Colonel Fisher smiled. "Major, the floor is yours. Let us hear about your wartime experience."

Hans picked up his story where he'd left it the day before. "I joined the SS after completion of three years of surgical residency at Kiel University Hospital. It was always my intention to stay in research, and I was given that opportunity after completing the required SS course work. I had been studying methods to help our airmen survive the cold ocean after being shot out of the sky. This sent me to Dachau initially, and later to Auschwitz to complete my studies."

"Doctor Bloch, what about the subjects you used in your experiments? I have heard some concerns raised about this issue."

Hans paused.

He knows, damn it... I can't hide anything... Maybe just soften it a bit.

"As you are aware, Colonel, Dachau and Auschwitz-Birkenau were work camps to provide labor for industry. The work was hard, and, frankly, the living conditions and food were, suffice it to say—poor. The German government did not put enough resources into the camps, and unnecessary deaths occurred. Some of the more fortunate inmates were allowed to participate in our studies and were well fed and kept healthy, sheltered indoors in our laboratory, out of the weather."

"So you are saying that the lucky ones became part of your study?"

"No, sir, not necessarily. But it was important to have healthy subjects for our study."

"So, Major, your studies didn't lead to any deaths. Is that true?"

"No, Colonel, I didn't say that. Yes, we did have some deaths, but not because of my cold immersion study," Hans lied.

Colonel Fisher's face suddenly became hard, and he looked at Hans directly with a cold stare. "Bodies were discovered, stacked up just inside the gates of the camps. Some of these poor individuals had scars from experimental surgery; others had enucleation of their eyes, and many had signs of direct inoculation of infections into their bodies. And you tell me none of your subjects died because of your study?!" Anger welled up inside the colonel; his face reddened, and he looked like he was ready to lash out physically at Hans. "And there must be a score more of SS doctors like you who butchered untold thousands of Jews with their worthless experiments!"

Bowing his head in feigned deference, Hans said, "The deaths bothered me greatly, as a physician... It was hard for me to accept that so many died unnecessarily. I was fooled by those SS physicians who carried out studies that were meaningless in the end. One doctor in particular stood out..."

"Yes, who? Which one?"

Hans hesitated a moment. "You may have heard of him—Mengele."

The colonel sat up quickly upon hearing that name. "Was this the SS doctor they called the 'Angel of Death'?"

"Yes, sir, I believe some of the inmates may have called him that. Mengele was important to the camp and supervised all human experimentation."

Hans chose not to mention his additional function as the chief officer responsible for selecting those sent to the gas chambers.

"Continue on, but I want to know as much about Mengele as possible."

Over the next four days, Colonel Fisher took extensive notes as Hans gave detailed descriptions of Mengele and each of the SS physicians, and he recounted their experiments on the prisoners. The colonel was surprised at the extensive knowledge Hans had about each study at Auschwitz-Birkenau, but he waited until the last day to ask him about the documentation he had to support this information.

Hans was ready for this moment, and had carefully planned his response. "Colonel Fisher, when you started the interrogation, I mentioned that I would expect some consideration in return for my cooperation. It is obvious that the information I have will be valuable to you and the OSS in the pursuit of war criminal charges against many of my former colleagues." Sitting forward, Hans leaned his arms against the desk and peered directly into the colonel's eyes. "However, I need some form of guarantee that I will be free from prosecution after we have finished. In addition, for my personal safety, I need to be sent out of Europe, away from the war and its memories. I want to start a new life."

The colonel tamped the bowl of his pipe and relit it. Through a cloud of smoke he said, "Yes, all this is valuable and could be helpful in our efforts, but we still need documentation. You've given me quite a complete account, but how am I to know that it's the truth? If you can confirm any of these experiments with written data, I can help you."

Hans let a few moments pass while he appeared lost in thought, as if trying to recall some important fact. He could sense the American becoming anxious as he kept tamping his pipe unnecessarily and relighting it, waiting for Hans's response.

"Colonel Fisher, I can lead you to copies of the experimental designs and data, after, of course, the appropriate guarantees are signed."

Fisher left the office and returned with blank sheets of paper for Hans. "Write out what would work for you in the future and sign it. I will bring it to my general for review. When you are finished, place this paper clip on the document and give it to the sergeant."

"...and to teach them this art, if they shall wish to learn it..."

32

April 18, 1948
Montreal, Canada

Exiting the Jewish Hospital of Montreal, Michel was beckoned by this beautiful April day to forego lunch and enjoy the change in seasons. He strolled alone, as he had often done in Lyon when he walked along the Saone River. The midday sun had just begun to give off warmth that he could barely feel under his jacket and the spring thaw had left the sides of the road stained brown from the sand used to de-ice the snowy streets in winter. A quiet hike along the riverbank was one of the few pleasures from the past he could still enjoy.

But this anticipated diversion was tempered by his ongoing worry of being discovered; the paranoia was intense—a constant fear that one day he would be recognized by someone from his past. It was eerie how so many people he saw on the street recalled painful memories of the camps. If their back was rounded or they used a cane, he would wonder; if their eyes were sunken or their cheeks hollow, he became uneasy as he passed them by.

Most camp survivors had physical changes that persisted after liberation and freedom; the camp diet had been devoid of calcium, and the daily meal of dirty bread and gruel was barely four hundred calories. The silent pain of spinal compression fractures was accompanied by a permanent rounding of the thoracic spine that was irreversible, despite an adequate diet during the years after liberation.

As he walked along the St. Lawrence River, he continually scanned the sidewalk, the roadway, and the adjacent park. He was a spectacle to behold, constantly moving his head from side to side, as if he were being hunted.

Michel easily understood why he would be disliked—even abhorred—by those who had come out of the camp alive. In many survivors' minds, he would always be associated with Mengele and the other SS physicians. He shamefully held secrets that few people knew; he had witnessed the method by which Mengele killed the children in his twin studies: chloroform injected with a long needle directly into their hearts. These poor young ones had been saved from the gas chambers, only to be used in his grotesque studies and then slain. But it was Michel who had opened up their bodies and took a piece of their shrunken liver; it was he who had cut a section of an atrophied sigmoid colon or prepared a slide of their spleen.

His only living patients had been the Sonderkommandos who worked in Crematorium III, but he knew that they, too, were destined to die. Ironically, it was his job to keep them strong and well, and he'd been given a great variety of medicines and bandages for these inmates—equal to those available to the guards and SS officers.

As he watched the winding river current carry the barges downstream, he mused about his own life's twists and turns.

Is this my penitence? Must I always wander in fear? Only thoughts of Tamara bring me brief respite from the painful judgments I have placed upon myself.

Each day, he hurried home from work, hoping to find a pale blue envelope with his name written in her artistic hand. In the two years after leaving Auschwitz, she'd graduated from high school and was awarded a scholarship to the Prague Institute of Art, where her skills had been honed and polished; her paintings, depicting scenes of the camps, had been chosen for display in the Institute's prestigious gallery. He recalled the opening paragraph of the last note he'd received.

Dear Michel,

I pray this finds you in good spirits. I am doing well here at the Art Institute. It's a little difficult to manage school and care for my younger brother Samuel. Nanny Freda had kept him safe from the Germans during the war and he was ready to come home and stay with me after hostilities ended. He is a good student and looks to be interested in engineering. I am hopeful for the future as there are many people attracted to my paintings, and I hear murmurings that someday I will be asked to participate in an art exhibition in America.

His replies had been brief, though caring. He could not share her optimistic spirit, and doubted that she would ever leave her home. His letters to her had a different tone and color, as if contrasting their new lives. Tamara's were a vibrant panoply of multiple bright hues; Michel wrote only in shades of white and gray.

He soon found it difficult to sit down and write, and months would go by without answering her. Tamara's life seemed to be expanding into something beautiful, while all he had to share was an empty life of dreariness and depression. When he did write back to her, he tried hard to minimize these feelings by sharing only minor details. He sensed that she understood he was battling his demons, and did not press him to reveal more. But he began to fear that reluctance to share his thoughts would frustrate her, and his sadness might, in some way, dampen her happiness.

Still, in a few weeks, his life was about to change, and he wanted to let her know this. So it was with hesitation that, one night in July 1948, he sat down to write...

Dear Tamara,

I hope this finds you well.

Each letter I receive from you seems to bring a fresh breeze into my existence. I do relish your words, as I see happiness growing in your life. I must say that my time has been sad. I have been rereading a stack of mail from you that I have saved, and must apologize for not responding sooner.

My letters to you are often brief and purposely bereft of details of my life. As I have already told you, I searched for my family and have been unable to find them anywhere, but I did not give you the details of my travels. My wife and children were not at Terezin, and I stopped at many displaced persons' camps and looked at so many lists, so many records, but could not find their names anywhere. I had hoped beyond hope, but now I believe they are dead. Upon returning to my home in Lyon, I discovered that my house had been ransacked and vandalized. I did learn that my uncle Stan and his wife had died in a work camp. My parents and sister are presumed dead, as well. There was nothing left for me in Europe.

I have just finished my required two-year training program at the Jewish General Hospital in Montreal. It has been an excellent place to work, and it was best that I did take additional instruction prior to entering into practice again. Being assigned to a general surgical service, I worked at the level of a senior resident. My responsibilities included running a surgical ward of thirty patients and supervising an intern and second-year resident in surgery. In addition, my team was responsible for caring for urgent cases admitted through the emergency room. It felt good to be helping people again—yet my nights are often filled with fear about someone discovering my past. I know it sounds crazy.

Do you recall Rabbi Rosenberg from Auschwitz? I received a letter from him last month. He left on that forced march from Auschwitz to Buchenwald, right before the Russian forces liberated the camp. I had talked with you about him, although you never were able to meet. He survived the march, spent one month in a hospital, and was able to immigrate to New York City. It was good to hear from him. I answered back and told him about your survival and hiding all those months in the attic until the Germans left.

And there is some good news. I was fortunate to be asked to join a surgical group in Milwaukee, Wisconsin, and will move there this month. I do look forward to restarting clinical practice and pray that I can, hopefully, put the past behind me and carve out a new life.

Please continue to write, as I prize each letter from you. And if the murmurings about coming to America are true, let me know when that might happen, as I would love to see you again.

Affectionately,
Michel Katz

33

May 18, 1945
Hamburg

The next morning, Hans was brought to Colonel Fisher's office for more questioning. He'd been unable to sleep or eat since he'd given the colonel the document detailing the information he would offer the Allies in exchange for his freedom. The colonel continued to tamp his pipe while Hans sat nervously in his chair, trying to appear relaxed.

"Doctor Bloch," the colonel said, "we have been meeting over half the night concerning you. We have read your demands, and there seems to be a difference of opinion among my colleagues about what should be done with you. The OSS is well aware of your past and wants to press charges against you for war crimes, specifically for your experimental work at the concentration camps. Also in question is your involvement in a particular top secret study; we are still pursuing more information on this."

Colonel Fisher hesitated and stared directly at Hans, looking for any reaction to his last words.

"In your favor, however," he resumed, clearing his throat, "there is a group of scientists working for the Army Air Corps who are interested in your cold immersion studies and any other experimental data you collected while at Auschwitz. If you work with us, we may be able to secure a position for you in America, but, upon completion of your project, you will then be deported back to Germany to go through a de-nazification program; we will outline the details later. Your cooperation could go a long way in reducing any punishment you are due."

Hans looked earnestly at his adversary. "I have told you I can be of great benefit to your country in terms of the information I have concerning the activities that went on at Auschwitz-Birkenau. Not only would some of the experimental data be important, but also the information I have on the other SS physicians would be quite helpful to your war crimes investigators. But in regards to *any* 'top secret study,' I have no information about that."

Silently, Hans prayed that the OSS had not learned of the God-forsaken radiation study…

I was the only doctor aware of its existence, having been recruited at Dachau. It was highly classified and Mengele had no knowledge of it. They couldn't possibly have uncovered any information.

Seeing little reaction from Hans, Colonel Fisher sat back in his chair and said, "We must review what files you have before I can promise you anything."

Taking a chance, Hans leapt to his feet. "Colonel, do I look like a fool to you? If I bring my information here, you can take it and do what you like with me, and I am no better for it. No, sir, I must have a complete guarantee that I will go to America and work with your scientists on my studies. Otherwise, I can't share a thing with you."

"Doctor Bloch, I won't send you, a war criminal, to the United States without any justification. We need to see this information in order to know how valuable it may be."

Hans reached inside his coat, ripping the inner lining. The colonel sprang back suddenly, and placed his hand on his holster, fearing Hans might be going for a weapon. But before he could draw his pistol, Hans pulled out two sheets of paper and handed them to the colonel. "This is a taste of the material I have collected," he said, calmly.

Colonel Fisher scanned the pages, quickly noting the name Josef Mengele, MD. His eyes widened as he reread the information. Included on the typed sheet were Mengele's home address and the names of his wife and children. On the second sheet, there was a list of Mengele's experimental studies.

Taking a deep breath, the colonel cleared his throat and looked at Hans with the hint of a smile, and conceded. "Doctor Bloch, my secretary will make up an agreement for you to sign. You must understand that, if approved, you will be returned back to Germany after your studies in the US are completed. Prosecution for any war crimes will be waived, but you must return for some routine processing that would allow you to work again in Germany."

Colonel Fisher left the room as Hans was escorted back to his cell.

After another sleepless night, Hans was taken to Kiel to retrieve the files he had hidden in a steamer trunk at his mother's home. Handing these files to the Colonel, a large paper clip was placed on the outside of the packet.

Staring earnestly into Hans's eyes, the colonel said, "You will not discuss our plans with anyone. Remember, 'Operation Paper Clip' is top secret."

Over the next several weeks, Hans was intensely questioned by several OSS officers and research physicians prior to getting administrative permission to travel to San Antonio, Texas, where an apartment would be waiting for him.

As he boarded the ship to New York, he looked back silently over his shoulder at the Port of Hamburg, knowing that this might be the last time he would see his homeland. But at least he was safe.

♦♦♦

HANS HAD NOT TRULY comprehended the size of the United States until he boarded a train and traveled eighteen hundred miles from New York to San Antonio in July of 1946. By European standards, the U.S. trains were of a lower class and did not give the service he was used to. Yet, he had little to complain about. He had escaped being tried for war crimes and was going to a place where he could continue his studies.

There was little fanfare upon his arrival in San Antonio. He was greeted at the train station by Private Marcus Shaver, a research assistant, and driven to his new apartment quarters on Randolph Air Force Base. Little was said during the ride. The private seemed kind and helped him unload, carrying the suitcases into his new home; he left him with typed instructions concerning the next day's schedule.

Hans finished unpacking and took a short walk around the base residences to stretch his muscles after the three-day train ride. Gazing up at the faded, light-green military housing, he was somewhat surprised.

So this is America!

Drab as it was, Hans realized that for him, this was heaven. He had been directed to meet with Brigadier General Robert Short at 9:00 a.m. the following day. Private Shaver arrived at Hans's quarters in the morning and escorted him to the general's office, then waited in the reception area as Hans was invited in. Shaking hands, General Short said, "It's good to finally meet you, Doctor Bloch. We've been expecting you for some time now. Have a seat."

"Thank you, General." Hans sat down. "I had hoped to arrive weeks ago, but small details had to be completed prior to my leaving Hamburg. I must say, your government is quite focused on the minutiae of one's past life. Everything I told them had to be verified before I was allowed to board ship."

"Well, you have discovered one of the secrets of our government, but I'll live with that," said the general with a smile. "Even though the war is over, these are still difficult times, and we all must adjust. Your placement here has stirred a lot of controversy among the Army staff and present administration in Washington, but similar issues were raised with many of the other scientists we've recruited from Germany under Operation Paper Clip."

Leaning back in his chair, the general folded his hands and continued. "We do have some rules you must follow, if you intend to successfully complete your work with us. Your travels are restricted to the City of San Antonio. You will be given a work card as identification and you must present it when asked by any authority. You are to work only for us, at this base. And finally, you do not have permission to travel anywhere else in this country, and you are not licensed to practice medicine here."

Hans shifted unconsciously in his chair.

"In addition, there will be no discussions of your work with anyone outside of your specific research team," General Short continued. "Your work is sensitive and may upset others who do not understand its significance. If approached by any member of the press with inquiries about the project or your past, you must plead 'top secret.' Do you have any questions?"

"No sir, I...have none," replied Hans, somewhat shaken.

He had not expected such restrictions.

The general stood up. "Good. Then it's time for you to visit room 12c, the laboratory home for your studies. Private Shaver has been assigned to help you, and he will take you there. Good day."

Hans spent the next thirty days organizing the research project that had been carefully vetted by many levels of military and government officials. He had wanted to continue with human volunteers, but his request was firmly denied by the base's Research Council. News of the concentration camp experiments was just making headlines and horrifying the public; Rhesus monkeys were to be used instead. His assistant, Marcus, was quite helpful in obtaining the immersion tanks, ice, and monitoring equipment necessary.

Private Marcus Shaver had been drafted and assigned to the Army Air Corps as a research aide. He had been in pre-medical studies at Duke University and was ready to enter medical school when his selective service notice arrived in September 1944. He had just fifteen months left on his military obligation when he was assigned to Doctor Bloch. His commanding officers had been tight-lipped about the doctor's past, and Marcus knew better than to ask questions; in fact, few on the base knew anything about Bloch's background. But at times, he wondered...

Why would they bring German scientists and doctors to this country after all the death and destruction caused by their actions?

This study involved vital sign documentation and interval blood tests on the monkeys during cold immersion. From time to time, one of the animals died during the experiment and autopsy studies were performed.

Private Shaver was responsible for the accurate recording of all the data collected, and the study progressed smoothly as he worked with the German doctor. He noticed that Hans Bloch spent many hours in the laboratory and socialized little on the base, other than joining a few colleagues for drinks at the end of the work week.

♦♦♦

GENERAL SHORT WAS GIVEN weekly reports of the progress of Doctor Bloch's study by Marcus, and after eleven months, enough data had been obtained to complete the cold immersion study. Hans was happy with this course of events. He had excellent help in his laboratory, and the support of the facility was without fault. Also, to his surprise, he became aware of another study on hypothermia at the University of Cincinnati, published in 1944. Sixteen mentally retarded individuals had been placed in refrigerated cabinets for 120 hours at thirty degrees Fahrenheit. This research had sparked fierce controversy in the medical community over the issue of informed consent. The stated goal had been to find out if cooling diminished or improved the subjects' mental capacities. The results were mixed, but the issue of human experimentation had generated much debate.

From his previous work at Auschwitz, Hans had gathered sufficient background material on cold immersion, and, with the new data obtained from the San Antonio study, his research was quickly written up. The Cincinnati experiment had been helpful, and Hans wanted to find out more from the study's authors. He contacted the university to get further details and quietly inquired about the possibility of further resident training in Cincinnati.

It was almost a year to the day he had arrived at the base when he received notice that on July 7, 1947 he was to present his completed study to the Army's Research Council in San Antonio.

"In conclusion, gentlemen," he addressed the group of military doctors, "our studies have now shown that Rhesus monkeys can withstand immersion in thirty degrees Centigrade water for three hours without ill effect. If the temperature is lowered to twenty-five degrees, forty percent of the animals will die. Adding natural fiber insulation to these animals will allow external cooling to twenty-five degrees for three hours, with just a slight decrease in core temperature."

Hans took his seat following a vigorous applause and expected to answer further questions, but none were asked.

General Short broke the silence. "It's clear, Doctor Bloch, that you truly have studied hypothermic effects on primates, and understand this as well as any doctor in the world. We are justly proud to have your work here and hope that someday secrecy restrictions will be lifted and this important scientific study can be published."

Hans went to bed that night feeling proud. His ego was restored to its healthy state, and he easily fell asleep. But a cold sweat woke him at 4:00 a.m., and he bolted upright in bed.

Have I finished the project too quickly? Will they be through with me?

He had difficulty falling back to sleep and spent most of the early morning outlining a plan to ensure his continued freedom.

His newfound confidence following the praise from his colleagues had relaxed his guard, and some of the former personality traits he had carefully hidden began to resurface. One day, as Private Shaver was cleaning up the lab, Hans stormed out of his office and yelled, "Private, you *Dummkopf,* where is that typed report? It was due this morning!" Raising his voice even higher, he said, "How many times do I have to tell you how important this project is, you damn lazy American?"

Brushing past him, Marcus entered Hans's office, pulled a folder from the top of the inbox, and slowly turned, burning inside, and handed Hans the completed report. "Doctor, it was done yesterday... *You* missed it. It was sitting right here."

Hans said nothing, but the look he gave Marcus made the private shudder.

The general's secretary, Mary Smith, had overheard the loud exchange. Later that day, she approached Marcus in the lunchroom. "That German doctor," she whispered, "I hear how he treats you. You might want to familiarize yourself with his past."

She quickly turned to walk away, but Marcus grabbed her arm.

"What do you mean? What can you tell me?"

"I can only tell you that it's top secret. That's all I can say. But you should go to the base movie theater tonight and see the Clark Gable movie, Command Decision. There is also a special edition of Movietone News detailing the liberation of the Buchenwald Concentration Camp. You'll understand."

◆ ◆ ◆

LATER THAT NIGHT, MARCUS left the theater, fists clenched, heart pounding.

That bastard! He did these experiments on humans, I know it! He worked in those concentration camps and we invited him here... I could kill him...

At first, his anger clouded his judgment.

I worry about Mary.

As the general's secretary, she had top-secret clearance. If he mentioned anything about Bloch's past or approached the general, an investigation could lead back to her.

I'll find a way.

◆ ◆ ◆

DESPERATE FOR MORE TIME in San Antonio, Hans asked to meet with General Short to discuss plans for further research.

"General, I was quite satisfied with our experimental model utilizing the Rhesus monkeys. Having this study as a baseline, I'd like to propose that we test various materials for heat retention, with direct applicability to the materials used in flying suits in our pilots."

"Yes, you did a fine job, and we are all quite pleased," said Short. "The difficulty, however, is that with the war over, scientific funding has been cut. I doubt if we can continue your project as you would like."

But Bloch would not give up. "Well then, perhaps I could become involved in another ongoing study? I could offer my assistance to...the high altitude study. Yes, that would be good."

"Doctor Bloch, I will do my best to find a way to keep you here, as you have proven your value. But you must understand...limits are placed upon us."

♦♦♦

LATER THAT DAY, MARCUS was sitting with Mary at lunch. "We must do something," he said, keeping his voice low. "We can't just sit here and allow this *bastard* to roam free."

Mary drew in a deep breath. "I shouldn't be saying any of this, my job is at stake." She took a quick gulp of milk before she continued. "He is trying to extend his stay here and work on other experiments. I cannot give you any details, but...you saw the news report on Buchenwald. He wasn't there, but there were other camps...horrible camps, like Auschwitz. I can't say anymore." She paused and moved her chair closer and whispered in Marcus's ear. "General Short is about to agree to grant him more time here, so we must intervene somehow and get him back to Germany, as per his contract. I know I am telling you too much, Marcus, but my best friend Rachel would be devastated if she knew. She lost both sets of grandparents in Auschwitz. We must find a way to stop him—now!"

While Bloch was planning his future at the base, Marcus knew he had to act. Anger continued to stir within, and he had trouble sleeping that night. *Auschwitz, that's where the Nazi worked. Millions were killed there.*

Marcus had two Jewish friends, enlisted soldiers, who he suspected would take a special interest in Hans and the "studies" he'd conducted during the war.

Hans often frequented a bar close to the base, The Army Roadhouse, and he'd made plans for the following evening with colleagues to celebrate the success of his project. Aware of Hans's schedule, Marcus invited his two friends to join him at the Roadhouse tavern for drinks that night.

It was a perfect summer evening. The day's warmth was dissipating as the three young friends entered the tavern. Marcus scanned the room until he found what he was looking for—Hans standing next to the bar, enjoying himself with several coworkers.

Marcus posed a question to his unsuspecting accomplices. "Robert, Jerry, what if I told you that man sitting at the bar just three stools away is Hans Bloch, a former German SS officer and a doctor who experimented on Jews at Auschwitz?"

They both looked at him as if he was crazy.

"I'm not kidding," Marcus continued. "And what if I also told you that Doctor Bloch works for our government, our Army Air Corps, continuing his experimental work here in San Antonio?"

Marcus could see rage building in the faces of his two friends. "Listen, he took Jewish men and submerged them in freezing water, killing many of them as part of a study, without any concern. He did this at the Dachau and Auschwitz concentration camps, where over one million Jews were killed. Just look at that arrogant bastard, sitting in our country, in our neighborhood bar, enjoying our beer and laughing—not a care in the world. What do you think? Maybe you'd like to ask him about his time in the war…?"

"But Marcus, how sure are you? Would our government really do this?" asked Jerry Schwartz.

"I have no doubts. A reliable source told me, someone close to a high-ranking officer on the base. Besides, I've seen his conduct, his anger and disrespect for others. It all fits."

Marcus had picked these two men carefully, knowing how inflamed and passionate they had become when they saw newsreels reporting the Nazi atrocities at the concentration camps. Now they sat in stunned silence. As he waited for his friends to digest the news and consider his challenge, he made eye contact with Hans.

I got you now, you bastard.

Hans, unaware of Shaver's thoughts, tilted his head slightly in acknowledgment.

Marcus excused himself and headed for the exit, but he didn't want to miss what would happen next. From the doorway, he could watch his friends in animated discussion with their foreheads touching—speaking in low tones. Robert's face was turning red and Jerry was pounding his right fist into his palm as he got up and walked straight toward Hans. Robert followed on his heels.

"Doctor Bloch," said Jerry, edging a little too close to Hans. "We are two soldiers interested in the war. I am Jerry Schwartz, and this is Robert Rubenstein... Are you getting the picture?" Edging closer, his face next to Hans, he hissed, "We'd really like to know what you did as a doctor in the war—or, rather, in the concentration camps, *you son of a bitch*... Just how many Jews did you kill?"

Hans started to stand, getting up from his barstool. "None of your goddamn Jew business!"

Hans's colleagues backed off as he tried to walk away. "Get out of my way...I'm leaving."

Neither of the two soldiers budged, blocking Hans's path. They stood there waiting for a response, and it came as Hans's fist struck out toward Robert, who easily ducked and delivered a crushing blow to Hans's right temple. Hans fought back but was pummeled with multiple blows from the two angry men. A crowd encircled the fight as Hans collapsed onto the floor. For a few seconds, Robert and Jerry stared at the helpless lump beneath them, saying nothing. Then they calmly walked away, as the knowing crowd split in two, facilitating their departure. Two MPs, whistles screeching, charged through the door but failed to notice the two soldiers making a casual exit.

Hans survived with a few nasty bruises and a small cut on his upper lip. What he didn't survive was the newspaper account of the brawl that followed, taken from an anonymous witness who described in detail what had been said and who threw the first punch. The headline read: "SS Doctor Attacked in Bar Fight." The article discussed Doctor Hans Bloch's presence in San Antonio and his past involvement in human experimentation at Auschwitz.

This quickly became a problem for the Army Air Corps and General Short, in particular, who suffered the most embarrassment from the incident. Radio and print reporters besieged him for interviews, but he declined them all. The White House sent him an urgent telegram: "Get rid of Doctor Hans Bloch. NOW!"

General Short sent a written communication to Hans:

"It is in the best interest of the US Army and our government if you are returned to Germany, as per the agreement signed by you. A reservation has been made for you to travel by bus to New York on July 9, 1946. You will be given transportation to the Port of New York and passage on the transatlantic liner SS Norway, departing July 12, 1946. In the meantime, you are confined to your quarters."

Hans had much to think about. He had let his anger get the best of him, but he couldn't let that little slip mess up his plans; he already had a backup scheme to keep him in the United States. His agreement under the contract he'd given Colonel Fisher allowed him to enter the United States for scientific studies only, similar to the contracts given to rocket scientists like Werner Von Braun. No time limit had been designated in his Operation Paperclip documents, but when the studies were completed, the scientist or doctor was required to return to Germany. It was clear that when the American government was through with these men, they were sent home.

But Hans had other plans.

Secretly, he had applied for a surgical residency at The University Hospital in Cincinnati, Ohio—the same institution that had conducted the hypothermic studies on retarded men. But the name Hans Bloch was nowhere on the application. He had carefully guarded the Hauptman diploma and documents, knowing that someday they would be useful to him. Jürgen Hauptman, MD was ready to become a surgeon in the United States, and Doctor Hans Bloch was about to disappear forever.

"Whether they be free men or slaves…"

34

July 11, 1946
Cincinnati, Ohio

T he seven rolling hills that embrace Cincinnati were a wonderful surprise for Hans. He had endured the flat landscape and colorless adobe-inspired structures and homes of San Antonio for the last twelve months and had hoped to find a real city in America where he could feel comfortable. Beyond the interesting geography, the metropolitan area of Cincinnati seemed to share some of the elegance and class common to European cities. This large city also afforded the opportunity for a person to be faceless, almost invisible.

As he walked along the narrow boulevard adjoining the Cincinnati General Hospital, a hot breeze caused him to remove his suit jacket. To the southwest, high, billowing thunderclouds filled the sky, promising a shower in the evening. He entered a park at the base of Dixmyth Street and sat down on a bench to reflect on the events of the last few weeks.

Free at last…no suspicious eyes following my every move. And I left there before those damn Jews could again come after me. How long will it take for anyone to miss me in Germany? No, I won't be found; even if they question my mother and grandfather…they won't know. I have told no one where I am. The party was fine, but Americans try too hard to be nice… It makes me gag.

Despite the furor surrounding Hans Bloch, the staff members in San Antonio had felt obliged to throw a modest farewell party to celebrate the successful completion of his study and his return to Germany. Only General Short was aware of the telegram from the White House that hastened Hans's exit. The other staff members had no idea that the agreement Hans signed in Hamburg with Colonel Fisher had stipulated that, upon completion of his initial cold immersion study, he would be returned to Germany for de-nazification. The exact details of this process were not spelled out, but after surrender, SS and prominent Nazis had already begun to be debriefed regarding their activities during the war.

But for Hans, it was simply deportation, and he wasn't going to let that happen. On the eve of the party, he received word from Cincinnati General Hospital that a position in their surgical residency had opened and that he should call to schedule an interview within the next two weeks.

Private Shaver's last chore was to drive Hans to the Greyhound station in San Antonio. Gloating internally, Marcus opened the rear door of the Chevrolet sedan for the glum-appearing German. It was an uncomfortable ride and not a word was spoken between them while Hans stared straight ahead at the highway. Dropping him off at the downtown depot, Marcus waited until he was sure Hans had entered the bus marked: "New York City." Ecstatic with his success and not wishing to stay a minute longer, Shaver stomped on the accelerator, squealing his tires, and sped away in the army sedan.

Good riddance, Nazi slime.

If he'd glanced in his rear view mirror even once, he would have seen Hans slip off the bus and board another one marked: "Cincinnati."

Finally, Hans was on his way to fulfill his dream. There were no guards to fool, no one demanding identification or travel papers. For the first time in two years, he felt totally free.

Arriving in Cincinnati two days later, he made his way by taxi to the Vernon Manor, an old but classy hotel. Although somewhat luxurious, he could afford to stay there a few days until he secured the residency position.

At the hotel desk he smiled at the registration clerk and signed in as Jürgen Hauptman, MD. "Might you have an inexpensive room, as my budget is limited?"

Casting a wary eye at this foreigner, the clerk said, "I do have one room that might be perfect for you."

A rickety, old elevator took him up to the fourth floor, where upon entering room 410, his senses were overwhelmed with a musty smell that suggested the room had not been opened or aired for many days. After a light meal at the hotel's restaurant, Hans settled back in his room, unpacked, and showered. Gazing out the south-facing window at the Ohio River, he was pleased by how easily he had escaped into his new life. Then he pulled a sheaf of documents from his briefcase, spread them out on the bed, and began preparing for his meeting with the head of the surgical program—scheduled for two days hence.

Rising late the next morning, Hans decided to become acquainted with this special old city and its unique charm. The downtown area was laid out in a grid pattern and easy to navigate as he walked outside his hotel. He made his way to Dixmyth Street, which wound up a steep hill to the Cincinnati General Hospital. Once away from the central city, curved roads intersecting at all angles with no apparent logic replaced the regular street pattern. He came across an attractive apartment building just two blocks from the hospital and decided to inquire inside. Within a half hour, there was a suitable unit on hold for him, pending the outcome of his interview.

"So, Doctor Hauptman, it is good to meet you," said Doctor Hugh Tackett, chairman of the surgery department, the following day. "I'm sure it was a difficult struggle for you in Germany, and I can understand why you might want to come to this country."

Hans sat quietly, head slightly bowed. "I can't tell you how fortunate I feel to be here, after going through what I have experienced these past four years, Doctor Tackett."

"Why don't you start by telling me about your education and where the war took you?" Tackett offered, trying to set him at ease.

Hans had prepared his Jürgen Hauptman story well, knowing it was important to include accurate dates, addresses, and other information that had been included in his application for the position. "I was born and raised in Hamburg, Germany," he began, "where I completed all of my secondary education. I was accepted into medical school at the University of Hamburg in 1941. I did well in my initial preclinical studies and started my clinical rotations at the University hospital. However, as the war intensified, medical students were drafted into the military to take over the duties of clinic doctors, as a shortage of physicians on the front began to mount. Early in 1944, I received my notice to join the military, just prior to taking my final examinations."

Doctor Tackett pulled his chair closer to his desk.

"I was attached to a naval unit, first in Rostock and later in Potsdam, as the fighting close to Berlin intensified," Hans continued.

He had rehearsed this narrative many times, but he was never able to get through it without finding himself back in front of the clinic, holding the near-lifeless body of the young man whose identity he now claimed. He could still hear the bullets clattering on the street and the frantic screams of civilians. "Our medical unit suffered tremendous casualties one day when attacked by Russian aircraft. Only two of us survived, and the unit was subsequently disbanded. I was sent back to Hamburg and worked again at the university hospital, where I was able to pass my written examinations just prior to the war's end."

Doctor Tackett sat quietly, leaning slightly forward, deeply engrossed in the details offered by Hans. "Doctor Hauptman, you've been through a lot and seem stronger for it. We have received information from the University of Hamburg confirming your education, and we look forward to having you here as a resident in surgery."

Hans's downcast eyes brightened as he looked up at Tackett.

"Please let me know of anything you might need," Tackett continued. *"We meet each day at six a.m. in the lounge to go over the cases of the day. Your position starts this coming Monday. Good luck. I speak for my colleagues and staff when I say we are so glad to have you join us here."*

◆◆◆

HANS HAD HEARD THAT July was not the best time to travel by train across the grand expanse of the United States to California, but with his three-year stint at Cincinnati General over, he moved on to his next position. His compartment was hot and stifling, and though opening the window allowed for a breeze, the exhaust from the locomotive blasted in with the hot air. For Hans, this journey was crucial and could not be avoided; it was the one last step toward securing his safety and sanctuary, five years after the end of the war.

Small cities dotted the tracks, the train stopping often to pick up and let off one or two passengers. Fortunately, the stopovers at each station lasted no more than ten minutes—until the conductor peered at his timepiece and yelled: "All aboard!"

As the train left the more populous areas of the Midwest, open fields of corn and grain filled the landscape and the train stops became less frequent. Hans had never appreciated the breadth of America, nor the great contrasts among the various geographic areas of the country.

A truly stronger nation defeated my Germany.

Closing his eyes, he succumbed to the rhythm of the tracks under him as he reflected on his time in Cincinnati.

It was good, as it had been too many years since I last worked in an operating theater.

Initially, he had been quite successful in the residency program, quickly earning a reputation as a dedicated surgeon willing to take on any case, often working late into the night. His skills were appreciated to the point that in his third year he was allowed to operate without the presence of a staff surgeon, and his hard work and exemplary performance earned him a promotion to Chief Resident. He ran an essentially flawless service in this role, but in time, he started to have difficulties with the attending surgeons. The stress of his duties began taking its toll, and it became difficult to suppress the arrogant Nazi persona that lurked just beneath the surface.

He was eager to restart his hypothermia cooling studies in a clinical setting, but understood the need to be cautious. Concerns still lingered in Cincinnati about the widely publicized experiments done in 1943 at the same hospital, and he did not want to ignite the old controversy. Determined to avoid any connection to that infamous study, he set about developing a cooling blanket with the help of the hospital engineer to aid in reducing stubborn fevers. He shaped a small, diameter rubber hose into multiple loops and placed them within a large sleeve of cotton fabric. The hose was fastened in place with the loops evenly spread along the approximate six-by-two feet length of this "cooling pad." A continuous irrigation solution of cold water ran through the device, propelled by a small pump immersed in a bucket of ice water.

Over the next two years he tested the pad initially in the hospital's infection ward to reduce markedly elevated fevers, and met with surprising success. With Doctor Tackett's approval, he began to look for the ideal case in which to try body-cooling in a surgical patient, a procedure that Hans was certain could save countless lives. By cooling a patient, the metabolic demand would be lessened and tissues could survive longer periods of time without adequate circulation.

He didn't have to wait long. An eight-year-old boy was hit by a car while riding his bicycle, sustaining multiple rib fractures, a contused left lung, ruptured spleen, left femoral fracture, and a brain injury—a subdural hematoma. The boy was comatose, with a falling blood pressure and rapid pulse. Immediately, he was taken to the operating room for surgery and placed on the cooling pad. Hans monitored the body temperature while a splenectomy was performed and drill holes placed in the skull to relieve the blood from around his brain. Following surgery, Hans continued the child on the cooling pad until his vital signs stabilized and neurological condition improved. The child's temperature was maintained at ninety-five degrees Fahrenheit for the next twenty-four hours.

Intent on achieving success with his experiment, Hans became quite compulsive during this initial clinical trial and spent a full day and night at the hospital monitoring the child. Sitting at the bedside, he took the young boy's blood pressure every ten minutes and checked neurological signs. Fighting fatigue, he became testy with his colleagues and ignored his other clinical responsibilities while focusing exclusively on the vital signs of this one patient.

When the child awoke from his coma the next day and his blood pressure and pulse were stable, Hans's newfound success went quickly to his head. It wasn't long before the other residents sensed a change in his demeanor. Rather than discuss a care plan with his junior residents, he would issue curt orders. If a problem with a patient occurred, he would openly reprimand the resident in front of his colleagues. The true Hans Bloch had re-emerged from his hiding place.

Noting the successful trial with the child, he asked to continue and apply the cooling blanket on elective surgical cases, but Doctor Tackett didn't support his idea. He was becoming somewhat wary of Doctor Hauptman's unpredictable behavior. Jürgen was displaying more and more arrogance, and his relationships with the attending staff were becoming increasingly strained.

Three months after Hans's success with the young bicycle accident patient, Doctor Tackett called him into his office and shoved a file folder across the desk in his direction. "Besides your deteriorating relationship with other residents and attending staff, our nurses have noted that at times, you sign the order sheets as 'Hans Bloch, MD' before correcting it. Perhaps you might explain that?"

Usually quick and prepared, Hans seemed taken aback, and appeared to fumble for an answer. "Doctor Tackett...after the surrender, the Allies detained anyone of question, including doctors in the military, and I used the name Hans Bloch, a civilian, to avoid that circumstance. I just made a mistake on some entries, that's all."

Tackett saw Hauptman's hands tremble slightly, allowing papers to spill out of the folder.

What is your real story, Doctor Hauptman? The name change, the age discrepancy, the Nazi arrogance... I wonder... No sense digging for the truth now...

Doctor Tackett watched Hans grab the papers before they hit the floor.

He has just a few more months here. Let him be someone else's problem.

"I have little time to look into such details as you have told me," Tackett said coldly. "I will assume your explanation is true and see no reason to question you further. However, I will remind you that your obligations here are almost complete. I suggest you mind your manners until you leave."

Hans's stomach began to ache as it often did when he was under stress. Getting up to leave, he locked eyes with Doctor Tackett, and a sense of understanding seemed to prevail between them.

I must take it easy, my past can haunt me.

Over the next four months, Hans assumed a more passive role with the other physicians, and the tension subsided as he readied himself for his next step. He had applied for a post with a hospital in Indio, California, and after forwarding the necessary documents from the University of Hamburg and Cincinnati General Hospital, a position was offered to him. Having secured his next job in America, Hans knew he must lay low and keep his ego in check. The time passed without any major blow-ups, and so, at summer's end, he packed his clothes and cooling blanket and boarded a train heading west. As the train roared across the Ohio River, he looked back at the city and smiled to himself.

Auf weidersehen, Cincinnati... Auf weidersehen Hans Bloch.

♦♦♦

July 5, 1950

THE CROSS-COUNTRY JOURNEY SEEMED endless. The landscape changed as the train entered New Mexico, and then Arizona, but an infinite dry desert was all he could see. The heat was unbearable. Water was served frequently to the train's passengers to try and quell the effects of the desert's furnace. Hans could only wish that the train would go faster and get out of this hellhole.

He had been warned to expect warm weather in Indio, yet had incorrectly assumed that the climate was more temperate, based on his knowledge of California. Hans had communicated with the hospital administrator only by mail, and arrived at his new post with little knowledge of the area. A brochure of the town and pictures of the hospital had sufficed; the setting was exactly what he was looking for—a small, rural hospital with a limited medical staff in a quiet city where his services were greatly needed.

As he stepped off the train, he was met by Gerald Adams, the hospital administrator, and ushered into his sedan. They spoke briefly before Adams dropped Hans at the Cactus Inn Motel, not far from Indio Community Hospital, with an invitation for dinner that evening.

Showered and refreshed, Hans ventured outside to get a feel for his new city. The sun reflecting off the pavement caused him to squint as he looked around. He was somewhat surprised to find out that Indio was indeed located in the hot, dry climate of the Sonoran Desert. The tallest building visible was the weather-beaten Southern Pacific Railroad station's two-story wooden structure. The rest of the downtown area had a distinctly Spanish Colonial look, including red tile roofs and stucco exteriors with wrought iron trim. Hot winds swirled dust into the air as Hans struggled to keep his hat on. No, it wasn't anything like the cities he was used to; it was, however, a place where few would be concerned about his past. He was safe.

Hans was graciously accepted into the small medical community of Indio. There was one other general surgeon on staff, Doctor William Casey, with whom he would share call and assist on surgical cases from time to time. The hospital had a medical building attached to the main facility in which an office had been set aside for him—for Doctor Jürgen Hauptman. The administration would take care of all billing and paperwork, freeing Doctor Hauptman to fully engage in his surgical practice. When he informed Mr. Adams that he was involved in an ongoing research project, his announcement was met with support and the offer of "whatever assistance Doctor Hauptman might need." Encouraged by this response, Hans wasted no time in briefing the anesthesiologist, Doctor Allen Homer, and his general surgical associate as to the nature of the hypothermic surgery study.

Ah, a perfect place to continue my work. These Dummköpfe will do what I want without fear and ask few questions.

"I will give no deadly medicine to any one if asked."

35

October 20, 1950
Milwaukee, Wisconsin

Michel relished his feelings of accomplishment that Friday afternoon. The hospital rounds had gone smoothly, and his remaining patients were discharged during the day. Mr. Phillip Johns, the gastric resection, and Mrs. Lulu Prentice, the mastectomy, had both returned with dry dressings and no signs of infection. Two patients had been referred today for surgery, and a hemicolectomy and thyroidectomy were scheduled for the following week.

It was time to enjoy a little of this pleasant weather and celebrate autumn. He left the office earlier than usual, pushing aside the chaotic stack of papers sitting on his desk. Briefly glancing through it, he decided that this mass of forms could easily wait—he would get to it on Monday.

Milwaukee had not been one of the American cities familiar to Michel. While hospitalized in Belgium, he had met a US physician who had volunteered to help treat Europe's displaced people. Doctor Ralph Cohen had recently finished his residency in Milwaukee and was working at clinics caring for holocaust survivors in Europe prior to returning home to practice. When Michel came to Montreal the following year, he contacted Doctor Cohen, who urged him to visit Milwaukee and look at the wonderful opportunities available in that city. And so, in the spring of 1948, as he was finishing his two-year commitment at Jewish General, Michel took a train to Milwaukee to visit his American friend. Impressed with the city and the medical community, he made arrangements with Milwaukee General Hospital to join their staff and begin practice as soon as his time in Montreal came to an end.

Milwaukee had been a good choice. Wisconsin's large European immigrant communities from Scandinavia, Poland, and Germany made it easy for a foreigner like him to remain invisible to the small Jewish community. No one knew him or knew of him. Perhaps inside the walls of Milwaukee General he could find a sanctuary from the past.

Michel stepped outside to a late afternoon sun. To his right, the sweeping blue of Lake Michigan merged with the azure sky that only fall can bring. The wispy, cool breeze formed whitecaps, swirling in fine, white lines—the only flaws in a sea of blue canvas that stretched to the misty horizon. Lakeside Boulevard was packed with the cars of downtown workers getting an early start on their weekend, but Michel was not in any hurry. He had no particular place to go, just ambling along the lakefront, letting his mind wander and escape. This sense of freedom was further expanded as he had taken the weekend off, signing out for the next two days to another surgeon, Doctor Gerald Winters.

The changing colors of the maple trees lining the boulevard served as nature's calendar this time of year. The leaves had not yet fallen from their branches, but were threatening to do so. Some things were inevitable.

He turned west up Belleview Street, as it rose slowly away from the shore, then south on Summit Drive, and climbed up a small hill on top of which stood an old, white building, maybe once a church. As he approached this structure, he could see its aluminum siding, which had fallen off in several places, and the drainpipes hanging lazily away from the sides, supported only from the roof. Weeds had grown up along the back of the building, reaching up under the loose siding. An attempt had been made to trim the grass and control the weeds along the front, yet the backside had been forgotten. The sidewalk in front of the building was uneven—the cement slabs forced upward over the years by large maple trees pushing their expanding roots under the pavement in search of water.

Michel had not ventured into this part of the city before. Several men with dark fedora hats were strolling toward the old building on the north side of the street. *Tzitzit* was hanging out from under their white shirts.

No, not here—now!

He stopped, frozen, unwilling to go further as sweat started to pour down his back and his legs seemed to lock in place. What had once been a church was now an Orthodox Jewish synagogue. Feeling ill, he became light-headed and felt a throbbing pulse in his temple. His legs couldn't move.

How long has it been since I have been to shul?

After leaving Auschwitz, he had purposely avoided the Jewish refugee camps; he believed he did not belong there.

At Auschwitz, there were no open Jewish prayers, as it had been verboten.

When was it that I last attended services? Oh, yes, it was Yom Kippur—but what year?

Time was a blur in his mind. Maybe it was 1942, in Lyon, in secret. Even then, they couldn't be seen having Jewish services. His family was always worried that the Gestapo or miliciens would burst in. And yes, he remembered now. It had been a short service, everyone wanting to get home fast as soon as it finished. That was his last time.

Freed from the concentration camps, many Jews hungered for the comfort of *Shabbat* services in the various Displaced Persons facilities. Throughout Europe, they had been welcomed into those houses of worship that were still intact, but Michel had chosen to avoid them, just as he avoided the DP camps. Disgraced and dishonored in his own mind, he had kept his distance from all religious services.

Michel walked across the street from the synagogue and entered a small park commanding a view of the lake. He sat down on a wooden bench facing the shul; all the men had entered, and the doors closed just as he lowered himself down on the bench.

He sat quietly, thinking back on his youth and all the happy times with his family before the war. Much of their social life had centered on their temple, as it was the focal meeting point for the community. Hebrew school was an integral part of the children's lives, even though the youngsters disliked it; still, it was a safe place to meet their friends.

As he rested on the bench, a sense of tranquility came over Michel. It was one of those rare times when nothing distracted him; his senses were keen, but he did not react to them. Rush hour sounds of engines and horns drifted up from the lakefront. Flocks of geese headed south, honking goodbye as they passed overhead. The smell of newly cut grass at the park, maybe the last cutting of the year, was refreshing. But suddenly this panoply of everyday sights and sounds seemed to reconnect him with the humanity he had abandoned in the camps in a desperate bid to save himself and his family.

He felt tears streaming down his cheeks, but did not try to stop them, as he had before. He allowed himself to cry, to let the tears fall without restraint. Everything dear to him had been taken away—his wife and children, parents, and relatives.

Did I not see how blind I was to life? Medicine was more important to me than family, and now look—my children and my wife are gone.

Looking back at his graduation from medical school, he saw himself reciting the Hippocratic oath, an oath he had violated each day he worked at Auschwitz. Other than Tamara, he had developed no friendships in the camps, and now it was even more difficult for him to establish relationships for fear that someone might recognize the spineless soul he had become.

There was little time for smiling each day; life's contentment came only through his practice and surgery. It was only in the surgical suites that he felt alive and valued. It was there that he commanded a setting where the nurses and other doctors responded to each of his requests without question. It was there that he could find respite from his past.

That professional commitment in his life had paid off, giving him a level of satisfaction each day, and it kept him going. It was when he returned home at night to his empty apartment that he felt that nothing in his life, beyond his work, seemed to matter.

As he gazed across the road at the rundown temple, he wondered if they knew, those men with covered heads.

Don't they recognize that across the street, sitting on a park bench, is a man who did nothing to stop the death and butchering of so many lives? Do they know that I am a monster who opened the bellies of children killed by Nazi doctors to see how they died? And could they believe that I, too, was once a Jew like them?

Just then, the fall wind picked up, as if trying to blow him off this safe perch.

Perhaps it was God telling him to leave, that he did not belong, not even here. Michel slowly rose up and retreated down the hill, back toward the shoreline.

"Whether in connection with my professional practice or not…"

36

April 20, 1954
Paris, France

"**D**amn, again!" Michel cried out as he balled up the letter and tossed it into the trashcan.

THE SAME MISERABLE RESPONSE from the French as last year.

Rubbing the back of his neck he walked around his office trying to figure out what he could do next as he mulled over the latest communiqué from the Ministère de l'Intérieur in Paris. Angrily digging into the trashcan, he retrieved the letter and spread it open to reread it: "Monsieur, we have no record that your home in Lyon was seized by our gouvernement. If you have such proof, you must present such documents to our office, immédiatement…"

♦♦♦

As THE LOCKHEED L1049 Constellation broke through the clouds, the Eiffel Tower caught Michel's eye, marking the finish of his ten-hour transatlantic journey from New York. He felt the hair stand up on the back of his neck and a chill course through his body as the plane landed at Le Bourget Airport in Paris, his first time back in France. The last to exit the plane, he walked slowly down the ramp steps, still uncertain of his decision to return and plead his case with the government. Yet there had been one beautiful reason to make the trip.

♦♦♦

Tamara was excited that Michel was coming to Europe and had made plans to arrive in Paris on October 4, two days after he landed. After obtaining a visa to travel to France, she indulged herself with a trip to the salon, new clothes, and perfume. Unable to control her elation, she talked endlessly to her friends about this chance to meet up with Doctor Katz. Having finished her course work at the Prague Art Academy, she was now working as a faculty assistant, helping students with their art studies and projects. The school allowed her a few days off.

♦ ♦ ♦

Michel felt a giddy excitement as he walked down the ramp; he would see Tamara tomorrow, the little teenager whose life he had saved and who had given him a reason to live on.

How old is she now...maybe twenty-four? A young woman.

He preened himself with new clothes and visited a barber in the Champs-Elysees who restyled his pompadour haircut. Her last letters were filled with an ebullience that, for the first time in years, brought a smile to his face. He would finish his business with the authorities in France and then reconnect with Tamara.

"Monsieur, il y a twenty thousand applications, and you must be patient and wait your turn for restitution," said the sweaty, overweight French official at the *Ministère de L'Intérieur.* Michel stood at the counter as this new glimmer of hope contrasted with the previous negative responses he's received from the government office and calmed his long-standing anger. "We have, with your *papiers,* acknowledged your ownership of a home in Lyon and its expropriation by the *gouvernement CGQJ (Commissariat Général aux Questions Juives)* in 1943. Our processors must finish their appraisal and will contact you by mail sometime later this year."

Leaving the stifling office with a mixed sense of accomplishment, he was elated thinking about Tamara's arrival the next day.

The clock overhead at the *Paris Nord* Railway station read 11:54 a.m.—ten minutes until Tamara's train would arrive. Michel had not felt such anticipation in years and instinctively brushed the front of his suit jacket while peering down Platform V, hoping to spot the train as it entered the station. He walked back to the tobacco shop and bought a pack of Gauloises, reached into his pocket for his lighter, and nervously lit the cigarette dangling from his lips.

The crowd surged past him as the sounds of the arriving train from Prague filled the station. He watched as the passengers exited the platform, studying each young woman's face as he tried to imagine what Tamara would look like now. With the train almost emptied, a downhearted Michel was about to leave when a young lady wearing a wide-brimmed hat brushed past him. He turned to race after her.

"Tamara?" He touched her shoulder.

"*Non monsieur,* you are mistaken."

Eyes downcast, he slumped on an empty bench. He'd wait for the next train.

♦ ♦ ♦

Two weeks later in his apartment, a letter was waiting for him when he returned home from work. Michel sat down as he anxiously opened the envelope.

My dear Doctor Katz,

Michel, please forgive me for not meeting you in Paris. I desperately wanted to reach you that day but did not know where you were staying and had no way to call you. As I boarded the train in Prague, the officer looked at my travel permit, checked his list, and told me that my authorization to travel had been revoked. I tried to explain through tears about our meeting, but he was under orders and I was to report to the local police station that afternoon. Later, I angrily boarded a trolley for downtown where I met with a Communist government official who advised me they had reviewed my paintings on display at the school and that my "art" showed indications of "bourgeois" influence; my travel was to be restricted until they were assured of my loyalty to the Communist Czech government.

I can't tell you how sad I have been as I cry myself to sleep each night, not being able to see you again. Believe me, my wonderful doctor, it may take a little while, but I know we will see each other, as the words "au revoir" translate to "to seeing you again."

His tears fell and stained the letter as he finished reading Tamara's words. Once again, Michel called on his protective internal shield and deftly set aside another of life's disappointments. He would awake the next morning to immerse himself back into his work.

"...and oath according the law of medicine, but to none others."

37

March 12, 1964
Milwaukee

"Quite a fine morning, isn't it, Doctor Katz?" was the greeting that stirred Michel's senses as he started his morning rounds. It was Sarah Goulding, a cheerful attractive nurse who got a kick out of making the usually glum Doctor Katz crack a smile as he marched into the nurses' station. The petite woman was pretty, with deep blue eyes, soft brown hair, and a curvaceous figure hidden beneath the generic white nurse's uniform. When he peered back at her a little longer than usual today, she noticed and walked up to stand close to him.

"Well, you do look alive this day, my good doctor! Was it something you ate, or just a grand time last evening?" There was a twinkle in her eye, and she smiled mischievously. "You know what I mean."

Michel remained as serious as ever. "No, Sarah, not me. That kind of life left me years ago. I'm just a boring old soul, married to my work."

She already knew this. In fact, all the nurses wondered why such a good-looking man like Doctor Katz had so little social life. They were aware he had immigrated from Europe, survived the concentration camps, and lost his wife and family.

But after nearly two decades, he certainly should be ready to enjoy life again.

Sarah had been secretly attracted to him since she'd started at the hospital five years ago and was sure she could be the one to bring him out of his shell.

I know I could help him forget.

"So, Doctor, should I accompany you on rounds and uplift your spirits, or would you like to travel alone?"

Michel could not answer right away. He had not noticed her interest in him before.

Is this just professional?

It had been so long since a woman had befriended him, he couldn't tell. "Why yes, I'd be de...delighted," he managed to sputter out.

They continued down the hallway, Sarah holding the charts and giving him updates on his patients on the floor. As they walked, she asked lots of clinical questions and he answered gratefully, as he had finally found someone who wanted to listen to him.

What if...?

"You look like you would enjoy getting out, and maybe we could share a meal or something?" she said, as if she had read his thoughts.

Struggling to know how to say yes, Michel nervously responded. "Oh, that would be so wonderful. Could you?"

They began seeing each other on a regular basis, going to restaurants and watching an occasional movie. Michel was hesitant to become romantic, as he found it difficult to abandon the deep emotions he still felt for Anna and the guilt he carried regarding her death. The thought of caring for someone new just added to his regret. The letters he received from Tamara reminded him that he could still find love in his heart for another person, but romantic love?

I don't know that I could ever go there again.

When it came to Sarah, he couldn't explain his feelings. He was still so bound up in the horrible web of shame and self-judgment he'd carried since Auschwitz. There was no place left in his soul to accept the loving feelings of another.

I'm not sure I deserve it.

Sarah recognized the slow pace of romance with Michel and wished to hurry it up, as her feelings for him were exploding.

If I could just get him alone, in bed, I would make him love me...

She was determined.

As Michel became more comfortable socially, they saw each other often and started to enjoy a few glasses of wine together. Michel opened up and haltingly began to talk of his past, including the camps. Sarah relished these moments and shared a few tears with him as Michel described his journey and the pain at the loss of his family. A warm bond was forming, and she knew it was time. They had been seeing each other for three months. He was ready. The next day at the hospital, she approached him.

"Michel, I have a wonderful night planned for us at…my place. A special dinner I am cooking to celebrate this Saturday night, okay?"

"Why…yes, but to celebrate what?"

A sparkle danced in her eyes. "You'll see."

And it *was* an extraordinary night. Champagne, fine Bordeaux wine, and Sarah in a sexy, low-cut dress. She turned on her charm and took every opportunity to tease him with her walk, her eyes, her smile, and a light touch on his shoulder while they talked.

Insulated by the wine and champagne, he could not resist. The passion and electricity were intense. Their lovemaking carried on into the night, until they both fell into deep slumber.

Michel awoke in the morning, confused, and rolled over to see Sarah sleeping naked next to him. His heart began to race as he remembered their evening and the hours of making love that had followed.

He rose quietly so as not to disturb the beautiful sleeping woman. Hastily dressing, he glanced up at the mirror beside the bed and paused. His guilty face stared back at him, and he shuddered.

Do you really even deserve to live?

He thought of Tamara and the monthly letters he'd received from her over the years. In his mind, she was the one person who truly cared, who could hold the small piece of his heart that was still alive. Again, the face of his lovely and gentle wife filled his vision, as he recalled the wonderful life they'd had together. He cringed, thinking of how he'd deserted her and the children through his naïveté, believing he could ensure their safety from the hate that had befallen their people. Images of the death and torture of so many Jews, some at his own assistance, made him cast his glance away from the traitor who lurked in the mirror.

What does love mean to me, anyway? I always placed my own needs in front of those I loved.

He couldn't make sense of his feelings for Sarah. What good could come of this liaison, this tiny hope of joy? Would this be more hurt and disappointment at the hands of the great Doctor Katz?

No, I will not risk that.

His only choice was to pull away before he caused another innocent's disappointment, so he dressed silently and took one last look at the young woman so peaceful in her dreams. On a scrap of paper that he found on her bedside table he wrote a quick note, and left it on the pillow beside her:

Sarah, I don't want to wake you, but I need to tell you, as I have shared with you in the past, it is difficult for me to love again and it is impossible for me to give you the love you deserve. Were we to continue, I would only disappoint you. I hope you can find it in your heart to understand. Michel.

After that night, he shunned any further interest from his female co-workers. When he crossed Sarah's path, he purposefully and shamefully avoided her gaze. Aware that his self-imposed loneliness was drawing him further into despondency, his isolation increased.

In the evenings, in the dark and quiet of his apartment, he found himself thinking more and more of Tamara, and it was in these few moments that he found solace. He knew that only she could understand the intense pain he was feeling. He remembered her tenderness, her unconditional caring. Her letters had continued to arrive, in spite of the fact that he had sent so few in return. In truth, he had reached the point where he couldn't find the strength to open them.

A bright, yellow March moon was rising in the east, bright enough to cast shadows as Michel took his evening walk, recalling the last night with Tamara before she left Auschwitz. He had promised to see her again and her eyes had lit up with hope, but this pledge remained unfulfilled, just like his promises to his family. Turning toward home, his gait became quicker as he again glanced up at the sky, knowing what he had to do.

Entering his apartment, he went directly to his desk and opened the right-hand desk drawer where he had stored the unread pile of letters. Slowly, one by one, he read them...

38

July 17, 1962
Buenos Aires, Argentina

Stepping out of the Boeing 707 onto the departure ramp, the blast of cool air reminded Martin Brosky it was winter in this part of the world. The twelve-hour flight from Miami to Argentina had left him tired and achy, but he was anxious to get on to business. The taxi dropped him off at the classy Intercontinental Hotel, and he quickly went to his room, unpacked the necessities, and took a well-deserved rest followed by a shower.

The preparations for his arrival had been made well in advance. The former OSS officer, José Mendoza, was already in Buenos Aires and would meet him in the morning. The culmination of months of research had resulted in the perfect plan, and now his prey was in range.

After a good night's sleep, Martin carefully unpacked the Lugar he had taken from the Auschwitz SS guard eighteen years ago and cleaned and oiled his favorite weapon. Leaving the room, he entered the waiting elevator and descended the five floors to the plush lobby and adjoining hotel restaurant.

♦♦♦

JANUARY 3, 1945, WAS the day Oberleutenant Kurt Werner knew the war was lost. He felt the coarse vibrations in the road as the Russian tanks rolled quickly toward his unit, and he and his men hunkered down in ditches, just west of Krakow. The Russians had easily cut through the German defenses in eastern Poland, causing a massive retreat of the Wehrmacht forces. Yet his troops had been ordered to hold their position at any cost.

Things had changed radically for Werner during the past year. After the final evacuation of Jews from the Lodz Ghetto, he'd been reassigned to command a unit searching for Jews hiding among the Polish population in various cities. He had been working in the Krakow district when an intense Russian aerial attack nearly destroyed an infantry division posted twenty-five miles east of the city of Krakow. With half of its officers missing following the attack, Werner was ordered to assume command of one of the battalions. It was somewhat unusual for an SS officer to run a Wehrmacht battalion, but the colonel in charge had no choice, and Werner was already stationed close by.

Inspecting his troops, he took stock of the remaining soldiers in his unit and left, shaking his head.

What were those generals in Berlin thinking? These are inexperienced young boys, many just sixteen years old and in their first battle. They all look scared.

Following orders from headquarters, he directed his officers to position his young soldiers along the highway on the outskirts of Krakow, hoping to halt the Russian onslaught. A fierce artillery bombardment ensued, scattering the troops and forcing him to jump into a truck and head west toward the rear. But Russian fighter-bombers unleashed a harrowing attack, just as he arrived at the command post, an area previously thought to be safe. Looking back toward the front, he could see the shells ripping up the road and everything near it. The vision of bodies strewn amidst the carnage along with the screaming cries of the wounded soldiers paralyzed Werner. Cold sweat engulfed his body as Russian shells obliterated everything in sight, and he ordered his driver not to stop, but to continue west toward the German border. He had no choice but to leave, as he would certainly be taken prisoner along with the few soldiers who were still alive. Some might call it desertion. Werner called it survival.

As he fled away from the battle towards Berlin, he reflected on the events of the past year. He had been promoted quickly because of his success in Lodz Ghetto, where he had managed to move all the Jews to Auschwitz in 1944 in a matter of days. When the bomb went off in Lodz during a staff meeting, he had acted without hesitation: in response to the death of twenty of his men, twenty civilians were selected for revenge. He'd actually enjoyed lining up those Jews, men and women alike, and killing them personally—a lesson from Lieutenant Werner, who had risen from a young dairy farmer in Wilster to Oberleutnant in less than two years. His last, almost pleasant, assignment was to search out Jews who'd hidden from the SS.

Kurt Werner could see that the Russians would shortly be in Berlin. He was equally aware that the Allied forces would be looking for him and other SS officers, especially when they discovered the concentration camps. Two weeks ago, a confidential message had been forwarded to him, asking if he could meet in Berlin with other SS to discuss the war's end and important decisions that had to be made.

I will be hunted down. I must leave Germany.

Arriving at night, he was greeted by smoke, rubble, and debris as he entered the capital, hardly recognizing this once majestic city. Threading his way through twisted piles of steel, he made his way to SS headquarters, where civilian employees were frantically throwing boxes of files into a bonfire in back of the building. After checking in at the front desk, he quickly went down the two flights of stairs to the SS bomb shelter and officers' lounge where he spotted a group of his colleagues gathered in a corner. One officer, Heinz Pohlman, yelled, "Kurt Werner, come join us! We have much to talk about."

These SS officers had arranged to meet on January 3, 1945. Their purpose was to plan for the postwar period and the continuation of the SS corps as a means to re-establishing the Fatherland in the future. The agenda was unwritten but determined. They needed to find ways to leave Germany and be harbored safely abroad. Large sums of stolen money and gold had been secretly deposited in Switzerland by German agents to be used at a later date to restore the Reich. The combined strength and covert participation of several large German companies, plus stolen wealth, had built a clandestine organization that made this possible. ODESSA, *Organization Der Ehemaligen SS-Angehörigen* (The Organization of former SS members), would be recognized around the world as the group that orchestrated the movement of Nazi criminals out of Germany.

Initially, safe houses would be established in Switzerland to avoid capture, and, later, secure locations outside Europe could be found. The planning was meticulous but they would require expert assistance to safely complete their travels. In preparation for travel to South America, new Identification cards, visas, and other documents had to be produced.

The men worked late into the night and early morning, going over details of their planned escape. A significant amount of groundwork had been laid, yet it needed to be refined. Guides had been contacted to secretly take them across back trails through the Alps and across the Swiss-German border. Once the spring thaw arrived; they would be lodged just outside Zurich.

The next morning, Werner reported to SS offices and learned that his Krakow brigade had been totally destroyed. He was then temporarily assigned to the Berlin headquarters unit where he had little responsibility. Spending much of his time in quarters, he studied maps of South America and looked to settle in an area where he could exploit his former skills as a dairy farmer. Over the next two months, secret meetings among the SS involved with ODESSA occurred weekly as they waited for their time to leave.

With Berlin in chaos in March 1945, Kurt Werner slipped out and successfully traveled to the Swiss border where he was met by members of ODESSA. He was kept in a safe house near Kloten, Switzerland, while papers were forged and travel arrangements made. His new identification in hand, he traveled across Switzerland into Italy where, with the assistance of well-placed individuals in the Vatican, preparations were made to leave Europe. On August 17, 1946, he boarded the liner "North King" in Naples, en route to Buenos Aires, Argentina, under the name "Eduardo Gómez." Upon arrival, he was met by several German nationals who had found him a place to stay in Bariloche, a city in the shadow of the Andes with a history of German immigration. On July 13, 1947, Eduardo Gómez purchased a dairy farm just outside the City of Córdoba.

♦♦♦

January 1, 1945
On the outskirts of Lodz, Poland

THE MEN GATHERED AROUND the open fire with blankets pulled over them to ward off the cold wind, each holding a bottle of vodka to warm his insides. Grabbing Martin by the shoulders, Stefan drunkenly pulled him to his side and roared, "So when, my tough Jew buddy, do you get a chance to join that ferocious 'Jew Battalion' in Italy you've been talking about since you got here last month?"

A rumble of laughter rippled among the men.

Martin, too, gave a short laugh, and pulled his good friend closer. "We can't talk here, but there is a chance for me to get out. Join me at the cook's tent in ten minutes."

◆◆◆

Leaning against the tent support, Martin whispered, "As you had advised, I've met here with Mark, the British contact agent of the Special Operations Executives."

Stefan edged closer as Martin lowered his voice to a whisper. "He told me about the British DC-3 Dakota secretly landing near here in Lublin last April and taking off with parts of the V-2 test rocket that had mistakenly landed in the muddy marshes."

"Yes," said Stefan, "that was code-named 'Operation Wildwood,' and the plane also took off with our AK deputy commander and two couriers... Went back to Italy, I think."

"Well, the Americans are sending another plane to land sometime this month, when the weather clears. As you must know, another misfired V-2 has been found, and Mark wants to deliver these parts to the Americans in Italy before the Russians get here."

Martin looked up and smiled. "He wants me to fly with him and talk to intelligence officials about Auschwitz. I can do that. While I'm there, I'll look up the Jewish Brigade."

◆◆◆

On January 10, the AK force rested hidden in the woods outside of Lublin. A code word had been broadcast on the BBC indicating that the weather was clear enough for the plane to land that evening, and Mark had received word from Italy that the American DC-3 was on its way. As the AK resistance had done back in April, green lights were placed along the dirt airstrip half an hour before the plane was to touch down at 11:00 p.m. Crudely crated, the V-2 rocket parts were covered with a blanket and hidden in the woods adjacent to the landing strip—guarded by twenty men.

The roar of an approaching aircraft put the men on alert, fearing Germans might also have heard it. The DC-3 landed, and ten men quickly carried the crates into the storage door on the side of the plane just as a cry rang out from the far end of the runway.

"Halt! I say, halt, or you will be shot," yelled a German officer grasping a semi-automatic rifle.

Two Wehrmacht soldiers who'd suddenly emerged from the woods manned a machine gun pointed directly at the plane. Holding their hands up, Martin and the men next to the plane feigned surrender and stood still. As the German lieutenant approached, a torrent of gunfire from both sides of the airstrip tore through the officer and the German soldiers at the end of the runway. Without missing a beat, the men continued loading the rocket parts as Martin and Mark ran up the ramp into the aircraft's hold. Within three minutes, the DC-3 had taken off, as Polish fighters combed the woods for any Germans who might have escaped.

The flight back to Brindisi, Italy was harrowing as the DC-3 Dakota had to dodge German flak while altering its flight path to avoid cities and strategic points where anti-aircraft batteries had been placed. Dawn was breaking as the plane landed safely in Italy and taxied to an isolated hangar at the far end of the field. The hanger doors closed as the men exited the plane, while a contingent of airmen opened the storage area to remove the rocket parts.

Martin was given quarters to rest in until he was to be interviewed by the OSS later that afternoon. Unable to sleep on the rough five-hour flight, he fell asleep quickly, but was awakened a few hours later by a rap on the door. A soldier's voice called out, "The colonel will see you in ten minutes. Please be on time!"

The interview lasted four hours. Martin was able to give the British SOE colonel and American OSS (Office of Strategic Services) commander names of guards, SS officers, and German physicians with whom he'd had contact at Auschwitz. They were particularly interested in the human experiments at the camp and the function of the gas chambers and crematoriums. He recounted his work with the Sonderkommandos and his escape following the October 1944 revolt.

As the meeting was coming to an end, Colonel Bostick said, "Thank you, Martin, for talking with us. It's been quite informative. Is there anything I can do for you, now?"

With no hesitation, Martin spoke up. "Please sir, yes. Can you get me to Tarviso, Italy? I want to join The Jewish Brigade based there."

Martin was accepted into the Brigade on February 2, 1945, and was given accelerated training and placed in an infantry unit in late March, where he saw action against the remaining German units in northern Italy.

This controversial Jewish unit was officially established on September 20, 1944, as part of the British eighth Army. Comprised of volunteers from Palestine and the Nazi-occupied countries of Europe, there were more than five thousand soldiers spread over three infantry units and one artillery unit. Just two months later, in late November, they went to battle against the Germans in northern Italy, where they fought with an uncommon vengeance. Following Germany's surrender, the Brigade assisted in moving Holocaust survivors to Palestine, against the wishes of their British sponsors.

"Operation Judgment" became the major activity of the Brigade in Europe at the end of the war. A group of soldiers who called themselves the TTG (*Tihas Tizig Gesheften*, or "Lick My Ass") rounded up senior SS and Gestapo officers and systemically killed them for their crimes against Jews. The Brigade was officially disbanded in 1946, yet many of its members continued to hunt down these murderers. Most of the Brigade's officers and enlisted men returned to Palestine to work for Israeli independence, and thirty-five of these former Jewish Brigade soldiers became generals in the Israeli military.

Martin chose not to go to Israel at the conclusion of the war in May 1945. He and several former Brigade soldiers continued their primary task well into the next decade. Working out of a safe house in Florence, Italy with a list of established Nazi criminals, they methodically hunted down and killed former SS officers in ways to make them remember the pain they had inflicted in the camps. The Brigade's activities ran parallel to the Nuremburg Trials of German war criminals, yet seemed far more effective in meting out appropriate punishment. Funding for this activity continued to come via courier from Israel, although no official connection to any government was ever made.

By 1952, over fifteen hundred Nazis had been tracked down and eliminated, but more than one hundred war criminals could not be found in Europe, and a great deal of effort was made by several groups to search these men out. Some German scientists had been sent to the United States to continue their research, and many had fled to South America, where they had adopted new identities.

Information about these war criminals had been obtained by the Brigade from captured SS officers during interrogation sessions prior to their painful demise. The CIC, the U.S. Counterintelligence Corps, provided useful information to Martin and his colleagues about SS officers who had fled Europe. This came from imprisoned war criminals awaiting trial. Passenger lists from departing ocean liners were perused. Applications for permits, licenses, and visas were inspected. It was arduous work for those sifting through mountains of paper, trying to track down the last of these wanted criminals.

By 1961, Martin had just two names left on his personal list. Number one was Oberleutenant Kurt Werner, the bastard who had killed his parents, and whose capture continued to elude him. He sought help through a well-funded private American organization called "The Owl," sponsored by Jewish groups that were committed to the capture of Nazi war criminals. The Owl had collected large amounts of data that Martin knew could be useful in his task. There was also a second name on his list, but Martin would leave that one for now.

In time… In due time.

♦♦♦

THE CROSS-ATLANTIC PASSAGE OF the vessel *North King* to Argentina in 1946 generated interest among those hunting down Nazi criminals. In late January 1962, The Owl obtained this ship's old passenger log revealing thirty possible names that could have been aliases for Kurt Werner. Martin turned to a former OSS officer working in South America, José Mendoza, who whittled the roster list down to three individuals and studied the Brigade's dossiers on each, including descriptions and current information available to pinpoint Martin's prey.

♦♦♦

REVIEWING REAL ESTATE TRANSACTIONS in the major newspapers of Argentina and possible links to suspects, José Mendoza paused at the photo of one "Eduardo Gómez," who had purchased a dairy farm near Córdoba in late 1947.

If the dossier details are correct, he has farming experience and bought this farm just ten months after the arrival of the North King.

Mendoza noted that Gómez was a member of the local German-Argentinean club in Córdoba.

◆◆◆

MARTIN CAUGHT HIS BREATH as he read Mendoza's letter.

That must be him!

Picking up the phone, his voice catching, he asked his contact for one more thing: "Mendoza, I need to see his picture so I can confirm—for myself...then, I think we are ready."

◆◆◆

EDUARDO GÓMEZ STOOD OUTSIDE, admiring the view from the back of his home. His *estancia* now extended over ten thousand acres, as far to the west as his eyes could see.

All mine. Just sixteen years ago, I left Europe and my old life behind. Maybe, someday, when German pride returns, we can rebuild the Reich, and I will go back. But for now, this is mine.

His business skills had allowed his small dairy farm to expand to one of the largest in the Córdoba province. Purchasing adjacent rangeland, he also started raising cattle, as there was an increasing world market for Argentine beef. Eduardo worked hard on his Spanish, successfully speaking it with just a trace of German accent. In an abundance of caution, he had hired men to enforce security on his property and patrol the ranch and living quarters on horseback. A short, dirt airstrip was set off to the right side of the main barn, enabling visitors to avoid a long, uncomfortable auto trip from Buenos Aires.

◆◆◆

MENDOZA WAS SITTING IN the hotel restaurant in Buenos Aires when Martin came down from his room. Wearing dark aviator glasses, he appeared stoic and showed no expression when Martin joined him. The man was well-built, with a broad chest and large, muscular arms. They spoke in Spanish.

"Just as I imagined you," said Martin, smiling. Mendoza had thick, black hair, neatly combed back. He wore a brown suit, white shirt, and striped brown-and-white tie. Martin had donned a dark blue suit and silk tie for the occasion, and looked the more uncomfortable of the two in his business dress.

"*Yo me siento lo mismo, Señor*. You could be a banker, lawyer, or politician with that get-up."

"That's good. If I could fool you, I can certainly convince *Señor* Gómez of my credentials," said Martin. "Is the plane ready?"

"Yes, it is, and we should get out to the airport soon. The skies should be clear within a short time, and we can go over the details while we're on the plane. The flight should last about an hour and a half."

Finishing their coffee and rolls, they walked to a car parked on the street and drove off to the airport.

Forty minutes later, the two men boarded the six-passenger de Havilland DHC-2 Beaver, with Mendoza in the pilot's seat. He had been flying for twenty years, serving in the U.S. Army Air Force, where he'd piloted B-17s over Germany during the war. Mendoza exhibited the kind of confidence one would expect from thousands of hours of harrowing flight time. Slightly injured during his last bombing run, he was recruited to the OSS in 1944. Martin, too, was well prepared for this mission. He had completed pilot's training and could back up Mendoza, if needed. He had perfected his Spanish with a crash course language program that left just a tinge of an unidentifiable accent in his speech. For this mission, Martin was "Señor Altancara," a wealthy Mexican-American interested in purchasing rangeland in Argentina.

The flight was uneventful, and the two men reviewed in detail how the "deal" would go down. Spread beneath them was the Pampas—an immense, flat South American lowland where abundant grains were grown and hundreds of thousands of cattle were raised. "That must be it," said Mendoza, pointing to a group of buildings corresponding to his map and directions.

Several large structures, dairy barns, could be seen adjacent to a large, red-tiled home. A landing strip was located next to the barn furthest from the house. Approaching from the south, they landed and taxied down the dirt airstrip toward a welcoming committee.

Two menacing *gauchos* on horseback met the plane with rifles slipped into leather pouches alongside their saddles as an older, well-dressed man walked slowly toward them.

"That must be 'Gómez,'" said Mendoza under his breath to Martin. "Chin up, my friend, the show is on."

"Buenos días, amigos. I assume your flight was fine," said Gómez as he strained to look into the eyes of the two men shielded by aviator glasses. "Come in for a drink, maybe *una cerveza* or cola?" The gauchos followed the men, stationing themselves outside the door as they entered the house. "Thank you, *Señor,* cola for my friend and me. We appreciate you showing us your property," said Mendoza. "We are interested in expanding our acreage here in the Pampas for cattle and would like to view the *estancia.*"

He gestured toward Martin. "Señor Altancara is part of an investment group that owns over one hundred thousand acres of rangeland, mostly in Mexico, but some in Brazil and Bolivia."

Mendoza paused to take a sip of his drink. Gómez noticed that Martin did not speak.

"Well, Señor Altancara, you have been quiet. What do you think of this area? You are the moneyman, I presume? You must have some thoughts."

"Es un lugar especial," Martin answered in his best Spanish. "Whether we come to a deal or not, *lo recordaré—por siempre.*"

Looking pleased, Gómez sprung out of his chair. "Come! Ramón will drive us around in his truck."

Mendoza spoke up and pointed to their plane. "Señor, we have little time. What do you think about conducting a tour of your beautiful estancia from the air?"

"What a grand idea!" Gómez smiled with childish delight. "Ramón, have the maid prepare some snacks out for when we return. Gentlemen, you will be impressed with what you see. *Vámonos!*"

A look of concern crossed Ramón's face, and he spoke a few words into Gómez's ear. Gómez paused for a second and looked up, surveying the two men closely. "Don't be silly, Ramón," he said finally. "It's fine... I'll be back in an hour."

Martin smiled.

◆◆◆

THE WIDE PASSENGER SIDE door of the Beaver slid open and Gómez settled himself into the back while Mendoza and Martin took the front seats. Right after takeoff, Martin slipped back into the left seat behind the pilot, next to Gómez, and smiled at him—maybe a bit too long.

Gómez shifted nervously and looked away.

That smile...

He started to talk, a kind of ramble. "Over there, the river outlines the western border of the property... What are you doing?"

Martin's hands were suddenly on Gómez's chest, feeling for weapons. "What is this? I don't understand!"

Smiling more broadly now, Martin said, "We know who you are, SS Oberleutenant Kurt Werner, and I, especially, know you... I'm quite sure you can remember."

Martin took out his Lugar and held it on Werner, who sat stunned. "What, what...? I don't know what you are talking about!"

He looked right, then left. As if looking for a way out, he put his hands to his face.

In perfect German, Martin said, "It was you who shot my father. It was only a leg wound, and he didn't need to die—but you let him bleed to death. And then, you bastard, you shot my mother in the head!"

Werner was gasping, trying to talk, "But...but..."

Sweat was pouring down his face.

"Think back, you son of a bitch. I'm sure you can remember Lodz... I was just fifteen. I tried to help both of them, but you... You wouldn't let me save my own parents. Did you think you had escaped justice? Well, perhaps you had—until *now*."

"But...but...I was under orders, yes, orders. You must understand. The solution, get rid of the Jews. I didn't...I didn't..." Werner sputtered, his eyes wide open, his mouth gaping.

"Shut up, you goddamn pig. I can't stand your squeals. You never gave them a chance, nor did you give a damn." Martin's face lit up red with rage. "You killed twenty innocent men and women in the forest, retribution for the explosion that killed those officers in Lodz—shot each of them in the back of the head. Were those 'orders,' too?"

Werner couldn't speak. He tried, but he started to cry. A muffled "please" was lost in his bawling.

"And I know that these were the least of the horrors committed at your hands."

Martin handed his gun to Mendoza. He took out a pair of handcuffs and fastened the Germans' wrists. The Lugar was back in Martin's hands.

"What what are you going to do to me?" begged the terrified German.

Martin shoved Werner toward the right side door of the plane, and slid it open. The wind howled through the opening as he placed his Lugar next to Werner's head and fired. The shot was skilled and purposeful, and the bullet exited the open door, as planned, without injuring Werner. An immediate fecal smell filled the cabin and the front of Werner's pants became soaked with urine. Martin pulled the trigger again, next to the skull. Werner passed out, but Martin slapped him hard across the face until he awoke. "Come on, Oberleutenant, we have so much more to talk about. You must stay awake or you'll miss all the fun."

Taking out a switchblade knife, Martin carefully carved the initials SS into Werner's forehead. Numb from the shots fired, Werner sat paralyzed with fear as the blood poured from his forehead across his face and onto his jacket. "It is important that you be readily identified when they find you, and that your neighbors know who you are. Oh, and thank you for your hospitality. We would now like to complete our joyride and take you back to your estancia."

Mendoza skillfully turned the plane around and headed back toward the runway.

Now alert, face covered with blood, Werner turned towards Martin and pulled his handcuffed wrists up to his chest, as if begging for his life, and sobbed as a combination of blood, tears, and mucus dripped from his chin. "But Señor, please don't… please! I have money, gold—anything you want…the estancia—it's all yours."

Werner was wailing now, his dark eyes pleading with Martin.

Flying at five thousand feet above the farm buildings, Mendoza yelled over the roar of the engine. "It's time for you to hurry back home."

Martin removed the handcuffs and stared directly into Werner's eyes.

A look of confusion crossed Werner's face. "But, but we haven't landed."

"No, not yet," Martin nodded his head in agreement, "but we're dropping you off—special delivery." And with a strong push, he sent Kurt Werner flying into the air—and plummeting home.

As soon as their passenger had departed, Martin moved back into the comfortable front seat, lit two Cuban cigars, and handed one to Mendoza. The plane turned back toward Buenos Aires, and the two men blew smoke rings to celebrate their victory. Martin smiled to himself once again.

Just one more task to complete…one more animal to hunt down.

"...and all the gods, and goddesses, that according to my ability and judgment."

39

February 1969
Prague, Czechoslovakia

In contrast to the despondency evident in Michel's letters, Tamara's life had blossomed with hope and some measure of cheer. Optimism ran high in Czechoslovakia as the movement called "Prague Spring" developed in January 1968. Articles expressing freedom of speech and capitalistic ideals were being published in the newspapers by the growing mass of intellectuals in the Communist-controlled government. This sense of fledgling freedom extended to the arts, and Tamara's drawings and paintings expressed this newfound liberty and could now be exhibited without fear of the censor's hook.

Steeped in her passion for art, Tamara had enjoyed few romantic relationships as a young woman. A brief romance with Vaclav Kryl, a progressive sculptor, came to a halt when he was arrested and imprisoned following a demonstration in downtown Prague in 1958. Brushing off this disappointment, she concentrated on her artistic career while also guiding her younger brother Samuel's education. After graduating from Czech Technical University, he landed a decent job as an engineer at an electronics factory in Holyne, outside Prague.

The loss of her family and the absence of any meaningful relationship left an emotional void in her life. Her heart would stir only when she thought of Michel, the one person she knew who could fathom the pain and loss she had endured. He'd written infrequently during the twenty-four years that had passed, and her heart ached for what seemed to be his sad, colorless existence.

I do worry about Michel... He seems to have no life outside of work, no one to love or to love him. Would it be too foolish for me to go there, to help him—or would it simply pull me down? Here, I have found my passion again. I stand at the easel all day and paint with my feelings, enjoying each season as it passes, from the blossoming of spring flowers to the colorful farewells of fall foliage. Can I leave all this beauty behind and go to him—with all the uncertainty that entails?

Her decision was made for her. With the sharpness of a sickle cutting through wheat, Soviet and Warsaw Pact forces invaded Czechoslovakia in the early morning of August 21, 1968, and the short-lived taste of freedom was suddenly removed and replaced with the iron hand of Mother Russia. Fearing that enhanced freedom in any one of the Soviet satellite countries could lead to the fall of their empire, the Russians reacted with force.

The sight of foreign troops on the streets of Prague brought back the same feeling of angst that had terrified Tamara when the Nazis arrived in Czechoslovakia thirty years earlier. The sounds of marching troops and tanks now filled her with fear and the unsmiling faces of foreign forces made her shudder inside. As these invaders passed through, she once again found herself hiding in the shadows.

For two weeks, martial law ruled the country. Schools closed, many businesses were shuttered, and all movement was strongly controlled, as troops were stationed at strategic intersections, railway stations, airports, and government offices. All gatherings were banned and exhibitions were cancelled. Artisans she knew were being questioned by the authorities about their political views.

Tamara retreated to her home in fear that her art might be considered anti-government and thereby confiscated. She had to make a decision. Composing a letter to Michel describing what was happening in Prague, she placed it in a drawer but resisted mailing it, as the authorities might open and censor it. The signs were clear: That short sense of liberty in the spring had been quashed, leaving her no alternative but to leave.

Five months later, the foreign troops had left, yet the feeling of suppression continued in Prague. Travel restrictions still remained in place. Tamara was especially nervous, remembering her failed trip to Paris to see Michel nine years previously, when the authorities had stopped her. Focusing on her future, she skillfully laid out a plan and took the first step in her quest for freedom.

Cautiously, she boarded the train for Vienna and showed the guard her passport and government authorization to travel to Austria for an art exhibition. Upon arrival at the station in Vienna, she hailed a taxi and directed the driver to go straight to the American Embassy. With suitcase in hand, Tamara approached the front desk and quietly asked to speak to an Embassy official. After a grueling four days of questioning and negotiation, she was granted refugee status, and two days later, on February 17, 1969, she flew to Detroit, the home of her cousin, Ruth Goldstein. She had shipped many of her works to Ruth over the past month as part of a "cultural exchange" program, and for the past year, in anticipation of a move, she had taken classes in English two nights a week. Hoping to surprise Michel, she sent him a teasing note:

"Michel, read the Sunday Milwaukee Journal, *March nineth and go to the Arts and Culture section and look for 'Holocaust Art.' I think you will be surprised."*

Michel immediately noticed the postmark was from Detroit, dated March 3, and a giddy excitement started to build. Grabbing the Sunday paper, he found the headline: "Exhibition of art created by Holocaust survivors on display at Fowler Hall, Marquette University, March 11-13." Glancing at the list of artists, he spotted the name, T. Lissner.

Tamara is here. It starts Tuesday.

With a sense of anticipation he hadn't felt in years, he quickly copied down the information and dashed to the closet that housed a broad, thin box marked: "Tamara's Drawings." He had often pulled out this carton with the thought of visiting her through her work, but on each occasion he would return it to the shelf unopened. This day was different. For the first time in so very long, a tiny spark of warmth flowed into his heart.

He prepared carefully before going to the art show. Surveying his closet, he picked out his best white shirt to go with his navy blue suit with the wide lapels. He studied his ties and chose one that picked up the deep blue of his suit—alternating stripes of blue and red dotted with tiny squares of white. Then he polished his shoes to a spit-shine equal to anything available on the street.

It was a large crowd of people at the exhibition; mostly older Jewish couples whose accents belied their Eastern European origins. The hall had been left plain and undecorated out of respect for the somber subject. A low murmur of quiet anguish travelled through the room as the crowd moved slowly, straining to cope with the unspeakable reality that lay naked to the world on each canvas. Many secretly hoped that somehow these paintings would bring their departed loved ones closer and help explain the unimaginable death of their family members. From time to time, a cry of recognition and pain pierced the hum of sadness.

The exhibition was arranged with each artist occupying a space next to the one where their art or sculpture was displayed on easels or tables. The lighting was generic from the ceiling lights, not the kind seen in a gallery; yet the effect seemed to maintain the necessary solemn atmosphere.

Michel strolled slowly through the hall, stopping whenever the art struck a chord of memories and emotions. It pained him to see the endless portraits of bedraggled faces and bodies amidst a palate of smoke and barbed wire. Children were depicted in only a few of the pieces, but they were all bereft of the joy one expects from childhood scenes. He cringed for a second, thinking he smelled the nauseating odor of the ovens. As he wandered among these nightmare recollections of the past, he felt his chest tightening, and a slight dizziness forced him to find a nearby chair and sit. He rested there a moment, eyes closed, breathing deeply to regain his composure. When he opened them, he felt a surge of life course through his veins at the sight he beheld just twenty feet away.

She stood gracefully in the corner, as if waiting patiently for a guest to arrive. He was mesmerized by her elegance. Her familiar light brown hair had been combed out to flow over her shoulders, and she was wearing a long, elegant black dress that flattered her womanly frame. Realizing that she was now in her late thirties, he calculated that twenty-four years had passed since they'd left the camps. She was more beautiful than ever, her face unblemished and still naturally smooth. Those almond eyes with the clear, light brown irises could belong to no one else but Tamara. His heart fluttered.

Ignoring the art in the foreground, the well-dressed Doctor Katz strode quietly toward Tamara's exhibit and stood silently, appearing to be deeply engrossed in the pictures. Before she even looked up, his presence was felt. Tamara's heart stopped. When she finally had the courage to raise her head, she saw only his back. But she knew. The man she had held so close to her soul for all these years stood before her. She moved nearer and touched his shoulder with the gentlest tap. He turned and faced her, and immediately their eyes met.

"Michel, Doctor Katz. It is really you?"

Words were not spoken for several minutes as they clung to each other. Tears of happiness stained each other's shoulders while they stood together as one. It was as if the tears held back for so many years were suddenly allowed to release at this moment only, saved just for them, together. It did not need to be spoken, it was simply understood: They would never leave each other again.

♦ ♦ ♦

DEPARTING THE HALL WITH Michel, Tamara was happy, yet concerned. There was something about him that seemed different. He looked smaller, shorter than she remembered. Maybe it was because of the way he held his head, more down than straight, as if watching what was directly in front of him, rather than what was to either side. He was jittery, always looking over his shoulder and staring at people they passed on the street. Sometimes, he actually stopped and moved into a doorway or shadow to hide his face from someone. At night, when his dreams came, he shook, cried out, and awoke covered with sweat. He was carrying a burden that he seemed unable to share. The Michel she'd known before had been a proud, smart man who'd functioned with confidence during that nasty, horrible period when others would have given up. Yes, he had become increasingly saddened and despondent toward the end—but this…

Something changed. Michel appears deeply depressed. I came at the right time.

He showed her to a second bedroom in his sparse but neat apartment overlooking Lake Michigan. They had talked little during the drive to his home, yet his eyes seemed to sparkle each time he looked over at her.

Tamara felt buoyant and began to believe that her new life had arrived. Yes, coming here, meeting Michel again, was something ordained by fate. The beacon that had guided her from the horror of the camp was her drawings, and then later the exhibition. But sadly, there had been no such guiding light in Michel's life.

Perhaps now, these drawings might help release him from his darkness.

She sensed that Michel had invited her into his life again without knowing exactly why. But what might be hidden from him was becoming clear to her: She was the only one who could help him complete his story.

To this man, I owe my life; for this man, I would give anything to help remove his sorrow.

At Auschwitz, he had been much like a father would be toward his child—protective and loving. But then, although she *was* only a child, he had confided in her as a friend. He'd had no one else to talk to during that dark period in his life, and he told her things a father would not normally divulge to a daughter. But her heart had listened and understood. Now, as an adult, it was her turn to give back to him.

Entering this new phase of their relationship, she worked hard to get Michel to talk about the camps in the hope that facing the past would help deal with his depression. "Michel, you need to open up. We can heal each other and put the shame and guilt aside as we restart our lives."

And so, as they had twenty-five years before, each night thereafter they talked. At first, they talked of today—of what she was doing with her painting and how he enjoyed his practice. Gradually, pressing back into time, Michel spoke of Montreal and moving to Milwaukee, but avoided any reference to his last days in Europe. Tamara felt restless and wanted to explore both of their lives after they'd left the camps, but while he seemed willing to set aside the time to do so, she sensed his hesitancy.

"Michel, we both need to face our past and discuss that painful time in both of our lives. Should we continue to bury it, it will act as a cancer to our souls and eat us up inside."

At those moments, Michel would look away; the pain was too great.

One day, while she was sitting at her easel, Michel came home from the hospital, kissed her on the cheek, and sat silently facing the window looking out at the lake. His eyes seemed vacant and distant. "Something upset you today?" she asked gently. "You're so quiet."

"Well, yes. I was rounding for Doctor Winters and checked on an older woman whom I had not seen before. And then suddenly, I couldn't...talk. She had...those numbers tattooed on her left forearm. I stared down at them and felt faint. I knew I was going to cry and had to sit down at the nurses' station. My heart was pounding so hard, my hands were shaking. They asked what was wrong, and I said that I hadn't slept well, but the way they looked at me... It was as if they knew..."

His voice trailed off.

Later that night, Tamara said, "Michel, you can't go on grieving each time a reminder of the camps crosses your life—the memories won't disappear." Sitting up, she took his hand and continued, "I have feared bringing up certain questions, but it's time to face those things that have so painfully affected your life."

"It's so hard for me...but, please go on and ask what you must...I might never be ready to talk about that part of my life, but I want you to help me. It's time."

Slowly, this must be done with care.

"You are willing to try, and that's good. Let's start...maybe tomorrow."

The next evening when he returned home, the words spilled out of her mouth before she could stop them. "Michel," she said sharply, "how could you do this...perform postmortem studies on these children each day...one after the other?"

His eyes glazed over as he answered slowly. "At first, I donned my doctor's cap and 'did my job,' something I had trained for so many years to do. In that mode, I couldn't cloud my objective findings with emotion. If I'd lost it—and believe me, at times I was close—I would have had to stop. I feared for myself."

"But those poor children, killed for no good reason—by that monster!" She stroked his hair and made him face her. "Michel, you know there was no medical justification for his studies... They were all just to satisfy Mengele's sadistic curiosity."

"We were surrounded by death... We saw it, smelled it, and heard the screams every day, and...I touched it too often. I had to block it out...I couldn't let it in."

Michel lowered his head. Reaching around his shoulders, Tamara pulled him toward her as tears welled in her eyes.

Emboldened, the next night she pressed on. "What about those ghastly cold immersion experiments you helped with that vile SS doctor, Hans Bloch?"

Michel swallowed hard. "Do you think I could've stopped helping him? You saw Bloch. Cross him once, and I would have been the next corpse engulfed in fire."

His face lit up in anger.

"But you *did* speak out, remember? And he listened—sort of."

"Yes, though I was trying to keep men alive for his experiment—to let them die would have meant the loss of a subject, not good for his numbers. And he did listen to me when I told him that submersing the subjects' entire neck in the ice water frequently led to their death."

"I remember now...you did get mad. Remember being so angry that one night? It was the first time I saw you react so strongly."

"Yes...yes...Hans was running out of adult males for his study, so he started to bring in children no older than twelve." Michel's voice was trembling. "None of them made it; each one died in the ice water. When I tried to convince him to stop, he looked at me with those cold, dark eyes and said: *"You should know, Jew doctor, they will all die, anyway, so what's the difference?"*

Michel slumped down in his chair and covered his face with his hands.

They will all die, anyway...

"I will give no deadly medicine to anyone, if asked, nor suggest such counsel."

40

March 30, 1969
Milwaukee

The cold, wet pillow lay matted against the side of his head. As he turned to find a dry spot on the pillowcase, he rolled into the moist, dampened sheets. Such a miserable, yet familiar, feeling. Some nights Michel remembered the dream vividly, but more often it was forgotten as he awoke still sweating. Waking up wet, he knew he had dreamt it again, as he had every night without exception since he'd left the camps. He shivered, not from the cold, but from the horrors of this persistent nightmare that stalked him.

As if watching a silent play, he saw a child, like so many who had perished in front of him, lain out on the autopsy table. She was a young girl, maybe eight years old, a twin—with light brown, curly hair, and fair skin. Her body was reasonably well-fed, as Mengele had ordered that all his twins get the same meals as the SS. The pale green eyes were open, staring innocently up at the white ceiling. He watched as she was killed by a chloroform injection into her heart from a hand that could have been his—he wasn't able to tell. All the instruments were carefully arranged to the side of the marble slab. He reached for the large blade and started his incision at the suprasternal notch, extending down through the abdominal wall to the pubis... Just then, the body suddenly sat up and cried out, "Mommy, Mommy!" and fell back down, silent.

He could not put aside the terror he felt with each repetition of that dream, yet it seemed to be forgotten during the day, as if he was permanently numbed by all the death and pain he had witnessed. But at night, his sensitivity to these horrifying events returned, and with it, the torment.

He was aware of how fortunate he had been and he never allowed himself to feel a patient's pain. Viewing empathy as a weakness, he sensed that any visible sign of sensitivity to a patient's discomfort could serve to diminish his standing before his peers. Within this protective cocoon, Michel hid behind his 'doctor's blinders,' so that he was immune from suffering the same anguish a mere mortal might feel.

♦♦♦

THEY HAD BEEN TOGETHER just one month, and each night they continued to immerse themselves in discussing the fears, pain, and losses of the past. It seemed that their liberation from Auschwitz had been merely a physical one, and that both their souls were still trapped in the harsh realities of survival.

That didn't seem right to Tamara.

We should have celebrated the joy of living and learned to relish the small blessings that have come to us over the years. But in the aftermath of the camps came news of the death of so many family members. We had to deal with the shock of our continued existence and the shame of our personal survival—with the knowledge that all those others we loved had perished.

Her own quest for freedom had been supported by her art, her drawings. What she couldn't express in words, she could paint in the hues and shades of human emotions. While hiding in the attic above Michel's laboratory, her drawings had been limited to black and white; life's colors had disappeared from her palette. Only after she resumed life again in Prague did she dip her brush into colors that captured the essence of her new reality. And this she did each day, alone in her studio, translating her fears, feelings, and failings into shapes and colors that resembled people, trees, or things not necessarily recognizable… It didn't matter. As she drifted into sleep each night, her emotional plate had been emptied onto a canvas so that someday others might understand what could not be written. And while she had not reached total freedom, she had found a level that at least allowed her to breathe, to experience joy in life again. Still, she knew that along her road to liberation, her art had led the way.

She feared that Michel's route was not quite so clear.

He told me once that he kept a diary. He showed it to no one, as it was his private place, alone. He knew that I expressed myself through art, yet he had not seen my paintings. Perhaps, he will now wish to expose his own art—the written page.

Shortly after Tamara arrived, Michel retrieved the unopened box containing her artwork that she had sent him years ago and lay hidden in his closet. As he took out the drawings, he arranged them on the dining room table in the order he believed they were finished. She watched silently as he studied them, the way an archeologist might look at ancient pictographs carved in stone. He spoke with his eyes as he looked up at her, and she knew in that moment that he understood, that the time she had yearned for had finally come. He studied her simple pencil drawings and knew they had captured the essence of their months together at the camp.

Michel spoke tenderly, but with purpose: "We must discuss each one."

He pulled a small drawing from the pile on the table between them and slowly set this one drawing aside, purposefully turning his back to her. Bending over, he cradled it between his hands and rested his head on it. After a few moments, he sat up, eyes reddened. He moved his hands away, allowing her to see what had touched him so.

Tamara was jolted, having not seen any of these images in twenty-five years. She remembered this one scene while peering down from the attic above Michel's laboratory. There were tearstains on the paper that depicted a young girl of about ten years, lying on her back. Partially blocking her view was the back of two heads: of two men observing a body outstretched on a marble slab. Gazing again at her drawing, she remembered that exact moment, and was visibly shaken as her feelings returned so clearly.

I was watching an autopsy of this young person. The watermark formed by my tears that fell on the drawing was of small stains, somehow authenticating my emotional presence.

Michel began to speak, "I never realized...the pain you must have felt in the camp. I was so wrapped up in myself that I did not think about you and your fears. Maybe, during our talks at night, I had failed to really listen. I may have foolishly assumed that you were grateful to just be alive. I was wrong."

"*You* gave me the pencil and paper," Tamara's voice was shaking. "And with it, you saved me for the second time. I had an easy outlet for my emotions; it was *you* that worried me. Even though I was so young, I saw you had no way to vent—to rid yourself of the suffering that plagued you each day. Yes, you expressed thoughts each night and you worried so about your family. But you never talked about your other feelings, the feelings you must have buried inside as you carried out the work of the SS."

Michel stood up and started to wander about the room, head down, as if thinking of something to say. "The pain is still here. As a doctor, we are taught to hold our emotions in check because they often get in the way of clinical judgment. I did that, I tried my best, yet I still felt those sensations deep within." Holding his face in his hands, he continued. "For me, it is so hard to express...I carry so much shame...I am worth nothing."

He sat down next to her.

"Michel, I, too, have a long way to go to accept the indignity of my survival—that I should be allowed to live while so many others died. And yet, I was given a second chance to live, and, later, to love again."

As she spoke, she moved closer to him and gently placed her arm around his shoulders.

He lightly moved her arm away and opened a drawer in his desk adjacent to his dining table. Reaching in, he pulled out a brown leather diary secured by a clasp. Warily, he opened it to the first page, dated July 8, 1944. Looking at Tamara, he started to read aloud:

"*This is my first day working in the laboratory. How things have changed! I can wear a white doctor's coat over my inmate clothing. There is no one else here to tell me what to do. I will spend the day exploring my new surroundings and be ready for Mengele's visit this afternoon.*"

Putting the journal down, he continued talking as he stared at the floor.

"A young Sonderkommando named Morris found this diary, still empty, among the belongings of a Jew who'd been gassed. He passed it on to me, asking me to write down what I saw at the camp and in the laboratory. He knew there would be few survivors left to tell the world, and that I would likely be one of them."

He lifted his eyes as Tamara moved closer to him. "I wrote my thoughts each day and hid the journal under my mattress. Six weeks later, Morris and his group were killed and replaced."

Tamara's drawings remained propped up on the table over the next several days, as the two started pouring through the daily entries in Michel's diary. One night, as they read and talked, Michel's attention became distracted and he seemed startled—halting mid-sentence. He was staring at a sketch of the inside of a cattle car that transported inmates to Auschwitz. Although drawn in pencil and charcoal, the figures were clear: A mother seated on the straw in a corner of the railcar holding two children.

"Was this scene in the car that carried you to Auschwitz?" he asked.

He was about to question her further, but stopped for fear of what the answer might be. Tamara did not look up. The woman looked like Anna, his wife.

Could this be my family?

Michel held up the picture with trembling hands and studied it further in the light. *My family! Yes, I can make out Aaron, taller and with longer hair than I remember, but Aaron, just the same. And Rachel, that looks just like her, snuggling up to her mother—Anna.*

He did not want to believe what he was seeing, yet he began to cry softly. He knew. The memories came flooding back, and he shook inside. Finally, he looked over at Tamara. She did not meet his gaze, but instead looked down at the floor, lost in her own questions.

Will he hate me for not telling him? Was this the right thing to do? I have kept this from him for so long. How much longer...? Yes, when he showed me their picture in his room at the camp, I knew...it was them.

Michel held his head in his hands and let the tears fall freely. He needed no words from Tamara to know the truth. And he understood.

She couldn't tell me...she wouldn't...she would spare me.

He slid over and embraced her. He felt no anger, just a desire to ease the painful conflict that he knew was tearing through her and that she had carried so bravely all these years. Once again, there was no need for words between them.

We both know the truth. Speaking it out loud can never change it.

Night after night they continued to sit quietly together, looking at the pictures and reading from Michel's diaries. At times, they discovered they could match a day's journal entry with one of Tamara's drawings. Each had recorded the Sonderkommando revolt in Crematorium II. Tamara had drawn a picture of smoke coming from a burning building, with inmates being summarily shot in the head against an adjacent wall; Michel's entry was full of angst and fear after Doctor Bloch's vicious assertion that he was part of the plot to blow up the crematorium. It went on to detail how Hans had forced him to march downstairs to be executed with the Sonderkommandos—only to be saved by Mengele. A few days earlier, Tamara had drawn a picture of the line of women and children being led into the "showers" downstairs, never to return. Michel's entry for October 30, 1944 described "the repeated cacophony of screaming, shouting, and wailing occurring several times today, followed by silence." These sounds marked the last day the crematorium was used.

As they paired their entries and talked openly about their feelings, both seemed to move emotionally closer. Their bodies touched more often, and the simple warmth of Michel's arm next to Tamara made her heart race.

For the first few weeks after Tamara's arrival, he would wearily suggest that he took responsibility for what he had done to "save his family." In time, however, he became more honest, both with Tamara and with himself, and admitted that it was his own survival that had driven his choice to assist Mengele. Tamara knew it was truly a milestone for Michel to start to take personal responsibility, and not to pass the blame off totally on Mengele or Hans Bloch.

There can be no more excuses for us.

As the days passed, they both began to accept that their own primal instincts had been the force that steered their choices, and were perhaps no different from what other inmates in the camps would have felt or followed, had they been given the same opportunities to survive.

One day, Tamara asked Michel, "Tell me, where does the hurt begin?"

"I lied to myself," he said slowly, "to my very core." Michel dropped his voice so low that she had to move closer to hear him. "I left my family behind to regain my doctor self, assuming so wrongly that I would save them, while knowing deep down I could not."

"What if you hadn't gone to Auschwitz from Terezin and didn't work with the SS doctors? Would they be alive today?"

He had no answer. What he knew for certain was that, in the camps, he had no power to save them. "I know only this. I still fear going out in the street today. I have this crazy belief that the whole world knows—that each passerby will recognize me as the Jew doctor who aided Mengele by doing autopsies on their children."

Tamara's cheeks flushed as her voice rose. "If you hadn't done it, would all those children have been saved? And those survivors who see you today, what did they do to stay alive? Did they steal jewelry from the suitcases of those led to the chambers that they could trade for food or medicine? Did they bribe the guards with stolen valuables for water, bread, or clothing? Would it have been better that we all were dead, so that we shouldn't suffer shame and guilt? Should I feel shame that I alone survived the gas chamber and lived?"

Sinking back in the couch, Tamara sighed deeply, exhausted.

Michel gently put his arms around her and pulled her close. As she looked up at him, he looked deeply into her eyes. Their lips met naturally. For the first time, Tamara felt Michel's kiss, the one she had dreamed of for so many years. She kissed him back, fully and completely.

"While I continue to keep this oath unviolated..."

41

August 12, 1953
Indio, California

Hans felt comfortable in his new identity. Two years after the arrival of "Jürgen Hauptman" at Indio Community Hospital, he had earned the respect of the other physicians in the community. It took some time for him to be accepted because of his German background, but it wasn't long before they began to notice and admire his direct approach to both the staff and his patients. He was not a "coddler"; he had his post-operative patients up and walking sooner and discharged his patients earlier than the other doctors. It was difficult to determine if his odd and quirky approach to patients was a cultural one, yet it yielded beneficial results. In any case, he was gracious to all, and the staff was glad to have him.

His use of a "cooling blanket" for surgical patients was new to the nurses and doctors who worked in the operating suites with him. Details of his research in hypothermia done in San Antonio were shared with Doctor Homer, an anesthesiologist. Contrary to his experience at Cincinnati General, there were no barriers to overcome in his determination to continue his study in this desert hospital. After just three months, he had easily convinced the doctors, nurses, and administration that surgical results would improve and the hospital's reputation would be enhanced.

♦♦♦

Hans Bloch's life had changed. No longer could he appear as the confident SS officer who demanded the total respect of others around him. The crisp, sharp uniform adorned with service medals that he wore with such pride sadly had been put away forever as he adopted the persona of Jürgen Hauptman, MD. Months turned into years until two decades had passed, and his concern for his own security had lessened.

Maybe no one is looking for me. Hans Bloch is not missed by the Germans, or by the Jews and their Mossad.

Continuing to celebrate his surgical successes, he had used his hypothermic cooling pad on over five hundred patients, dutifully recording his data. He was encouraged to publish his results early on by Doctor Homer, but was hesitant for fear of exposing his past.

Looking back over the past twenty years in Indio, his surgical results were decent, indicating a reduction in operating time and average blood loss, but there were a few complications directly related to the cooling blanket. These included superficial frostbite, slowed heartbeat (bradycardia), and ventricular arrhythmias. There had also been ten cases of ventricular fibrillation in which eight patients died. Spreading out these complications over the years, little attention was raised, and Hans continued his program. Since this cooling device was not manufactured, government approval did not seem necessary in the eyes of the hospital. Despite these significant difficulties, Jürgen Hauptman remained convinced that his cooling device was highly effective for his patients undergoing surgery.

In 1970, he felt secure and confident enough to publish his results in the *California State Medical Bulletin*, an obscure but respected journal with minimal circulation. During these two decades in Indio, Hans led a quiet life and allowed no one to get too close to him. Being obsessed by work, Hans stayed aloof from the social scene around the hospital and remained a bachelor. He lived in a modest home surrounded by a wrought iron fence and electronic gate in a housing development at the southern edge of the city. He was not exactly a hermit, but few people were invited into his house, and he rarely entertained. From time to time, he had brief relationships with women, but avoided any serious long-term romance. For the first few years, it had been difficult for Hans to accept himself as "Jürgen," but as the years passed, he readily slipped into that mold and welcomed his transformation. Also, any reference to Hans Bloch had been removed from his office files and from his home.

He had developed a close and most trusting relationship with Allen Homer. The anesthesiologist had been in Indio for five years prior to Hans joining the medical staff and his path to the desert community had also been a rocky one. Originally practicing in Riverside, California, Homer was on the verge of losing his credentials to do anesthesia at Riverside General Hospital following the death of two patients within a relatively close period of time. Before that hospital's executive committee could meet, he resigned and moved on to the small desert hospital in Indio.

Doctor Homer saw Hauptman's research as a chance to professionally redeem himself, and he offered to support him in any way he could. He did wonder, however, how a colleague could refrain from publishing such a brilliant, successful, long-term study in a journal such as the *Annals of Surgery*, but he chalked it up to a unique form of modesty. Doctor Homer was also privy to the occasional flash of arrogance from that German temperament. Above all, he was overly impressed with his colleague's depth of knowledge, and he suggested that perhaps Jürgen might consider presenting a paper at a surgical convention.

This made Jürgen's pulse race. He had wanted to present his work before a large audience, and his friend's suggestion rekindled that desire. Then, as if by uncanny coincidence, he received an announcement of a call for speakers for the upcoming meeting of the National Trauma Society in San Francisco in May 1974.

"Gaining the respect of all men for all time…"

42

March 10, 1974
Milwaukee

This was a day that would change Michel Katz's life. The exquisite lounge of the Milwaukee Pfister Hotel beckoned the weary, thirsty traveler to sit in its deep, cushioned armchairs and escape the woes he had plodded through this day. Seated around Michel were young and middle-aged men in suits, some together, others alone, looking quite comfortable in these surroundings. Michel felt strange here, in the middle of the afternoon, enjoying the perks that only business people indulge in when he should have been back in his office or in the operating suite. But Martin had said it was important, a matter of life or death, and that Michel must meet him immediately, and alone.

He ordered a Perrier while he awaited Martin's arrival.

A Scotch would be great, but I still have patients to see.

The light in the room was muted, so Michel kept his eyes on the entrance to the lounge, searching each face to identify his former campmate.

I remember him only as a boy… What does he look like now? I do remember that smirk, his crooked smile when he talked of escape from Auschwitz.

His intense concentration on the door was broken when Martin, as if emerging out of thin air, slid silently into the chair beside him.

"My God, where did you come from? You scared the living shit out of me! I have been watching the entrance for five minutes and didn't see you come in," Michel gasped, trying to keep his cool and not draw attention to their meeting.

"In my business, it often pays to arrive at my destination early and observe the crowd. There could be someone around with an interest in one of us," Martin whispered, as if he had actually spotted someone spying on their meeting.

"Well, that's reassuring, I think. But what is your business?"

Martin did not answer immediately, and in the silence, Michel studied his old nemesis. Time had not changed him; he still carried those boyish looks he had back at Auschwitz. His thin, inmate body, however, had been replaced by a fit, muscular frame that exuded strength and power. Although he was pleasant in appearance, his eyes held a somewhat menacing look. Michel wondered what was coming next.

Motioning to the waitress, Martin ordered a vodka tonic, then sat back and began: "How long has it been—maybe thirty years since I left Auschwitz?"

"Yes. You escaped in December, 1944. After that, we met briefly again at the DP camp in Belgium when I was ill."

"We didn't have a chance to talk then, so you know little about my escape or my life since then, correct?"

"No, and the Nazis never said a word to me. They jotted down the number of the dead man they thought was you, and nothing further was said," Michel grinned. "You were never missed."

Martin shifted around in his chair, attempting to get comfortable. "You're wondering why I looked you up."

Michel nodded.

"Remember Hans Bloch, that murderous doctor who killed all those young men with his cold immersion studies?"

"Quite well," answered Michel without hesitation.

Martin looked up, then straight at Michel. "He was also involved in a top secret study concerning the effects of radiation exposure on children. If you recall, he was absent two days each month for his 'clinical rounds,' and we always wondered what that meant. We now know that Bloch would fly to Ohrdruf Thuringia, just ninety miles southwest of Berlin, where the Germans were in the early stages of developing an atomic bomb. The concentration camp located there provided inmates, including children, for radiation exposure experiments. Over two hundred of them were studied."

"Well, go on... I assume that, just like Mengele and his cohorts, they killed children with their horrible experiments, correct?" Michel asked, knowing the answer could not be a good one if Hans or Mengele were involved.

"Death, experiments on children, yes—all of it was monstrous. But this...this was different, and those bastards like Hans were more inhuman than even Mengele himself. No one made children suffer like that animal Bloch did. At least Mengele didn't try to create painful torture on his victims. He killed them with phenol or chloroform to the heart, and boom—they were dead. Hans's children were exposed to one thousand millicures of radiation, and their burn development was recorded on film."

Michel started to feel faint and put his head down as he fought the nausea rising from his stomach. "Oh God, so much horror, over and over. How did you find this out, if it was so top secret?"

"Only a few selected, ardent Nazis in the SS were knowledgeable about this highly secret program. But one of the captured SS officers who participated in the study came forward in an attempt to plead for his life. He smuggled out a single copy of a film and exchanged it for a reduced sentence in prison. The film is so inflammatory, we did not release it to anyone, let alone the Americans."

"But why are you telling me this now?"

"Let me finish," Martin said quickly. "Our group has identified each of the SS involved, and we are tracking them down, one by one."

"But you're like vigilantes, without state connection or authorization to do so, correct?"

"Not entirely. Let me give you some history. When the Jews of Palestine understood what was happening to European Jewry, they formed a British unit called the Jewish Brigade that fought alongside Allied forces in Europe. When I escaped the camp, I traveled to Lodz and joined up with the Armia Krajowa, a Polish resistance group. From there, I was flown by the British Secret Service to Italy, where I was debriefed about Auschwitz, my escape, and the Polish resistance activities. The Brits directed me to Tarviso, Italy, where I joined the Jewish Brigade. As the war ended, the Brigade refused to break up, and many continued on in a clandestine fashion in Europe. Some of us helped arrange transportation of Jews from Italy to Palestine, avoiding the British ships trying to intercept them. Most, however, were involved in trying to help the Americans and Brits capture the Nazi war criminals."

Martin leaned forward and Michel saw anger burning in his eyes. "I was on the hunt for one of these animals when I saw you in the hospital in Belgium. As the details of the concentration camps came out, and the magnitude of the Holocaust became apparent, a profound sense of rage set in, and we changed our tactics. We couldn't wait for the Nuremburg trials to be completed; the proceedings seemed to drag on beyond reason. We wanted immediate retribution and did this quietly, without headlines. When a targeted criminal was found, we didn't kill him right away. It was important to recreate a period of pain and suffering with each Nazi bastard so that he would experience exactly the agonizing process of slow death they had inflicted on others."

Michel closed his eyes and breathed deeply, then stared at Martin for perhaps too long before asking, "You're not Mossad—not connected with Israel in any way?"

"The government of Israel would disavow us publicly—yet privately, our actions are encouraged. Funding our mission has never been a problem."

Martin went on to regale Michel with an unbelievable tale spanning twenty-five years. In order to get close enough to the Nazi criminals and gain their confidence, he had assumed identities that required specialized knowledge in a number of fields and professions. In his short life, he had taken on the roles of accountant, banker, aerospace engineer, pilot, and even a nurse. "I've become quite an actor. I think I can do just about anything, at this point. Our methods may seem coarse, but they are effective, and that Nazi officer who came forward with this info on Bloch won't even have to finish his twenty-year sentence, as one of our 'stress-relief' officers paid him a brief visit yesterday and found a way to shorten it."

Martin stared at Michel, who was now obviously shaken.

"So, what does this have to do with me?" Michel asked, clearly afraid to hear the answer.

Now Martin leaned closer, looking directly into his eyes. "We thought we had that bastard Hans Bloch in San Antonio, when he was brought in by those forgetful American generals under Operation Paper Clip. They saw him as a ticket to their next star. Here they had the world's leading expert on radiation injury to help the United States secret program develop an atomic bomb. There was no question that he had to come to the US. If not, the Russians would have certainly stolen him away. In fact, when he arrived at the Air Force base in San Antonio, guards were assigned to watch over him. Isn't *that* a laugh?'"

Martin paused long enough to take a swig of vodka. Rage filled his face, as if he was ready to strike out at someone, anyone. "Politically, the staff at the US air base opposed any radiation experiments, and the Truman administration supported that decision, but Bloch was able to continue his 'cold immersion studies' on primates. Fourteen months later, though, he had become an embarrassment to the Air Force after getting into a fight with Jewish soldiers in a bar. They planned to return him to the Germany for de-nazification, but, like other Nazi scientists they recruited, this sly fox evaded the authorities, and, for the past twenty years has been practicing under a different name in a hospital in Indio, California."

"And how did you find all this out?" asked Michel.

"Early on, our organization began routinely screening applicants with foreign credentials for all state licensure requests in any profession. When the name 'Jürgen Hauptman' surfaced, our records matched it to a German medical student killed at Potsdam. We checked with the student's medical school, and they reported that they'd received a request for his records to be sent to Cincinnati General Hospital. The copies of the university transcripts were so poor that no one would be able to detect a changed or forged signature. Someone calling himself Doctor Hauptman finished a surgical residency there. It wasn't until this year that we found him in California, practicing surgery. We identified him by his picture on the Indio hospital brochure."

"So again, I ask you—what is it you want of me?"

Michel felt his anxiety escalating.

"We know you have registered for the National Trauma Society meeting being held in San Francisco this year from May seventeenth to the twentieth. Coincidentally, Hans Bloch is presenting a paper at the conference on "Hypothermic Surgery," and we need you to help us capture him."

"Whoa, wait a minute! This is way out of my league. I'm just a middle-aged doctor who is in no shape to be a policeman. Why can't you just capture him where he lives?"

"Yes, we could do that, but we prefer to do our work in large cities, where the circumstances of the death will attract little publicity. And, you must understand, we do not wish to broadcast our methods to the world."

Michel, seized by another wave of panic, made a move to leave. But as he rose, he felt Martin's hand firmly gripping his shoulder, bringing him back to his chair. "It's been so long," Martin hissed in his ear. "Maybe... time has caused you to forget, *Monsieur le Docteur?*"

Yes, Martin was there when I helped the Nazis with their experiments. I even had him hold down inmates in cooling tanks for Hans's hypothermia studies. I am sure he watched as I reviewed data with Mengele on his twins' research. In fact, he may have been present when Mengele killed those children by injecting chloroform into their hearts.

Michel remembered how, when Martin demanded to be hidden in the attic above the lab, he'd threatened to expose Tamara if he refused. It was all so long ago, and yet...

What else does Martin hold?

A cold chill ran up his back. Martin was the only one, other than Tamara, who knew of his role, his work, at Auschwitz. A mountain of shame, once suppressed, began to rise again inside him.

"We need you to see and confront him," Martin was saying. "It won't take him long to understand. You will threaten to expose him, unless he agrees to donatefive hundred thousand dollars to a Holocaust victims' fund. You will refer only to his changed identity and cold immersion studies, and will not mention the radiation experiments. His deepest fear is that he will be connected to the radiation exposure work, and he will not take that chance. In fact, I have no doubt he will cooperate. All you need to do is set up a meeting time and place, and we will take over from there. Nothing will be traced to you—nothing. Your job will be done. Once we enter the picture, we will put the issue to sleep."

The two men talked a few minutes longer, and then Martin excused himself. Michel sat, as if paralyzed. A myriad of thoughts coursed through his head while he tried to reconstruct what had transpired these last few minutes with Martin.

Is this blackmail? If I don't help him, will I, too, now be exposed? And Tamara, she had nothing to do with this. How do I tell her?

Walking out of the hotel into the late afternoon sun, the last thirty minutes seemed to blur.

Did I agree to be part of a plot to murder? So Hans Bloch has a new name. I didn't catch it.

His head was pounding hard with this new twist life had thrown him, and he was sure he wasn't ready for it.

43

May 17, 1974
San Francisco, California

I should not be here, this is foolish.
Other thoughts wildly crisscrossed his mind as he stood in line with Tamara to register at the San Francisco Hilton.

Maybe he won't come, and it was just a ruse. Or I'll be dragged down into Martin's fiendish plot. No…can't think that way. But, somehow, I had to come.

"Sir, we have a room on the seventh floor. Would that be satisfactory?" offered the hotel clerk as he motioned to the bell captain to take care of their bags.

"Yes," answered Michel. "Very nice."

The bags were deposited in their room, and the bellman had left. "Oh Michel," said Tamara standing at the window, "the Bay bridge is right out there…marvelous."

Putting his arms around her waist, he said, "I've always loved this city. Look at the buildings, the architecture—reminds me of Europe, and yet different in many ways."

"Maybe it's these hills, so steep and with buildings tottering on top—as if they could fall over," said a smiling Tamara.

"I see that," as Michel craned his neck toward the south. "Look, people are bustling along the sidewalk…they seem to have a sense of *joie de vivre* and adventure."

For Michel, this particular surgical convention was important as the field of trauma was a new subspecialty in surgery. In Milwaukee, he was active on the trauma team and spent many nights caring for victims of gun-shots and car accidents. Following Martin's visit, he had considered not attending this conference, but it was too important for him to miss.

He had avoided answering any of Martin's calls after their meeting in Milwaukee, and even changed his home telephone to an unlisted number.

If he thinks I might not help him, maybe he'll go away. I can't let this lust for vengeance rule my life. Over the past five years, Tamara and I have worked hard to escape from the prisons of our own making. We have allowed each other's love to heal us. We have not buried our pasts, but learned to live with our actions and the painful guilt of being survivors. For either of us to join in on Martin's dreadful plan...could only give rise to yet more regrettable grief.

♦♦♦

WITH 250,000 SQUARE FEET of space, the San Francisco Convention Center could accommodate the largest of medical specialty meetings and conferences, including multiple halls for scientific presentations and vendor exhibitions. Immense and imposing, it loomed as a storehouse holding acres of exhibits and displays set to trap the wandering doctor with the newest devices—much like the Sirens of *The Odyssey* with their beautiful voices snared the unsuspecting sailor. It was here that the National Trauma Society had chosen to hold its annual meeting. Over eight thousand doctors were gathered at the Convention Center, while a cast of twelve thousand exhibitors all vying to market their medicines, wares, and devices to the captive physicians.

For Michel, there were a variety of educational activities available. The classic ten-minute doctor presentations went on all day in three different lecture halls simultaneously. And one could walk for hours in the exhibit hall, going from one booth to another to learn about the latest tracheotomy procedures and other surgical advances. New instruments and scores of other medical devices were thrust at the curious doctors from both sides of the aisles. At times, it was exhausting for Michel—so much information being cast at him at once. The exhibit hall resembled a circus, with large tents and striking female models posing in the latest thigh-high stretch compression hose. The more glitz and glamour, the better it sells... That was the takeaway message.

Walking through the hallways and exhibit center, Michel continued nervously to scan the floor for Martin, while reflecting on the surreal atmosphere of these conventions. The crowds of doctors were most interesting to observe and could appear, at times, peculiar. First, their look was predictable: The older physicians wore the unremarkable dark suit with conservative tie, while the young practitioners and residents sported the almost uniform blue blazer and khaki slacks. They moved hastily, as if on a mission to get to some place they had yet to identify, and all shared the same dour all-knowingness and deep responsibility that lined their faces.

The doctors carried similar canvas bags, decorated with the logo of one exhibitor or another, and stuffed with all sorts of papers, free pens, aspirin, clips, and samples. Many sat to the side, enjoying coffee and reviewing the scheduled activities. A few wives could be seen heading towards the area marked: "Spouses' Programs and Tours."

On the first day, Michel had elected to attend a symposium on "Pulmonary Embolism." He had purposely sought out this topic as just two weeks prior, he had treated a young, thirty-two-year-old, healthy female who died suddenly of a pulmonary embolism while recovering from the repair of a liver laceration and fractured femur. She had been run down at dusk by a car while doing her nightly jog and ended up at Milwaukee General, where Michel was the surgeon on call. Her death left a two-year-old daughter and six-month-old son to be raised alone by their father. Even though Michel and the staff had treated her appropriately, she developed a blood clot thrown from her iliac vein into her left pulmonary artery, and died.

Could I have saved her life?

It was a question that dogged him, and he looked forward to the lecture by Howard Edwards from the University of California, San Francisco, who was scheduled to speak on the surgical approach to massive pulmonary embolism.

Unfortunately, Doctor Edwards's enthusiasm about surgically extracting the clots from the major artery of a lung was not strongly supported by his data. Of the seven patients he had operated on, only three had survived. Based on the clinical description of these three patients, Michel surmised that they might easily have lived if treated with the usual anticoagulation methods without the surgery recommended by Doctor Edwards.

Perhaps this procedure should be abandoned.

As he was leaving the hall, Michel noticed a man about six feet tall walking straight and purposefully ahead of him. He recognized something about his gait—so correct, almost robotic. He was maybe between sixty and sixty-five, and in good physical shape with a slightly thinning mound of white hair combed meticulously—not one hair out of place. Michel couldn't see his nametag, but an uneasy feeling alerted him. Then the man turned slightly, and, on the left side of his head, starting at the hairline and proceeding up to his scalp, was a bluish stain, or hemangioma. He knew it could be only one man.

It's Hans Bloch.

He almost reached out to say something or to stop him. A painful knot developed in his stomach and a cold shiver ran through his body as he followed the doctor out the side door of the convention hall and into the San Francisco Hilton. He quickly looked back and scanned the lobby—sure that Martin would show up any moment. Quickening his pace, he kept directly behind his prey, maybe twelve steps back, careful to keep others between them as he tried to stay calm and control his rapid breathing.

When the doctor stopped at a bank of elevators, Michel ducked behind a ficus tree and watched. His prey soon disappeared amidst a throng of suited men, and the elevator door closed. The next elevator took Michel to the seventh floor and he entered his room—his pulse racing.

♦ ♦ ♦

HE WAS RELIEVED. TAMARA had not yet returned, as she had chosen to spend her day on a spouses' excursion. Collapsing onto the bed, his whole body began to tremble.

It's starting again.

His thoughts became erratic, spinning out of control, and consciously he forced himself once more to slow down his breathing. He'd had a chance to glance at Hans's face before the elevator doors closed, and was able to verify it was the same arrogant bastard.

I can still see him sneering at me in his SS uniform.

His mind switched to Martin.

I know he's here, and he will find me. What did I tell him? Time is a blur… I can't remember. But if I said I would help…I can't.

His shaking intensified as he sat there weighing his thoughts while his mind raced through the gamut of possibilities. The brief meeting with Martin had only confirmed that this former Sonderkommando hadn't changed. He had threatened to expose Michel before, at Auschwitz, and he was doing it again, now. But this time his pursuit of vengeance would not only extract the wrong form of justice, it could enslave him and Tamara again, plunging them back into the survivors' guilt they'd worked so hard to escape.

Tamara arrived an hour later and was excited to tell Michel about her day, but her spirits immediately dampened—seeing him slouched in a chair.

"Is it Martin?"

"No, not him—yet. But I did...see Hans Bloch."

"Did you talk, say something to him?"

"No, I followed him into our hotel and I lost him when he went into an elevator. That's all."

"That means that Martin is somewhere...near us." Tamara looked at the door. "Michel, he worries me so."

"I expect that we will see him soon... He doesn't give up."

Michel stood up and paced the room.

"You must confront him, Michel, tell him it's over...*over!*"

Michel didn't answer. With shoulders slumped he slowly sat back down on the bed and hung his head.

He looks beaten, and I'm afraid for him. He's lost that spark that had come back over the past few years. Since seeing Martin two months ago, he doesn't leave the house, other than go to the hospital and office.

She had suggested that he not go to the meeting—that he stay home and avoid Martin. But he had made the decision to go. And now here he was, just sitting there with a clenched jaw, staring at the wall. She knew that Michel had worked hard to climb out of the morass of personal doubt and found himself on a higher plane of self-awareness. He had fought his way through the stages of denial, anger, grief, and finally achieved self-acceptance. He was now able to see himself as not just "the doctor," but as a feeling, sensitive person—not much different than anyone else. She feared that everything he had done in the hopes of finding himself again was now at stake.

They both knew Martin was coming any moment.

♦♦♦

THERE WAS A SHARP rap on the door. Michel sat quietly and stared at it—another rap, then a whispered, "Michel, open up! It's Martin."

Tamara clung to Michel, wrapping her arms around him and burying her head in his chest.

Michel gently released himself and stood up, eyes fixed on the door. Fear fully enveloped his body. The sweat under his arms became cold, and he stood there, paralyzed.

Another loud hammering at the door; then a third one—this one hard enough to loosen the door trim.

"Michel," Tamara was shaking. "You probably should let him in."

Michel, his face fixed in a stony glare, slowly walked over and opened the door, allowing his nemesis to enter.

Martin burst in quickly, his red face exploding with anger. "You knew I would find you! Did you think you could hide?"

It was then that he saw Tamara sitting on the couch.

"Tamara? Is it you?" Martin walked closer to her. "Tamara! I am surprised. I did not expect to see you here. What I have come to say is between Michel and me, so I ask that you remain silent. Or better yet, perhaps you will leave."

Tamara coolly ignored both his question and command by making no move to stand. "Martin, I will stay. There are no secrets between Michel and I. Let's hear what you have to say."

Martin was breathing hard. "It is time, Michel, and I must have your assistance. As I told you, we've planned to carry out this 'retribution' in a large city such as San Francisco, where it will attract little attention. We must complete this task now and move on to our next target."

Michel sat stoically, staring at Martin, who continued to talk.

"You will help us bring justice to this animal. He deserves no better."

"Have a seat, Martin, and let us discuss this matter," Michel said, his voice surprisingly calm, considering he was shaking internally. "Time has passed, and so must our emotions be tempered. It is no longer revenge that continues to ravage my mind."

How can I make him understand?

"I have tried to make peace with myself for my actions at the camps—and so should you."

Martin's face reignited with anger, as he fought to control his speech. "Remember, I watched you every day serve the wishes of Hans and the other SS animals who called themselves doctors. You must remember! Those were days you couldn't be proud of, and they will continue to stain your person and follow you forever."

He paused and gave Michel a penetrating look. "Some people might even see *you* as equally guilty for the experiments that took place."

As he spoke, Tamara looked away, tears in her eyes.

"But..." Michel rose to his feet, and looked down at Martin, now seated. "Do you think *you* were the only one who suffered? We all lost our families... although I did try to save mine—and, yes, by working with the SS. And, after the war and the camps, I merely endured...day after day...sometimes hour after each damned hour...until Tamara came back into my life. We have both struggled so hard to heal. Do not ask us to go backwards!"

Martin jumped up and began pacing the room like a caged animal, pausing only to stare out the window and look down on Market Street. "This may be our only chance to get him," he said coldly, his voice like steel. "I have an assignment back in Europe, and I must leave in two days. My team is assembled here. You will contact Bloch tomorrow for a meeting later that evening."

Martin smiled, and his voice became overly conciliatory. "I'm quite sure you will help us. Otherwise, I will have no choice. Doctor Michel Katz will be known to the world as the Jew doctor who helped Doctor Mengele, the Angel of Death, in his murderous experiments at Auschwitz. You will attend a lecture Thursday morning at ten a.m. by Doctor Jürgen Hauptman. Hans Bloch will be there. You will then..."

"Stop, Martin, stop!" Michel held up his hands. "How will I find him?"

"You won't miss him, trust me." Martin bared a sinister smile. "You will approach Bloch and give him this."

Martin held up a sealed, white envelope. Michel looked at Tamara and shook his head slightly. "There is a demand inside that orders him to meet with representatives of the Holocaust Survivors' Fund tomorrow night at the Bridge City Café at the west end of Golden Gate Park, where Doctor Block will happily donate five hundred thousand dollars to that fund. All you have to do is give him this envelope, and your part will be over."

He placed the envelope on the desk next to Michel. "But your presence will certainly augment its importance. Don't worry. One of us will be in close proximity to protect you, should he respond violently. The letter will also tell him that if he does not cooperate, the FBI office in San Francisco will be notified that a wanted Nazi SS criminal is visiting their beautiful city."

Martin strolled toward the door. "Of course, he won't have to pay the money, nor will he need it. Our methods will be simple. There won't be the luxury of a quick death. My teammates know how to end life slowly with knives—piece by piece—allowing the victim to revisit the pain suffered by so many at his hands and those of his murderous SS cohorts."

Tamara listened silently and turned her head away from Martin.

We have both worked so hard… Please, not this now.

The door closed and Michel put his arm around Tamara, holding her tight against him. Closing his eyes, he tried to understand what had happened in these last few minutes.

How can I be part of this madness? And yet, he is right… I may have no choice.

His thoughts drifted back to the camps and his meeting with Rabbi Israel Rosenberg after dealing with the deranged Sonderkommando who relentlessly screamed, "They will kill us, every one of us… We will all die in the ovens!"

He recalled how the rabbi had to lie to this man and tell him it was not true, much like Michel had to lie to himself every day in the camp about his own actions.

The Red Cross had forwarded a letter from Rabbi Rosenberg to Michel when he was in Montreal, noting that he had come to the United States and settled in Brooklyn. Michel had answered him then and copied down his phone number and address. The rabbi had been the first person at the camps to whom he'd expressed his anguish over his involvement in the experimental studies. Rosenberg had been his mentor and his personal sanctuary. Michel leaned back, still cradling Tamara, and rested for a moment, gathering his courage.

He finally got up, moved over to the desk where he rummaged in his briefcase, and pulled out his phonebook. A yellowed piece of paper napkin with Rosenberg's phone number was folded between the pages. Rubbing his forehead he dropped back into thought. *Will he remember me? God, I hope he can help.*

Looking over at Tamara, he said, "Remember the rabbi…Rabbi Rosenberg at Auschwitz?" Not waiting for an answer, he picked up the phone, "I will call him."

As he dialed, Tamara sat listening from across the room.

"Hello, Rabbi, this is Michel Katz, from so long ago, at...the camps. I'm sorry to bother you at this hour. I know it's been a long time."

"Doctor Katz, it is so good to hear your voice again! Tell me, what would entice you to call me at midnight—after thirty years?"

Michel glanced at this watch: 9:00 p.m. "Rabbi, please forgive me! I am in California and forgot the time difference. If it is late for you, I can call tomorrow."

"Oh no, my old friend, I was up finishing a sermon for Saturday's service. Go ahead, what's on your mind?"

With the precision of planning a complex surgical procedure, Michel described how Martin had suddenly shown up in his life and the dilemma he was causing. He recalled back to his time at the camps, quickly recounting the subsequent years of his own life, reuniting with Tamara, then moving on to Martin's escape, his work with the Jewish Brigade, and his obsession with revenge.

Much of this was new to the rabbi, as he'd assumed that all the Sonderkommandos, including Martin, had perished after the failed revolt. He was, however, familiar with the attempts by clandestine Jewish groups to capture Nazis who had escaped from Germany after the war. He listened quietly, not interrupting. When Michel stopped talking, he finally spoke.

"Michel, you've described your life, your reunion with Tamara, and the events that have occurred, and it sounds as if you have put it all back together since you left Europe. What I didn't hear, though, is how have you *felt* through it all? How is your inner self?"

Michel was slow to answer. Clearing his throat, he began. "It has been hard to forget the loss of my family. I thought I had saved them...I was wrong. I was wrong about so many things when I helped the SS doctors in their beastly experiments."

He stopped for a few moments, choked up with emotion.

"Go on, Doctor Katz, I am listening," said the rabbi.

"After I left Auschwitz, I felt as if I should have died there with the others. I may as well have been burned, much like the rest, as I made myself an outcast from my profession and from Judaism, too. I was certain that someday I would be recognized as that monster that helped the Nazi doctors in their experiments and betrayed his own people."

Michel paused, looking over at Tamara, who had moved closer to him.

"Like many others, I directed my anger against the Nazis and their criminal guards, trying to fend off criticism of myself. I carried this weight with me to America. I wore the impenetrable cloak of my profession, in which I could hide and be safe from others' questions. As long as I did my job and buried myself in medicine and surgery, I could avoid discussing my life and feelings with anyone."

"Well then, Michel, one would expect that you might welcome this chance for revenge," Rosenberg offered.

"Yes, Rabbi, at one point that would have been true." He reached out and pulled Tamara next to him. "But Tamara and I have spent so much time working through it all, and we are different now. I can't be part of Martin's plot to kill Hans Bloch. It would destroy all that Tamara and I have worked for. We have both carried the burden of being survivors and the internal angst that came with it. We've spent many hours speaking openly with each other, and have come to understand and accept that, as mindful as we were of those we lost, we could not have affected what happened. There was nothing we could have done to save her parents, her older brother, or my wife and children. We are ready to embrace life now, together."

Michel was surprised to hear sniffling on the rabbi's end. "Are you okay, Rabbi Rosenberg?"

"The tears still come each day for me as well, my dear friend. My family was all murdered. I have yet to find someone to share those feelings with, as you did."

The rabbi fell silent for a moment as Michel heard what sounded like a few muffled sobs. Then he continued. "For those of us who outlasted the camps, it is natural to carry feelings of hatred and hope for revenge on those responsible for the deaths. Yet for many, that is not the answer, nor would forgiveness be appropriate. Revenge does not equate to justice. All we can do is ask and believe that justice, in some form, does prevail for those responsible for our horrific tragedies."

Michel listened intently as Israel Rosenberg went on to cite biblical references from the Old Testament when dealing with the horrors both men had experienced. "Above all," he said slowly, "we both must reestablish personal dignity and self-worth to complete our lives. You are right to have made this choice to forego revenge as justice."

Thanking the rabbi profusely for his time, Michel placed the phone back in its cradle, then moved into Tamara's waiting arms. She looked at his face and saw no fear, only confidence and decision. Relaxing into her embrace, he pictured Hans freely walking across the convention floor. The solution was clear: It was his time to step up. Martin would not have his moment.

44

May 18, 1974

San Francisco Convention Center

"A nd, in conclusion, this study has allowed us to develop hypothermia as an adjunct to surgery to improve our results."

Appreciative applause filled the hall as Doctor Jürgen Hauptman masterfully concluded his presentation, "Hypothermia in Trauma." The audience of surgeons had stayed riveted, especially following the opening slide of the Messerschmitt fighter crashing into the ocean.

Michel had chosen to sit close to the podium, just three rows back from the stage.

Fear rose up his spine as the man masquerading as Doctor Jürgen Hauptman stepped onto the stage.

Yes, it is him. The unmistakable, ugly birthmark. This is the same man I followed to the elevator yesterday at the Hilton. It is Hans Bloch standing at the podium, just fifteen feet away.

Michel's heart pounded like a hammer and his head throbbed as he searched the room for Martin.

Is he here?

Martin's murderous plans contrasted with the rabbi's wise words that "revenge is not justice." Conflicting thoughts crowded his pounding head.

So why did I come here? Do I "out" him here and rob Martin of his prey? Can I live with another death? Or am I just trying to save myself—again?

Closing his eyes and relaxing his hands on his lap, he inhaled slowly, resting for twenty seconds. Slowly, a faint glow of light appeared, though his eyes remained shut. His angst let up, and a feeling of calm surrounded him. As the glow grew brighter, a sense of clarity came with it, growing stronger as Hans finished his talk.

I now know what I must do.

When the moderator called for questions, Michel confidently approached the microphone stationed at the aisle and stared directly at Hans Bloch.

What should I say? Am I crazy? No, I have to do this.

He paused as an eerie silence filled the room. Then he spoke slowly yet clearly, for all to hear: "I am Doctor Katz, Michel Katz. The studies on humans were not done in Texas. They were done in Poland—in Auschwitz, to be exact—some thirty years ago."

A soft murmur rushed through the audience.

"I should know..." Michel went on.

Oh my God. What am I doing?

"...because I was there as an inmate and a doctor. I did the autopsy and tissue studies on the twenty men who died after he chilled them. And his name is not Jürgen Hauptman; it is Major Hans Bloch, an SS physician." He paused, his throat tightening up. "I still carry the shame and guilt for my role in these experiments, and worse...for my lack of courage to try and stop them. And you, Hans Bloch, Nazi murderer, your life is a lie!"

No sooner had the last word left Michel's mouth then Bloch pulled a stiletto out of his jacket, and, to the horror of the attendees in the front rows, charged off the stage towards Michel yelling, "Lousy Jew pig!" before tripping over the outstretched leg of tall Texas surgeon, Roger Allen.

The crowd of physicians in the San Francisco Convention Center Hall froze in stunned silence as Hans tumbled to the ground, the stiletto piercing his neck, while Michel, clutching his chest, bent over the old Nazi, sneering, "Too bad it's just a flesh wound... I believe your real pain has just begun—and, just as certainly, mine has finally ended."

♦♦♦

DOCTORS RUSHED TO SURROUND the two men as the convention's security force burst in. Minutes later, a squad of paramedics arrived and dressed the superficial wound on the right side of Hans's neck and examined Michel, who was suffering chest pains, to make sure he was okay. Police quickly followed, dispersing the crowd around the two men and ordering everyone out of the hall except for Michel, who was helped into a seat and briefly questioned by the police before agreeing to come to the station later to file a full police report.

The hall had finally emptied, leaving Michel alone. He leaned back in his seat and willed himself to breathe. It was over. He could hear the commotion in the lobby, as hotel guests mingled with doctors attending the conference, gawking at the sight of several burly policemen escorting a handcuffed physician cursing in German to a waiting van. A few media reps assigned to the meeting attempted to get statements from the officers, but were rebuffed.

Michel stayed inside the hall, hoping to avoid the circus going on with the police, reporters, and doctors milling about. His chest pain had eased and he sat quietly, at peace with his actions and ready to answer for any consequences his admissions might bring.

After ten minutes he got up to leave, but a man slid deftly into a seat next to him and put a restraining hand on his shoulder. "Please continue to sit," said Martin. "You will not leave without hearing what I have to say. You bastard, you were going to deliver him...We were ready... I saw your performance, well-orchestrated, just like the gutless do-gooder I always knew you were."

Michel shifted in his chair so he could look Martin in the eye. "Revenge is not my path to justice, my friend. You wanted to kill, and thus satisfy your deep thirst for personal vengeance." He brought his face close to Martin, his voice steady and low. "But you must understand: By putting him and these murderers in the glare of the press and in a courtroom before the world, their actions will be remembered. Now, Hans will be locked up for the rest of his life and be forced to look back at the horror he helped to create. And that, Martin, is *true* justice."

"I am a patient man," hissed Martin, his unblinking dark eyes staring directly into Michel's. "I can be anywhere and make myself into anybody in order to deliver my message—and I will. Your way is not enough. Trust me, Hans's time will come."

With that, Martin rose up calmly, walking out the side entrance of the hall.

♦♦♦

The San Francisco Journal, May 19, 1974
Nazi War Criminal Apprehended at Medical Convention

Doctor Hans Bloch, a German general surgeon from Indio, California, was arrested by local police and FBI agents Saturday for war crimes against humanity as he presented a research paper to a gathering of physicians at the National Trauma Society Meeting at the San Francisco Convention Center. Doctor Bloch, who was brought to the US in 1945 by the government to work on secret medical studies, is accused of murder and human experimentation while working as a SS physician at the Auschwitz-Birkenau Concentration Camp from 1944-1945. Doctor Bloch failed to return to Germany as ordered in 1946, and instead remained in the US, continuing to work on his experimental studies. He began surgical practice in Indio, California under the assumed name of Jürgen Hauptman, MD, in 1950. Charges are pending following a review by the Justice Department. Doctor Bloch was attending the National Trauma Society's annual meeting here as a speaker under the alias of Doctor Hauptman, who perished in World War II. He was presenting a paper on "Hypothermia in Trauma" when he was recognized as Doctor Hans Bloch by Doctor Michel Katz, a French-Jewish physician who had been an inmate at Auschwitz-Birkenau. German authorities have been contacted and an extradition request is pending. Bail has been denied.

"May the opposite be true…"

45

September 24, 1991
Munich, Germany

I t is the silent scream that is most painful. Somewhat like dreams filled with fright and fear, you cannot yell out, your voice won't work. But Hans Bloch was not having a dream.

Following his extradition from San Francisco to Germany and conviction for war crimes, he'd spent the last seventeen years locked up in a cell. So it was with mixed emotions that he left the Munich Stadelheim Prison under guard and entered the hospital for surgery.

Just the chance to see the daylight and walk outside of this place…I'll take the risk of this operation.

Greta had expertly placed the intravenous needle in his arm in the pre-operative area of the Munich University Hospital. She was a once-pretty lady, now in her fifties, with deep blue eyes. "Is that okay, Herr Bloch? I tried to be gentle," she said, "but sometimes it does hurt just a bit."

In his most patronizing way, Hans answered, "Yes, your technique is quite good…for a nurse."

As he was being wheeled into the operating room, a fit man in green scrubs entered the surgical suite. Greta had heard that a new anesthesiologist was coming, but had not yet worked with him. She watched as he introduced himself to his patient.

The mask hid his face, yet something about his eyes was familiar to Hans.

Do I know you?

Hans's frequent episodes of pain and bleeding from peptic ulcer disease had not cleared with rest, medications, and nonsurgical care. His ulcer history dated back thirty years, but it had been kept under control until this past year. Lately, he continued to bleed, despite the best medical care. Surgical excision of a large part of his stomach was necessary, and he had agreed to the procedure.

The anesthesiologist described what Hans could expect next. "First I am going to give you succinylcholine, a muscle relaxant. I'm sure you are familiar with this drug, Herr Doktor Bloch. This will enable us to more safely intubate you and paralyze your muscles to allow the surgeon a more relaxed abdomen to work on. Don't worry if you can't move. "

Hans nodded.

Greta moved across the room to help set up the surgical instruments. As the medicine was slowly being injected, Hans mumbled, "Doctor, I didn't get your name."

Continuing to infuse the medicine, he spoke quietly. "My name is Martin Brosky... Perhaps you forget, but we have met previously."

Hans tried to connect his memory to the man behind the mask, but he was slipping into a narcotic haze from the pre-operative medicines. He sensed something different about this doctor—something unsettling. He looked anxious, unsure.

Is this man really a doctor? Where would I have met him?

"Think back. You may remember me from many years ago, in the camps. One day, in the laboratory at Auschwitz, you held a gun to my head and assigned me to the death detail, the Sonderkommandos. You always assumed I had died after the revolt at Auschwitz, but, Herr Doktor, it was someone else...I escaped."

He could see fear growing in his patient's eyes as Hans searched his memory. But Martin was through talking. He placed the anesthetic mask on Hans's face just as the surgeon entered the operating room.

Hans tried to move, but couldn't; he was physically paralyzed by the last injection. He tried to talk, but no sound came out; his chest wall and vocal cords were paralyzed. He could feel the beads of sweat coursing off his naked body; there was a dull ache where the intravenous needle entered his right arm. He was unable to move, but he had sensation...

I can feel pain.

He wanted to make sure that more medicine would be given.

Where is the anesthetic medicine to make me sleep and take away any pain?

The inhalation mask was filling with an odorless gas, but the familiar smell of an anesthetic was absent. Panicking inside, he needed to tell this anesthesiologist he forgot something—forgot the halothane or some other anesthetic gas that would take away the pain. His heart started to race out of fear of death and of...imminent pain.

Holding an inhalation mask tightly over Hans's nose and mouth, Martin's left hand grasped the bag that carried only oxygen into his airway. He gave three strong, forceful thrusts, watching the chest expand with each squeeze of the bag and then forced the endotracheal tube down the trachea and inflated the cuff. The only sign of Hans's anguish were tears flowing from the inner corner of both eyes.

He well understood the impending agony that was coming. Hans struggled to talk, despite the tube in his throat...

Where is the pain medicine? He didn't give it... There is no anesthesia.

It was then that Martin lowered his mask to reveal his full face and noted the hint of recognition and surprise that filled Hans's eyes. As if to comfort the patient, Martin Brosky leaned down and whispered softly into Hans's right ear, "I have nothing left from the camps—all my family was tortured and killed. Nothing will ever match the pain they went through, nothing. You were one lucky son of a bitch, as that gutless doctor, Michel Katz, saved you from death in San Francisco seventeen years ago. We were ready then...but Katz turned you in before we could get to you, and I had to become a patient man. Now, it is time, Hans Bloch, you bastard; it is your turn to endure the unbearable pain."

Looking over to the waiting surgeon, Martin Brosky declared, "You may start your incision, Doctor. The patient is ready."

EPILOGUE

November 1, 1992

MICHEL'S HANDS TREMBLED AS he navigated his arthritic fingers to open the envelope that had just arrived. It had been many years since the Department of Justice had contacted him. Last year Martin shocked him with a note saying: *"Hans Bloch's time has come"* as he reveled in describing the somewhat tortured details of Hans's surgery. Handing the Justice Department envelope to Tamara, he asked that she open it; there was a hint of fear in his eyes at what the contents might contain. Unfolding the letter she read it first to herself, then aloud to Michel.

Dear Doctor Katz:

We have been asked to relay information from the German Justice Department about Hans Bloch. They have told us that he passed away on October 12, 1992, while still imprisoned at the Munich Stadelheim Prison. He died as a result of extensive complications following abdominal surgery for bleeding peptic ulcers. Unfortunately, his course was prolonged and painful and he was confined to his hospital bed for the greater part of one year. He was lucid until the end and asked that we contact you upon his death and that his medical information (enclosed) be given to you. When asked who else should be contacted concerning his condition, he gave your name alone. He stated only, "He will understand."

Sincerely,
John Linkner
War Crimes Division

Tamara saw the tears streaming from Michel's eyes. "Tell me, my love—say something, anything to help me comprehend what you are feeling."

Struggling to speak, Michel said, "The suffering really never stops, does it?"

He got up and walked towards the window facing Lake Michigan. "But though some might think it's poetic justice for this horrible being, this 'doctor,' to suffer as millions did before him, and hundreds did because of him, what does that do to all of us? Did his pain and infirmity lessen what happened to my family or yours? Will his tortuous journey help the world understand any better what has gone on here? In the end, Hans died as his inmate subjects did, painfully; no one heard *his* screams, either."

Tamara walked up and stood next to Michel. "No, Michel, there is not a good answer, but you have grasped it better than most."

She knew.

Michel has truly completed his passage, for he has traveled from the very nadir of guilt and personal responsibility to the summit of one man's character: the acceptance of his and other's past deeds and the person he is now—just a man, like anyone else.

Moving close to Michel, she took his hands in hers. "Michel, I have tried to understand what happened to us, to the world, yet it makes so little sense, and I have no words. Do you think we can ever explain it?"

Michel stared out the window as the sun was setting, and spoke to the sky. "It is not about forgiveness or forgetting the horrors of this time; it's about acknowledging that this demonic plague, this Holocaust, was far beyond the control of any one single man, but dependent upon the actions of millions and the inactions of millions more. In concert, they all allowed these unspeakable, horrendous deeds to happen."

He turned from the window to face her, catching a spark of light from the sun in her eyes. "Only one thing is certain: mankind will be stained and haunted for eternity. But will it learn from this?"